# BLOOD TIES

# BLOOD TIES

a novel by

# SIGMUND BROUWER

WORD PUBLISHING
Dallas·London·Vancouver·Melbourne

*Dedication*

*To Kip and Kathy Jordon*

**Library of Congress Cataloging-in-Publication Data**

Brouwer, Sigmund, 1959–
  Blood ties / Sigmund Brouwer.
      p.   cm.
    ISBN 0–8499–1294–6
    I. Title.
  PS3552.R6825B58   1996
  813'.54—dc20                                          96–23396
                                                            CIP

*Printed in the United States of America*

6 7 8 0 1 2 3 4 9 BVG 9 8 7 6 5 4 3 2 1

# Acknowledgments

Joey and Lana—as always this project is as much yours as mine.

Ray and Mary, and Bob, and Cova—thanks for fact checking. Any mistakes are mine.

Danelle and Nancy—only you two will fully know how much your perception and skill transformed and polished this book.

Also, I leaned heavily on C. S. Lewis in attempting to make sense of the mystery of evil. I appreciate his wisdom and insight.

# Prologue

## Kalispell, Montana—June, 1996

As Kelsie McNeill reached across to the glove box of her BMW, she had no reason to expect anything inside but registration papers and the sunglasses she needed for a relaxing ride home in the bright afternoon sun.

It had been a difficult day. As she was the first McNeill in McNeill, McNeill & Madigan, she'd spent nine, solitary, intense hours preparing a complicated class-action lawsuit.

When she had arrived just after seven that morning, her car had been in the shade of a tree. Now, afternoon heat had baked the black car, giving it a thin blanket of shimmering air.

As she stretched across to the glove box, she smiled at a realization. When was the last time she'd actually driven her car with the convertible top down? Was life so serious she couldn't try to lose herself in the sensation of wind and sun on her face? The impulse to rebel against her rigid self-discipline in such a minor way was so strong that she abruptly pulled her hand back from the glove box and unbuckled her seat belt.

She stepped out of the car again and scanned all directions for the towering thunderclouds that often rose during hot summer afternoons. She saw none. Twenty miles away, the mountains that walled the eastern side of the Flathead Valley were clear lines of granite against blue Montana skies.

Definitely a convertible day, she decided, worth the effort of unfolding the top, worth the effort of folding it back into place fifteen miles ahead when the asphalt ended and the gravel began for the last five miles of her drive up to the ranch.

Once she had securely fastened the convertible top back, she took off her suit jacket before getting inside again. She threw it onto the passenger seat beside her shoulder bag, amused at her rebellious satisfaction in not folding the jacket neatly.

Behind the steering wheel, Kelsie took off her high-heeled shoes, which she tossed onto the floor of the backseat. She unclipped the wide barrette holding her hair back and shook her hair free. She then gripped the steering wheel with both hands to stiff-arm herself against the seat back. Eyes closed, she straightened her legs and flexed her thighs and calves, tensing hard until the muscles burned. Then she relaxed the muscles.

Kelsie was wearing a sleeveless blouse—Saks Fifth silk, ivory colored, which matched her silk pants and the cream-colored leather shoes now on the floor behind her. The sun felt good on her shoulders and the bare skin of her upper arms. She allowed herself the luxury of an entire half minute of rest, concentrating on the warmth of sun against skin. She exhaled, wishing she could rid her mind of the lawsuit details as easily as she released the breath from her lungs.

Finally ready to drive, she opened her eyes and again reached across to pop open the glove box, thinking of sunglasses.

Movement caught her eye, but it was too late. She could not react. She could not even scream. She was frozen, conscious of every minute detail, as if a spotlight were slowly moving across a darkened stage.

From inside the glove box, the trianglular head of a snake arched forward in time-freeze frames, its eyes a brief black glitter, its body colored in the dust-green-and-brown diamonds of a rattlesnake. The snake's head slammed into the flesh of her forearm. The force of its strike hammered her arm against her side.

Unbelievably, she felt no immediate knife thrust of poisoned hollow fangs. Still, the rattlesnake clung to the flesh of her right forearm.The bulk of its body fell flat across the center armrest.

Kelsie half twisted, her instinct for survival surfacing. With her left hand, she grabbed the snake behind the head. It flailed and coiled, sending its spasms of rage up through her arm. Three, maybe four feet long, it was heavier than she thought. It took all her strength to squeeze the contracting muscles of the snake's body.

The snake's power shook her from side to side. Its rattles slammed against the dash. For a sickening moment, she was eye to eye with the snake. Then, finally, it opened its mouth wide, showing the gray pinkness of its palate and throat.

Quickly she lifted the snake above her head. She tossed it up and backward over her shoulders. Seconds later, it slapped the asphalt with a light thud, twisted, and streaked for the grass of the far side of the parking lot.

Kelsie gasped for breath. Her heart was racing, and she was shaking, but still she began to list her priorities: medical attention first; call Clay on the cellular phone as she drove to the hospital and tell him to start dinner without her; leave a voice-mail message for Lawson asking him to cancel the next day's appointments; and book a room at the hotel so that Clay wouldn't know what had happened.

How long, she wondered, before the swelling went down and she could return home? That was, if she lived.

She looked down at the spot on her arm where she had been bitten. Incredibly, she saw no blood and no puncture wounds. The skin was red and pinched with slight ridges as if a toothless baby had bitten her. But there were no puncture wounds.

She flexed her fingers. The muscles of her forearm quivered, and she began to feel an ache, as if she had been hit by a hammer. Long sleeves, she decided. Heat wave or not, she'd have to wear long-sleeved blouses to hide the bruising from Clay. He had already asked too many questions.

There was more to explore. She dreaded what else she might find in the glove box. But it had to be done. She leaned over to look inside. Her fears were confirmed when she saw a solitary eagle feather. Beneath it was a folded piece of paper. Before she opened it, she knew she would recognize the handwriting.

> Darling, please show how truly you love me. Delay my request no longer. It is tedious and dangerous work to remove snake fangs. Next time I may not have the patience. Next time I may leave the gift for someone close to you. Remember the others.

She folded the note and shoved it deep into her shoulder bag. She knew it was a foolish hope that someday she might be able to use it against the sender, but Kelsie badly needed hope of any kind.

She waited a few moments, struggling for composure. She told herself again and again that she was a fighter and a survivor. When she finally believed she could speak without a tremor in her voice, she picked up her cellular phone. She felt as if another woman were dialing, another woman listening to the first few rings.

"Hello," her husband said.

"Clay, it's me."

"It is," he said, his voice cool. "How are you this evening?"

She hated his formality. She hated the reason for it. "I'm fine," she said, finding the strength to stop her voice from shaking. "I'll be at the office awhile, all right? Don't hold dinner for me."

"Sure."

If he had stayed on the line another few seconds, if there had been some warmth in his voice, she might have folded, might have cried, might have finally asked him for help. Instead, he hung up without a good-bye. She didn't blame him.

Kelsie stared sightlessly through her windshield.

Something nudged her ankle. She looked down between her legs. *No!*

Another rattlesnake slithered out from under the driver's seat.

She couldn't find the breath to scream. When she finally unfroze, Kelsie lifted her legs and dove toward the passenger door, scrambling over the armrest in her panic to get out.

She leaned against the fender of her car trembling, struggling to breathe, her knees nearly buckling.

After all these weeks of vigilance had she left the car door unlocked?

Kelsie wanted to believe she'd been stupid and careless. Because if she had not left the door unlocked this morning, that could mean only one thing: The man who had been stalking her all this time had somehow managed to copy her keys.

# PART ONE

# Kalispell
# July, 1973

# Day 1

In room 27 of the Bluebird Motel Doris Samson screamed soundlessly into the duct tape across her mouth. Smelling her cheap, rose-
based perfume, the Watcher drifted back into boyhood, remembering
another woman—white, and much older than this frightened
Flathead Indian. The Watcher remembered how as a boy he had
breathed in the smell of cloying rose perfume during long, frightening nights.

In the Watcher's memory, those nights were never far away. Nor
was the old woman . . .

*Her perfume had overwhelmed him when she surprised him and pulled*
*him onto her lap. She held him tight, burying his face in the wrinkled cleav-*
*age exposed by her half-open housecoat.*

*"Little Bobby, I love you," she crooned, holding him so firmly he could*
*not push himself away. "I love you so much. Mommy just wants to hold you*
*again."*

*She finally relinquished her smothering grip, and he was able to draw*
*air. "I am not little Bobby!" He squirmed to get out of her lap.*

*She squeezed his face between her hands. If she was aware that it hurt*
*him, it didn't show in the tender love on her face.*

*"Little Bobby, it's all right. We're together again. Let your mommy give*
*you love."*

"I am not little Bobby!" He wiggled his head, trying to pull loose from her hands.

She leaned forward and kissed his forehead. With the blond wig over her gray hair, the makeup she'd applied with shaky hands, and the light dimmed low enough, she might indeed pass for thirty years younger.

"Little Bobby, let me help you into your pajamas."

"My name is not Bobby! My name is—"

"Hush," she said, pulling his face into the wrinkled valley of her chest. "Hush, little one. First I'll bathe you. I'll wash you everywhere. Then I'll dress you in your favorite pajamas. We'll spend the night together. Oh, yes, we'll spend the night together."

She rocked the little boy back and forth. "And it will be like you were never gone."

## 6:30 A.M.

Clay Garner stepped out of his Chevrolet sedan in the parking lot of the Bluebird Motel. He had no difficulty figuring out which was room 27. A sheriff's car was parked at an angle directly in front. One deputy, tall and massively fat, stood in the open doorway of the room, facing inside. Another sat behind the steering wheel of the sheriff's car, lips close to the radio mike he held in one hand.

There were no flashing lights, however, and no rope or yellow tape cordoning off the parking stalls and sidewalk outside the room. At 6:30 A.M., perhaps, the deputies cared little about any risks from curious bystanders. Or, he thought, the deputies had just arrived and hadn't had the time yet to mark off the crime scene. Or the deputies were sloppy or uncaring, or both.

Clay decided they were sloppy *and* uncaring. They'd parked the sheriff's car so close to the room that any evidence found on the asphalt beneath would be suspect at best, and at worst, disallowed in court.

The deputy turned as he heard Clay's footsteps. Recognition came a half moment later.

"Hoover's boy," the deputy said derisively.

Clay ignored the sarcastic tone. A man didn't scrabble his way this far from West Virginia coal country without thick skin. Clay also knew in this situation his special agent's badge worked against him. He was twenty-six; that was the second strike. As an outsider meddling in their jurisdiction, he knew the ball had crossed the plate long before he'd had a chance to step up to bat.

"Who's the investigator in charge here?" Clay asked.

"Not you, hillbilly." Slowly, the deputy used his tongue to shift a wad of chewing tobacco from one cheek to the other.

"Who's the investigator in charge?" Clay pushed back a flare of temper. Gangly, knobby at the joints, big-nosed, and just starting to fill his frame, he'd borne plenty of insults during his awkward teens. Work-hardened knuckles might have been a solution at county dances ten years earlier. Now, however, a fistfight would only mean paperwork and a reprimand in triplicate.

"Come to step your FBI shoes over everything?" the deputy responded, pushing back his wide-brimmed hat.

"Who's the investigator in charge?" Clay was the same height as the deputy but probably a hundred pounds lighter. He didn't flinch, however, as he stared into the deputy's deep-set eyes.

The deputy spat a stream of tobacco juice onto the toe of Clay's polished right shoe.

"I'll look forward to the day we meet and you aren't wearing a badge," Clay said quietly. "I'll invite you to try that again."

"Then what? You gonna—"

"Back off, Two Car." A hatless man, past fifty, barrel stout in a flannel shirt, suspenders, and blue jeans, squeezed between the deputy and doorframe into the sunlight. "Here's the situation, Mr. FBI. I got called from a warm bed at six. Had an entire day planned flyfishing on the South Fork. Instead, I get this stiff, a real bleeder. If you had any brains, you wouldn't add to my considerable irritation."

Sheriff Russell Fowler wore his gray hair in a military crew cut and had a small balding circle on the top of his skull. Clay knew this, because at six-foot-one, he looked down on Fowler's five-feet-eight inches—a fact that almost certainly had brought a fourth strike into play during their first meeting the day before.

"I'll remind you the same as yesterday. I have no interest in scratching dirt like roosters in a circle," Clay said. He spoke slowly, acutely aware that his West Virginia accent, with consonants polished like stones in running water, set him apart as surely as did his badge. He was too proud, however, to deny his heritage by snapping his vowels short. "I believe this here"—*here* came out in two syllables—"is a matter that involves the Federal Bureau of Investigation."

The deputy in the sheriff's car stepped out silently and joined the first deputy in staring at Clay.

"A matter for the FBI. I find that of particular interest," Fowler said. "Not only do you manage to get here a half-hour after we do, but somehow you already know enough about the crime to tell us who's in charge." Fowler rubbed his nose, then grinned. "With knowledge like that, we should check your fingernails for blood, boy. Maybe it was *you* gone knife crazy in there, instead of one drunk Indian against another."

"I doubt it was a knife," Clay said, wondering why Fowler had tried to mislead him.

"No?" Fowler's voice lost its insolent tone and became threatening. "I don't like it that you're so certain for someone who has no business here."

"How many knife fights have you tended to, Sheriff?" Clay asked.

"Over thirty years? You obviously don't limit your useless questions to train wrecks."

"Then you know enough to recognize the marks a knife leaves." Clay regretted his first question, knowing it had sounded like a challenge. But he wasn't going to back down now.

"I know the marks. And I'll bet my pension you ain't seen real blood or real death since graduating, Special Agent Clay Garner. One year out of the academy, and most of that year on backdated draft-dodger files." Fowler's grin returned. "Don't let the size of this state fool you, son. Took just one phone call to find out exactly how you've spent your time in Great Falls. You've been no closer to blood than a paper cut or a stapled finger."

To Clay Garner's frustration, he couldn't truthfully argue with the sheriff. After years of undistinguished trafffic duty as a state trooper, his fledgling FBI career had not yet been much: Nine weeks training in Quantico, Virginia; a brief swearing-in ceremony, devoid of the presence of J. Edgar himself; immediate transfer to Great Falls, Montana, and its backwater office of three; and fifty-four weeks of 25s—the Selective Service Act cases that meant trying to locate local draft dodgers—mainly by telephone, with all fifty-four weeks in discomfort because of J. Edgar Hoover's enforced personal dress code: dark business suit, white shirt, dark conservative tie, dark socks, black shoes.

Clay Garner hated his suit. He'd spent the previous two days visiting ranches and Indian reservations and had been greeted with suspicion or laughed at outright because of the cheap suit that barely reached his bony wrists. Only bankers and lawyers wore suits in this county, and both were welcomed like scorpions in a sleeping bag. Thinking of his age, badge, assignment, accent, and dress, Clay doubted he could deliberately find any more ways to make his job any more difficult in the Flathead Valley.

"Knife wounds," Clay continued, refusing to rise to Fowler's bait. "Look for stab, puncture, or slice. Double-edged or single." Stiff-suited and stiff-lipped, Clay would not concede this was memorized book knowledge, taken from grainy black-and-white textbook photos.

"Take notes," Fowler said to the deputy in a condescending tone. "Now we're getting a lesson from a graduate."

"As you well know," Clay said, "the corkscrew was still in the body."

"President Nixon himself don't interfere with my investigation and get away with it," Fowler said angrily, "let alone some wet-behind-the-ears ugly duckling with a memo from Hoover. If you stepped so much as a hair into this room before we got here—"

"George Samson called me."

"Samson? How's he know? We haven't notified him yet." Fowler's face was blotched with red patches from barely contained anger.

"Clerk at the front desk saved you the trouble." Clay thought it interesting that Russ Fowler had no need to ask who George Samson was. "Same clerk who probably called you. From what I understood from George, the clerk knew his granddaughter. The clerk also saw enough to know it wasn't a knife that killed Doris."

"George Samson don't know you from Adam. What's he calling you for?"

Clay had been asking himself the same question, a fact he was not going to share with Russ Fowler. "As you might recall from yesterday's conversation, my assignment here is the train derailment adjoining his property. I interviewed George last evening. He called my motel room a half-hour ago and asked that I come down here."

"We've got this investigation under control," Fowler said, not budging from his position.

"Mr. Samson seemed to think you might be less than thorough. I find that interesting, especially in light of your less-than-thorough approach to the train derailment investigation."

"The derailment was an accident, and I refuse to waste time on it. George is a crazy old Indian who belongs in a Wild West show. And you belong back in Washington. This is beyond your jurisdiction. Clear this investigation site, or I'll make sure you don't last another week with that tin badge."

This was something Clay understood. Intimidation. It usually meant the intimidator had something to hide—fear, maybe, or guilt.

Clay was also a stubborn man. If these local boys had treated him with any courtesy, he might have left them to their work and gone to his, futile as it was. Instead, he smiled and held his ground. "I had an interview scheduled with Doris Samson later today, Sheriff. So her mysterious death ties this into my train investigation. Also, this is a non-white murder victim. That, too—"

"Non-white?" the first deputy echoed in disbelief. "Some Flathead squaw gets stuck like a frog, and you want to talk like a government clerk?"

Clay would not give them the satisfaction of knowing how badly he wanted to shuck his starchy role and respond like the backhills boy he'd left behind. Instead, he chose his language carefully. "Doris Samson is from the Flathead reservation. That, too, makes it my business, according to federal statutes that grant FBI jurisidiction in government and Indian reservation matters."

"Get someone in Washington to send me a memo to that effect, son," Fowler said, thumbs hitched behind his suspenders. "I can always use more toilet paper. In the meantime, why don't you just get into your car and leave us to our work."

"You're barring me from stepping inside the room?"

"I'm telling you this is local sheriff's business. I don't even want you peeking inside the doorway."

It was almost comical, Clay thought, the way the two deputies shifted to block the doorway, like two boys playing king of the hill and daring Clay to try to take the top.

Clay Garner drew a deep breath. An unsolved murder and an interjurisdiction dispute, all before his first cup of coffee.

"Sheriff," he asked, "do you have a photographer on the way? Coroner? Crime techs?"

Sheriff Fowler shook his head. "You been watching too much television, son. This one won't be tough to solve. Tonight, some brave will get drunk and tell his pals about a squaw who gave him so much grief he had to shut her up for good. We'll hear, track him down, and sweat it out of him. Case closed. Not that anyone cares."

Clay studied the sheriff. Clay had his first tingle of excitement, as if an instinct he didn't know he possessed was coming to the surface. "From what Mr. Samson told me," Clay said, keeping his slow drawl even, "whatever you have in this motel room didn't happen because a drunk lost control."

"Son, not only did you get beat good with an ugly stick when you was little, someone knocked the hearing out of your skull. I just said nobody cares about a dead Indian."

"I do."

"Your point being?"

"Obstruction of justice. Another federal statute that puts this within FBI jurisdiction. Unless you deal with this crime scene properly, I will investigate and charge you and your deputies with said violation." Clay winced inside at how pompous he sounded. But at his age and level of inexperience, he had little else but rules, his badge, and the weight of the organization to give him confidence and authority in this unusual situation.

Fowler watched Clay to see if it was a bluff.

Clay reached into his suit pocket. Much as he hated the jacket, it was handy for holding a notepad and pen. He pulled out his notepad, flipped it open, and recorded the time and date.

"Fowler," Clay said, looking up briefly. "F-O-W-L-E-R?"

"Boys, let him inside," Fowler said after a long pause. He directed his next words to the largest of the deputies. "Two Car, get back on the radio. Make the calls for a forensic tech to be flown in from Missoula. If they squawk, tell them the FBI will cover the expenses."

Fowler lifted his jowly face to look at Clay again. "Right, Mr. Special Agent?"

"Right." Clay knew he'd be lucky to get this one past the paper-pushers. But he was angry and stubborn, and if he had to, he'd pay for this himself before letting Fowler find an excuse to file this as just another knife fight.

"Go on in," Sheriff Fowler told Clay. "It ain't pretty. You know the rules. Don't touch anything. If you feel queasy, make sure you get clear into the parking lot before losing your breakfast. Be a real shame, wouldn't it, if you messed up all your fine evidence?"

# 11:14 A.M.

"Here's a twenty," Harold Hairy Mocassin told Johnny Samson. "Go in and buy some gum. Got it? Costs a dime. Make sure you keep all the change. Then meet me down at the hotel in five minutes. I'll show you a good time then."

"I don't get it," Johnny said, folding the money and placing it in the back pocket of his blue jeans. "You wrote a phone number on the twenty. How does that double our money?"

Harold Hairy Moccasin stubbed out his half-smoked cigarette on the sole of his work boot. They were standing in sunshine two doors down from a five-and-ten store on a street with little pedestrian traffic. It was past eleven o'clock, a time crucial for Harold in two ways. Enough of the morning had passed that Harold expected the cash register in the five-and-dime to carry a necessary reserve of cash; the Kalispell Hotel bar was open and waiting for their triumphant entry with some of that cash.

"Johnny, there's plenty you don't get," Harold said. "Blame it on your grandfather. It ain't hard to tell this is your first day alone in the white world. You stick with me, man, and you'll get an education worth something."

"Hey, man. You watch what you say. My grandfather—"

"Be cool, Johnny Samson. Be cool. All I'm saying is there's two worlds. You know the hills. Now you get to know the streets."

Johnny Samson drew a deep breath. Harold Hairy Moccasin, in a deerhide jacket, was short, skinny, with a half-dozen straggling long chin hairs. At nineteen he had been out of boarding school long enough to have grown his braided hair below his shoulders. He had his own truck, a '64 Chevy, and he'd been with a dozen women already, even had a couple of children, if a person cared to believe him.

About a hundred years earlier, Harold was proud to tell people, a Crow named Hairy Moccasin had scouted for Custer. Hairy Moccasin had not been suicidal enough to stay put when he saw the odds at the Little Bighorn, and as a result Harold was able to include himself among the great-great-grandchildren who bore the scout's name. The privilege of such a background more than made up for the dignity he lost when people called him Hairy instead of Harold.

Johnny was honored that a person of Harold Hairy Moccasin's stature would give him any attention at all, let alone invite him into town to celebrate Johnny's seventeenth birthday with his older sister, Doris. Johnny would have felt less honored if he'd known Harold Hairy Moccasin had designs on Doris and that Harold intended to lubricate the day's celebration as much as possible with their twenty dollars doubled.

"Nothing can go wrong, Johnny. You're just buying a pack of gum. They can't stop Indians from doing that. Just be sure to use the twenty I gave you."

"Yeah," Johnny said. "I'll be sure."

"And don't look my way when you leave. Got it? When I walk in after you, she can't know we're together."

Johnny Samson nodded in agreement.

Johnny left Harold and walked the short distance to the storefront. He wore cowboy boots, jeans, a jean jacket, and a Stetson. Johnny's hair was longer than Harold's, but Johnny had been raised in the hills, not in a boarding school, and no one had ever forced him to cut his hair like a white man's.

The doorbells jangled as Johnny let himself into the store. He stood for a moment, letting his eyes adjust to the darkness. The store window was jammed with cheap merchandise, so little sunlight made it through, and the light fixtures were cheap and far between.

Johnny approached the cash register. A brown-haired girl his age stood behind it. She had waxy white skin, pimples, and square glasses, which added pudginess to an already overly pudgy face.

"Gum," Johnny said. "I need some gum."

"It's on the shelf beside you," she said in a tone of voice that indicated he was an idiot for not noticing.

Why was he so nervous he couldn't see the gum himself? Harold was the one taking a risk. Right?

Johnny Samson grabbed a pack of Wrigley's Juicy Fruit and threw it on the counter. He dug Harold's folded twenty out of his back pocket as the girl regarded him in silence. She handed him the change, and he left the store, turning toward the Kalispell Hotel. As instructed, Johnny did not look behind him for Harold Hairy Moccasin.

Five minutes later, Harold Hairy Moccasin met Johnny at the curb in front of the side-door entrance to the hotel. Two older Indians sat on the curb, heads down to keep the sunshine out of their eyes.

Harold was eating from a one-pound bag of raisins as he joined Johnny Samson.

"Raisins?" Johnny asked. He badly wanted to know if and how Harold had doubled their money as promised but felt more compelled to ask why Harold had stopped at a grocery store when all Harold had talked about the entire morning was whiskey and draft beer.

"Raisins," Harold confirmed. "Man, don't you know nothin'?"

"I know I don't eat raisins. When I was little, one of my cousins told me whites made them by catching flies and pulling off their wings and legs. I never touched them since."

"Eat them and your blood clots better," Harold replied with a superiority granted by knowledge. "Nobody can say Harold don't think ahead."

Harold maintained his master-to-pupil tone. "See, tomorrow I sell blood. Four bucks a pint, man, that's what you get. Thing is, they don't let you donate more than once every six weeks. It's hard to make money that way. And they got this test to make sure your blood's thick. There's an easy way to beat that, though. Eat plenty of raisins, and next day you pass the clotting test. I go in every ten days, give 'em a different name. To them, we all look alike. Raisins cost me fifty cents; I get four dollars, plus plenty of cookies and Kool-Aid. Good business, I figure."

Johnny nodded, not sure why he was smiling. Could it be healthy for a person to give away that much blood? But if Harold Hairy Moccasin moved that easily through the white world, Johnny needed to pay attention.

"You get another twenty dollars?" Johnny asked, knowing he had more to learn from Harold Hairy Moccasin.

"Close enough." Harold discreetly unfolded a handful of bills. There was no sense flashing wealth with the bar right up the steps, not when so many friends somehow always managed to appear to share good fortune.

"Did you use a gun?" Johnny was amazed.

Harold grinned and puffed out his chest. "I case the stores downtown. See, when a cashier gets a large bill, she's supposed to put it on top of the register when she makes change. That way there's no mix-up. Some places though, the cashier's lazy, throws the bill in right away. She can never be sure what you just handed her. Like in the store we just visited."

"Yeah?" Johnny wasn't following. He didn't want to show it though.

"You went in," Harold said, "bought gum, gave her the twenty, got nearly twenty back. I waited a few minutes, bought a candy bar, gave her a dollar bill. She gave me change and closed the drawer. I tell her, look, I been ripped off, what happened to the rest of my money? She says what do I mean? I say I gave her a twenty. She says no, it was only a buck. I tell her I know for sure because I had a girl's phone number on it. I close my eyes and tell her the number, like I memorized it. She looks at the bill on top of the stack of the twenties, sees the one you gave her, and it's got the phone number I wrote down when we were standing outside. I tell her it ain't right, trying to rip off an Indian. She's all sorry, gives me another nineteen bucks to make up the difference."

Johnny shook his head, half in admiration, half in worry. "Kind of like stealing but different."

"You sound like the Flatheads I left behind. Too respectable. Me, I figure nothing you take from the whites is stealing. Think what they took from us. Maybe you should spend less time with your grandfather, hang out with some of us braves who ain't scared to fight for the old ways."

Johnny Samson wondered what to say to that—he loved his grandfather—but he didn't have to worry about a reply. Harold Hairy Moccasin already had him by the arm and was pulling him up the steps into the Kalispell Hotel.

"Let's get this celebration started," Harold said, already dreaming of Doris Samson and a variety of possibilities with her. Some were saying she'd changed her ways, but Harold was optimistic the rumors about her and church weren't true. "She knows you're in town. She'll find us or we'll find her, I promise."

Inside the hotel, they walked down a narrow corridor to the barroom. Nobody challenged Johnny for age identification, which raised his esteem for Harold, who had earlier told him not to worry about it. The bartender, however, cigarette hanging on his lip, took a little wind out of Harold's impressive momentum to this point.

"Hey, Harry Hairy," he called as they stepped into the yeasty smell of old, spilled beer soaked into wood floors. "No money, no service."

Harold shrugged it off and tried to get back into his role of master by throwing a ten carelessly onto the bar. There were maybe a half-dozen other people in the room, all nursing drinks at tables with Formica tops. They were wise—getting drunk too early meant waking up sometime in the evening with too much time to kill until the next morning, wasting all the booze it had taken to get them senseless in the first place.

"Couple of whiskeys with beer chasers," Harold said. "And I told you plenty of times already, it's Harold."

"Sure thing, Harry Hairy."

Johnny was watching carefully. He expected Harold to get angry at this white insolence, but instead Harold accepted the drinks meekly.

Harold showed Johnny how to gulp a whiskey shooter and follow it with draft beer. Johnny learned fast. In fact, within the hour, he had guzzled four whiskey shooters and six beers and was well on the way to being drunk for the first time in his life when a Blackfoot Indian he did not know sat down beside him and asked if he was Johnny Samson because if he was, his sister Doris had been murdered and word was out that the sheriff had already put her in a body bag and the FBI was out looking for her friends, relatives, and boyfriends.

## 2:01 P.M.

At age forty-four, along with holding considerable power over two local banks, James McNeill ruled seventy-two hundred acres of Flathead Valley foothills, fifteen hundred head of grazing and feed-lot cattle, one hundred horses, thirty employees, two bunkhouses, an eighteen-year-old son, a nineteen-year-old nephew, and a sixteen-year-old daughter. In turn, he was ruled only by the memories of his wife, Maggie, buried three years earlier after succumbing to a brief and painful fight with bone cancer.

James sometimes found himself at a loss to deal with Kelsie, his daughter, in direct contrast to the ease of dealing with his son and nephew. His son, Michael, loved the ranch in the same way he did, and they rarely found cause to disagree. As for Lawson, James had become his nephew's legal guardian a week after the boy's tenth birthday, following a house fire in which he had lost his mother. The decision to adopt Lawson had been easy. Lawson's mother had been Maggie's sister, and family was family. Now best friends with Michael, Lawson proved to be amiable company for James and was smart enough to listen carefully on the few occasions when James felt pushed hard enough to raise his voice. A day didn't go by that James wasn't grateful both boys had ignored any fool notions about going down to San Francisco and joining the long-haired movement of hippies, communes, and dope-smoking.

But Kelsie?

James sat at the dining-room table, facing business ledgers and a midafternoon coffee, which cooled untouched as he looked through the ranch-house picture window. With the panoramic view of much of the valley below, he had eyes only for the activities at the horse corral near the main barn, some hundred yards down from the house.

He spotted Kelsie leaning against the wood railing, mesmerized by three cowboys who whooped and hollered as they took turns riding green horses to a standstill. One of them, a good-natured neighbor boy named Rooster Evans, was not even part of the ranch but showed up often to throw a hand in with work, simply to be close to Kelsie. The other two cowboys were ranch hands, paid to work, not to perform in front of his daughter, who had been standing there for nearly two hours.

Lord, James thought, how he wished for Maggie. She would be able to talk girl things with Kelsie. Whenever James tried, he fumbled so badly it embarrassed both of them.

What James wanted to do was to go down there and order Kelsie to leave and let the ranch hands get on with their work. He knew it would be futile, though. Kelsie, a dreamer so much like her mother, also had her mother's stubborn streak. If he told Kelsie not to do something, it would only give her more determination to do so. If he told her to stay away from the cowboys, that would only add to her romantic notions of true love. And James was sure she'd set her heart on one of the cowboys—he just didn't know which one.

Of course, he could wait until she made it clear who she was dreaming over, then ask that cowboy to stay clear of her. But he knew that even the most resolute young cowboy would have difficulty staying away from her.

At sixteen, Kelsie looked twenty-one, almost identical to Maggie in a wedding photo taken nearly three decades earlier. She had the same shoulder-length blonde hair, same slim waist, same heart-breaking smile.

Kelsie, like her mother, did not have a model's flawless cheekbones and skin. Instead, her eyes were slightly wider and rounder, slightly farther apart than they should have been. Her mouth, too, was slightly too wide. The not-quite-perfect symmetry had a startling effect, as did her green eyes and the pouting curve of her lips.

While Kelsie's fashion choice tended toward work jeans and men's shirts, the bulky clothing was incapable of hiding the considerable promise of a body far too developed for the peace of mind of her father, who with great clarity remembered the passion he'd never lost for her mother and her giving, loving body. He also remembered his wild cowboy days before meeting Maggie and becoming a one-woman man.

James hoped Kelsie was as innocent and unaware of men's glances as she seemed to be. He told himself, as he watched her leaning against the corral, it would be far worse at her age if she already possessed enough feminine wiles to realize her best chance at landing a cowboy was to pretend to ignore him instead of mooning about in such an obvious fashion.

Still, as he remembered so well, cowboys and young women were a dangerous combination.

He'd have to think of something, and soon.

## 7:45 P.M.

Kelsie's most precious possession was a gift from her mother, a musical jewelry box with a tiny ballerina on top. When the mechanism was wound, if the lid was opened and then shut, the ballerina would spin to tinkling music. The jewelry box was velvet lined and had a false bottom an inch deep; it was Kelsie's habit to save small bills until she had enough to exchange for a fifty-dollar bill. She had four fifties in the music box now, along with her favorite Valentine's cards, a letter from Maggie, sweet poems from her brother's friend, Rooster Evans, and her first real love note, from a handsome cowboy named Nick Buffalo.

No one knew of the note or the money or even of Kelsie's deeply sentimental and romantic side, which led her to save all that she did in the jewelry box. On a ranch with three males, she'd learned early to hide her softness and her secret yearnings.

Instead, she confided to her diary. This, too, was a secret. It felt right that she spend time with her diary in the one spot that Kelsie and her mother had shared with no one else—under their favorite tree. While Maggie was alive, they had visited the tree often, especially on clear blue summer evenings when the day's breeze dropped to a whisper.

The tree was a granddaddy poplar—silver, old, and dead—sitting alone on the edge of a hill two miles from the ranch house by horse trail, seven miles from any other house in the valley. Its broad trunk had been worn smooth of bark by cattle rubbing itchy hides against it. Higher up, the scars of bears' claws could still be seen; grizzlies over the years had stretched tall and ripped at the bark to mark their territory. The tree was just wide enough to allow Maggie and Kelsie to sit between its gnarled roots and watch the shadows that lengthened across the valley with the setting of the sun. There would be a special moment—the one Maggie and Kelsie always waited for in silence—when the sun dropped behind the western edge of the valley. At that moment, the light would diffuse into golden softness so pure the entire valley seemed like a new, untouched land.

Kelsie believed fully in God and Jesus and angels, and because of it, ever since her mother had died, she often rode Saber, her black ten-year-old gelding, to the tree for evening conversations with her mother. Kelsie knew Maggie was looking down on her and would appreciate hearing her thoughts on the day.

Kelsie also shared these thoughts with her diary. She liked it best when she got to the tree early and was able to sort out her thoughts by talking to Maggie, with time after to record her thoughts in the diary while she waited for the special moment when the last fire of the sun disappeared.

In the summers that had passed without Maggie, Kelsie discovered that when the golden light turned soft, she often strained her ears for the rush of air against angel wings, so great was her feeling of peace and the presence of her mother.

Kelsie swayed with Saber's slow walk as they neared the tree. Her mind was on Nick Buffalo. When he accepted a glass of water she had fetched for him while he was breaking horses down at the corral, they'd shared a secret smile. Although he hadn't been able to say anything—not that he said much anyway—she knew he was thinking what she was thinking. For what they felt for each other, words weren't needed.

It made Kelsie dizzy to daydream about Nick's lips on hers. Something like this—when the thought alone caused her stomach to tremble—had to be right, didn't it? It was a question she intended to share first with Maggie, then with her diary as she enjoyed the peacefulness of the valley below.

As usual, Kelsie looped the ends of Saber's reins over a tree branch of a smaller poplar at the edge of the clearing surrounding the big, dead poplar. And, as usual, Kelsie grabbed a small stick as she walked toward her favorite tree.

In the summer, because it might lead to awkward questions if she was seen with her diary going to or returning from her tree, Kelsie preferred to leave it in a hole in the side of the dead poplar. Come fall, she would take the diary back to the house and leave it in a secret spot in her room, for the weather then forced her to write there.

Kelsie, for all her dreaminess, was still McNeill enough to have a practical streak. She always rubber-band-wrapped the diary in a plastic bag, so it wouldn't get moldy or wet or infested with bugs. There was also a reason she carried the stick. She'd reach in with it and rattle the hole first, so that she would not be surprised by a sleeping squirrel, a mouse, or by wasps or bees.

After satisfying herself that she could reach in without getting surprised, Kelsie took the diary from its hiding spot. She pulled it from the plastic bag, then eased herself into a sitting position against the broad trunk.

Before opening the diary, Kelsie said a small prayer, thanking God for the day and for her health and asking God to keep looking over her father, Michael, and Lawson as they tended to the affairs of the ranch.

Her prayer finished, she spoke to Maggie for a while, telling her about the tabby with four new kittens and how James seemed to miss Maggie still. Kelsie took time, of course, as she'd done for the past week or so, to slip in a few words about Nick Buffalo, wondering if it mattered that a man had red skin or white and then answering her question by saying probably the important thing was that the man made his woman happy, which Kelsie knew by instinct would happen when she spent more time with Nick.

Finally, she opened her diary. She gasped.

Bent and broken, just inside the leather cover, was a feather. She plucked it out and straightened it. If she was guessing right, it was an eagle feather.

*But how could—*

The diary had been wrapped in a plastic bag and sealed shut with the heavy rubber band. Someone must have placed the feather inside her diary, which meant someone knew where she hid it. And for that matter, knew what she'd written.

*But who could—*

She had never told anyone about this tree, not even her father. It was a secret more precious because of her memories of being there with her mother.

Kelsie stood quickly.

The soothing whispers of breeze and leaves became haunting reminders of her isolation. Kelsie told herself it was her imagination. She told herself the silent stands of trees above and below her hillside perch contained only small birds and rabbits. But someone had followed her there once. And someone had watched her once. Because someone had found her diary, and that someone had left the eagle feather as a message to let her know she had been watched and followed.

Never before had Kelsie been frightened to be alone in any corner of the vast ranch lands. She hadn't been scared of bears, and she hadn't been worried about getting lost.

Fear now shivered through her. Was someone watching her at that very moment?

## 10:20 P.M.

A few hours later, when Lawson McNeill reached the final crest of the winding forestry road, four other pickup trucks parked among the trees gleamed in his headlights. He parked his own truck, flicked off his headlights, and saw the glow of a campfire ahead. Obviously the others had decided the weather was so fine there was no need to use the cabin behind the campsite.

Lawson stepped out of his truck and walked unhurriedly toward the men waiting for him. He guessed there might be a rifle trained at his chest, so he spoke.

"Sorry I'm late," he said as he approached. "James had a few things he wanted done before I could leave."

"Don't sweat it, son," one voice said from the shadows at the side of the fire. "Fowler's got no business calling us all together anyway on such short notice."

Lawson spotted the dark outline of an ice chest nearby, opened it, and threw in a dozen cans of beer—minus one for himself—then found a large chunk of firewood in the grass. With one hand—he held the aluminum beer can in his other hand—Lawson rolled the firewood toward the fire. With his toe, he flipped the firewood on its end to use it as a low chair. He plunked himself down beside a familiar figure and snapped open the beer top, nodding and smiling at the six other men already seated.

"Hey, bud."

"Hey, Rooster," Lawson said right back, just as quietly. Even if they hadn't been neighbors, there would have been a bond between the two. All the others around the campfire were middle-aged. Rooster and Lawson, who were the same age, were the only two young wolves who had been granted the privilege of admission to the select group.

Lawson let the flow of conversation wash over him, half listening to the talk about deer hunting, loose women, money, and local politics. The other half of his attention was on the fragrance of fresh pine and the crackle of pine sap burning in the fire. He tilted his head back for a swallow of beer. Straight above was a piece of starlit sky so black it felt inches from his face, so clear the smallest stars appeared as dust among the constellations.

He enjoyed being at the gathering, not only because of the surroundings, but also because it filled him with pride to share the company of some of the most powerful men in the Flathead—Rooster Evans and his father, Frank, along with Bud Andrews and Freddie Dubois, who were on the county council, Judge Thomas King, and Wayne Anderson, a banker. It felt good to be a man accepted so casually by those he admired.

Lawson was in no hurry to drink his beer. The last thing he wanted was for them to think drinking beer was important to him. These weren't the kind of men who approved of drunkenness.

Ten, maybe fifteen minutes passed. Wayne Anderson, the banker, handed more cans of beer to Lawson and Rooster. "Can't let this stuff get warm," he said. "No telling when Fowler will get here."

"Three minutes away," Lawson said, accepting the beer. "I'm guessing he's already crossed the Diamond Creek bridge."

"No kidding?" Anderson said, his tone friendly, not disbelieving.

"Heard his motor." Lawson corrected himself, trying to cover all bases. "Unless it's someone else."

The judge slapped Lawson's back. "Hey, boys, how would you all like to be a puppy again? Back when a feller had sharp eyes, sharp ears, and a tail ready to wag at anything."

The others chuckled dutifully.

Lawson shrugged away his pleasure at the attention. By example, James McNeill had taught him well over the years. Any show of emotion was a show of weakness. And he wanted to be, if nothing else, known as James McNeill's boy.

Within minutes, as Lawson had predicted, a new set of headlights appeared over the crest of the road. The group waited for the slamming of the truck's door. Then the judge, a skinny man with a lion's head, set down his beer and grabbed a rifle. He held it ready until Fowler called out his howdy then leaned the rifle back against a piece of firewood.

Fowler declined an offer to sit and declined a beer. Standing above the small group, Fowler wasted no time. "I'll get right to it," he said. "You all probably heard by now about the Flathead squaw we found early this morning at the Windsor Motel."

"Old news, Sheriff. Don't tell us this is the reason you dragged us up here."

"Cork it, Frank," Fowler told the rancher. "The reason I dragged you up here is because we need to talk some about what this means."

"Like what?" This from the judge, Thomas King.

"Like how we all agreed the first rule was nothing public. How do you expect me to cover something like this?"

"Hold on," Frank said. "Are you accusing one of us?"

"No," Fowler said. His tone suggested a bull pawing at dirt. "I'm not going to accuse any of you. Fact is, I don't want to hear one of you did it. What I saw this morning was more than I'll accept, and I'm telling you now if I find out who did it, I'll take—"

Fowler stopped short. A Winchester 30-30 leveled chest high has that effect on a man, no matter how sure he is of himself.

"That sounds real close to a threat," the judge said, standing with his legs braced.

"This ought to be good," Fowler said. "All day I've been looking for an excuse to lose my temper."

"Tommy, put the gun down," the banker said without rising. "This is not the OK Corral. Russ here wouldn't ever do anything as foolish as make threats. Just like we don't threaten him."

Frank burped to show his casual regard for the situation. The two councilmen watched with the same rigid silence they were famous for during town meetings and poker games. Lawson held his breath, fascinated by the palpable will of the strong men around him.

The judge finally lowered the rifle.

"Russ," the banker said, "Tommy's a little high-strung after last night's poker game. Forget his crankiness and tell us what bee is buzzing under your skirt."

"Two things." Fowler said. "The first is this: In my business, coincidences are disturbing, because they are rarely coincidences. All of you here have a good acquaintance with Doris Samson." Fowler jerked his thumb in the direction of the cabin in the darkness behind them. "I don't have to remind any of you about your week-long hunting trip last fall and how Doris and three of her friends provided entertainment the entire week."

"She's turned born-again," Rooster blurted. "Won't have nothing to do with that stuff anymore."

Fowler paused and let his words drop slowly. "Which is the coincidence I don't like. What if someone here took that personal? Wouldn't be the first time a man took it hard when a woman said no after saying yes real easy."

"Hang on," the banker said. "It was only a party here at the cabin. That don't mean—"

"Second thing," Fowler said. "The FBI is in on this now. Which means—"

"Russ, you promised to handle that for us," the judge said, anger in his voice.

"No," Fowler said. "*You* made the promises."

"Which I delivered. They sent in a rookie on a short leash. You handle the rest and keep a potato sack over his head."

Fowler didn't reply immediately. His labored breathing was audible above the crackling of the small fire. "I can't stop him from asking questions," he said at last. "And I got a bad feeling about him. He's got bulldog determination. If he learns enough to land on your doorstep, I want you warned. Which is part of why we're meeting tonight—to get some stories straight and ready for him. If worse comes to worst and it gets out she was up here last fall, we can't let it mess up the land deal." ▨

# Day 2

*"You remember this suit, don't you? Easter Sunday you wore it to church. All the other mothers were jealous of us. You were so handsome. Me—so beautiful."*

*He shivered, hopping from foot to foot on the tile floor beside the empty-ing bathtub.*

*She held a shirt out for him and smiled at his small naked body. It made him feel strange, strange like when she slept with him.*

*"These clothes smell funny," he said. "I want to go home."*

*"They smell like mothballs. And I want you to remember you are home, Little Bobby."*

*"I am not Little Bobby. My name is—"*

*Her hand moved so quickly, he didn't realize at first what had happened. It sounded like a thunderclap, and the blow rocked him sideways. He began to wail.*

*She folded the clothes neatly, set them on the edge of the counter, and when she was satisfied with that, finally scooped him into her arms. She kissed the top of his head. "There, there, Little Bobby. See how Mommy makes it right?"*

*She pushed him back to study his face. "See how Mommy makes it right?" Her question became a threat.*

*He wanted to tell her she wasn't his mother. But then she would hold the*

23

*candle flame beneath his palm again. She became angry when he didn't call her Mommy.*

*"Yes," he said, "Mommy makes it right."*

*"Mommy's glad Little Bobby knows who loves him." She patted his bare bottom. "Let's get you dressed now. All the other mothers will be so jealous of us."*

*He held out his small arms and let her pull a starchy shirt onto his upper body . . .*

Although the memory bothered him as he lay in bed waiting for the new day to begin, the Watcher smiled at a new thought. Maybe he should no longer think of himself as the Watcher, for he had finally gone beyond watching, hadn't he?

## 6:01 A.M.

"Behavioral science. Flannigan." Not even a full ring had passed before the curt answer.

"Mr. Flannigan," Clay said into the telephone, "I am Special Agent Clay Garner, calling from Kalispell, Montana. The first thing I should tell you is that I have not cleared this call with my special agent in charge."

Clay sat at the small desk beside his motel bed. He had a notebook open in front of him, the left page covered with writing, the right page blank. There was a large brown envelope beside the notebook. Clay had the telephone in his left hand, a pen in his right hand. Straight ahead he had a view of concrete blocks painted dull brown. By shifting his head to the right, he could admire less than ten feet of orange shag carpet and a window curtained with red fake velvet. If the FBI wanted to encourage agents to roam the field instead of camping in a hotel room, cheap accommodations were certainly incentive.

"Who's your SAC?" Flannigan asked.

"Warner, sir. Edward Warner."

"Great Falls, right?"

"Yes sir." Clay remembered Flannigan as a white-haired chain-smoker. The raspy voice on the other end reflected years of cigarette smoking.

"So why doesn't he know about this call?"

"Well, sir—"

"Cut the sir business. Try Dennis. You'll get further. Why haven't you cleared this call?"

Garner paused to gather his composure. It wasn't that he allowed any man to intimidate him; it was the pettiness and unpredictability of the FBI that bothered him. In the ninth and final week of training, Garner's instructors had told him and the rest of the class that they were about to face their most important exam, a test by J. Edgar himself. If they passed his personal inspection, they were in. If not, they were gone. On the day of the exam, all thirty-five of them waited in single file. Dark suits, dark ties, white shirts, black socks, black shoes. As the director, a man more powerful than the president, passed by, each candidate was supposed to say nothing more and nothing less than: "Hello, Mr. Hoover, my name is _____." One agent, nervous to the point of fainting, managed to stutter out, "Hello, Mr. Jones, my name is Edgar Hoover." The agent was fired immediately. Two others, deemed pinheads by Hoover, were fired later simply because their hat sizes were too small for someone who should represent Hoover as a Bureau man. It had filled Garner with gratitude for his own granite skull and a 7¾ hat size.

Thinking of Dennis Flannigan at the other end of the country and the other end of the line, Clay reminded himself that a frightened man spoke quickly. Clay made a conscious effort to drawl his words. "I haven't cleared it because I'm in the field and hope to speak informally."

"In other words, you don't want to get tied up in proper channels. Is that it?"

Garner couldn't tell if the question was meant as a reprimand. All he could do was plunge ahead. He barely remembered to bite off the word *sir*. "That is exactly it."

"Well, you do have me curious. By my watch, I'm guessing it's 0600 your time. Plenty early for a field op. And not every special agent thinks behavioral sciences is worth risking a reprimand. Why the call?"

Garner relaxed. "A murder here. I sat in on a lecture of yours. I—"

"Hoover's said behavioral sciences reflects its initials. I wouldn't have lectured a rookie class. Where'd you hear me?"

"D.C.," Garner said. "Convention for municipal police."

Dennis Flannigan's voice warmed. "A little above and beyond the call, wouldn't you say?"

"Just seemed prudent. I was in the area anyway."

Flannigan let that pass. Nobody merely crashed a police lecture. "You're calling me on a murder, huh? What makes you think the FBI should be involved?"

"It's what you were saying about serial killers."

"How many dead before?" Flannigan rapidly fired off questions. "Over what period of time? What do they have in common? Why haven't the locals called me?"

"Only one dead," Clay answered. "Yesterday morning. Locals want to believe it was one drunk Indian stabbing another. I don't."

"Hang on," Flannigan said. "If you sat in on a lecture, you know what we're about."

"Criminal psychology. Sex crimes. Hostage negotiation." Clay paused. "And serial killers."

No pause from Flannigan. Instead, an amused snort. "One dead body does not make for a serial killer."

"I believe it's a serial killer in the making. At least, if I remember right from your lecture."

Through the receiver, Clay heard the sound of a door closing. Then he heard a loud voice, although he couldn't make out the words. There was a long pause as Flannigan listened to the same voice. When he came back on the phone, he was curt again and businesslike.

"Look," Flannigan said, "nothing personal, but a few things are busting loose here. I don't have the time to sit and talk that I thought I did. Pitch me. If I buy into it, I'll call you when I can. If not, we both drop it. Either way, this call stays between you and me."

"Three things," Clay said without hesitation. He was reading from the left-hand page of his notebook. "Stab wounds with no bruises. Coin-sized marks on the carpet. And a feather."

"Keep going. You've got less than a minute."

"Murder weapon was a corkscrew," Clay said. "Yet the autopsy shows no signs of bruising around any of the puncture marks."

Clay swallowed. Yesterday's memories of the motel room and the Flathead woman's gory body were too vivid. "There were twenty-two punctures," Clay explained. "Each exactly two inches deep."

There was a ten-second pause. Then Flannigan spoke. "No bruises. In other words, no thrusting stabs with the corkscrew. Your guy leaned into her and slowly twisted the corkscrew in. Sounds like he was enjoying himself."

"My guess, too." Clay said. In the autopsy photos, the wounds had been swabbed clean. They looked innocent, tiny breaks in dusky skin. But they had allowed Doris Samson's heart to pump itself dry.

"Two inches deep," Flannigan continued to muse. "Perp didn't penetrate any vital organs. She bled to death slowly. He wasn't in a hurry, was he?"

"It doesn't seem so." Clay swallowed again, then said, "There was blood everywhere, except for three nickel-sized marks near the bed. Perfect circles, no blood, as if dimes had been placed there, gotten splashed, and then taken away after the blood began to dry."

"How far apart?" Flannigan asked.

Clay had the crime scene photos, too, but he didn't need to refer to them. "Twenty inches. In a perfect triangle."

Through the receiver, Clay heard several more sharp knocks on the door to Flannigan's office.

"I don't have time to guess," Flannigan said. "In fact, I'm standing right now and reaching for my jacket. What's your read on the circular marks?"

"I'm not sure yet," Clay said. "I was hoping you could help."

Flannigan paused, then spoke again. "Not right now. But I will. It's an easy guess that you've got someone killing for the fun of it, especially if he took his time. Because of that, you're right, it probably won't be the last. Give me your number and a time to call back."

Clay grinned at the depressing brown wall in front of him. He gave his number and told Flannigan that after dinner would be fine.

"Hey," Flannigan said, "I really gotta go. But what was that about a feather?"

"Crime techs found a feather in the dead woman's mouth."

"A feather? From a pillow, right? He gagged her with the pillow, and she swallowed a feather."

"No," Clay said, "more like a pinion feather. He had to make an effort to fold it up to get it into her mouth. The crime techs are guessing it's an eagle feather."

"Eagle feather?"

"Eagle feather," Clay said. "Like maybe he's leaving a message. But what's he trying to say? And who's supposed to get the message?"

# 10:05 A.M.

"Daddy," Kelsie said, "isn't it about time we took a break?"

They were standing at the side of the first grain shed in a row of four, all needing new paint. Flies buzzed and settled on the rough walls and buzzed again. Halfway up a stepladder, Kelsie pushed back a strand of hair and streaked red paint across her forehead as she looked down and waited for James McNeill to answer.

Standing several feet down from her, and in charge of the lower half of the shed, he set his brush across the top of the paint can. He *had* been working her hard, his solution to keeping her away from mooning over cowboys. His plan was to paint this grain shed with her, and if she wanted to talk about anything that was fine, but he wasn't going to press her. When this shed was done—and when he'd shown he was willing to work hard, too, instead of just handing her a project—he'd let her move on by herself to the other three sheds behind the main barn, and pay her well for her time.

"A break?" James said. "Why not? I'm due for a coffee and a smoke."

"I wish you wouldn't." She climbed down from the ladder.

"Coffee won't kill a man," he said, grinning as he reached for his tobacco pouch.

"But cigarettes will. And you knew exactly what I meant." Kelsie tried to act angry, but when her father grinned his watermelon-stealing grin, the best she could do was a halfhearted stamping of her foot. It was no wonder her mama had fallen for him, she thought. Her daddy was tall, rugged, and confident. Hat, boots, and all, he was like the cowboy from those cigarette ads. His hair had gone to gray, and his wrinkles had deepened, but Kelsie still thought he was the handsomest man in the world—and the most exasperating.

"Go on," he said. "See if the mail's here. I'll meet you up at the house."

Kelsie nodded and began a half-jog toward the corner of the barn. From there, her father knew, she'd go past the corral and, if it was there, to the old Ford pickup where the keys always rested in the ignition. She'd be gone at least five minutes, down to the end of the driveway to the mailbox and back, plenty of time to finish a cigarette before he joined her in the kitchen.

James McNeill absently rolled a cigarette as he watched his daughter leave. She'd been unusually silent this morning. He fervently hoped it had nothing to do with any of the cowboys.

Kelsie hopped into the truck. She'd been driving it since she was eleven, although her daddy made it a strict rule she couldn't take it onto county roads—not until she officially had her driver's license in a few days.

As usual, straw and chunks of dried mud were scattered on the floor of the cab. Pieces of twine covered the seat, and the ashtray overflowed with cigarette butts. The dash was covered with dust. This was not her father's traveling vehicle—he wouldn't tolerate the mess—but an old truck he made available for odd jobs around the ranch. All the hired hands knew it was there for short-haul trips, and it was used often. It didn't make sense to try to keep it clean.

Kelsie grunted as she moved the stick shift into gear, double-clutched as she backed the truck onto the driveway, and wrestled the steering wheel into a turn to follow the driveway. She could see flashes of the Flathead Valley between the tall spruces on the downhill side of the road. The cobalt of the lake below was a teasing reminder of how hot she was beneath her coveralls.

From the last turn of the driveway, Kelsie saw that the flag was down at the mailbox. It didn't fill her with anticipation, for she didn't expect mail for herself. The only person she wrote to was a pen pal in Australia through the 4-H club, and Kelsie had sent her a letter only the week before, so she knew it would be at least two weeks before she heard anything in return.

The sheaf of letters she pulled from the mailbox looked like the usual assortment of bills, bank notices, and business correspondence she picked up on other days. As she flipped through them, one envelope caught her attention. It had no stamp, no return address, not even the address of the McNeill ranch. All the envelope had on it was her name, spelled wrong—KELSY MACNEILL—in thick block letters. The lack of postage on the envelope told her that someone had slipped the letter among the other mail.

Her first impulse was to look around. The experience of the evening before was fresh in her mind.

Should she open it now? Later? Throw it away?

Kelsie climbed back into the old pickup and locked the doors for perhaps the first time since James McNeill had purchased it at an auction five years earlier. She sat behind the steering wheel, staring at the letter. At last curiosity mixed with dread overcame her, and she slowly removed the letter from the envelope.

The letter was also written in pencil, in thick, block letters.

> Kelsy, I have been watching you with the love that our souls have been destined to have sinse before time began. Why do you hurt me by looking at others? I am the only one for your affektions. Our spirits are like eagles sircling the sun. If I have to pull your soul out of your body to keep you, I will make myself dy too and we will have life together beyond the flesh. Forever. That is what our love means. Don't hurt me by thinking of others, or they will see the feather. The feather is your warning. And that is their punishment. If you don't believe me, remember that Doris died to punish him for taking your attention. This is my first letter to let you know of our love. Keep it secrit. Don't let our secrit go beyond. If you tell anyone of our sacrid bond, I will visit them and they will be harmed too, just like Doris. Remember, the eagle leaves a feather when it takes its prey. I am your Watcher. Forever.

Kelsie was shaking so hard that she was barely able to grind the stick shift into gear. She stalled the truck twice. This must have been the person who placed an eagle feather in her diary, she thought. Who was Doris? She couldn't really be dead, could she? And who was being punished with the supposed death?

All the way up the driveway, she fought with a decision. Should she tell her father about the letter? She'd been warned to keep it secret or others would be punished. But how could this awful person get close to her father to punish him?

Her decision was taken away from her.

She parked the pickup then walked into the kitchen to see her father already at the table, two coffee mugs and a plate of cookies in front of him, hat hooked behind him on the corner of his chair.

He was twirling a large feather in his hands.

"Strangest thing," he said. "I think it's an eagle feather. I found this by the coffeepot when I walked in. Any idea how it got there?"

# 11:50 A.M.

Russ Fowler locked himself in the one-car garage in the back of his yard. He'd told his wife he needed to tinker on the carburetor he'd pulled from his '60 Corvette parked in the driveway. She cared so little about his passion for rebuilding old cars, if she did open the hood to check his story, she'd have difficulty pointing out a spark-plug wire, let alone a carb.

Before beginning his task, Fowler switched on a bright overhead light and pulled down the blinds. He didn't even want a passing glance from a neighbor. In this town, word got around quickly, and the sight of the sheriff facing a workbench lined with a couple dozen beer cans might be misinterpreted. Or worse, interpreted correctly.

Satisfied that he had both privacy and time, Fowler plugged a Johnny Cash eight-track into the stereo player and adjusted the volume to a background level. He hummed along as he began his task. Fingerprinting.

The night before, after the campfire discussions had ended, Fowler followed all the trucks back down the forestry road to the main highways. Once the vehicles scattered, he had turned around and retraced the route into the hills, all the way back to the campfire. It had meant an extra forty minutes each way, but he felt it worthwhile, for it gave him the chance to collect all the evening's empty beer cans, which were now in front of him. He'd picked each one up by inserting a pen into the open tab and lifting it upside down; dregs of beer ran down the pen and onto his hand each time, but it ensured he did not contaminate the cans with his own prints.

In the garage, Fowler used a pair of alligator pliers to hold the first can by the rim. With his other hand, he used a small brush of soft fibers to apply finely ground carbon powder to the aluminum. He was confident he would find latent prints, caused by a transfer of the skin's oil onto a clean surface.

The first set of prints emerged, and he was careful to brush as much as possible in the direction of the ridge details of the prints. Brushing crossways might destroy the print, and although it had been awhile since he'd been called upon to fingerprint a crime scene, to Fowler a lesson learned was not forgotten.

Once a set of prints emerged—carbon dust clinging to the finger-print oil left on the can—Fowler peeled a small strip of transparent acetate tape from its roll. The tape, similar to Scotch tape, was two inches wide and capable of covering one single print. He pressed the tape on the first clear print and lifted it away. His final step was to transfer it onto a three-by-five card. He did this for each print on the can. The entire process took him close to fifteen minutes.

Fowler took a deep breath, mentally crossing his fingers. With all the other beer cans remaining to be tested, it would be nice if these prints matched those on another file card beside him.

He held both cards up to the light, comparing each set of prints. It had been awhile, too, since he'd done this kind of exercise, and after a few minutes of squinting, he decided they did not match. The first set of prints consisted mainly of whirls; the second, taken from the beer can, revealed a loop pattern of ridges.

He grunted. He hadn't expected to get lucky on the first try. He had little expectation to get lucky at all at the end of dusting all the beer cans, but it had to be done.

The first set of prints—Fowler's comparison set, a partial of a thumb and forefinger—came from the corkscrew that had been found in Doris Samson's body.

While he would have much preferred to be tinkering on a carbu-retor, Fowler knew it would be worth his time if he discovered any of the beer-can prints matched those lifted from the corkscrew.

Fowler also knew it was a long shot. Chances were the murderer was not one of the men at last night's campfire. On the other hand, in his career Fowler had seen weirder long shots break the ribbon. Everyone in the group had known Doris. After last fall and the stag party, all were in a position to be compromised. Maybe a few had seen her later. Maybe she'd made some threats. Maybe there was something with the land deal that Fowler didn't know about. This was a small community. Even Fowler, closer than most to the under-currents, didn't understand all of what roiled beneath the surface. It wouldn't hurt to eliminate the long-shot possibility—or to confirm it.

Fowler continued his work. He knew full well that establishing a match would not give him the murderer's identification, for at this point, of course, he had no way of confirming who had held which can of beer. Yet, if he did find a match on one of the cans, he would know for certain the murderer had been one of the men at the campfire. If the long shot came in, man by man, he would find a way to get each man's fingerprints and narrow it down.

Fowler took another deep breath and bent over the next aluminum can. Yes, if one of the seven had indeed killed the Flathead woman, the knowledge would be leverage of incredible value against men with far more money and connections than Fowler. If anything went wrong with the land deal, Fowler would have something with which to protect himself.

Six more cans and nearly two hours later, Fowler banged his fist on the workbench in triumph. He'd found a match! One man out of the campfire's seven was now only a sheriff's report away from a conviction of deliberate homicide. And in Montana, that meant execution by rope or lethal injection. How much more power could Fowler ask for?

## 5:20 P.M.

Harold Hairy Moccasin led Johnny Samson to a grassy knoll above Flathead Lake. Two men stood in the clearing and waited in silence, each carrying a rifle.

The first, Nick Buffalo, wore a cowboy hat, jeans, and a red-and-black flannel shirt. He was of medium height, with a body that was muscular, yet graceful.

Sonny Cutknife, slightly taller and much slimmer than his partner, did not have the luxury of a hat brim over his face. A yellow headband covered most of his broad forehead; a choker of shells covered his neck. He'd woven his hair into two long braids, and he was dressed in buckskin leggings, a clean white T-shirt, and a buckskin vest.

Two days earlier, Johnny Samson might have been intimidated by the two men, who were a good ten years older than he was; he might have been intimidated by their rifles and their silence. Not now. Yesterday had aged him. Miserable from a hangover, and much more miserable because of his sister's death, he hardly cared that they wanted to see him and had chosen a lonely spot that was a two-mile hike up from Harold Hairy Moccasin's truck.

"Nobody followed you?" Nick asked Harold.

Harold waved carelessly behind him. "You think maybe they can sneak up on us? Remember, we're the redskins."

"That's not what I asked," Nick said, unamused.

"Cool it, Nick," Sonny said. "Harold's not the one that took out Doris."

Harold gave a lopsided grin of submission to both of them. He reached into his back pocket and took out a flask of rye whiskey. He unscrewed the cap, took a hit, and passed the bottle to Nick. Nick flung the bottle without watching its flight through the air.

"Harry, get the party thing out of your head," Nick said. "That's not what we're about."

Harold stared after the bottle, pulling nervously at his nine straggling chin hairs.

Sonny addressed Johnny. "Don't let Nick give you a bad impression. Normally, he doesn't say much. Maybe you didn't know. He was sweet on Doris. Helped her move into her apartment even. Did you know that?"

"Shut up, Sonny." Nick said to Johnny, "I was just being nice. Nothing happened between me and her. Sonny's got a big mouth."

Sonny shrugged. He rested his rifle in the crook of his left arm. "So you tell him what we're about."

Nick glared at Sonny and moved away from the three of them to sit on the grass and stare at the lake. Harold went in the opposite direction. He hadn't heard the smash of breaking glass and was hoping the bottle had dropped through some bushes to land intact and upright.

"Go ahead," Sonny invited Johnny. "Sit down. Relax. I want to talk to you."

Johnny had a half-frown on his face as he looked at Sonny.

"I know," Sonny said, "Sometimes I sound different. Blame it on the university. I slip up and talk educated white."

Johnny's frown deepened.

"Bureau of Indian Affairs broke up my family when I was a baby. Sent my older brothers and sisters to boarding schools. Me, they put in an orphanage. I was adopted by a white family," Sonny explained. "Christian do-gooders, determined to do mission work at home. They sent me to college." He grinned. "But don't worry. I'm no apple."

"Apple?" Johnny said. Events seemed to be happening all around him, and he was doing his best to keep them straight. Home schooling was good, he knew, but sometimes he had a difficult time with lingo that others took for granted.

"Apple. Red on the outside, white on the inside. Someone who has sold out to the European colonizers. I ditched my family the day I graduated."

"Oh," Johnny said.

"Yeah. See, what I learned in school was how badly we'd been treated. The first step to freedom was to set myself loose. Get back to our traditions. That's what we're about. There's not many of us yet, but give us time."

"Oh," Johnny said.

"Second step . . . well, that's why we asked Harold to bring you here."

Johnny waited. What could they want from him? He didn't have money. He'd worked at the McNeill ranch two summers now. So had Nick and Sonny, and they had never bothered to talk to him much. Not that Johnny expected it, being so young and all.

"Are you angry?" Sonny asked.

Johnny thought that through. Doris was dead. He still couldn't believe it. He wanted to find the person who killed Doris. Then everyone would see how angry he was.

"Of course you're angry, Johnny. Ever heard of the American Indian Movement? The leaders, they got it right on. You live in a system that puts you in the ghettos, man. They throw a few material possessions at you and expect you to be happy. You see families on the reservation living in abandoned car bodies all winter long. There are boarding schools with teachers who abuse young boys. I could tell you things that would make you scream with rage. And the things they did to put us here. Broke treaties. Killed us with their whiskey and disease. When that didn't work, they starved us and raped our women. Of course you're angry."

Johnny Samson thought of his grandfather, of his slow, dignified ways, and his calm acceptance of life in the hills. Maybe the old ones didn't see the world in the way that they should.

"Not only have they have robbed us of our land, but worse, of our tradition. They want to Europeanize us. We, who have lived in harmony with the Great Mother Earth for centuries. We know that humans do not have the right to degrade Mother Earth. Europeans have not only abused us, they have abused the earth and poisoned the air. They do this and feel no sense of loss. They turn the mountains into gravel. The lakes become coolant for their factories, and we are shoved aside to live in ghettos."

Johnny wouldn't ever brag he knew much, but he was willing to guess Sonny had made this speech a few times before. It had that kind of cadence. Still, it was impressive.

"Europeans, they know nothing of truth," Sonny said. "To them, truth is what they tried to teach me in college. Truth to them is the latest theory. But as soon as the theory is improved, the truth changes. So for them, the truth shifts. We know truth, Johnny. Our tradition teaches us truth. Truth of spirit, truth of the earth, truth of the ages. We are part of that truth. It does not change. Johnny, are you angry?"

"I could be, maybe, if I work at it," Johnny said because he felt some reply was expected. "Let me get a hold of the one who killed my sister. That's where I'm mad."

Sonny wasn't listening. "The do-gooders, they sent me to Sunday school. I learned about Moses. He had his own tribe, captive in Egypt, long ago when our people were free to roam this great land and hunt the buffalo and to fish clean lakes. Moses went to the pharaoh and said, let our people go. That's what we have to say, Johnny. Let our people go. The pharaoh didn't listen to Moses, not until the plagues. Well, you look around, you see plenty of plagues inflicted on the whites: Violence in the cities, people homeless, parents abusing children, hospitals filled with people dying of cancer from the poisoned air and poisoned water. Trouble is, man, those same plagues have been inflicted on us."

He shook his head in theatrical anger. "That train, man? The one that crashed last week? You know how bad it was, spilled those chemicals on reservation land."

"I know how bad it was," Johnny said. "Some of it spilled on my grandfather's land."

"See?" Sonny said. "See? A plague inflicted right on you."

Sonny paused and beamed his wisdom at Johnny. "What's right and true is that we find a way to inflict plagues on the whites. Until they set us free."

Sonny patted Johnny on the back. "We want you to join us, my young brother. Make them pay the price for what they did to your sister. Make them pay the price for taking our land. Help us set the plagues loose."

"How do I do that?" Johnny asked.

"For a start," Sonny said, "you don't do anything different, except at the ranch. Hang out more with us instead of going back to your grandfather's cabin every night. Maybe we'll work it so you spend time with me and Nick."

"Nick?" Johnny wondered how much fun it would be to work with Nick.

"Sure," Sonny said. "We're going to let you join our little club. All you got to do then is wait for what happens next. We promise, it will be worth the wait. Whites will pay. For everything—including your sister."

Johnny thought about it for a moment. He didn't really want to be part of any war, but he'd be putting in his time as a ranch hand anyway. And if along the way Sonny and Nick happened to give him the chance to get the person who got Doris, so much the better.

"Sure," he said. After all, what harm was there in going along for the ride? He could always hop off later, couldn't he?

## 6:20 P.M.

"Garner," Flannigan said without preamble, "make any progress today?"

"Sure," Clay said. "This phone call."

"Eh?"

"You called back. It's the best I've been able to do today. You'd think I'd rolled around with a dead skunk as much as I could find anyone who wanted to answer questions."

Flannigan laughed. "Looked in a mirror lately?"

"This motel wall is bad enough." Clay was leaning forward at the small desk, frowning at the dull brown paint. "I don't need my reflection to make it worse."

"Suit and tie and haircut, Garner. You might as well stamp FBI across your forehead. We're not the most popular law enforcement agency in the country. And this is at a time when *pig* is the nicest name they'll give anyone with a badge. If you've been asking questions of reservation people, that's tougher yet. Wounded Knee is barely over, and they won't have forgotten it, not by a long shot."

Clay sighed. "Thanks for telling me something I didn't know."

"Ask Warner to free budget money for informers."

Paying for information was a common FBI tactic if the money were available or if the special agent in charge cared. Clay Garner wasn't about to tell Flannigan that SAC Edward Warner was a not-so-secret drunk counting out his days until retirement. Many were the agents who wondered what Warner had on the boys at the top to be able to remain entrenched in Great Falls.

"I appreciate the suggestion," Clay replied. "But I'm not even sure how long Warner will leave me here in the field."

Flannigan laughed his raspy laugh. "The old souse won't give you a penny. But next report, write some hogwash about the possibility of the American Indian Movement conspiracy. Make sure the report gets past him to Washington. Someone will find money quick enough. Nothing gets wheels turning faster than the threat of commies or revolution. And everyone is still nervous about Wounded Knee."

Clay found himself nodding and smiling.

"Let's get to it," Flannigan said. "My wife has threatened to divorce me next time I'm in the office later than nine P.M. I might be able to get away with it twice this week but not three times."

"I've got the report in front of me," Clay said quickly.

"Forget the report. Tell me what you remembered. Reports are for later, when you're out of gut reaction."

Clay began to describe the room and how the sheriff's men had found Doris Samson, answering Flannigan's occasional questions as well as he could. Bitter sadness filled him as he spoke. He could not shake his anger at seeing the dead woman, pain twisted on her face.

"She was fully clothed?" Flannigan interrupted, as if he wasn't sure he'd heard Clay correctly.

"Fully clothed. No signs of sexual assault." She'd been bound to the bedposts with strips of towel, and her killer had punctured her clothes and skin with the corkscrew. The blood had seeped through her clothes and soaked the bed as thoroughly as if buckets had been poured on her. But there was nothing to show crazed lust.

"That definitely points to a first-time kill then," Flannigan said. "If there is a next time, he'll be bolder, more sure of himself."

"Meaning?"

Flannigan sighed. "There's got to be something about the feather in her mouth. If there's any key at all to understanding serial killers, it's some kind of sexual frustration. Something in their past keeps them from being able to form a healthy relationship. Your man—"

"Is that a safe assumption? That the killer is male?"

"Ninety-nine percent safe assumption. Female serial killers are almost unknown. Figure on male until you see something to indicate otherwise."

"Sure," Clay said. "Sorry for interrupting. This man—"

"—is inexperienced," Flannigan said. "He's maybe fantasized about something like this for years. Then one day he has the chance and makes it reality. Only he was nervous. He didn't prepare for it. He was afraid of getting caught."

"Didn't prepare?"

"You said her wrists and ankles had been tied with torn strips of towel. He improvised—did what he could with the material at hand. I'm guessing the same with the corkscrew. Maybe he found it in her purse or in the motel room. This first one, it's almost like an accident. He gets a kick from it, begins to plan the next one better. He'll make a killing kit to suit his style. Maybe throw in pieces of rope or a roll of duct tape. Murder weapon. Some we've seen make their vans an entire kit. The interstates have become a hunting trail. Once a serial killer pulls a woman inside, no one sees her again."

Clay swallowed hard. In the lecture, Flannigan's theories had been interesting on an intellectual level. Now, however, with the vision of the dead woman so real in his mind, Clay felt chills of horror to think of human predators roaming the highways to pluck victims at random.

"Can we be certain it will happen again?" Clay asked.

"Pray it doesn't. Don't be surprised if it does. And don't be surprised if it gets worse. With practice, he'll be more relaxed, more sophisticated. He'll have had time to think about it, and he'll have new ways to experiment."

"Flannigan, I want to throw up." Clay swallowed hard. "How can anyone be so twisted? So evil?"

There was silence, filled only by the slight static of the long-distance phone call.

"God only knows," Flannigan finally said. The barrier of distance could not disguise the quiet anguish in his answer or the fact he meant his statement literally. "I've been asking Him the same question myself for years and still haven't heard back."

More silence. Clay thought of the countless times he'd flung a single angry question upward in the past few years, only to be answered with the stone-cold silence of his own heart.

"Here's what you need to do." Flannigan spoke quickly, as if regretting his lapse into emotion. "Find out as much about her background as possible."

"I'm driving out to see her grandfather tomorrow."

"I'll be surprised if he can help you with the questions you really need answered. Was she a barfly? One boyfriend? Or lots of men? Either way, you're looking for a killer who is smooth with women. Someone smart and probably charming."

"The booking of the motel room," Clay said. It had been one of Flannigan's first questions earlier.

"You catch on fast. She signed for the room and the key. Either he had talked her into doing it, or later he talked himself into her room."

"Any thoughts on the coin marks?"

"Marks?" Flannigan repeated.

"Three circles in the blood."

"Oh. Right." Short silence. "No thoughts. Look, send me all the photos and reports you can. I'll do my best from here. In the meantime, you have a lot of old-fashioned legwork ahead of you. Let me give you three pieces of advice."

"Sure."

"First piece you probably know, and I hope the local law knows it. Don't release anything to the public about the feather in her mouth or the three circles in the blood. More often than not, you'll have some loony making a confession. Hold back the details, and if the confession doesn't match, you know you've got someone looking for attention. Also, that way you won't be fooled by any copycat killings."

"Nothing's been released yet. Not even the murder weapon."

"Good. Second piece of advice. I've gone through your records here. Impressive. Impressive with the West Virginia state police force. Impressive in training here. It won't surprise me to see you moving up quickly. Don't ruin your chances by spending so much time on this that you forget about the reason Warner sent you in. He might not care, but some paper-pusher somewhere will, and all your reports stay on file forever. If you can tie this in to what you're doing, fine. If not, go slow. Nothing gets you a red flag quicker in this organization than a reputation for playing the game outside of the team. Got it?"

"Sure," Clay said slowly. He wondered why Flannigan had gone to the effort of pulling his records. He wondered if Flannigan had read far enough to know about a loaded coal truck on two-lane asphalt shiny with rain, and how badly ten tons of equipment at fifty miles an hour had crushed a Datsun pickup truck with Clay's wife and daughter inside.

"Third piece of advice," Flannigan continued, "keep yourself out of what you do."

"I don't understand," Clay said, grateful Flannigan hadn't brought up the subject of the accident.

"Don't let any of today's liberal psychology fool you. If you're up against a serial killer, you're not up against someone who society has forced into wrongdoings. You're up against evil. Real evil. If you let it get inside, it's like letting him inside."

There was a long pause before Flannigan spoke again. "I want you to know something a philosopher noted," Flannigan said softly. "When you look at the monster, it's looking back at you. And, Garner?"

"Yes?"

"This one's not in its cage."

# 8:40 P.M.

The Watcher stood among the trees and watched Kelsie's bedroom window until the light was finally turned off. There was always the hope she might walk past her window. Out here she had no need for privacy. The Watcher smiled a love smile as he waited and hoped for a glimpse of her. She had not spoken to anyone about the letter. And because she had not spoken about the letter, The Watcher knew Kelsie understood their secret love and that it must be kept secret. The Watcher had learned well from the woman in his past, hadn't he?

*"Do you love this kitten, Little Bobby?"*

*The boy nodded. It had been days since he had tried to tell her that his name was not Little Bobby. He almost believed he was Little Bobby, but he could still remember his own mother, and he missed her badly.*

*"Say it, Little Bobby. You love the kitten."*

*"I love the kitten."*

*"'I love the kitten, Mommy.'" She shook her finger at him in mock anger. "Don't forget to call me Mommy."*

*"I love the kitten, Mommy."*

*The kitten was gray. He had played with it all day. In the afternoon, it had fallen asleep on his chest. The boy had listened to the kitten purr as it curled up against him.*

*"I'm glad you know what love means," she said. "Do you know what dead means?"*

*"That's when you go to sleep and wake up in heaven."*

*"No," the woman said. "Dead is much, much worse. Be a good boy, Little Bobby, and watch your Mommy. She'll show you what dead means."*

*She scooped the kitten in one arm, and with her other arm, took Little Bobby by the hand. She led him into the kitchen.*

*The kitten meowed as she set it down on the cutting board.*

*"Little Bobby," she said, "if you close your eyes, I will get the clothes-pins again. You must watch. It is important for you to know what dead means."*

*The boy did not take his eyes off the kitten. He wanted to hold it again.*

*"Good," she said. "Remember, you must watch to learn."*

*She grabbed a large butcher knife from beside the sink.*

# Day 3

As the lawyer approached on foot, George Samson was leaning back in a rocking chair on his wide front porch. His eyes were closed, his breathing deep. To the lawyer, George Samson appeared to be asleep.

The lawyer coughed. George remained undisturbed.

The lawyer flicked his eyes beyond George to the small cabin. It was tucked into a hill, facing south toward the lake. By the saw marks on the weathered, peeled logs of the cabin, the lawyer knew they had been cut by hand. The chimney was made of irregular-sized stones set in concrete, and the lawyer could imagine this older man, working on a similar sunny July day decades earlier, taking joy in building his own house.

The lawyer knew exactly how long George Samson had lived on the edge of the reservation, for he had personally searched the deed to this land and seen Samson's signature etched in black ink nearly thirty years before. The lawyer even knew some of the story behind it: Five machine-gun bullets had stitched through George's right leg as he pulled a fellow soldier away from oncoming German tanks. He had taken home a Purple Heart, and he had also taken home four years of army wages and poker winnings, which he had used to buy the land. It was an extremely mature decision for someone only twenty years old.

Looking at the man and his cabin, the lawyer envied George Samson the apparent simplicity of his life. The lawyer also felt some regret for the man. Samson's simplicity was about to end.

The lawyer coughed louder. George Samson opened his eyes without alarm.

"Good morning," the lawyer said. "My name is Earl Madigan."

George Samson watched the lawyer. He was not hostile, merely curious. It discomforted Earl. The older man had not yawned, nor blinked, nor shifted, nor stretched. Yet he seemed totally alert.

"I have business with you," Madigan told Samson. "County business."

"Join me up here," Samson replied. "It's a long walk from where you must have parked your car. I'll get you some water."

Earl did not want to accept the courtesy, not with the business he needed to discuss. George Samson's words, however, held a measured peace. Refusal seemed ridiculous in the presence of the man's dignified strength.

Earl climbed the short steps onto the front porch. George Samson rose to greet him, extending a hand, which, again, seemed ridiculous to ignore.

The older man wore jeans and a faded denim shirt. His hair was a brilliant white, corded into a ponytail. Although the skin on his face and neck had loosened with age, he was still straight-shouldered handsome. The steadiness of his posture and the unwavering confidence in his black eyes gave him an aura that mesmerized Earl.

"I'll have no quarrel if you loosen your tie, Mr. Madigan," George said as he stepped toward the cabin's front door. "We're not in your law office."

Earl loosened his tie and stared at Samson's back. How did this backhills Flathead know Earl Madigan was an attorney?

George Samson returned a few minutes later with two Mason jars of water and a plate of sliced apples. He set them on a stool and gestured for Earl to take a chair on the other side of the stool.

Earl sat.

George pulled up another chair and faced Earl. "How old are you?" George asked. He offered the plate to Earl.

"Thirty-five." Earl took a slice of apple and bit into it.

"Family?"

"Yes." He chewed and swallowed. "Two young boys."

"See much of them? Or does work keep you from them?"

"I provide," George said defensively. How had the conversation gone this far this quickly?

"I imagine that is a considerable load on your shoulders."

"No more than any other father. In this world, you do what you have to."

"I meant it literally," George Samson said. "Tight muscles. You carry your shoulders high. Your head is almost hunched from the strain. I saw it as you stood and now as you sit. You have my sympathy."

Slowly, Earl relaxed his shoulders and discovered the old man's observation had been correct. The difference in position was considerable. How could he not have noticed the strain himself?

George Samson smiled and offered more apple slices. "Mr. Madigan, good news is never important enough for anyone to visit here. What bad news do you bring?"

Five minutes before, Earl might have stalled for time by countering with a question. Five minutes before, however, he had regarded George Samson merely as an older Indian.

"The county wants to annex your property," Earl answered, surprised at how refreshing it was to speak without games. He braced himself, though, for outrage.

"I would prefer not to sell, Mr. Madigan." George Samson spoke calmly. "I am fond of this land. I built this cabin myself, and it has many memories for me."

"You're in a difficult position, Mr. Samson. There are provisions in the land-act laws. Moreover, there are now environmental issues resulting from chemical spillover from the recent freight-train derailment. By the time the dust settles, you may have no choice. My advice to you—"

George Samson held up a hand. He smiled as he spoke, voice still level. "If you are representing the county, wouldn't any of your advice to me be a conflict of interest?"

"Well . . ."

"I know you are a younger man, Mr. Madigan. So please understand I am taking liberties because of our age difference."

"Yes?"

"My advice to you is to listen carefully before speaking. I told you I would prefer not to sell. That doesn't mean I will fight you to the end on this. If if seems more sensible for me to sell, I will. Save your impressive threats until you need them."

"Yes sir." His own words surprised him. Earl wondered when he had last called anyone "sir."

"Why don't you leave your papers with me," George Samson said. "Let me consider the county's offer before you and I decide what to do next."

"You and I? It's the county. They sent me—"

"You and I. There will be much to discuss. I cannot talk to a county. I can, however, talk with you."

"You and I," Earl said, hiding a smile. This man had put him off balance from the beginning and, in lawyer's terms, had handily won every round of the first fight.

"One other piece of advice," George Samson said. "As you walk back down to your car, look around you with new eyes. There will be a day when you are not young and healthy. You will wish then you had enjoyed the sun on your face and the cries of the birds in your ears. There will be plenty of time later in your office to worry about this matter."

Had the old man just warned him to expect a battle? Or was this a firm dismissal? Either way the conversation seemed over.

Earl stood and thanked George Samson for the water and sliced apples. Then the lawyer walked back down the hill, wondering if he should have offered the old man condolences on the death of his granddaughter, Doris Samson.

Long before the lawyer was out of sight on the winding path that led down from the cabin, George Samson closed his eyes and returned to the time of prayer that the lawyer had interrupted.

## 1:05 P.M.

Sheriff Russell Fowler walked into the Kalispell First National Bank carrying a small briefcase. It was new, made of simulated leather, and the lights of the bank interior reflected dully on the material.

Fowler nodded at a few tellers. They smiled back. Although Fowler was in uniform, they saw him often and found nothing alarming about the presence of the sheriff.

"Marge, is Wayne in?" he asked a woman who was flipping through ledgers at a desk to the side and back from the tellers' counter.

"Go on back, Sheriff," she said without looking up from her work. "It should be fine."

Fowler stepped past her and into Wayne Anderson's office. Anderson was standing near a window staring down the street. He was a tall, thin man, clean-shaven, with lines beginning to show around his mouth and eyes. His hair was still glossy brown, although Fowler believed some of the color came from a bottle. Anderson wore one of the new-fangled leisure suits and burnished cowboy boots. He nodded at Fowler.

"Morning," Fowler said. He tossed the briefcase in a slow, high arc toward the banker.

Anderson caught it easily.

"Just like high-school football, Wayne. You had the surest hands in the county."

"And you had one of the worst throwing arms, I recall. It's a miracle we won the three games we did." Wayne set the briefcase on the desk. "What's with this?"

"Look inside," Fowler said.

Wayne flipped open the latches.

Fowler glanced around the office. Anderson's desk took most of one side. There were two chairs near the door. A high bookshelf, filled with hardcovers, stood against the far wall. Diplomas and community service awards hung on the walls, including a photo of Fowler and Anderson holding a string of thirty lake trout they'd caught on a trip into the Northwest Territories of Canada well before either had grandchildren.

"What am I supposed to be seeing here?" Wayne asked, looking down at the now-open briefcase.

"That stuff is from the motel room where we found the dead squaw. See if any of it looks familiar to you."

"I don't like that talk," Wayne said. "I like it less in the bank."

Fowler shrugged. "In those plastic evidence bags, you'll see a jackknife, some cuff links, and a piece of a ripped tie. Chances are, they came from the killer. All I want is for you to take a close look. See if it belongs to anyone you know."

Wayne frowned. "Russ, you're flogging a dead horse. None of us did it."

"Wouldn't you like to be certain? If I've got to cover up a mess, I need to know who to cover." Fowler paused long enough to make it significant. "Chances are if one goes down, all of us do."

Wayne stepped away from his desk, moved past Fowler, who remained motionless, and closed his office door.

Wayne returned to the briefcase and sifted through the plastic bags. "No," Wayne said at last. "Nothing is familiar. I haven't seen any of this with anyone we know. Satisfied?"

Fowler shrugged again. He'd have been surprised if the banker recalled ever seeing any of the items. None had come from the motel room murder scene. Fowler had accomplished his goal, however. By now the briefcase and the evidence bags carried plenty of Anderson's fingerprints.

"Hope you don't mind," Fowler said. "I'm going to have Larry take a look."

"Do you think that's wise?"

"Sure." Fowler grinned. "That way he can tell me none of this belongs to you."

"Is that an attempt at humor?"

"A bad one," Fowler said. "Sorry." He reached across the desk, snapped the briefcase shut, and picked it up.

"How's the FBI making out on the train wreck?" Wayne asked.

"Stonewalled. The judge arranged to have him called back in the next day or so."

"Good," Wayne said. "Everything is going as planned."

"Not that you were ever worried."

Wayne gave a small, cool smile of triumph. "Don't lose the evidence that puts Rooster and Lawson at the train site though. It never hurts to have a couple of fall guys in place."

Fowler thought of the beer can and corkscrew sets of fingerprints he had waiting to compare against the banker's and smiled an equally cold smile in return. "You're right, Wayne. A fall guy or two for backup never hurts."

## 2:31 P.M.

"Hey, Johnny," Sonny Cutknife said, "you think staring like that is good for you? You're gonna scorch your eyeballs."

Both men were well past the main barn. They stood at the side of a pickup truck, its back end filled with fence posts. They had unloaded less than a quarter of the posts and were pausing to allow Sonny a cigarette break.

Johnny Samson looked away from the blonde girl in jeans and a T-shirt where she was putting a coat of paint on a shed a couple hundred yards closer to the ranch house. "I wasn't staring."

"And my lips don't move when I talk. If Old Man McNeill finds out you're thinking those thoughts, he'll bury you ten feet under."

Sonny took a long drag, squinted his eyes against the cigarette smoke and hot afternoon sun, and changed the subject. "People in this valley, they're going to learn the price it costs to oppress the native sons."

"Yeah," Johnny said, although his heart was not in it. Sonny's diatribes were becoming tiresome. He had listened for an hour on the way into Kalispell to go to the lumber yard and an hour on the way back. How Johnny figured it, you had white skin or you had red skin. White or red, you did the best you could with what life gave you. Without complaining.

Johnny pulled on his leather work gloves and reached for a fence post.

"Not so fast," Sonny said. "Still got my smoke."

"You finish, then. It don't mean I can't start unloading."

"Johnny, I got a lot to teach you. White man, he works against a schedule. You got to learn to be natural. Relax, man, get into the rhythm of the day, don't worry about no time clock."

"My rhythm tells me we got to unload these." Johnny grunted and pulled at two fence posts. "Nothing natural about expecting them to jump out themselves."

"Johnny—" Sonny did not finish his sentence.

Johnny lifted his head to see what had interrupted Sonny.

A man was walking toward them, a tall, gangly man in a suit and tie. He stopped to talk briefly to the rancher's daughter.

Johnny watched as she pointed up at them and the pickup truck and the small stack of fence posts already on the ground. The man nodded. It looked like he handed her something before he continued his way toward them.

"Watch where you step, city boy," the older one said. "Around here, cows ain't been potty-trained."

Clay didn't rise to the bait by looking down. He smiled blandly and hoped the one with the attitude was not Johnny Samson. His headband, the tattoos, the silver and turquoise jewelry—all of it reminded Clay of the photographs he'd seen of the American Indian Movement guerrillas who had occupied the church building at Wounded Knee. Clay's patience was wearing thinner by the day, and the last thing he wanted to face was a radical.

"I'm Clay Garner," he said to them both. "Federal Bureau of Investigation. Mr. McNeill said I'd be able to find—"

"Show us your badge," the older one said. "Like on television. You know, how that Zimbalist stooge does his authority thing and scares all the bad guys."

"Are you Johnny Samson?" Clay asked.

"No."

"Then you must be Sonny Cutknife. I kindly request you to shut your mouth."

"Free country. Isn't that the way you European colonists want it? Free for you to take? What's good for the goose is good for the gander, man. I don't have to shut my mouth for anyone. 'Specially no European."

Clay thought through his options. Because the last few days had been so frustrating, he was tempted to reach into his suit jacket, pull his pistol free from his shoulder holster, press it against Sonny's nose, and cite federal regulations about obstruction of justice. While that might shut Sonny up, it might not, and either way would show as much weakness as making another futile request for cooperation.

Clay noticed the younger one, Johnny Samson, was sweating freely, like maybe he'd been doing most of the work while Sonny took it easy. Maybe the kid didn't share Sonny's bad attitude. Should he appeal directly to the kid?

No, Clay decided. Don't make the kid choose between a show of support for Sonny or for an FBI agent. Sonny would definitely come out ahead, and Clay wouldn't have a chance to ask his questions.

"I'm here," Clay said, forcing himself to speak in a relaxed tone so there would be no hint of challenge in his voice, "because George Samson sent me here looking for his grandson."

"We don't need your help, man," Sonny spat. "I've seen what you FBI pigs did at Wounded Knee. We—"

"You talked to my grandfather?" Johnny asked.

"Twice," Clay said, grateful the kid had spoken. The first time had been the brief interview before Doris Samson's death. The second time had been after, an interesting hour at Samson's hillside cabin, plenty of it in shared silence. Many of the questions Clay had wanted to ask about Doris, however, he hadn't felt comfortable inflicting on the gentle old man.

"You talked to him up at the cabin?" Johnny asked.

"Yes. He's hoping I'll be able to help the local authorities look into the murder of your sister."

"Did he invite you inside?"

"Yes," Clay said. "He has a wonderful collection of books. Your grandfather is a remarkable man."

And a remarkably astute man, Clay thought. He'd foreseen the sheriff's lack of interest and been politically smart enough to find a way to apply pressure through Clay's involvement.

"Grandfather doesn't invite anyone inside unless he respects that person," Johnny said.

"Man," Sonny said, "this dude is white. Don't that tell you anything?"

"My grandfather didn't notice his color," Johnny said. "Probably because this dude didn't notice my grandfather's color. That tells me plenty."

Sonny opened his mouth to try another tact then realized he was losing ground, so he shrugged and lit another cigarette.

Clay saw Sonny's work gloves on the ground. He shucked his jacket, setting it on the hood of the truck. Then he grabbed the gloves without asking permission, slipped them on, and pulled two fence posts from the truck bed. He dropped them on the small pile beside the truck.

Johnny grabbed a couple and did the same.

"I know your grandfather raised you and Doris," Clay said. "Taught both of you until you each had high-school diplomas."

"Boarding school wasn't right," Johnny said. "He'd heard too many bad stories about them."

"And Doris moved into Kalispell two years ago, right?"

"Right. She worked as a waitress at Clem's Diner, a pancake house."

Clay pulled a fence post and handed it to Johnny, who in turn twisted and dropped it on the pile on the ground. When Johnny straightened, Clay had another one ready to pass along.

"Did you stay close?" Clay asked. "Even with her in town and you still with your grandfather?"

A small spasm of grief on Johnny's face gave Clay all the answer he needed. How could he now ask the kid the same questions he had avoided with the grandfather?

"She was my sister. Our parents died in a car wreck. All I had was her and Grandfather."

Clay passed him another fence post, then another. He waited five fence posts, giving Johnny time to shake off the tears that had threatened his eyes.

"She have a boyfriend?" Clay asked

"I think she was trying to stay away from guys," Johnny said. "She started going to church and everything."

"Can you think of anyone she might have seen lately?" Clay asked. "Or anyone who was interested in her? Interested in a good way? Interested in a weird way?"

"Nick—" Johnny started to say.

"Johnny," Sonny warned. "This dude is from the Federal Bureau of Investigation. He's got no business poking around with us."

Clay decided this would be a good time to change directions. He'd already learned plenty. There was someone named Nick, and Sonny didn't want it discussed. Clay decided he'd wait until he could talk to Johnny without anyone else around.

Clay tossed the gloves back to Sonny and walked to the front of the cab for his jacket. He didn't put it on, but reached into the vest pocket and pulled out a a business card.

"If you remember anything else, call this number and leave a message. I'll get back to you."

He tossed the card onto the front seat of the cab. There was no sense in giving Sonny a chance to refuse or drop the card.

# 8:07 P.M.

"What's troubling you?" George Samson asked his grandson.

George sat in his rocking chair on the porch of the cabin, sipping hot tea, watching the last of the sun streak the horizon clouds. Johnny sat on the floor of the porch, his back against the railing. He had not spoken in twenty minutes.

"What's troubling me? How can you ask that, like maybe you've forgotten Doris," Johnny replied angrily. "Someone took her away.

First my mother and father. Now my sister. What is the fairness of that? To them—or to me."

"I have not forgotten Doris," George said gently. Although he didn't share Johnny's anger, he understood it. "I grieve her death deeply. Nor have I forgotten your mother and father. Remember, I, too, lost what you lost."

"And you think it's fair?"

"Is this something you are telling me," George said, "or asking me?"

"Asking," Johnny said with sudden challenge. "You tell me how you can sit there and drink tea. Me, I want to kick in doors and break windows."

George considered his answer carefully. He knew Johnny well. The boy would listen, but he would not blindly accept. George also knew Johnny was like a young wolf—restless. He was still polite and respectful; by schooling him at home, George had kept him from running with the wilder boys on the reservation. But Johnny was growing restless, as he must, simply because he was reaching adulthood. George had no intention of trying to chain his grandson. Nothing could stop the boy from roaming on his own—George had smelled the liquor and seen the pain of a hangover on the boy's face after his trip into town. George had not reproved his grandson, for there were difficult lessons he would have to learn, and all George could do was trust he had managed to help the boy build a strong foundation to help him make his own decisions.

"I will try to answer," George finally said. "But you must understand, first of all, I will answer from my faith, which may not seem like a practical answer, but unless faith can be applied to practical matters, it is useless."

"White man's faith," Johnny sneered. "Small enough to fit into a building one day of the week."

George had taken Johnny and Doris to church every Sunday until each reached their sixteenth birthdays then allowed them to decide for themselves. After not attending for years, Doris had chosen to return. On Johnny's sixteenth birthday, he, too, had chosen not to attend. Would he return? George believed it futile to force religion on a person, and up to this evening, he had waited until Johnny wanted to discuss his decision, thinking Johnny would not be open to listening unless he wanted to listen.

"Truth is blind to color, Johnny. And many whites are blind to the truth of their faith, which is why they rely on a church building to shrink the truth to something they can control. But that has nothing to do with faith."

"Our ancestors found faith outside the church," Johnny said. "That should be good enough for me."

George was glad for the implications of Johnny's statement. Despite Johnny's silence on this subject since announcing he would not be attending church, the boy *had* been thinking and questioning. It was far better that the boy be searching than to accept life as something that merely consisted of what was visible.

"Our ancestors worshiped creation, which is understandable," George said. "It is a reflection of the creator and as such cannot help but be glorious. But it is merely a reflection. I choose instead to worship the creator."

"A creator who stands aside while someone murders my sister."

Again, George took time to form his answer. He felt Johnny was on the cusp, ready to turn away from a spiritual search. George doubted anything he said could convince Johnny tonight, but George wanted the boy to continue searching and wanted to give the boy something to consider as he searched.

"Johnny," George said, "nothing I say will make sense unless you believe we are eternal beings. It is one or the other. Your body carries an eternal soul, or it does not. I believe it does."

Johnny shrugged.

"If you want to think of this world as a place that was intended for your happiness, or even to be fair to you, this world will always disappoint you. If you think about it as a brief apprenticeship to your eternal journey, that the situations and events in this world are meant to train and correct you for eternal life, you will never lose hope or peace, even during the most unhappy moments."

Another shrug.

George set his tea down and leaned forward. "If half the people in a building expect it to be a luxury hotel, they will grumble their entire stay. The half who correctly view it as a prison—which this body and earth surely are for your soul—those people will be grateful for the small, unexpected comforts they find during their stay. If you think this world is meant to train you, in the end, what seems ugly and painful about this world strengthens you. Johnny, I take hope and peace in understanding that pain molds me for eternity. On the other side, I will look back and not remember the pain. Like having a tooth pulled, Johnny. Even in this life, the sensation of pain is long forgotten in the relief that follows."

Johnny said nothing.

George realized that words, any words, were hollow against the memories of Doris and the horror of how she had died. For George, however, he would have been infinitely more inconsolable without the understanding and peace that faith gave him. This was what he wanted Johnny to possess.

George did not want to preach—that might push Johnny away—but he had one more thing he wanted to say. "Johnny, I can tell you words all evening, and they will be like bothersome rain pouring down on your shoulders. Your life lies ahead of you, and I feel I can teach you nothing, for living seems to be a matter of coming to realize ancient truths that are so simple they seem meaningless when spoken. They seem like meaningless platitudes to those who have not had the experiences to teach them those truths. You, like every new generation, must learn these truths as if you are the first to learn it. All I can ask is that you keep searching, remembering that each choice you make leads you closer or away from your eternal God. It is like good or evil. A good man becomes practiced in choosing good. An evil man has made so many choices to the bad, that he can no longer recognize good. Can you promise me to remember every choice you make matters on your journey?"

"Doris is dead," Johnny replied. "I can promise you I will remember that."

Johnny rose abruptly, shoved his hands into his pockets, and without saying good-bye, marched down the porch steps and away from the cabin.

George lifted his cup from the porch floor and held it without drinking until long after the tea had turned cold. He, too, could not forget that Doris was dead.

# 11:59 P.M.

*"Mommy kept you safe all night, didn't she?"*

*The boy shivered. He hadn't slept at all. He was afraid she would roll over and crush him. Her perfume had made him want to throw up, but he could not imagine how angry she would become if he did that. So he had tried to breathe through his mouth the entire night and had curled himself into a ball, trying to become smaller and invisible. Worst of all, he could not forget the kitten.*

*"Little Bobby, did you hear your mommy's question?"*

*The boy stared at his feet.*

*She lifted his chin, and he was forced to stare into her face.*

*"Now you will be gone for a while, Little Bobby. But I don't want you to cry. Mommy will miss you too. But Mommy will be waiting here for you."*

*"My real mommy is coming to get me," the boy said. "I'm going home today."*

*"I'm your real mommy."*

*"No. My real mommy—"*

*She squatted, held his shoulders, and gazed straight into his face.*

*"Little Bobby, you must keep our love secret."*

*"My real mommy loves me."*

*"Little Bobby, you must keep our love secret." She repeated as she straightened his collar. As she spoke, her tone of voice remained calm and affectionate. "If you tell our secret, whoever hears that secret will die. Do you understand? Do you remember what happened to the little kitten? If you tell someone our secret, that will happen to them too."*

*The boy nodded. He knew what dead meant.*

The Watcher walked among the hillside trees beneath clear skies and a half moon, remembering the woman and what she had taught him by example with the kitten.

The power of death was the best lesson he could have learned from her. The threat of death could make people do what you wanted them to do. It was an even greater power when you went beyond the threat and were able to give or take life by your own decision.

The woman had taken the kitten's life, by her choice, and later he had done the same to other animals. He could let them live if he decided or make them die. And when he killed them, he felt the surge of power fill his veins, as if their life power was transferred into him.

Then he had begun to wonder what it might feel like to take life when a person could beg to keep it. The animals had said nothing. They hadn't known the Watcher had the power of choice. A person *would* know, and the person's fear would confirm the Watcher's power.

And he had been right in his guess. Seeing the final spasm of the woman in room 27 had given the Watcher a surge of power infinitely more thrilling than any of his earlier experiments.

The Watcher was glad he'd had the foresight to take photos. Just looking at them returned to him the tremors of that surge of power. He especially liked the photos of him and the woman together. Behind him, in the hills where he traveled more comfortably at night than during the day, he had a special place to keep those souvenirs.

He would take another souvenir that night. Not a photo, but something more special. From her, the one he loved.

It would be a thrill, wouldn't it, standing above her and knowing her life was in his hands? He smiled at the thought of his power, and his teeth gleamed in the moonlight like those of a wild animal. He broke into the clearing above the ranch house and held himself perfectly still as he waited for signs of any trouble.

The cattle were silent in the corral. The dog wouldn't be a problem. Aside from the buzzing of mosquitoes around his head, there were no sounds.

The Watcher took his first step toward the ranch house. It would take cunning and skill to get into her bedroom without waking anyone. But that was all part of power, wasn't it? And wasn't power the real way to love?

# Day 4

Kelsie woke with a slight headache and sunlight across her face. She frowned. She was almost certain she had closed the curtains the night before. Maybe her father had slipped into the bedroom earlier and opened them. With his wry sense of humor, he would find it an amusing way to tell her to quit wasting the day.

She sat up in bed, stretched, and yawned into awareness. As she woke, all the fears and worries and guilt she'd carried with her into fitful sleep returned in a tumbling flood. All she could think about was the reason that Doris Samson had been killed.

At lunch the day before, it had come up in conversation with the McNeill men, the murder she had read about in the papers. There were plenty of rumors already that it had not been typical. Michael had commented that Nick Buffalo had been real quiet all morning— with Lawson laughing and pointing out that must have been some kind of quiet because Nick never said much any way. Nick Buffalo? This coming in a thoughtful question from their father, who looked up from buttering a slice of bread. Michael had gone on to explain he'd heard Nick was sweet on Doris and how choked up Nick must be about the entire situation. Sonny Cutknife had let it slip that Nick felt it was his fault because he had been catting around somewhere instead of meeting Doris that night like he'd promised her. At that

59

point, all three had stared at Kelsie because she'd been pouring coffee into her cup and was still pouring as coffee overflowed onto the table.

As they stared, Kelsie thought all three would read guilt on her face. Instead, their father had commented sharply to the boys that the lunch table was no place for talk about murder. Lawson had rushed to get a dishtowel to mop up the spilled coffee. And Kelsie had smiled a weak apology as the full impact of the news filled her with horror.

Doris. Nick Buffalo's girlfriend. It was a double shock to Kelsie. Painful as it was, the first shock had been the lightest to bear. Nick Buffalo sweet on Doris? The two-timer. He'd been with her, Kelsie thought, and he'd betrayed her. And he'd betrayed Doris, too. It shattered Kelsie's romantic illusions about sweet kisses in the moonlight.

The second shock was worse. There had been a woman mentioned in the letter as punishment to Nick, a punishment because Kelsie's attention had been on Nick. And to make it worse, it had happened the night she and Nick were kissing in the moonlight.

It was Kelsie's fault that Doris Samson had died.

Sitting back from the table, staring sightlessly as Lawson mopped up the spilled coffee, more of the horror dawned on Kelsie. Whoever had read her diary knew about Nick. Whoever had read the diary had left her the warning letter. That meant whoever had written the letter had killed Doris.

Who? Why?

Kelsie had never felt more like a little girl wanting to throw herself into her daddy's arms. But she couldn't. She couldn't confess. She couldn't ask for help.

Hadn't the letter also told her to keep it secret? Hadn't the letter warned of more punishment? If she told her father, he might be killed next. Or Michael. Or Lawson.

Instead of blurting out her fears, Kelsie had blamed her near hysterical reaction at the kitchen table on her monthly cycle—she'd discovered the subject unnerved her normally fearless father—and had excused herself, saying she needed to get back to painting the next shed.

Then, that afternoon, the tall FBI man had arrived asking after Johnny Samson. He hadn't been much to look at, but she'd sensed an undercurrent of strength similar to the one her daddy had, and on an impulse, without explaining why, she'd asked the FBI man for a way to call him.

He hadn't asked for an explanation but had handed her a card with a number where she could leave her name and a message if he wasn't there.

The FBI man had smiled as he said good-bye. Kelsie had noticed the smile had done something nice to his eyes and the angular lines of his cheekbones, and she had wondered about the sadness in his smile. She'd wondered and watched after him all the way until he reached Johnny Samson and Sonny Cutknife.

Now, in bed with the sunlight across her face and the headache she wanted to ignore, she found herself thinking about the man's unhurried, easy manner of speaking and how for a moment the sad smile had transformed his face. Maybe she read too many romances, but she was willing to bet there was a story in that smile.

Aside from that, of course, was the card he had given her. She'd thought plenty about it before falling asleep. There was no way she could call Sheriff Fowler and tell him about the letter. The sheriff knew the family too well. Maybe this FBI man would swear an oath of secrecy and help her. How could the mysterious watcher person find out then that she had told someone about the letter?

On the other hand—Kelsie swung her feet out of her bed—whoever had written the letter was beyond creepy. If he actually did find out, there was no telling what he might do.

Kelsie smoothed down her T-shirt—extra large, it served as a comfortable nightgown—and moved down the hallway. She had this end of the house to herself and enjoyed the privacy of her own bathroom.

She wanted a cool drink of water then a good, hot shower. She stepped into the bathroom and locked the door.

She rubbed the sleep from her eyes then reached for the glass on the sink. A large feather was propped upright inside it.

*No!*

She took a deep breath, trying to calm herself.

There was a folded piece of paper beneath the glass. Her legs began to buckle. She sat on the closed toilet seat and pressed her hands beneath her knees to keep them from trembling.

It must have been five minutes before she found the courage to open the note. The paper shook so badly in her hands she had to place it on the sink counter to read it.

You are safe because I am watching over you. All through the
night. Remember our sacrid bond and keep it secrit.

The doors to the ranch house were never locked. Last night
someone had crept inside to this bathroom, Kelsie thought, past the
bedroom where she slept. Who? Why?

Somehow, she found the energy to stand. She told herself to pretend everything was normal. She told herself to shower, to concentrate on an ordinary task to take her mind off this horror.

It didn't work. All she could think about was that a killer was
stalking her, slipping into the house as she slept. He had invaded her
house, and worst of all, she could not tell anyone. She was alone,
with no place to hide. Her father, the one person who was a rock of
strength through everything, could not help, close and comforting as
his presence might be.

The fear nauseated her, and her stomach began to heave. There
was no time to lift the toilet lid. She lurched to the sink and emptied
her stomach, running water as much to disguise the sound of retch-
ing as to clean the sink.

When she had finished, she kept leaning against the sink, willing
herself to find the energy to straighten.

And when she did, she stared at her reflection in the mirror in
disbelief.

Part of her hair had been snipped. He had taken hair from her
head during the night; he had been that close to her.

But that wasn't the worst.

The man had written in lipstick across her forehead. The letters
were written in reverse so that the sentence blazed back into her eyes:
I LOVE YOU.

What had the note said? *I am watching over you. All through the
night.*

He had stood over her during the night. He had stared down on
her. He had listened to her breathe. He had reached down and
touched her.

Kelsie fought an urge to scream. It might bring her daddy. If he
asked, she would have to explain, and her father would go looking.
And then the stalker might kill her father because she'd told.

The urge to panic rose. She grabbed a hand towel, held it against
her mouth, and screamed.

# 9:50 A.M.

"What's the word from J. Edgar today?" Fowler said into the telephone. With his free hand, he scratched the back of his head in unconscious irritation. The sooner this FBI rookie left the valley, the better.

"I talked with some of the waitresses Doris worked with down at Clem's diner."

"Yeah?"

"They said she used to be real wild. You know anything about that?"

"Some." Fowler's heart responded much differently than the boredom in his voice might have indicated. This would be a good time, he thought, to cooperate enough to keep the rookie from thinking anything was strange and begin his own digging, yet not so much cooperation that Clay could ever make a link to the cabin in the hills. Even if none of the men had done this to Doris, it didn't need to get out that their hunting trip had been an expedition for two-legged Bambis.

"We're looking into it," Fowler continued. "But we also heard she stopping running wild about six months ago."

"She joined a church," Clay said. "But you probably knew that."

"Once we get the reports typed up, look through 'em." Fowler kept his voice surly. Too much sudden cooperation would also seem suspicious.

"Yesterday I heard she might have had one recent boyfriend. A guy named Nick."

"Nick. That helps. We'll APB statewide for someone named Nick."

"He knows a Sonny Cutknife, who works for a valley rancher named James McNeill," Clay replied. "I was thinking it might be easier for your men to track him down than me. And her boyfriend is the logical place to start asking questions."

"Keep that manual open," Fowler said, still sarcastic. "What's it say on the next page?"

"Treat local authorities with the respect they deserve—which in this case, leaves me some room for interpretation."

Fowler could not help but chuckle. The ugly, tall, serious-looking kid hadn't seemed capable of humor, and the surprise was as effective as the reply. "Score one for the FBI. We'll send someone out to the ranch to ask this Sonny Cutknife about Nick."

"Thank you," Clay said. "By the way, Sheriff, any progress on the fingerprints your report showed on the murder weapon?"

"None," Fowler said, "none at all. Trust me; we'd let you know."

"Two Car." Sheriff Fowler made it sound like an order, not a question, as he paused at the reception area of the downtown office. Two Car had the desk farthest away from the door. Fowler preferred anyone else to deal with people who walked in.

"Chief?" Ronald Duggan said in response, sitting well back from his desk because of his girth. Duggan drove the second of the force's three cars. Over the radio once, the dispatcher had called for Two Car to report, instead of calling for Car Two. Because of Duggan's size, the nickname had stuck. Duggan weighed 280 pounds. Little of it was muscle, because Duggan was not an athletic man. Physically and mentally, he was overwhelmingly unqualified for police work. As a rookie ten years and one hundred pounds earlier, however, he'd had the good fortune of walking into Wayne Anderson's First National Bank during a bank robbery and getting shot twice in the abdomen. Although the two robbery suspects got away to be caught at the next bank down in Helena, and although Duggan received a reprimand for attempting to make a personal bank deposit on duty, the severity of the wounds made him an instant hero and guaranteed him life-time employment, regardless of the coming and going of any town administration, regardless of how much it irritated Fowler to be called "Chief."

"I don't hear the typewriter," Fowler said. "And I know you've barely got half the report done."

"Half? Chief, I—"

"You spent two days knocking on doors, calling every person who had been registered at the motel, and going through the reservation talking to friends and relatives of the deceased. I know you didn't learn a thing. That's not the point. The point is I want the name of everyone you spoke to, where they were at the time of death, the weather, what you ate, how often you changed your underwear, and anything else you can think of to make it the longest report in the history of this department. Don't you get it? If Hoover's boy is going to look over our shoulders on this, we're going to bury him in paperwork. I expect a report in triplicate, and I want it on my desk by morning."

Fowler grabbed his hat from the coatrack. "I'll be gone the rest of the day. Don't even think of looking up from your desk, let alone going out for coffee and doughnuts."

Two Car knew better than to ask where Fowler was going. When the Chief was in this kind of mood, the less said, the better.

"Sure, Chief."

Fowler walked out without replying. His mood, though, was much better than it appeared to Two Car. Once Fowler was outside, heading toward the patrol car, he actually began to whistle.

Out of the seven others at the campfire, he'd already eliminated four men in his search for the owner of the fingerprints on the corkscrew murder weapon in Doris Samson's death. These were the four men easiest to reach first, the four men who lived and worked in Kalispell—Wayne Anderson, Judge Thomas King, and the two county council representatives. None of their prints matched the ones on the beer can. Yet one set of beer-can prints matched the murder-weapon prints. So he was down to three—Lawson McNeill, then Rooster and Frank Evans at the ranch that neighbored the McNeill spread.

Fowler would visit each in turn. Then, since he'd be in the foothills anyway, he'd spend a few hours fly-fishing. After that, he'd return to his one-car garage, dust whatever objects he had chosen for fingerprints, and discover which of the three had murdered Doris Samson.

Simple. And he was looking forward to the results.

Fowler was a betting man, and he'd give odds his man was Frank Evans. The old crank had always grumbled at James McNeill for "hiring no-good redskins" and was the mean-spirited, vindictive kind able to give you a long, detailed grievance list of who had done him wrong, when, and why over the last twenty years. Besides, both boys were as unlikely a candidate as Frank was likely. Lawson McNeill didn't have the guts and backbone of the old man. The boy did have a high opinion of himself, but it was based on what he'd been given in both money and name when the old man adopted him, not by what he'd earned. As for Rooster, that kid was so good-natured and quiet, it was inconceivable he'd puncture a woman's body with a corkscrew.

Nope, it wouldn't be the boys, Fowler thought. The murderer had to be Frank Evans, whose neck was far redder than any Flathead skin.

Fowler continued to whistle tunelessly as he drove out of Kalispell toward the wall of hills at the edge of the valley. As always, it amused him to see the flash of brake lights and the sudden caution in driving habits as people noticed him in their rearview mirrors.

Once out of town, Fowler let his mind drift away from the fingerprints and Doris Samson's murder. There was this one pool where he'd spooked a big brown a few weeks earlier, and if he got what he needed from both ranches early enough, he'd have a chance to try again, and this time he'd be a lot more cautious on his approach. All it took was a shadow on the water or the vibration of heavy walking to warn a smart fish. Fowler was determined to hook the brown by the end of the summer, even if he had to crawl a half-mile to do it.

Thinking of what joy it would be to battle the trout, Fowler stopped whistling long enough to grin with self-satisfaction. Life *was* like fishing, wasn't it? That was something Frank Evans was about to discover. Whatever you did, it paid to make sure you were on the right end of a fishing rod, where you had your hand on the reel, not your mouth around a sharp hook.

## 12:12 P.M.

Sonny backed a red Massey-Ferguson tractor toward the fence posts he'd watched Johnny and the FBI pig unload from the truck the day before. Johnny Samson and Nick Buffalo were standing to the side of the pile, waiting for Sonny to reach them.

Sonny watched for Nick's hand signals and maneuvered the tractor's rear end into position near a hydraulic post driver. Then Nick waved for him to cut the motor. Sonny switched off the ignition and hopped down. He grinned at Johnny.

"Too bad your girlfriend ain't up there painting sheds. I noticed you looking for her. I been wondering why she ain't there. She's got two sheds left to do. Maybe she decided to go for a nap this afternoon instead. Think of that, Johnny. Her sleeping cute and cuddly, just waiting for a big buck like you."

"Sonny," Nick said, moving to the back of the tractor. "Shut up. You talk too much."

"Sure, Nick." Sonny didn't pause a beat as he continued speaking to Johnny. "You ever put posts in before?"

Johnny shook his head. He noticed that while Sonny was lighting another smoke, Nick was kneeling to attach the hydraulic system of the post driver to a shaft sticking out between the big back tires.

"He's hooking it to the PTO," Sonny explained, exhaling smoke. "You know what that is, right?"

Johnny shrugged, not committing himself to an answer, in case Sonny challenged him on it.

"PTO. Power takeoff. The PTO's like a drive shaft. Gun the tractor motor, and it drives whatever you attach to it. Like this post driver."

"Sure," Johnny said. It was beginning to bother him that Sonny had this need to show off how much he knew.

"PTO." Sonny laughed. "I love that phrase. It's like when I'm smoking a joint, I'll lay back and wait, thinking to myself, PTO, come on and get me."

Johnny didn't laugh.

"Hey, Nick, get it?" Sonny laughed again. "Drugs and PTO. You get high, it's like a power takeoff."

"Got it," Nick said, sounding angry.

"Get Doris out of your head," Sonny told him. "It's filling you with bad energy. You can't help it she died. You can't bring her back."

"I miss her," Nick said, straightening from the tractor. His hands were dark with grease.

"Don't be stupid. You can always find some other honeypot to—"

Johnny tackled Sonny. They hit the ground hard, rolling into the stacked fence posts.

"That's my sister you're talking about," Johnny said, his face right in Sonny's, surprised he'd jumped Sonny, wondering if he was supposed to take a swing now.

Effortlessly, Sonny pushed Johnny off. It surprised Johnny how strong Sonny was.

Sonny wasn't angry though. He stood and brushed himself off then reached down for his cigarette, bent but still smoldering, and took a drag without straightening it. "You and me, we're even, all right? I should break your nose for jumping me, but I was out of line saying what I did about your sister. I forgot you were there."

"All right," Johnny said, hands at his side and trying not to pant for breath. There was something spooky about Sonny's flat eyes and his steady stare. Angry as Johnny was, he couldn't forget how easily Sonny had thrown him to the side.

Nick ignored them and started the tractor.

Sonny and Nick showed Johnny how to put in a fence post. The bottom ends of the posts, of course, had been pre-sharpened so they looked like giant pencils. After the post was set into position, Sonny or Nick would adjust the driver and hold the post steady.

The driver itself was like an upside-down L with a bucket-sized weight of concrete on top. When the hydraulic handle was released, the length of the driver would slide down the length of the post and slam the weight into the top of the post, driving the post deeper and deeper with ground-shaking force. They set the posts in the ground every twenty-five feet. Michael McNeill had instructed them to make a giant perimeter for a new corral three hundred feet long, a hundred feet wide.

An hour into it, Sonny abruptly stepped away from setting the posts, reached up to the tractor ignition switch, and cut the motor. The sudden silence rang in Johnny's ears.

"Smoke break," Sonny said. He offered one to Nick, who accepted. He offered another to Johnny, who declined.

While Nick and Sonny lit their smokes, Johnny let his eyes wander. The lake far below glinted mountain blue, disappearing down the length of the valley against a backdrop of mountains. A few hawks circled high, black dots against the sky bowl. Johnny breathed in the scent of pine needles, and as the cigarette smoke reached his nostrils, he glanced at Sonny and Nick.

Johnny thought it was curious, watching them together. Nick, strong and silent, always seemed a physical threat. But Sonny, always talking, made the decisions, like when to take this break.

"Here's what I been thinking," Sonny said as he looked past them toward the ranch house. "We need to make a statement."

Sonny waited for someone to ask what statement. Nick, of course, didn't. Johnny was still thinking how Sonny had talked about Doris and was in no mood to talk at all.

"This spring it was Wounded Knee," Sonny said. "Remember, Nick? We're holed up in a church in the middle of nowhere Dakota, fighting over nothing, and we had the FBI and army all over us like we'd taken Fort Knox."

Sonny drew a long drag. "Best of all, they had reporters and cameras in there like it was a new civil war. You tell me, wasn't that some kind of statement?"

Johnny had listened to Sonny before and still didn't know exactly what it was they wanted to make as a statement. After considering that for a few seconds, he expressed his question out loud.

"That we can't be pushed around, man. Right now, there are a couple hundred broken treaties. Government should be delivering on promises. We can scare them into it. That's just a start." Sonny's voice picked up speed. "What I figure is we make Wounded Knee look like it was a friendly party. We got to go further, man. Make a real impact."

Sonny made a righteous fist and pumped it a few times. "What I'm saying is we do what's happening across the world. Terrorism." He grinned at Johnny and Nick, who both looked surprised. "You heard me right. Terrorism. Bulldoze power lines. Pollute *their* drinking water. Burn buildings. Whatever it takes. We go traditional, man, like our ancestors. We play with their stupid heads, like the Sioux and Apache. Strike fast, then leave. Like a whirlwind, hit and go, become invisible so they wonder if it really happened, except just like the old days, they see the burning wagons and know the terror is real."

Sonny's eyes blazed. "Thing is, we'll be a spark. There's plenty like us in other tribes. They can keep the fire going where they live. Then the whites will know what an uprising is all about. We'll unite all the tribes. Whatever we demand, we'll get. Treaties honored. Our land back."

Nick remained expressionless. Johnny couldn't believe he was hearing right. He wondered if his friend Harold Hairy Moccasin knew these two would go as far as Sonny was suggesting.

"First thing," Sonny said, "is we call ourselves the Native Sons. We leave notes or send letters every time we strike. Before long, we'll be headline news." Sonny was nearly at the end of his cigarette. He pulled a last drag. "Maybe we should start by claiming the train derailment as ours. Gives us a track record. Gives us credibility. The media like that."

Sonny's eyes narrowed. "You in, Johnny?"

Johnny realized Nick was watching him closely, too.

"You in?" Sonny repeated. "Think what happened to Doris. You can get them back."

Johnny thought it was convenient for Sonny to remember Doris now, when he wanted something from Johnny.

"Let me think about it," Johnny said.

Nick and Sonny exchanged glances.

"Told you," Sonny said to Nick.

Nick shrugged.

Sonny ground his cigarette out beneath his boot heel. He pointed at the post pounder. "I saw this guy once, he was holding a post to steady it, let his thumb rest on the top of the post. Weight came down, no more thumb. Plenty of blood and yelling, but no more thumb."

Ever since they'd put the first post in, Johnny had thought of nothing else but that possibility.

Sonny shook his hand with theatrical hurt. "Hard thinking about something that painful, ain't it?"

Johnny nodded agreement. There was something weird about the way the conversation had turned.

Nick walked over to the tractor and started it. The engine throbbed. Nick turned on the PTO, and the hydraulics engaged.

Sonny walked a few steps away and found a rock the size of a softball. He set it on top of the fence post underneath the post pounder.

Nick released the weight, and the hydraulics slammed it downward, crushing the stone on top of the fence post. The exploding stone sounded like a gunshot. Granite dust sprayed across Johnny's face.

Sonny moved beside Johnny. Nick moved on the other side.

"Johnny," Sonny said above the sound of the tractor engine, "yesterday, you talked a little too much to the FBI pig. What you got to decide is who you're with. Us? Or them?"

Sonny took Johnny's right arm. Nick took the other.

Johnny tried to pull free, but they were bigger and stronger.

Sonny wrapped Johnny in a bear hug. Nick let go of Johnny's arm. He reached into his back pocket for a short piece of rope. Within seconds, he had trussed Johnny's ankles, using a flourish as if he had hogtied Johnny in a rodeo event.

Nick went to the tractor, took a coil of rope from beside the tractor seat, and wrapped it around Johnny's arms.

"You ain't saying much," Sonny said. "Something you should have done yesterday."

Johnny was more frightened than he had ever been in his life but saw little use in protesting or begging. It was obvious they'd planned this; he doubted he could get them to change their minds. Nor did he want to give them the satisfaction.

They lifted Johnny and carried him horizontally toward the fence post. Finally, Johnny squirmed and kicked, but it was too late. They placed the back of his head where the softball-sized stone had rested a minute earlier, leaving him to stare upward at the hydraulic weight.

They set his feet down, but Sonny grabbed his hair and pulled it down hard to keep his head on the fence post, and Johnny couldn't move. He was half crouching, with his back to the pole, and had no choice but to keep his head tilted all the way back, with the weight poised only a few feet above his eyes.

"Don't blink," Sonny said. "Otherwise, you might miss the fun."

Nick had his hand on the switch. Johnny couldn't see it, but he sensed it.

"Think of a watermelon," Sonny said. "That'd be your skull. Busted like a watermelon under a baseball bat."

Johnny felt an intense urge to urinate. He concentrated on holding his bladder and tried not to cry.

"That's enough," Nick said to Sonny. "Let go."

Sonny released Johnny's hair. Nick unwrapped the rope around Johnny's arms. Johnny pushed off the post and straightened, wobbling to keep his balance. He bent down to untie the rope that was around his ankles.

"You don't know it," Sonny said, "but you're already in. You were in the day you started working here. You try backing out, you talk to the FBI pig again, we'll take you into the mountains and let the wolves pick your bones clean."

Sonny hit the switch, and the hydraulics drove the weight down, shuddering the fence post another six inches deeper into the ground.

Understand?" Sonny said. He grinned. "Can you live with it?"

"Yeah," Johnny said. "I understand."

# 3:38 P.M.

Kelsie McNeill waited until the back end of Michael's truck rounded the corner at the end of the block, then crossed the street to the department store. On the other side, standing on the sidewalk, she looked both ways. Nobody was watching her. But then, that was little comfort. To this point, she had not once known when she was being watched.

After taking a deep breath to calm herself, she walked into the department store. She glanced at an old-fashioned round clock above a pyramid display of discounted disposable diapers. The clock read 3:40. She had twenty minutes until Michael was to return for her. She prayed the FBI man would be waiting.

He was. Standing exactly where she had asked, in the sporting-goods department, test-casting a fishing rod. He wasn't wearing the suit that made him appear awkward. He'd replaced it with faded jeans and a lightweight tan sweater.

He hadn't noticed her yet, and the lines on his face were soft with thoughtful sadness, as if his mind was far from the fishing rod in his hand. She wondered if that was his usual private face and decided, impulsively, that she liked him, although in his twenties, he was definitely ancient.

Kelsie took another deep breath and tried to make her approach casual, examining prices on tennis equipment and pretending not to notice him until she was nearly upon him.

"Well," she said, loudly and in false, brittle tones, "what a surprise. Aren't you the man who stopped by our ranch yesterday afternoon?"

He squinted at her and snapped his fingers in recognition. "McNeill, right?"

She was grateful he caught on so quickly. She hadn't left much of an explanation in her message, only a time and place to meet. She hadn't even left her name. Instead of playing along, he could have just as easily replied by asking her why she'd asked to meet him here. Which could be a disaster if the watcher was nearby and listening.

"Right," she said. "I'm Kelsie McNeill. Hey! Thinking of buying the fishing rod? Up in the hills you'll find great spots for trout. Ask my daddy; he'll tell you where."

A strange expression crossed his face, and he set the rod down. "Not buying," he said. "Just remembering."

"Oh." There didn't seem anyplace to go from there. Standing beside him, she picked up a plastic tackle box and flipped through the empty trays.

"You could have left a number for me to call you back," he said quietly. "A telephone conversation is much more private than pretending all this."

"No!" Then, realizing how intensely she'd spoken, she softened her voice. "I was afraid someone else might answer when you called."

Clay regarded her calmly. "That should tell me plenty—but it doesn't. Miss McNeill, what is this about? Why are you afraid someone in your family will know we talked?"

Aside from television, Kelsie had never known anyone to speak in the slow, drawn-out fashion of this man. She enjoyed hearing the soothing cadence of his voice.

"It's not that I'm afraid they'll hear. It's that I'm afraid for them."

"You have me at a loss, Miss McNeill."

"I need help," she blurted. "But if I don't keep it secret I'm asking for help, someone else might be killed."

He took the tackle box from her hands and set it on the shelf. She hadn't realized she'd been snapping the lid open and closed while she spoke.

"I still don't understand your problem," he said. "But if I can help, I will."

She began to relax. There had been no disbelief in his reaction to her comment. One of her fears had been that he might laugh at her, call her suspicions ridiculous. After all, he worked for the Federal Bureau of Investigation, and she was just a hick from a Montana ranch.

"Someone is following me," she said.

"Right here? In this store?"

She smiled. It seemed like her first smile in years. "No, at the ranch. He leaves me creepy notes."

"Miss McNeill, I appreciate your trust in my badge. However—"

"Last night, he snuck into my house and watched me while I slept." She twisted the bangs of her blonde hair. "He even took some of my hair."

"Miss McNeill, please don't misunderstand me. When I said I would help if I could, I meant it. Unfortunately, the Bureau is limited by jurisdiction. I cannot involve myself in something the local authorities should handle."

"They can't!" She heard the edge of hysteria in her voice and forced herself to speak calmly. "Sheriff Fowler knows my daddy. Just today, the sheriff dropped by the ranch out of the blue and had coffee with him and Michael and Lawson."

"Michael and Lawson?"

"My brother and cousin." Kelsie said. "If I went to Sheriff Fowler," she continued, "he'd go to my daddy, and then Daddy would go crazy trying to catch this guy, and then this guy would know I had told about the letters, and he would find a way to kill my daddy."

"Miss McNeill—"

"No," she said. "You have to believe me."

"What I believe doesn't matter," he said. "This is still a local matter."

"But you're looking for whoever killed Doris Samson, right? That's what my daddy told me. And that's why you needed to talk to her brother Johnny yesterday, right?"

"Yes, but—"

"Whoever visited me last night was the one who murdered Doris Samson," Kelsie said. She didn't want to tell him. It was too awful, feeling like she was the reason Doris Samson had been killed. She knew, though, she couldn't do this alone. The tall, shy FBI man seemed to be her only hope, and it seemed he was slipping away. "He wrote about it in one of the notes. He said he was jealous because . . ." Kelsie swallowed a few times. She definitely didn't want to talk about Nick Buffalo. But if that's what it took to convince this FBI man, she would have to do it. "Because, well, there's this guy I thought I liked. Nick Buffalo. But Nick Buffalo liked Doris."

"Nick Buffalo."

There, she thought, she had his attention. "Nick and I were kissing that night. Someone saw me with Nick. At least, that's what the note says. And that someone went and killed Doris to get back at Nick and to teach me a lesson, and the note said I couldn't tell anyone or other people would get killed, and I was thinking that since you're in the FBI, maybe you can keep it secret and no one will know you're helping . . ."

She stared at the floor, leaving a long pause in their conversation, long enough for them to hear an entire announcement over the intercom about a blue-light special in kitchenwares.

"Note?" Clay finally said. "I would appreciate the opportunity to read it."

She put her hand in her back pocket and almost pulled it out to hand him. Then she remembered that someone might be watching and resisted the impulse.

"Where is that tackle box?" she asked. "I might buy it for my daddy's birthday after all."

She smiled sweetly and reached for the tackle box he had returned to the shelf. She opened it again to inspect it. As discreetly as she could, she palmed the note with her other hand and as she closed the tackle box, slipped it inside.

"Nope," she said. "I don't think this is big enough for all the tackle my daddy has."

She placed the box back on the shelf, maintained her sweet smile, and lowered her voice to a whisper. "It's in there. Read it and meet me in the record department. I don't have much time left."

In a louder voice, she continued. "Well, it was nice meeting you."

She stuck out her hand to shake his good-bye.

"Nice seeing you, too, Miss McNeill. Take care."

Clay managed to hide his smile until she turned her back and walked away. *Sweet kid,* he thought, *but she's watched one too many spy movies.* Of course, the charade was so obvious, any Russian agent would have died from the strain of trying to hold in his laughter. And that move slipping the note into the tackle box; she had telegraphed it like a Charlie Chaplin routine.

A watcher? In her bedroom last night? It didn't make sense. Maybe she was looking for a way to explain how a boyfriend had ended up there. If that was true, it bothered him that she had brought in Doris Samson's death. A kid that sweet and innocent-looking, a person would hope for more from her.

On the other hand, hearing Nick Buffalo's name had certainly been a jolt. If the sheriff hadn't learned Nick's last name yet, maybe Clay could find Nick and talk to him first.

Clay reached for the tackle box. He opened it, unfolded the note, and began to read. He felt his half-smile freeze as he read several sentences into the note.

*If I have to pull your soul out of your body to keep you, I will make myself dy too and we will have life together beyond the flesh.*

This was a death threat.

*. . . the feather is your warning. And that is their punishment.*

Adrenaline hit Clay in a burst.

*. . . Doris died to punish him.*

Him? Nick Buffalo?

*The eagle leaves a feather when it takes its prey . . .*

Feather! Unless there had been a leak somewhere in the sheriff's office, the killer was the only person outside of the investigation who would know of the feather found in Doris Samson's mouth.

*I am your Watcher.*

This guy was for real.

Clay refolded the note and put it in his back pocket. He wanted to run to the record section of the department store, but he managed to make it look like a stroll. He saw Kelsie McNeill standing at the far wall beneath a Beatles poster. She smiled hesitantly in his direction at his approach.

Every once in a while, when he failed to guard against it, Clay would see a girl and wonder how his own daughter might have looked had she reached that girl's age. Now, seeing Kelsie flipping through the records, he pictured what his daughter might have looked like in her teens. He was sure she would have been equally pretty and equally innocent, and he thought of how he'd fight for her. In that moment, a white rage against the Watcher filled Clay Garner, and he knew the fight had become personal.

"Kelsie?"

"You read the note?" she asked.

"Yes," he said. He thought of Flannigan and what he'd said. The monster wasn't in its cage. "I'll give you all the help I can."

# 10:50 P.M.

*"Fran, we can't tell you how much this break meant for us. How can we thank you enough for baby-sitting?"*

*"Pish-pash," the old woman said. "It was no trouble at all."*

*"How about him? Was he any trouble for you?"*

*"The best behaved five-year-old anyone could ask for. You're a lucky mother to have someone so sweet."*

*His mother, his real mother, kept smiling. "I think so too. I missed him so much. You know, I wanted to call every day to see how he was doing, but my husband told me I'd have to learn to let him be a little man."*

*The boy wanted to throw himself at his mother's legs. He wanted to clutch her and sob and cry with relief. But he didn't dare. She might ask him what was wrong. And if he told her the secret, his mother would die. Just like the kitten.*

*"Did you miss me?" his real mother asked, squatting and opening her arms to him. "Did you miss your mommy?"*

*The boy allowed himself to nod, but he didn't run forward to her.*

*"Then come to Mommy," his real mother said.*

*The boy looked at the old lady to see if it was all right. She nodded her head slightly.*

*The boy took hesitant steps forward and let his real mother wrap her arms around him. Before, he would have hugged her back. But now, remembering how the old lady clutched him in her arms in the darkness of the night and remembering the hated smell of her rose perfume, the boy had the sensation of being trapped.*

*Trapped . . .*

The McNeills, the ranch workers, and most of the local people referred to the cabin as Mad Dog's Doghouse, partly because of its size and partly because of the hermit trapper who had built the log structure at the turn of the century, long before horseless carriages had invaded the valley. It was set in a natural hollow facing a stream; its roofline was almost invisible against the hillside, especially since its remaining split-wood shingles were gray and mossy and blended into the alpine grass and low shrubbery of the hill itself.

The cabin had weathered well, a testament to the painstaking labor of the trapper, who knew his life depended on how well his shelter bore the brunt of long, lonely winters. He had chosen his lumber so well and built it so solidly that the cabin walls were still strong and whole. The only concession to time, in fact, were the gaps between the logs where the mud chinking had crumbled over the decades.

The cabin's doorway was barely larger than the entrance to a doghouse, designed not for convenience but to block as much of the harsh winter as possible. The cowhide flap that had served as a door had long since rotted, and now the short, square entrance seemed like the entrance to a dark tunnel.

The cabin had served the trapper well. Winter was the time for prime fur, and he had used it as a base camp, which allowed him to run traplines in all directions, the length of one day's snowshoe travel. The trapper had made it a habit to camp overnight at the end of a trapline, returning to the cabin the next day, through each winter until 1905, when he went crazy and earned his Mad Dog nickname.

There was no one living, of course, of the men who had found him in the cabin that winter, but the story had been passed on again and again with ghoulish satisfaction, usually at campfires. Because the truth of the story was bizarre enough, little of it had been distorted over the generations.

In short, the trapper had chosen a poor location. Although the cabin faced south, had the north winds blocked by the hill, and had easy access to water, the hills formed a gigantic natural funnel, something the rescuers were clearly able to see as they looked upward at the path of the avalanche that had covered the cabin.

The rescuers had been summoned by another old trapper who had stopped by his friend's cabin with mild concern over a missed rendezvous. The friend had seen the tons of snow and wisely gone for digging help, with no idea how long the cabin had been buried.

As the searchers dug, so the story went, a strange, faint noise grew stronger and stronger until they recognized the sound as howling. It took them thirty more feet of digging to reach the cabin, and when they pushed aside the last of the snow, they realized the howling was coming from the man they were rescuing. They later guessed his candles had run out long before his food and that by the empty jars and cans, he'd spent five to six weeks trapped in the complete sensory deprivation of darkness and silence, his only company the carcasses of dozens of yet-to-be-skinned animals he'd trapped.

Whatever demons the howling man had seen, he never shared with anyone, for he never spoke again. No one knew what to do with him, so they eventually returned him to his solitary cabin, where, during the next full moon, he hung himself, designing the noose as an identical match to the noose he'd used to snare rabbits and mink over the years.

No one had lived in the cabin since. Even though it was on the McNeill property, only two miles above the ranch house, it was rarely visited. Most of the cowboys and ranch workers believed it to be haunted and stayed away.

One person, however, regularly enjoyed the solitude and ghostly echoes of imagined howling. The Watcher.

He especially enjoyed it at night. And on this night, walking to the cabin beneath a full moon that decades earlier had witnessed Mad Dog's final night, the Watcher thought of the legend of the howling, insane man. And smiled.

Soon there would be another man to add to the legend of this cabin, a man who deserved to die.

# Day 5

Clay slept poorly. The fishing rod in the department store had reminded him of another fishing rod, back in West Virginia, set on the front porch alongside his tackle box, thermos, and paper-bag lunch. He'd stood at the front window, staring at the sheen of green leaves and mist cloaking the holly trees. Sherry had come up behind him and run her hands up and down his chest, teasing him to stay at home for a romantic, cozy day under a roof sounding of steady rain instead of going out with Bud to get wet and cold chasing after slimy fish. Samantha was in the crib, Sherry had said, and how long had it been since they'd lost themselves in each other like newlyweds. If he'd have turned to kiss her, he might have stayed, sending Bud on alone when he arrived. But Clay had been unwilling to make up so easily from their fight the night before, and when Bud had turned into the drive, honking the horn of his '65 Valiant, Clay pushed away his wife's arms and went to the fishing rod and his friend. If he'd have turned and kissed her and allowed his stubborn heart to show his love, Sherry wouldn't have loaded Samantha in the car an hour later to go into town to get groceries. If he'd have turned and kissed her, there would have been no loaded coal truck missing a turn on slick asphalt. If he'd have turned and kissed her, there would not have been the stricken horror on the lieutenant's face as he came to deliver news they all dreaded giving after a fatality crash, only this time it had to be delivered to one of their own. If only he'd have turned and kissed her . . .

Clay slept so poorly, when the alarm rang at 5:30 A.M. he was awake and staring at the ceiling, wallowing in images and memories and wondering why he was in a run-down motel room thousands of miles from the mobile home in West Virginia where in another life he'd slept every night with the woman he loved, unaware in his complacency that God would savagely and abruptly take her and their baby away from him.

Clay punched the alarm clock off with gratitude at the excuse to begin another day and hurried into the shower, putting his thoughts and energy into the phone call he planned to make.

"This is pretty early. Even here on the East Coast," Flannigan said as a greeting. "Bucking for overtime? Or a GS-11?"

"How about both?" Clay said into the telephone. Moving from GS-10 upward meant an annual salary raise of $1,000. "Can you arrange it?"

Flannigan snorted. "You have me mixed up with someone who has pull around here. Like I said before, because of Hoover, everyone thinks we practice voodoo—you know, a process difficult to fathom, with questionable results. You're one of the few who takes us seriously, and from what I hear, you don't have any other straws to clutch."

"I'm not sure how to take that."

"It's nothing against you," Flannigan said. "It's what you've been thrown into."

"Thrown?" Clay felt stupid, echoing Flannigan.

"Notice there's no team of investigators on your train derailment? Politics, my young friend. I've been around long enough to have my own little grapevine. This one's a token investigation. No people killed by the derailment, only a couple of cars derailed, no special media attention. Thus, no showboating by the FBI. Why else pull a rookie—again, no offense intended—out of Great Falls and let him sniff around for a while? If this was a priority, you'd be flooded with leeches, trying to look good from the disaster. So don't sweat it. As long as you file lengthy reports, your butt is covered."

"What about a serial killer? Cover my butt there?"

"I finally got your package with the autopsy report and forensics," Flannigan said, not committing himself. "It's interesting. The sadism is there. But it also could be just a one-time thing. Someone may have hated Doris Samson. Find me something else, and I'll be prepared to believe this was more than just an ugly murder. Tell me more. I assume that's why you called."

"The killer left a note," Clay said.

"What?" All casualness left Flannigan's voice. "To you?"

"No, to a girl."

"You have the note?"

"Yes. But by the time I got it, she'd handled it plenty. My fingerprints were on it too. I doubt—"

"Clay, cut the forensics stuff. Our job is to get into his mind. Understand? We try to think like them, then anticipate them. It's his words that are important, not the ink and paper. What'd he say?"

Despite the seriousness of their conversation, Clay smiled. Flannigan had come to life, had dropped his defenses of cynicism and banter. The hunter was on his quarry's trail.

Clay reached for the paper on his desk and turned it to the lamp to be able to read clearly. "Kelsy, I have been watching you with the love that our souls have been destined to have since before time began. Why do you hurt me by looking at others? I am the only one for your affections . . ."

He finished reading the note.

"Again," Flannigan said. "Read it once more."

Clay complied. When he finished, Flannigan was silent, and Clay decided not to break that silence. He knew Flannigan was hooked on this now. He didn't need prompting or pulling to keep him involved.

"It's the part where he tells her that others will come to harm," Flannigan finally said. "That's enough for me to believe he might kill again. In other words, you've got my attention."

"It has her attention, too," Clay reminded Flannigan. "She's scared to death."

"You're right," Flannigan said, chastised. "Sometimes when I'm dealing with information, not people, this becomes a game. Gruesome, but a game."

Flannigan took a deep breath, clearly audible over the phone. "I've got another concern, but let's spend some time with the note. It had bad grammar. How's the spelling?"

"Poor."

"How? Which words?" He spoke with impatience, as if he wanted the note in his own hands on the other side of the country.

Clay explained the spelling errors.

"All right, Clay," Flannigan said, hardly pausing after Clay's answer, "now tell me who you think did this. Not his name—that would be too much to expect—but what kind of person."

"Young unmarried blue-collar worker," Clay said.

"Why?"

"Why did he kill? Or why is that my guess?"

"Why is that your guess? What makes you say he's young?"

"This is a first-time kill. From what you said in your lectures, most begin in their late teens, early twenties. Also he's young because he shows stupidity. By telling Kelsie he's been watching her, it narrows our search considerably."

"And he's a blue-collar guy because—"

"Bad spelling and bad grammar," Clay said, feeling this was an exam. "White collars and professionals would write differently."

"Obvious conclusion, but not necessarily correct. What if he's so young he still isn't out of high school?"

"Then he's a big kid. I'm guessing him for a worker for two other reasons. First, he had to be strong enough to subdue Doris Samson without hitting her across the head. That suggests someone physical. Second, is where the letter was delivered. No postmark, left in the mailbox at an isolated ranch. If he's been watching her a lot, I'm guessing he works on the ranch. Or at least he has work that takes him to the ranch frequently."

"Interesting," Flannigan said. "We'll get back to that and the narrowed field. Why unmarried?"

"He had no one to report to. They're saying Doris Samson was killed early in the morning. If he has a wife, chances are he wouldn't have that kind of freedom. He'd have to explain why he was gone."

"I like your thinking, Clay. Although I want to disagree with you about your guess on his age. I believe you're right, but not for the reasons you said. When you get another chance, look at the crime-scene photos. You'll notice the buttons on her shirt."

"Cross-buttoned," Clay said. "Like when you start the bottom button in the second from the bottom hole, and every button after it is wrong all the way up."

"Glad you noticed," Flannigan said. "Now tell me what it means."

"She buttoned herself in a hurry. He walked in and surprised her, and she didn't want him to see her body. Which means they weren't intimate partners."

"Maybe not. And that's why I think he's young. My guess is he wanted to look."

"Look?"

"Maybe before he started stabbing her. Maybe after she was dead. Probably after. He undressed her to take a look and then dressed her again. That tells me he's young. It also tells me something else. He's curious enough to look, awkward enough about it to dress her again. He's inexperienced. Sad to say, but we're in a society where kids get experience in a hurry. If he's missed out on all this free love that the hippies are into, he's either a loser with psychological problems or a kid with religion. I'd choose the first, obviously."

Flannigan spoke rapidly. Clay realized the older man had spent a lot of time thinking about this.

"Anything else?" Clay asked.

"You can generalize serial killers into two types. Unorganized and organized. Unorganized killers tend to have low mentalities. They blitz-attack, killing quickly because they don't have any sense of control, often don't want to know the victim, and hide or mutilate the face to make them an object. An organized killer is smart, able to control the victim, wants the victim to remain alive as long as possible. It's power over the victim's life he wants."

"But the poor spelling in the letter . . ."

"A bad writer is not necessarily a dumb person, Clay. Education and background play a big factor. That supports your theory he's in menial labor."

"Fair enough."

Clay glanced at the motel curtain. Dawn had arrived. "I've taken plenty of your time. If you need to go, I understand."

"If I need to go, I'll let you know. Trust me," Flannigan said. "I want you thinking about a couple of things. The biggest is the trigger factor."

"Something to set him off."

"Exactly. Think of a time bomb ticking. This is someone with violent fantasies. There're plenty of potential young offenders like that, kids who come from bad homes and have been abused themselves. But not many of them step over the line and commit their fantasy. Usually what it takes is something to trigger them, say, loss of a job or a 'Dear John' letter—maybe even a humiliating experience on a date."

"It's safe to say this person is obsessed with Kelsie, right?" Clay said.

"Definitely."

"So if this person saw Kelsie with another man, it might be a trigger factor."

"More than definitely."

Clay began to feel some of the hunter's excitement he sensed from Flannigan. "What I learned from her was that she spent time with one of the ranch workers. She wrote about it in her diary, and she believes the person who is watching her has read the diary."

"How's that?"

"Two words," Clay said. "Eagle feather."

"Feather!" Flannigan couldn't keep his excitement hidden.

"That answers my other concern. The biggest one. I was wondering how you were so sure that the person who wrote the letter to Kelsie was also Doris Samson's killer. The eagle feather is the link."

"Which is why I'm taking all this so seriously," Clay said. "And there's more. Kelsie not only wrote about her feelings for her new boyfriend. She let me know she spent time with him—moonlight time. Doing some innocent kissing."

"If the killer had not only read the diary but followed her that night . . ." Flannigan said.

"Exactly. I gather from Kelsie this is her first boyfriend. If she's never kissed anyone else, this watcher would never before have had a reason to be jealous. But this would trigger him."

"Who's her boyfriend?" Flannigan asked. "Maybe it's one and the same. Maybe they argued after kissing. Maybe—"

"A guy by the name of Nick Buffalo. Who was also Doris Samson's boyfriend. You see how it all falls together?"

"If Nick isn't the killer, his girlfriend was offed as revenge. If Nick *is* the killer, he could have done it, then sent the letter to make it look like some weirdo's in on this. Which might explain the handwriting, like someone took pains to disguise it."

"I'll be looking into the timing," Clay said. "From what Kelsie was saying, Nick was with her the night Doris died. But maybe he had enough time to make it into town after."

"Good start," Flannigan said. "See if you can get all the names of the ranch workers. I'll do what I can to pull records, look for anyone with violent histories, jail time, that kind of stuff."

"I take it you're in," Clay said mildly, smiling on his end.

"Not only in, but thinking if you do a good job out there, I'll get you into my department."

That had never occurred to Clay. It had a good feel to it, though. There was something about the hunt that was getting into his blood.

"Let's get back to the autopsy," Flannigan said, hardly pausing. "Those coin-shaped marks, what do you think?"

"Same thing I think about the eagle feather. Big mystery."

"It'll fall into place," Flannigan said. "Just learn as much as you can and get into the killer's mind. That's what behavioral science is about. And you need to get there in a hurry."

"Hurry?"

"Everything points to a first-time kill. Everything points to someone who enjoyed it. You guessed early it might be a serial killer in the making, one of the reasons I'm interested in having you in my department, Clay. This note and the obsessive jealousy backs you up even more. Whoever did this crossed the line. He's not coming back, Clay. He's out there and ready to do it again."

# 3:30 P.M.

As if there weren't enough to worry about, Nick thought, after dealing with Keslie McNeill and her crush on him, there was still the bad news that Sonny had given him an hour earlier, that men from the sheriff's department had come calling at the ranch to ask about Nick and his relationship to Doris Samson. Sonny's advice had been to head into Kalispell as though Nick didn't have anything to hide, but Sonny, Nick had decided, was thinking more about protecting his dream of the Native Sons uprising than protecting Nick.

Cops would be easy compared to facing Kelsie and telling her it was going to end between them. Nick Buffalo went through the list of how stupid it had been, why it was time to end it, and how he was going to tell her. He hoped he would be strong enough to tell her fast and not get involved further with any of the things she had promised in her note he had found in his car, asking her to meet him that afternoon.

He knew he had time to plan what he wanted to say. He was in no hurry—definitely in no hurry—so he'd keep the horse to a walk. On the unlikely chance James, Michael, or Lawson happened to be up in these hills, he'd say he was on his way to check the upper limits of the range for signs of grizzly, and he had his rifle in the saddle scabbard as proof. Nick figured if any one of them knew his true intentions, they'd hang him from the nearest tree branch. As fair and as blind to skin color as James McNeill was, his fairness probably didn't extend to hired hands who played kissing games with his daughter.

And that was the problem. They were just games.

Nick's gut ached to think of how stupid he had been. Sure, he knew why he'd first allowed himself the danger of spending time alone with Kelsie McNeill. She was white, and she was James McNeill's daughter. There was power in that, wasn't there, that a Flathead like Nick Buffalo, without the advantages of white skin, name, or money but simply on his own merits, could have someone like Kelsie McNeill? Of course, it wasn't enough to think it possible; he'd had to let it go far enough to prove it, blocking Doris out of his mind by telling himself that no woman owned him.

Plus Kelsie was beautiful. Doggone, she was beautiful. No man alive could watch her walk by and not snap his head for a second look. If Nick had first seen her at a rodeo dance, he would have guessed her to be his age, twenty, not sixteen. If he had first seen her at a rodeo dance, he might have chased her, instead of the other way around.

Even in chasing him, though, she hadn't been aggressive the way some women were. Instead, she'd been shy, hanging around him while he worked before finally suggesting they meet that night. Part of Nick's excitement was in realizing that she herself didn't realize what was happening, as if she had the equipment and the desire, but lacked the know-how.

It turned out, though, her desire was different from the blood-quickening hunger he'd tasted with other women. During their first kiss, Nick had understood it was like a fairy tale to Kelsie—romantic longing, not the hard-edged desire of the experienced rodeo women who slipped into the backseats of their cars with him at the end of dances.

He'd not taken advantage of Kelsie's innocence. That was how

Nick appeased his guilt. He told himself he'd done the right thing. Anyone else would have tried to give her the know-how, trampled over her dreams for the ugliness of satisfying lust. Instead, Nick had held himself back, allowing her to feel joy in her tentative kisses and murmured puppy-love ramblings.

He deserved some credit for that, didn't he? Nick knew a lot about women, how what they often wanted was the strength and roughness promised by his almost savage features and their image of him as a cowboy and rodeo bull-rider. Since the time he was old enough to drive, plenty of white women had found ways to throw themselves at him. He knew what pleased them. Yet walking alone with Kelsie among the trees at night—older, experienced, aflame with the effect of her kisses as he'd been—he'd nobly restrained himself for the sake of her innocence and feelings.

What had it got him?

Doris, dead.

If he'd gone into Kalispell that night and met Doris, she would still be alive. Instead, he'd kept walking with Kelsie, unsure of how to get away gracefully.

The worst part was, the instant Kelsie had nuzzled in close to his neck and lifted her lips to his, he'd pictured Doris. In that moment, the intense guilt of being in another woman's arms—something that surprised him because he'd happily played around on all his previous girlfriends—had led him to another surprising realization.

He loved Doris deeply. They'd only been together a month, hardly enough that people knew they were an item. Beyond soul-searching kisses, they hadn't done anything serious physically—Doris said she was through with that, and maybe that was one of the reasons he'd fallen for her . . .

As Nick rode his horse beneath the sharp, blue sky, following the gurgling of a mountain stream up a valley toward distant peaks, whiskey-jack jays flitted in nearby thickets, calling alarm in their peculiar raspy cries. Another man might have gloried in the beauty. All Nick could think of was Doris: her insistence on candles set in empty wine bottles whenever they sat on her apartment couch at night; her pride in that couch and the other used furniture she'd bought with cash earned by tips at the restaurant; how the candle shadows flickered on her face and how she kissed—wordlessly, soft, and slow—with her eyes closed in that candlelight.

He'd betrayed her. Because Doris was dead, he'd never have a chance to make it up to her. He'd never be able to tell her about his love for her.

The way Nick felt, no amount of sunshine and blue sky would lift the grayness from his soul. No amount of salt would add taste to his food. And no amount of prayer to a God he wasn't sure existed would erase his guilt.

At the very least, though, he was going to end it with Kelsie, even with the risk that she might get so upset she'd run to her father, who would fire him—or worse. In this valley, he might get rednecks running him off the road or beating him up once they knew about this. Or maybe some white judge would find a way to throw him in jail. He'd done absolutely nothing to Kelsie except fumble through a few kisses, but maybe he'd get accused of worse.

The day before—knowing of his decision to tell her it had ended and merely delaying the unpleasant task—Nick hadn't been worried about Kelsie taking it wrong. The note from her that he had found sticking out of his car ashtray in the morning, though, made him wonder now.

She'd probably copied some of it from one of her romance books. It was steamy, among other things telling him to meet her at Mad Dog's cabin because it was so far away from anyone that she'd be able to cry aloud her ecstasy at their lovers' reunion and they would have the entire afternoon to satisfy each other's longings.

Nick had had to find Sonny in the equipment shed and ask him what ecstasy was—without telling him why, of course. If it meant what Sonny said, even allowing for his tendency to exaggerate, Nick guessed Kelsie was intent on turning her desire into know-how in a big hurry.

Well, not with Nick Buffalo. A simple kiss had brought him more grief than he wanted to face again in his life. Besides, as a way to make it up to Doris, Nick was swearing off women for as long as he could manage it.

Nick rode slowly around a final bend. It didn't surprise him to see Kelsie's saddled horse nearby, hobbled and grazing in the meadow grass on the bank above the stream.

Nick looped the reins of his horse over a tree branch. There was no sense unbridling the horse, he thought. He wouldn't be at the cabin long, just enough to tell Kelsie it was over before it got started.

Nick approached the low, square doorway of the cabin.

"Kelsie?" He called her name softly, as if he were afraid his voice would carry several miles down to the McNeill ranch house and James would know he was meeting Kelsie in daylight.

"Kelsie?"

Nick didn't like the black interior of the cabin. He'd heard all the stories about it being haunted by Mad Dog, how people had found him hanging inside.

"Kelsie?"

The voice that replied did not come from the interior of the cabin. Nor was it Kelsie's.

"Drop to your knees."

Nick half turned. A thunderclap roar deafened him. It took the acrid smell of gunpowder for him to realize the person behind him had fired a shotgun.

"Next shot is in your back. Drop to your knees."

Nick lowered himself, wincing at the pain of a rock pressing against his kneecap.

"Now on your stomach."

Nick knew that voice. It was such a surprise, he felt his first chill of fear. "I don't get it," Nick said, on his belly with his face pressed against grass. "You? Why? I mean, how many years have we been friends?"

"Hands on your back."

Nick hesitated. This was getting serious.

The kick into his side came without warning. It was vicious, rib cracking.

"Hands on your back." As brutal as the kick had been, there was no excitement in the voice. That scared Nick more than the kick. He lifted his hands and put them on the small of his back.

He felt a cord being slipped over his wrists and tightened, looped in the knot rodeo riders use to hogtie a calf in roping competitions.

"Lift your feet."

Again, Nick hesitated. The next kick took him across the jaw.

He leveraged his feet upward, hurting his bruised knee as he pressed more weight on it.

After his ankles were trussed, he was rocked by a few more kicks in his ribs.

"My little note made you pant like a dog in heat, didn't it, Nick

Buffalo? Thought she was calling for you and you came running. Thought she was yours, didn't you, Nick Buffalo?"

"It's not what you think," Nick said, suddenly crazy with hope that this would become a good beating and nothing else.

"No?" The voice was softer. "Not what I think? Listen to me, Nick Buffalo. What I think over the next couple of days is going to matter very much to you. I have a secret little place nearby, a place where no one will find you even if they're looking. Your life is my power. Doris took two hours to die. If I do it right, you'll take two days."

# 4:01 p.m.

The extension phone in Russell Fowler's garage rang. He ignored it. Let the wife answer. She wasn't doing anything except putting a big dent in the couch cushions as she cheered on Phil Donahue.

Yeah, Fowler told himself, he was in a bad mood all right. He had done the field work to get seven sets of fingerprints. Each set had a corresponding name. Wayne Anderson, the banker. Judge Thomas King. Both councilmen. And his most recent prints, Lawson McNeill and Rooster and Frank Evans. It couldn't be, he thought; no prints in front of him matched the print on the beer can that, in turn, matched the partials on the corkscrew.

Impossible. There had only been those seven men at the campfire. Fowler himself made eight, and he didn't need to fingerprint himself to know he wouldn't match the mystery prints.

So what on earth was going on with—

He cursed the ringing phone. Why didn't Thelma answer? How was a man supposed to concentrate?

"What?" he snarled, grabbing the receiver off the hook.

"Hey, Russ." Fowler recognized the voice. It belonged to Tad Weslo, the portly administrative assistant at the courthouse who was on the verge of retiring. Tad loved trying to make inside straights and always bet as if he had; he hadn't yet figured out the weekly gang had long ago caught on to that bluff and loved it.

"Tad," Russ acknowledged.

"You sitting on a cactus? Or Thelma got you cleaning silverware?"

"I'm not in a joking mood."

"Like I said, cactus or silverware?"

"I'm in the garage, Tad. Cut to the chase."

"Got the carb apart again? I told you a dozen times to flat out buy a new one. No man needs the aggravation of trying to—"

"Tad."

"Almost sounds like you want me off the phone, Russ."

"I do, Tad. Thelma is dancing in front of me. She's wearing boa feathers, and she's real frisky."

Tad cackled. "Only if that's Donahue's latest advice. Thelma was over the other day, and that's all she and the old lady talked about for two hours. I swear, a hundred million woman in this country have dropped everything to turn on the television to watch that man. Economy grinds to a halt for one hour every day. No work gets done; no shopping gets done. And you should watch the show, see some of the things we get blamed for. Like they figure it's impossible for the rest of us men to be be aware of their feelings. Stupid broads, they—"

"Is this about tomorrow night's game? You deciding to hold on to your money and stay home?"

"Nope."

Tad had this aggravating habit of letting a person know he held a secret then forcing it to be dragged out of him.

"What then?"

"Got a call today."

"Yeah?" Fowler ground his teeth. Tad wouldn't call unless he had something of interest. It just seemed a man had to pay more than it was worth to get it. "From who?"

"Some starched collar on the East Coast. A muckity-muck from the FBI."

"Yeah?" Fowler didn't want to betray the interest that had bumped his pulse rate.

"Wanted me to search the files. Gave me the names of about two dozen men. Told me he needed to know if any had faced local criminal charges."

"Yeah? Tad, this carb, it's all over my workbench. Maybe tomorrow night you can fill me in on the rest." Fowler hoped he hadn't pushed so hard his bluff was obvious.

"I don't know, Russ. It just seemed strange, especially when I figured something out later."

Fowler grinned. Tad remained true to form, showing the inability to read people, an inability that got him invited back to the card table week after week.

"See," Tad continued, "I knew a couple of them by name. They all work at the McNeill ranch. So I gave Randy a call over at motor vehicles, fed him the names. Turns out every single one of them call James McNeill boss. What do you think is happening out there?"

"Probably nothing, Tad." On his own end of the phone, despite his casual response, Fowler was frowning in concentration. This didn't look good. "I'll keep my ears open. If I hear anything, I'll let you know." In a dry voice, Fowler added, "After all, you're good at keeping a secret."

"Town this small, you got to," Tad said, taking it seriously. "Rumors can do pretty bad damage, you know."

Fowler shook his head at Tad's opinion of himself. The rumor would probably reach James McNeill by dinnertime.

Fowler managed to cut his good-bye down to a couple of minutes. When he hung up the phone, he stared at the fingerprint cards.

What was going on at the McNeill ranch?

Fowler gave it some thought. Hoover's boy was mounting some kind of investigation that covered the hired hands at the ranch. Had the rookie made a connection of some kind to Lawson McNeill and his involvement in the group? Had he learned something about Doris and the stag party? Or, worst of all, had he somehow learned something about the train derailment?

Either way, it bothered Fowler—almost as much as an unidentified fingerprint on the beer can matching the one on the corkscrew.

Well, Fowler told himself, he wasn't imagining the matched prints, so there had to be an explanation. The conclusions he could draw for certain were that the same person who had once touched the beer can from the campfire had also once handled the corkscrew. He knew for certain that person was not one of the men at the campfire. So this person had handled the beer cans *before* it reached the campfire.

This was getting complicated. Fowler would have to find out who'd brought the beer that night and work backward from there. Worse, it didn't seem like the payback would be worth the work. If it wasn't one of the seven who had killed Doris Samson—it mattered far less; while Fowler would not mind putting the case to rest, he wouldn't lose sleep if he never did catch whoever had killed Doris Samson. Just a Flathead Indian, right?

He sighed. He wasn't ready to give up yet. First thing he'd have to do was dust the remaining beer cans. The other night, he'd stopped as soon as he'd found a print to match the corkscrew print. He'd have to keep looking; if he found a ninth set of distinct prints on the cans, it might prove his theory that the murderer had handled the beer cans before they reached the campfire.

In the meantime, he had the FBI to worry about. The kid was sharp; there was no telling where he was headed. He'd have to assign one of the deputies to dog Clay Garner, keep tabs on him, and report back.

Nor would it hurt to rain on the FBI parade. If rumor was going to reach James McNeill anyway, Fowler might as well get credit for it.

Fowler picked up the telephone and dialed a number he knew from memory. "James," he said to the answering voice. "Russ Fowler here. Look, there's something you should know about . . ."

## 10:27 P.M.

Behind the steering wheel in the cab of Harold Hairy Moccasin's '64 Chevy pickup, Sonny Cutknife grinned at the darkness on the other side of the cracked windshield. One headlight was gone on the truck, and the other threw out a poor yellow color in a losing cause against the black of night. It took concentration to follow the faded center line on the buckled asphalt of the back road, but Sonny was grinning because, aside from Nick Buffalo's absence, all his calculations had fallen into place.

Johnny Samson, leaning against the passenger door, had joined them at Harold's mobile home. All day, Sonny had worried that Johnny might not show. Sonny figured it would be a reflection on his leadership if he couldn't maintain power over some kid.

Harold, sitting between Sonny and Johnny, was burping happily, a result of all the beer Sonny had given him over the previous few hours. Earlier, after the first couple of beers in the cramped living room of the trailer, Harold had agreed to read Sonny's note into the tape recorder. Sonny had to coach him through it on nearly a dozen trial runs and suspected Harold had memorized the note instead of actually reading it. No matter. Sonny now had five cassettes, all with the same message. If something went wrong, there was no way Sonny could be tied into this; it wasn't his voice on the cassettes.

After a couple more beers, Harold had also agreed that Sonny could drive his truck, saying with owner's pride that sure, it needed new leaf springs and there were a few rust holes, but it got him where he needed to go. Which suited Sonny fine, getting where he needed to go with Harold's truck. If anybody remembered a vehicle near the construction site, it wouldn't point back to Sonny, and, after all, Harold's voice was on the cassettes. If anything went wrong, Sonny had planned, Harold could take the rap. Say it went to court; it would be Harold's word against Sonny's. Johnny wouldn't testify against Sonny; because he'd shown up, obviously he believed if he crossed Sonny he would find his head in the post pounder.

For a first raid, this one seemed almost perfect. Except for Nick. Johnny and Harold were worried about Nick's absence, and Sonny had lied, telling them Nick would meet them at the construction site, where the Native Sons would make their first strike. He thought that once he got the two of them that far, it would be too late for them to back out.

Sonny was a proud man, a warrior chief going into battle, and although at the moment he only had two misfit followers, after tomorrow, there was no telling where he'd go. Other warriors from across the nation were certain to join his cause, inspired by his brilliance and vision. Sonny knew that thirty years from now, people would look back and see how obvious it was that he had been destined to lead a national revolt to avenge white men's injustice.

Sonny grinned even more until a few miles later, when Harold Hairy Moccasin cracked a can of beer, sending spray into Sonny's right cheek. Sitting Bull or Spotted Tail or Red Cloud would never have had to endure an indignity like that, Sonny thought.

"Hey, Sonny," Harold said, nervous from the silence on both sides of him, "you like the way the truck handles? I'm thinking, soon as I get some money, I'm gonna slap in a V-8. You'll see this baby hum then." He burped and laughed. "Chicks love a man with power, if you get my drift."

Sonny said nothing, but his grin returned. *Power.* Right on to that. This was just the beginning.

Sonny drove them past the construction site and continued for a half mile before pulling down a side road. He pulled over as far as he could and parked.

"Why didn't you just have us walk from the trailer?" Harold complained, working at acting cool. "I could have saved gas money and spent it on beer."

Sonny decided to allow Harold the bravado. Instead of smacking Harold for questioning his authority, Sonny chuckled. "Harold, after tomorrow, we're gonna have money pouring in from all across the country. Brothers everywhere are gonna support our cause. You wait and see. Then you can have all the beer you want."

"Yeah, cool," Harold said. "Women too, right?"

Johnny didn't join in.

Sonny wished he could trust Johnny enough to give him the keys to the truck. It'd be a lot easier to have someone drop them off then swing back and pick them up again when they finished. Johnny, though, was too hard to read. Sonny needed to be sure Johnny wouldn't change his mind and drive off, especially after seeing the damage that Sonny intended. The last thing Sonny wanted was a get-away vehicle that got away before he did.

Doing it this way—and Sonny had thought it through—was best. If anyone showed up, the three of them could scatter in the woods and sneak back to the truck. The other way, with the truck right there, parked in front, it would be too easy for someone to follow them once they got in the truck, since the only place the truck could go was down the road.

It would have been better, of course, if Nick had been there. Nick could be trusted to drive. Not Johnny, though, and certainly not Harold. Harold would get lost in a parking lot. Sonny often figured it was a good thing grocery stores were invented for Indians like Harold because if Harold went looking for deer or buffalo, he'd never find his way back.

"Where's Nick?" Harold asked as they began the hike back toward the construction site. It was eerily quiet out there, some ten miles from the nearest town, three miles beyond the last house they'd passed. The tall spruce trees on both sides of the road were outlined black against the starry, clear sky, like sentinels along the roadside.

"He'll be there," Sonny lied, trying not to let Harold's reminder of Nick's absence irritate him. "If not, we don't need him. And he'll miss all the fun."

As a construction site, it wasn't much. During the day, Sonny had checked it as well as he could, considering he didn't dare drive by too slowly or too many times. He didn't want to raise suspicions, as there wasn't much traffic out this way.

All Sonny had seen on a half-acre freshly cleared in the trees were stacks of pipe, assorted piles of lumber, a construction trailer, a few pickup trucks, and a parked semi-trailer, probably loaded with other construction materials. Sonny had also noted with satisfaction a D-8 bulldozer chugging black smoke as it ripped a raw path through the trees and flattened the entire construction area.

At night, Sonny couldn't see that anything significant had changed since his day trip. The pickups were gone; that was to be expected. The workers didn't have any reason to camp out here. Everything else was in place, however. The D-8 bulldozer was parked beside the trailer.

Sonny assumed, because of an oil company sign at the road, that the multinational was getting ready to bring in a rig for a test well. During the last hundred yards of their approach, Sonny vented rhetorical anger about the raping and pillaging of ancestral land. Aside from that, Sonny couldn't care less about the oil company's intentions; he only cared about his.

Their eyes had adjusted to the darkness by the time they arrived at the construction site; a dozen times Sonny had warned Harold and Johnny if any headlights approached to hide in the ditch and look away so that their night vision wouldn't be spoiled. His warnings had been as unnecessary as they were tiresome. No vehicles had passed them.

"Where's Nick?" Harold asked as they surveyed the silent shadows of the construction sight.

"Yell for him," Sonny suggested sarcastically.

Harold drew a lungful of breath, and Sonny had to elbow him in the stomach to keep him from taking the suggestion.

Johnny still hadn't said anything. He hadn't said a word since leaving Harold's trailer, which began to worry Sonny. He'd have to make Johnny a part of this so that Johnny couldn't turn back.

"You and me," he said to Johnny, "we'll take the dozer. Harold's gonna watch the road."

"What about Nick?" Harold asked.

"What about your busted nose?" Sonny asked. "Cause that's what you're going to get if you don't stop crying about Nick. We got a job to do." He pushed Johnny toward the dozer. "Let's go."

Over his shoulder he told Harold, "Wait there. You see head-lights, you whistle."

It took Sonny less than five minutes to hotwire the bulldozer. There wasn't much to it, and he'd had experience working a dozer on the McNeill ranch.

The diesel engine chugged. Sonny didn't want to let it warm up long. Isolated as they were, there still was the chance someone might drive by.

"You get on with me," Sonny said to Johnny. "Harold, you watch for traffic. Come running if you see headlights."

Johnny found a perch beside Sonny, who was already at the con-trols. Sonny launched into action, shifting levers with no hesitation, getting the dozer blade high in place and rumbling forward. "Watch this, man," he said. He pulled a lever down, reversed one track, and spun the dozer toward the trailer. Seconds later, the massive blade pierced the thin metal wall. The dozer continued through as if the trailer was an egg carton.

"You like that?" Sonny asked. "This baby has got some power, don't it?"

"Sure," Johnny said.

"Well, you ain't seen nothing yet."

Sonny picked a crash course through a stand of saplings, popped the bulldozer through without slowing, and throttled it to full speed, straight uphill, straight toward a gigantic steel tower that carried electric power lines to feed power into the entire valley.

# Day 6

2:00 A.M.

"We're only going to be gone a week, my little sugar," Mommy said. She was in the front seat of the car, looking into the mirror of the passenger visor and adjusting her lipstick. "You have all you need in your suitcase. And some nice surprises that you can unwrap when we're gone."

"I want to go with you," the boy said from the backseat.

"You're almost a man," Daddy said, hands on the steering wheel. "Keep your chin up."

"For goodness sake, he's five. Don't place that kind of pressure on him."

"And bribing him with new toys is the solution? I'd rather raise a soldier than a wimp."

The boy fidgeted. He was small for his age, and with his legs straight ahead, his feet barely stuck out beyond the seat. It gave him the tips of his shiny black shoes to stare at as a distraction. He didn't like it when his parents spoke in those tones.

Finished with the lipstick, his mother snapped the visor into place. "Look, we've got one week. Do you want to spend the first two days fighting?"

"I'm only saying—"

"Honey, try to understand." His mother spoke softly. "No matter how much sense it makes, a mother stills feels guilty leaving."

The boy lifted his head just as his mother leaned over and kissed his *father on the side of his neck. "An entire week, hon. Maybe we can find a way for the stork to bring him a brother or sister."*

*"Or just practice." She kissed him more passionately, giggling slightly.*

*It caused the boy more discomfort. He didn't want to watch, but he couldn't help himself. He never liked it when his father got the kisses. Especially because his father wasn't always nice to her. Once the boy had walked into their room in the middle of the night to tell them about a bad dream and had found them fighting. His father had been on top. He had tried to pull his father off his mother. His father yelled at him, and his mother sent him away, and they had shut the door on him without listening to his scary dream.*

*"I want to go with you!"*

*His mother turned to look into the backseat.*

*"Sugar, Daddy and I won't be gone long. We'll call you every day to tell you how much we love you."*

*"I want to go with you!"*

*"Son, if you keep yelling," his father said, "I'll have to put you over my knee."*

*"No, hon," she said, "not now. He's upset. Go easy on him." She leaned over and began nuzzling his neck again.*

*The boy went back to staring at his shoes. He didn't look up again until the car stopped and his father opened the door for him. The boy saw the house, past his father, at the far end of the sidewalk.*

*He remembered the house. It was the house of his bad dreams. "Please," he said, "don't make me stay here."*

*"She's a nice lady. She took care of you last year, remember? You'll have lots of fun."*

*The boy opened his mouth to tell what he remembered about the old lady, but the house triggered another memory—of a kitten and what dead meant.*

*So the boy silently let his mother hug him good-bye. A few tears trickled down his cheek as he clutched her hand and let her lead him toward the house. His father walked behind them, carrying the suitcase packed with clothes and wrapped presents.*

*The door at the far end of the sidewalk opened, and the old lady stepped out and began to wave at them. His mother took him closer.*

*At the doorway, the boy smelled the rose-colored perfume on the old lady. He wanted to scream and cry, but the old lady had promised to make his parents dead if he wasn't quiet. He remembered that. So he let his mother push him into the house. He watched after her with tears streaming down his face as she walked away with his father.*

On his return well past midnight, the Watcher rigged a gas lantern to hang from a hook on the wall. It threw a surprising amount of intense white light, which the Watcher liked. The shadows were darker as a result in these cramped quarters, more surreal. The way the lantern hung, its light etched exquisite lines across the far side of Nick Buffalo's face.

"She has been mine from the beginning," the Watcher told Nick. "Or have you already realized that?"

Nick spat. He was still hogtied, of course, his hair matted with dirt, his pants stained where he'd been forced to wet himself while waiting for the Watcher to return. Nick's spitting was an act of defiance that pleased the Watcher. Doris Samson had been too frightened too soon. If Nick remained unafraid, there would be more power to take at the end.

Much as the defiance was pleasing, however, the Watcher wondered if he should go over and cut Nick to show him who was in control. He finally decided against it. Blood might lead him to a frenzy earlier than he wanted, and Nick Buffalo's escaping soul was an event to be anticipated and savored.

"Let me show you something," the Watcher said. Much as he hated Nick Buffalo, he found it exciting to finally be able to share his trophies, especially since it would only remind Nick of what the Watcher was taking away from him.

The Watcher stepped over Nick toward an old apple crate in the corner. He took the crate and sat cross-legged in front of Nick, setting the crate on the dirt floor between them.

"Photographs," the Watcher said, holding them up and spreading them like cards in a deck, with the back of the photographs toward Nick. "You can't look closely, though. They're for my eyes, not yours."

The Watcher paused to smile at each photograph: Kelsie walking by a stream; Kelsie under her favorite tree; Kelsie at her bedroom window; Kelsie swimming in the lake; Kelsie asleep. All of them had been taken without her being aware; all of them showed his power over her.

Reluctantly, he set the photos back in the apple crate.

He took out a white T-shirt. "Hers," the Watcher explained. "She was fourteen. Very beautiful then. See how large the shirt is? She used it as pajamas. Often, I wear it myself."

Nick Buffalo spat again.

The Watcher smiled at Nick's jealousy. The shoe was on the other foot now. The T-shirt went back into the crate. The Watcher lifted out a dog collar. "She had a dog named Louie. Altogether, it was taking too much of her time. So Louie had an accident. All the love she put into Louie returned to me with his life's blood."

"You are crazy," Nick said. "Nutso. Do you know that?"

"My perception of reality is different from yours. Don't feel at fault, though. It takes years of experimenting to get the force and understand it."

The Watcher gently set the dog collar down into the crate. He took out an envelope. "Here are some photos I *will* allow you to see."

He took a photo and held it in front of Nick's eyes, adjusting the angle so that the lantern light clearly illuminated a photograph of Doris Samson, gagged, eyes bulging with fright.

"It looks like ink," the Watcher said. "Unfortunately, I was forced to develop these in black and white. You don't get the full effect of the blood, and it looks like ink. Disappointing."

Nick's eyes were closed. One glance at the photo had shown him too much.

"Open your eyes," the Watcher ordered. "I want you to share these with me. Trust me; if I have to, I'll cut off your eyelids."

Nick opened his eyes. The Watcher took satisfaction in that. Nick finally understood the Watcher's seriousness and the Watcher's power. Whatever the two of them had shared before this evening mattered no longer, and Nick knew it.

"Good," the Watcher said as Nick kept his eyes open.

Photograph by photograph, he showed Nick the last moments of Doris Samson's life. When the Watcher was finished, he calmly placed the photographs in the envelope and put the envelope back into the crate.

The Watcher had much earlier decided he would first show Nick Buffalo the photographs of Doris Samson. That would make the final two items in the apple crate much more significant to Nick.

The Watcher kept his eyes on Nick's face as he took both items out and silently set them on the floor in front of Nick. First a 35mm camera. Then an eagle-feather headdress.

The widening of Nick's eyes showed that he understood.

"Yes," the Watcher whispered, his pleasure growing at Nick's fear, "I will remember you with fondness, too."

## 5:48 A.M.

The terrible sound of someone screaming took James McNeill from his wife's arms. Groggy, he sat up in bed. The dream had seemed so real that it took him a moment to realize she wasn't there.

And the screaming continued.

*One of the boys! Down the hallway!*

James pushed away the covers and hit the floor at a run. The house was dark. He made it to the bedroom door on memory and hit the lights for the hallway.

Nothing.

He cursed. What a time for the bulb to be burned out.

James continued in the darkness, stumbling down the hallway toward the screaming. *Lawson's room.*

Two steps later, he almost collided with Michael, who had burst from his bedroom door. Neither said a word; they hurried together to Lawson's bedroom at the end of the hallway.

The roaring continued on the other side of the bedroom door.

Michael tried the door. It was locked.

"Lawson!" James shouted. "Open up!"

The screaming grew louder. The door remained closed.

"Dad?" Michael asked.

James backed up two steps, then rammed his shoulder into the door, busting it off the hinges.

Enough of the faint dawn spilled into the bedroom to allow them to see Lawson's silhouette at the side of his bed. He was hunched over, jerking and shaking.

"Son!" James shouted. "What is it?"

Lawson roared louder, but his frantic jumbled words made no sense.

James fumbled for the light switch and finally found it. He clicked it, cursing again when the light remained dark.

"Flashlight, Michael," James ordered. "Back porch."

On the ranch, there were many occasions when a flashlight was needed in the yard or at the barns. Michael knew exactly where to find it. He dashed away.

James advanced on Lawson, who kept screaming. James placed a hand on his back.

"Let go, let go, let go, let go!"

James finally understood Lawson's frantic words and dropped his hand away. "Lawson? What is it?"

Only more screaming.

The flashlight beam bounced into the bedroom ahead of Michael. James stepped back to avoid blocking the light.

Michael turned the beam on Lawson. It took Michael and James a few seconds to comprehend the situation.

Lawson was clutching at the calf of his right leg, futilely pulling at the large iron jaws of a rusty bear trap. The chain attached to the bear trap had been secured to a bedpost. Lawson must have stepped out of bed, into the trap.

"We're here, son," James McNeill said. The how and why of something this bizarre he would find out later.

Lawson kept screaming, kept pulling at his leg, as if no one was in the room with him.

"Relax!" James shouted. "I can't step on the release unless you stop moving."

Lawson was in full panic, unable to understand.

"Hold him," James told Michael, taking the flashlight from his son.

Michael moved quickly, taking Lawson from behind and grabbing his arms and wrestling him to a standstill.

That was how Kelsie found them when she stepped over the broken bedroom door a few seconds later: her father in his boxer shorts, Michael in a pair of sweatpants holding Lawson, who was wearing pajama pants and screaming in pain.

James pointed the beam downward and stepped on the release spring of the giant trap. "Pull the jaws apart," he ordered Kelsie above Lawson's screaming.

Kelsie didn't hesitate.

Lawson was so panicky he didn't realize his leg was free until Michael lifted him from the trap. Then Michael let go, and Lawson collapsed onto his bed, moaning and holding his leg.

James pushed Lawson's hands away, and pulled up the pajama leg. He shone the flashlight to see that the skin on Lawson's leg was a deep, angry red where the teeth of the trap had closed on it. In some places, where the notches had dug deep, pin-pricks of blood oozed from the skin.

"Water," James told Kelsie. "He needs water."

Lawson probably didn't need water, James thought, but he wanted the boy to stop his feverish moaning. Drinking water might be a normal enough act to snap him from his panic.

Kelsie ran to the kitchen.

"Hey, bud," Michael said. "You're fine."

Lawson writhed on the bed.

A minute later Kelsie returned with the water. James handed the flashlight to Kelsie then took the glass and forced it to Lawson's mouth, pouring the water in when Lawson refused to hold the glass himself.

It seemed to help, for Lawson began to calm himself.

"That's better," James said. "And I think your leg will be fine. Your pajamas saved most of the skin. It was an old enough trap that much of the snap was gone. A new trap would have broken your shin."

"Trap?" Lawson's forehead was beaded with sweat. "I was going to the bathroom. I stepped down. It . . ."

It wasn't hard to figure out the mechanics of stepping in a trap. What bothered James far more was how the trap had gotten there— and why.

He didn't need to puzzle about it for long.

Kelsie screamed. It was a short, brief, high-pitched note of terror. She'd let the flashlight wander. It now pointed at a large feather on the floor beside the bear trap. Kelsie screamed again then fled from the bedroom.

## 9:23 a.m.

Russell Fowler faced the three men who sat in his office. He would have preferred to meet them elsewhere, but on short notice he could think of no better place. Restaurants were too open. Renting a meeting room at a hotel might have worked, but in a town this small it might not pay for folks to see all of them together. He was praying no one of importance walked in now and that if someone did, Two Car would be smart enough to handle the problem in the reception area without sending anyone back here.

"News conference, Russ?" Andy Summit asked. "Like the big city?"

"Sure," Fowler said. "You'll notice the coffee served in china and, of course, the big platters of hors d'oeuvres."

"Coffee?" Andy said. "That would be a treat. It's tough to percolate anything when everything electrical is shut down."

"I made it over a campfire," Fowler said. "The old-fashioned way."

Andy and the other two joined in the slightly nervous chuckles at the sheriff's attempted humor. They needed a release in tension. It had caught each of them by surprise, seeing the other two. Wasn't this the first time they been brought together by the sheriff? Into his office? Something had to be up.

Andy Summit was news director at KJIK, an FM country-music station. Tom Ramsey filled the same position at the local AM station. The third, Eddie Lewis, was editor of the *Kalispell Times*.

"Boys," Fowler said, "about an hour ago, I got a call from Seth."

He didn't need to explain more about the caller's identity. All the media people in the valley knew one another. Most Friday afternoons the various reporters and other news people got together at the Kicking Horse Saloon to trade gossip and war stories. Seth Williamson, news producer for KJOH-TV, had a reputation for buying more than his share of the rounds of beer on Friday afternoons. He was well liked as a result.

"Seems somebody dropped off a cassette tape at their front office today." Fowler watched for any reaction. This was a trade-off. He didn't like the prospect of releasing information they might not have. On the other hand, it would be surprising if they hadn't gotten a copy of the same cassette, and if not, each of them would eventually hear anyway.

"Native Sons?" Eddie asked. "I was on the verge of getting one of my reporters to call you to confirm some facts, but you reached me first. So I decided to come and find out for myself."

Eddie grinned. He was close to Fowler's age. His thin hair was plastered sideways over his shiny dome. "And now that I hear you mention cassette, I'm sure glad I'm here."

The other two wore puzzled expressions. Fowler pulled a portable cassette player out from under his desk. He set it on top of the desk and punched the play button.

"This is a call to all the native sons of North America," the voice said. "It is time to reclaim our land. If we unite, we can defeat the European colonizers who have raped our heritage. Wherever you live, join the fight. Derail the white man's trains. Knock down his power lines. Poison his water. Burn his factories. Strike and run in the honorable tradition of great warriors. And when the white man is filled with terror, he will honor treaties and return to us our heritage. We are the Native Sons."

"Power lines?" Andy said. "Utility company told us the power's out because a transformer blew. This have anything to do with that?"

"They agreed to send the transformer story out as the official press release," Fowler said. "Truth is, someone knocked down an entire hydroelectric tower. Whoever did it used a bulldozer from a nearby construction site."

"Bulldozer?" Tom Ramsey blurted. "Tower? Utilities said it would be a matter of hours before power was restored. You have an idea how many lines one of those towers supports? You can't just splice something like that together. We could be out for days."

"Half-day tops," Fowler said. "They're putting up temporary poles."

"Time doesn't matter," Andy said firmly. "The entire valley's out. We have a right to know why, especially if it's part of a terrorism thing. You can't hold that stuff back on us."

Fowler took a breath. This was the payoff moment. "I want to make a deal with you guys," he said. "That's why I've called you in for a discussion."

At the word *deal,* all three lost any animation or friendliness in their faces.

"Come on," Fowler said. "I'm going to tell you as much as I know. All I'm going to ask is that you guys keep it quiet for a while."

"This is terrorism," Andy said. "What if these guys strike again? People need to be able to protect themselves."

"The cold truth is that if we don't know where they're going to strike next, people can't protect themselves anyway." Fowler put up his hands to fend off any remarks at his callousness. "I've got a real good reason for asking."

They waited. He drew another breath.

"First of all, it will throw everybody into a panic. Do we want to start a small war?"

No reply. The newsmen could well picture good old boys packing rifles and heading out to the reserve in a convoy of pickup trucks.

"Second," Fowler said, "what happens if you put this out? How long's it going to take for the wire services to pick this up and spread it across the entire nation?"

Again, no reply. They all knew the answer.

"Don't you think that's exactly what these Native Sons want? Why else leave a cassette on the seat of the bulldozer? Why send out copies to the media? If every newspaper in the country picks this up, if every national network runs it in prime-time news, it's only going to encourage these guys to do more. And what about natives in the rest of the country? Remember Wounded Knee? Plenty of other hotheads on other reservations might think this is a great idea and do the same thing in their areas."

Fowler paused for breath. "There's not much we can do to secure a valley this big against random acts of terrorism. You might think these Native Sons are nuts, but the idea is good. Scary good. If we can't secure this valley, how about other towns and cities near other reservations? Same problem. If this got any momentum at all, it could snowball."

He shook his head. "Snipers. Fires. Dynamite. Get the natives across the nation wound up in a cause working together, we might see real trouble. Like brush fires springing up all over until you have a forest fire beyond control."

Fowler measured his small audience. They were listening intently. "Here's what I'm asking," Fowler said. "It's only going to work if all of you agree to sit on these cassettes. That way, no one gets an unfair jump. Give me as long as you can. All it might take is a day or two to get these guys. If I can stomp this bushfire before any others start, the forest is saved."

"I don't know," Andy said. "It's like a conspiracy. What if there's a leak about the conspiracy? Then where will all of us be in the eyes of the public?"

"Three days," Russ said. "I've told you enough at this point, any one of you could walk out and write a major story this afternoon. But if all of you hold off three days, what could be the harm in that?"

"It would have to be all of us," Eddie said, looking at the others.

"If one jumps the gun, the rest of us look bad. And the one who jumps the gun looks real good."

Fowler knew this was not the time for him to speak. He'd presented his case. It would be dumb to oversell it.

"It's not like this is New York," Andy finally said. "We know each other. We should be able to trust each other. And I think all of us want to do what's right for the community."

"Three days," Eddie said. "But if anything else happens, the deal's off. What do you guys say to that?"

The other newsmen agreed.

Fowler's grave nod hid a fair degree of triumph. He did care some about the Native Sons, and he knew there was a lot of truth in his argument. Media play would be throwing gasoline on the fire.

But there was more, much more that he didn't want these guys to know. The worst thing that could happen was more outsiders in the valley snooping around, especially if all the outsiders were professional media trained at turning over rocks. Fowler—and the people he worked for—would rather see a hundred FBI agents bumbling around than a dozen journalists armed with tape recorders and cameras.

"Thanks, gentlemen," Fowler said, standing. "You've helped more than you can imagine." He didn't know what might happen over the next three days, but three days was better than nothing.

# 10:47 A.M.

Clay recognized the back of Kelsie's head. She was sitting at a booth at the far side of the diner. It surprised him that she wasn't alone. It surprised him more that the man in the cowboy hat across from her was James McNeill, her father. It explained, at least, why she'd ask to meet him at a restaurant. If she didn't feel this needed to be secret any longer . . .

Clay walked through the cigarette smoke, passing cowboys and truckdrivers who were too intent on their own conversations to notice him.

James stood at Clay's approach, extending his hand in greeting. "I don't know if I should take a swing at you," James said, "or write a letter of thanks."

"Then I guess I'll ready myself to duck or fetch my reading glasses."

"Go on. Sit down." James waved a hand at a young, gum-chewing waitress leaning on the counter. "Chrissie, how about some coffee?" To Clay he said, "You do drink coffee?"

Clay nodded. He didn't know which side of the booth to choose. It didn't seem right to plunk down beside Kelsie, but he wasn't anxious to let James squeeze him in on the other side.

James saved him the decision by sitting beside Kelsie. Clay took the opposite seat and faced them both, holding any words until after the waitress poured coffee and swished along to the next booths in her too-tight polyester dress.

"I'd like to take a swing because I don't care for folks—especially eastern folks—inquiring after my business. I want to thank you kindly, because just this morning I discovered why you've been looking into the records of the men who work at my ranch."

"There's a lot I find interesting about that statement, Mr. McNeill."

"I told him about the notes, Mr. Garner," Kelsie said. "I couldn't help it."

"Call me James," the rancher said, squeezing his daughter's hand affectionately. "And I imagine your first question is how I knew about your inquiries of the men who work at my ranch. It's a small town, so small a two-bit rancher like me can still be considered a man of influence. As a result, it don't take long for word to reach me about anything of importance."

Clay winced. He should have foreseen that. "And Kelsie told you the why."

"Exactly," James replied. "Kelsie told me the why. You don't know it yet, but this morning, just before dawn, she got a good reason to tell me."

James explained the bear trap and the confusion around it without electricity to provide lights. He told about Kelsie's reaction to the feather they found beside the trap and how he'd asked Kelsie to explain what she knew, especially since she'd been acting strange over the past couple of days.

"She was scared," James said. "Scared about the situation, scared to tell me. And I don't blame her. Fact is, I believe without the family conversation at lunch yesterday, I doubt she would have told me anything."

Kelsie broke in. "Then last night, Daddy called us together—me and Michael and Lawson—and asked us if we knew anything about the Federal Bureau of Investigation looking into ranch matters. I didn't say anything because I was too afraid one of them might get hurt if I didn't keep the secret like I was told. But after Lawson stepped into a bear trap in his own room . . ."

She dropped her eyes to the table. Her shoulders trembled. Clay wondered if she'd gone as far as confessing to James her midnight walks with Nick Buffalo. He decided it didn't matter. That was between them. Besides, regardless of what she did, she wasn't responsible for a lunatic's jealousy or actions.

"If this weirdo got into our house twice . . ." James grimaced. "She told me about the lipstick writing on her forehead. If he got in twice, she felt it was more important to warn us than try to protect us. And she figured we already knew about the FBI, so a part of the secret was out anyway, and it couldn't hurt too much more to tell me. I'm sitting here with you because if any folks put together that you're FBI, they'll think you're asking me train-derailment questions."

"Michael and Lawson know about the notes?" Clay asked. "Did you tell them what Kelsie told you?"

"Nope. Before she said a word, Kelsie made me swear on a Bible that all this would stay between you and me and her. Which is one of the reasons I'm here with her. First of all, I'd like to thank you. I understand you agreed you would help as best you could, and you agreed to keep it quiet for her. Seems to me that's stepping past the boundaries of your job."

"Nothing to thank me for," Clay said. "You have another reason for being here?"

"Another note. Tucked into the paws of her favorite teddy bear."

"He'd been in my bedroom again!" Kelsie said. This time there was anger in her voice, not fear.

James unbuttoned his vest pocket and pulled out a piece of paper. Silently, he handed it across the table to Clay. It took Clay a few minutes to decipher the handwriting.

The trap of steel was a sign for you. Now you know anytime I can take anyone from you. If you don't keep our sacrid secret, I will rilly hert him. Maybe your father next if you are not careful. It is time for you to prove you love me. Tonight, when all are

asleep, go to your bedroom window. At two a.m., because I am
an eagle of the night. Open your curtins. Put on a show for me.
You know I will be watching. My love will be reaching acros the
darkness to you. If it is a good show, then I know you will also be
sending love to me. If it is a bad show or if you don't go to your
window for me, I will be forced to leave another feather. Only
this time someone will dy. Remember, I am the only one for you.
Your Watcher.

"Well," Clay said, "at least he's still convinced Kelsie's kept this
to herself."

"But for how long?" James asked. "I'm talking to you instead of
Fowler because this is less apt to get out, but eventually, it will."

Clay remembered his coffee and took his first sip. It was luke-
warm. "The answer is obvious, isn't it?" Clay said after further
reflection.

"Trap him," James said. "That's the third reason I'm here. To ask
you for help. We know where he'll be tonight. And when. You and I
are going to trap him like the animal he is."

# 1:10 P.M.

Russ Fowler hung up the telephone and returned to staring at fingerprint cards scattered across his desk when Two Car squeezed
through the office doorway.

"Yeah?" Fowler said, not looking up. By going back to the
remaining beer cans he'd ignored after first finding a match to the
murder prints, he'd found a total of twelve sets of prints on the beer
cans. There had been seven men at the campfire. The eighth set was
probably a grocery store clerk. One set, of course, was the clear and
definite match to the fingerprints on the corkscrew. But how much
backtracking could he do with casual questions?

As much as the coincidence bothered him, Fowler wondered how
much further he should push it at this point. He could make one trip
out to the ranch, but after that . . .

He'd learned that Lawson was one of the people who'd brought
beer that night. Could the killer have been one of the ranch hands? It
would be hard to casually get all their fingerprints—maybe even
impossible. It was driving him nuts, and to add to his aggravation,

he had to deal with the media, some crazed Indians called the Native Sons, and with Two Car's unappealing body odor, which filled the entire office. Maybe Fowler should clip out an Ann Landers column on the subject and stick it in Two Car's message box.

"Yeah?" Fowler repeated, his tone surly. When there was no answer, he finally looked up.

Two Car was extending a piece of paper, ripped from a message pad.

"Yeah? Can't you just read it to me?"

"Just came in. While you were on the line."

Yeah, Fowler thought. On the line with yet another problem: the judge, anxious that no national media would be hitting the valley and needing to be baby-sat about it.

"Read it," Fowler almost snarled. It seemed like years since he'd been in a good mood.

"Tonight. Saint Andrews Church. Midnight. Like the power-line trouble. Expect a fire."

"What!"

"Some weirdo probably," Two Car said, scratching his belly.

Fowler pushed back from his desk and stood quickly. He marched around the side of his desk and grabbed the paper from Two Car's hand. *Tonight. Saint Andrews Church. Midnight. Like the power-line trouble. Expect a fire.* "Anything else?"

"Nope. Some guy called, told me to have a pen and paper ready and to write down every word he gave me. Said you'd find it important."

"Who?" Fowler said. "Who called?"

"Chief, he said it was an anonymous tip. That was all. Then he told me to have a pen and paper ready and to—"

"Anything strange about his voice? Young? Old? Accent?"

"Just told me to—"

"Enough," Fowler said. Two Car didn't know about the cassette and the message from the Native Sons. Fowler had learned early that Two Car passed everything on to his wife, who was a hairdresser, which was more effective and less costly than an ad in the newspaper.

"Anything else, Chief?"

"Aside from not calling me chief?" Fowler looked at Two Car's uniform. The huge man was sweating giant half moons beneath his armpits. "Yeah," Fowler said. "There *is* something else."

Forget the Ann Landers approach, Fowler thought. He dug into his front pocket for a couple of dollar bills. He held them in front of Two Car's wobbling chin until the big man took the money.

"Buy some deodorant," Fowler said.

He only felt half-sorry for the puppy-dog hurt that crossed Two Car's face.

# 4:12 p.m.

*Outside the old lady's bedroom window, a full moon hung white and clear. The boy knew, because he'd been watching it from the moment she clicked off her bedside lamp and curled beside him, holding him against her stomach, with him staring away from her in silent misery, his head barely above the covers. For a while, in the darkness, she had kept whispering the name he hated in his ear, telling him she loved her Little Bobby, uncaring that his entire body was rigid.*

*Eventually he was able to tell from the even rise and fall of her chest against his back that she had settled into sleep. He had tried to shift a few times; but even asleep she sensed his movement and clutched tighter. So he had given up and tried to remain motionless, watching the moon and waiting for night to fade so that morning would return.*

*She clung to him with her withered arms. The boy could not remember being more miserable.*

*Later, when the moon had moved beyond the square frame of her bedroom window, a new thought occurred to the boy.*

*His father had taken Mommy away, hadn't he? She didn't want to go. She'd said that. It was his father who had done all this. Because of his father, the boy was forced to stay behind and sleep at night with the old lady who followed him around the house all day crooning the name he hated.*

*A sleepless hour later, the boy's body was still rigid, and he was still thinking angry thoughts about his father.*

*"I wish Daddy was dead," he whispered.*

*The thought scared the boy. It was wrong to wish someone would die. He told himself never to say that again. When dawn arrived, he was still staring out the window, trying not to say it.*

When the Watcher returned again, shotgun in one hand, flashlight in the other, it appeared Nick had not moved from his position against the far wall. He was still on the floor on his side, facing the small entrance.

"Roll over, Nick." Funny, wasn't it, ordering him like a dog.

"Man, the least you could do is untie my hands. I gotta go real bad."

"Roll over on your stomach, Nick." He wanted to determine from the doorway that Nick's wrists were still bound. "You're alive at my whim, and you probably understand I'm not big into predictability."

Nick obeyed.

The Watcher stood above Nick and turned the flashlight beam downward to make a visual inspection of Nick's wrists. They were dirty but not frayed. Nick hadn't found anything to rub the rope against.

"That's a good boy," the Watcher said. He used his foot to turn Nick on his side again.

"I gotta go," Nick said. "Come on."

"I'm not stopping you." The Watcher decided that inflicting small indignities was almost as enjoyable as torturing the man with knife cuts. Probably it was the sense of control. Later, he'd have to ponder the reason for this unexpected pleasure.

"Nice seeing you," the Watcher said, stepping toward the entrance.

"Water then," Nick said, unable to hide his begging tones. "I'm dying for a drink of water."

The Watcher laughed. "Key word there, wouldn't you say, Nick Buffalo? Dying?"

Nick's head slumped onto the dirt floor.

The Watcher pushed the door open and stepped out. Daylight poured in.

"You should know there's been a change of plans, Nick," the Watcher said. "You haven't shown up at the sheriff's office to answer questions about the night Doris Samson died. The rumor is you split because you're the one who did it."

The Watcher noticed that Nick was too tired to spit defiance any longer. That was another small pleasure, seeing the man slowly weaken.

"That works out great for me, Nick. This get-together was something I had planned just for payback. But I think I can do more with it now."

The Watcher glowed inside. Draining Nick of power had given him more strength.

"So," the Watcher continued, "now you write a note of apology to the world. And trust me, you will. If you don't, every person in your family will die. You don't want that, do you?"

"Just a drink of water."

"No, Nick. No water for you. Anyway, I'm telling you all this so you won't get nervous when you hear the chainsaw outside. My plans have changed, but not to the point where I've decided your end will be quick. Messy, I hope, but not quick. I won't cut you with a chain saw."

With that, the Watcher turned and stepped outside, letting the darkness inside settle upon Nick again.

A few minutes later, the roar of a chain saw echoed through the small valley, spraying sawdust into the grass at the back of the cabin.

# 11:45 p.m.

Johnny Samson stood hidden in the shadows of an industrial trash bin in the alley behind an all-night convenience store. The smell of sour milk and rotting cabbage nauseated him. He was tempted to pour some gasoline onto his sleeve from the can at his feet then hold the sleeve to his nostrils to mask the smell of the trash bin.

Bad thought, he told himself. He would escape the rotting smell as soon as he walked away, but once he poured gasoline on his sleeve it would follow him everywhere. Besides, Johnny figured, since he only had to wait until the church clock chimed at midnight, he had less than ten minutes of suffering the trash bin anyway.

Sonny had told them the plan would work because it was simple, with Harold coming at the church from one direction, Sonny from another, and Johnny from the third, using this dark alley to reach the back side of the church.

Sonny had told them it would be too suspicious if anyone saw the three of them together, especially at this time of night in this WASP neighborhood, especially since they were carrying cans of gasoline.

The plan was genius in its simplicity, Sonny had said again and again. By starting the fire from three sides, the historic old wooden church would be engulfed almost instantly.

Over at Harold's trailer in the early afternoon, when they were discussing it, Johnny had asked about Nick. Two nights in a row, and Nick wasn't around to do his share, Johnny had said. Sonny had nearly punched Johnny for asking, but then Sonny was in a bad mood anyway. He'd been listening all day to radio and television news, and not once had the Native Sons been blamed for the power outage that had put the entire valley down for hours. That, of course, was the reason for the spur-of-the-moment decision to burn the church. If a bulldozed power line didn't get the message out through the media, Sonny vowed, burning Kalispell's most beloved church certainly would.

Harold, splayed across his couch, happy with the beer Sonny supplied him, had agreed to the plan easily. Johnny had hidden his doubts.

Sonny had left Johnny to baby-sit Harold for the rest of the afternoon and evening and returned around eleven that night with gasoline and more beer. The truck ride into town had taken half an hour, with Sonny again behind Harold's steering wheel. Sonny and Johnny had dropped Harold off at a park opposite the church. Right after, Sonny had driven down the alley and left Johnny at the trash bin, where he'd been waiting since with the gasoline can at his feet, one hundred yards down the alley from the church he was supposed to set on fire.

The sound of slamming car doors reached him from the front of the convenience store, followed by loud male laughter. White kids, probably his own age, Johnny thought. White kids, in a white world, happy with their activities, sure of their actions, confident of their places in the world.

And what was he? An orphaned Flathead Indian, alone in their world.

At that moment, Johnny felt disconnected. There seemed nothing real to him about the cold metal of the trash bin against his back, nothing real about the dark, deserted alley. Wasn't his own world the sharp white points of stars against a deep black sky, the sway of pine treetops in the wind, and the creaking of his grandpa's rocker on the front porch of the two-room cabin?

An incredible wave of homesickness washed over him, a yearning to be at peace from emotions, thoughts, and wishes he only vaguely felt and understood. He wanted to be tough, standing strong alone, needing nobody. Yet instead of feeling strong about being alone, he felt lonely and afraid.

At that moment, it finally occurred to him to wonder exactly what he was doing, standing and waiting to pour gasoline on a church and light it with a match.

All afternoon and evening, while Harold dozed off the effects of a six-pack lunch, Johnny had mindlessly stared at the black-and-white television in the corner of the tiny living room, keeping his thoughts away from the past, which included memories of his sister, and away from the future, which seemed empty and hopeless. Because he'd managed to keep his mind blank, he hadn't much considered what the three of them planned to do at midnight.

Now, however, midnight was only minutes away.

Johnny realized he really didn't want to light the match. The night before, Sonny had said nothing of his intentions to bulldoze a power line but had kept them involved by saying he wanted to do some harmless pranks at the construction site as a way of getting attention for the Native Sons. By the time Johnny understood exactly what Sonny meant to do, it had been too late.

This was different. *Burn a church?*

He asked himself what would happen if he simply walked away. Well, Sonny would be angry, no doubt about that. So what? Johnny asked himself. The threat of sticking his head in the post pounder had just been Sonny trying to look tough in front of Nick. Johnny did know that, just as he knew Sonny was vaguely afraid of Johnny and his silences.

He'd lose their friendship. Harold, Sonny, and Nick wouldn't let him in their group anymore. So what to that too, Johnny decided. What kind of friends tried to get you to burn a church with them? Johnny would be better off staying in the hills with his grandfather. At least he could be himself there and not find himself holding his nose against the smell of rotting cabbage and sour milk in a cause he didn't care much for anyway.

The bells of St. Andrew's Church rang the stroke of midnight.

Johnny lifted the gasoline can at his feet and heaved it into the trash bin.

He stepped into the light at the edge of the parking lot and walked away from the convenience store. Three white kids, getting back into their car, paused to jeer at Johnny's retreating back. He ignored them.

Five minutes later, Johnny stopped and looked back in the direction of the church. No flames rose into the night; no firetrucks wailed to break the silence of the peaceful small town. Maybe Sonny and Harold had changed their minds, Johnny thought. It wouldn't have surprised him. Until Sonny actually put the bulldozer into gear the night before, he'd figured Sonny to be more talk than action.

Johnny shrugged. Either way, burned church or not, he was out of all this.

He began to walk again. Even though he had hours to go to get to his grandfather's cabin, and most of it hitchhiking along dark country roads, he already felt better.

# Day 7

The Watcher smiled from his vantage point at the front of the loft of the barn. He'd been sitting beside the open window up there for nearly an hour, so still on a bale of straw that five minutes earlier, a mouse had darted over his feet.

He smiled because his gamble had paid off. After following Kelsie to the department store and seeing her with the FBI pig, it was an easy guess that she had told him about the note. The Watcher had wondered if she would disobey him again, so he had written another note telling her to go to her window. He had hoped she would take this note to the FBI man, and she had, bringing her father along.

It hadn't been much of a gamble though. If Clay Garner and James McNeill did not appear, the Watcher would get the show from Kelsie he wanted. If the two men did appear, all the rest of what he had planned could fall into place.

Now, as he watched, Clay Garner and Kelsie's father moved past the corrals toward the stand of trees on the hill above the ranch house. As the Watcher had anticipated, both men were carrying rifles. He could see their outlines silhouetted against the yard light.

He smiled because they were early, and he had anticipated that, too. He had not, however, anticipated the man standing directly behind them and his two bloodhounds. But he continued smiling because this was a pleasant surprise.

It could only be Caleb Latcher, a short, intense man with a beard so high only his eyes and forehead showed. Once they found a quarry's trail—Caleb had a fondness for tracking bear—he and his celebrated bloodhounds rarely lost the scent. Fortunately, Caleb had a reputation for never letting them off the leash to run ahead. They were too valuable to risk losing to a bear's claws or teeth. It was a safe assumption that Caleb would not let them off the leash tonight either, which meant there was no need to fear any physical danger as the Watcher allowed the dogs to follow.

He began to relax. Now everything would work out fine, for his biggest worry was that the FBI man wouldn't be able to keep up in the darkness. After all, not everyone gladly embraced the night. Not everybody had the Watcher's gift of understanding shadows. Now, because of the bloodhounds, he wouldn't have to stoop to clumsily moving through the woods with enough noise to lead his prey to his lair.

The edge of the barn cut them from his line of vision.

The Watcher rose from his bale, walked softly through scattered straw to the side of the loft, and resumed watching them from a window there. He watched the men until they chose their hiding positions.

They moved into a triangle that would give each man a view of Kelsie's bedroom window. Each of them settled into the dark shadows of a tree.

The Watcher smiled again. It was exactly how he had planned to manipulate them.

His biggest regret regarding the events about to unfold was that he wouldn't be able to savor the death of the FBI pig. Yes, he had to die; Kelsie had turned to him and in so doing, betrayed the Watcher once more. The pig would die as punishment. Unfortunately, the bullet from Nick's rifle would be far too merciful. Yet, justice, as with Nick's death, would be served, and Kelsie would have no one left but her true love, always watching, always waiting.

Watching. Waiting.

Much as the Watcher would have liked to begin his plan now, he had written in the note that Kelsie should be at the window at 2 A.M.

If he made his move before that time, they might have suspicions later.

To pass the time, the Watcher closed his eyes and enjoyed blood-soaked memories of Nick Buffalo's final moments. Because he was able to use Doris as a comparison, the Watcher had discovered that he did prefer killing women. Still, Nick had served well, holding to his life force so long and with such fierceness and fury that the Watcher had absorbed much power.

He was learning and accepted that there would have to be trial and error involved. He would have to find women who matched Nick in their reluctance to relinquish their life force. He would have to find a way to test these women to his satisfaction beforehand. Because of the time and effort it took to prepare, there was no sense disappointing himself by discovering too late that he had taken a weakling.

For the Watcher did know with absolute certainty that after he completed his plans tonight, there would be a next victim to give him the life flow of power. And another. And another.

## 1:58 A.M.

Clay Garner wanted to stand and adjust his undershorts. Somehow—and it should have been impossible because he'd held himself still for three-quarters of an hour—the stupid boxers had managed to bunch themselves like an accordion up the legs of his blue jeans.

Because James McNeill had earlier warned him not to anticipate the night temperature from the day's heat, Clay had prepared properly for extra warmth by wearing a bulky sweater and a borrowed hunting cap. So, aside from the undershorts and aside from the reason he was sitting motionless on a stump beneath the boughs of a large spruce tree, he hadn't minded the vigil.

Several times coyotes had howled beyond the crew's bunkhouse. A distant jet had hissed as it passed high over the valley. Other than that, the air around him had been silky in its quiet. Unlike the muggy, hot summer nights of West Virginia, no incessant creaking and chirping of crickets and bugs disturbed the silence.

By tilting his head slightly, Clay could see a piece of sky between the boughs of the tree above him. He'd never realized a sky could be so dark, never understood how numberless were the stars. He liked it here.

Clay wondered how it might be to find enough peace to make a home in the valley, without the steamer trunk of memories and regrets included with the possessions he dragged along from apartment to apartment, peace like the peace he'd sensed from that old man, George Samson.

Clay let his thoughts stray. He'd begun to enjoy his daily travels in the valley, fruitless as they were in the course of his train-derailment investigation. They'd given him an excuse to range the Montana hills and mountains.

Much of his driving had been on Highway 93, the two-lane pavement running most of the length of the western edge of the valley. South, the highway skirted Flathead Lake for nearly fifty miles, dipping and curving through the rocky bluffs that dropped to the resort cabins on the shoreline. North, beyond Kalispell and the ski resort town of Whitefish, the highway turned into a sixty-mile funnel between two mountain ranges.

There was a seven-mile stretch of highway between the north end of Flathead Lake and the commercial spillover at the south end of the town of Kalispell, where Highway 93 was uncharacteristically straight and flat, with uncharacteristic fields of grass and wheat arranged in uncharacteristic neatness, as if Dutch farmers had invaded to form an enclave against the ruggedness of the Montana hills and mountains.

The stretch of flatness, unbroken by buildings or trees, was nearly his favorite piece of road because it gave him a sense of the panoramic scope of wide sky and freedom of the land. He remembered how he'd stopped along it early one morning, awed by the view of dawn clouds streaked with pale yellows and tinted with rose hues above the far mountain walls on the other side of the valley.

Something about Montana had captured his soul, he decided. Someday, he'd be back. Someday . . .

A square piece of light appeared, more intense because his eyes had become accustomed to the night. Immediately, he focused on the light.

Kelsie had turned on the light in her bedroom and was now standing at the window, opening the curtains, then the window itself.

Although her outline against the light revealed little more than a cutout figure, Clay knew she was wearing a full-length robe with pajamas underneath. James and Clay had both been adamant about her apparel and about her actions. Kelsie was *not* to do anything remotely suggestive. The thought of it filled both of them with rage and revulsion; not even to trap this killer and pervert was she to compromise herself. Moreover, if they did not catch the Watcher, they didn't want him encouraged to try again later.

Instead, they had instructed Kelsie to do exactly what she did next. She pulled a chair close to the window and sat. She rested her forearms on the window sill and leaned her chin on her arms, to stare out the window.

If he called out to her, she was to remain silent. They wanted his curiosity to drive him forward, not perverted desire. She was to be a beacon to bring him in closer, anything to get him to move and betray his position.

Five minutes passed.

To Clay, it seemed as if he hadn't breathed in that time. The slightest crackle of branches, the slightest motion of shadow, and they would move.

Noise and lights would be their first weapons. Clay and James had powerful searchlights and $CO_2$ airhorns. They wanted to confuse the man, panic him, freeze him, making it seem as if people were coming in on him from all directions. If he managed to slip away, Caleb and the hounds would track him down, and they'd have the lights to help follow.

Another five minutes passed.

Clay's senses were heightened to the point he believed he would hear a spruce needle as it fell through branches and dropped to the soft forest floor. He smelled his own sweat of adrenaline, found himself tasting the night air for clues to the prey, was conscious of the pressure of the weight of the rifle slung across his back, was aware of the pressure of his fingertips on the cool metal skin of his flashlight.

It dawned on him: He was juiced. This was hunting—far, far beyond his teenage memories of deer season. It was hunting at its highest level, stirring a primal instinctive lust he'd never known existed within him. It both excited and repelled him.

He was stalking a stalker. Was this what the stalker felt in pursuit of his victims? Was Clay himself becoming a monster in chasing a monster?

Yet another five minutes passed. Then . . .

*To the left of the house! A crouching figure, stealing forward.*

Clay grabbed his airhorn in one hand and his flashlight in the other. He pushed forward, keeping himself stooped until the rifle across his back cleared the low branches of the tree.

Clay rose into a sprint and burst forward, clicking on the flashlight. "Down here!" Clay shouted then pressed the button on the airhorn. He reached the open ground near the house.

On cue, James hit his own airhorn. Caleb hit his from the other side. The dogs howled, and noise filled the valley.

Clay's light bounced off the figure moving back into the trees above the house. The man was ducking and weaving, and Clay couldn't pin him with the light.

Another light bobbed through the trees. It was James coming down.

"To your right!" Clay shouted, trying to keep pace with the figure. "He's moving up and to your right!"

Caleb kept pressing his airhorn. The dogs kept howling. Lights appeared in the bunkhouse at the far side of the buildings.

James and his bobbing flashlight beam stopped, something Clay didn't note until after the roaring crash of rifle fire sent peals of thunder among the trees. There were two more rifle shots.

It crossed Clay's mind—*the rifles were only meant for backup.* But he himself didn't stop running, trying to keep the figure in his flashlight beam.

*Uphill.* The figure stayed on the uphill course, away from the road and buildings, losing himself in the surreal shadows of spruce and pine boughs that reflected as sheer white in the flashlight beam.

Another two rifle shots. *McNeill wants to kill him.*

Clay reached the trees again and crashed through some branches. He had no choice but to take the flashlight off the disappearing figure and concentrate on moving through the trees.

"McNeill!" Clay shouted, stopping suddenly. "Hold your fire!"

The last thing Clay wanted was to get shot himself, especially now that it appeared the initial attack had failed.

"Hold your fire!" he shouted. "Got that?"

McNeill turned his flashlight on Clay. Clay was surprised that James was so close. He hadn't realized he'd already covered so much ground in his stumbling pursuit.

"I got it," McNeill said.

Clay heaved for breath. McNeill pushed through some branches and reached Clay.

"Well, son," James McNeill said, "looks like we got some tracking ahead of us."

"You wanted to shoot him." It came out as an accusation.

"You'd shoot him, too," McNeill said. "If it was your daughter, you'd shoot him and hope for a gut shot that kills him slow. Fact is, I sent both my sons to Great Falls for a cattle auction tomorrow because if they were here, they'd do the same. If I can get him, I'll be the one to carry the burden, not one of them."

"I can't let you do that," Clay said. "I'm here as a law enforcement officer, and I can't let you take justice into your own—"

"You don't think I couldn't have set this trap by myself or with a few friends? That's exactly why I wanted you here—as a law-enforcement officer, someone trustworthy who could testify in court that I shot him in self-defense."

McNeill stepped away from Clay and toward the sound of Caleb Latcher's bloodhounds.

"I'm going to the bunkhouse. I need to talk to the hired men," McNeill said without looking back. "In the meantime, you make up your mind. You stay back here, or you come along and track him with us. But if you join us, son, you remember, we are after an animal. And first chance I get to make it happen, he'll die that way too."

# 2:05 A.M.

Neither councilman had been able to escape their families for what Fowler had told them at dinnertime would be an all-night poker game at the cabin. Nor had Frank Evans been able to leave the ranch on short notice. Michael McNeill was in Great Falls for a livestock auction along with his cousin Lawson.

That meant, aside from Sheriff Russ Fowler, who in this case had a valid reason to plead work, only two others had been able to find excuses to leave their respective families for an entire night. Actually, the two had not needed excuses. Banker Wayne Anderson's wife was out of state visiting her elderly parents. Judge Thomas King's wife tended to drink heavily—Fowler suspected it was because the judge often beat her—and wouldn't even be aware her husband had stayed away the entire night.

Both men were seated and waiting in the cabin when Fowler arrived. A half-empty bottle of Jack Daniels rested in Judge Thomas King's lap. Light from the single gas lantern hanging from the rafters glinted off the amber contents of full glasses in both men's hands.

The cabin was hardly more than a shack with a tarpaper roof. It had one double-paned window from which, in daylight, one could see a small lake framed by trees growing down to the shore's edge. On the other side of the cabin was the campsite where days earlier the judge had aimed a rifle at Fowler's chest, something that Fowler intended to remember and pay back when the opportunity presented itself.

The cabin's interior matched the spartan exterior, with bunkbeds on three of the roughhewn walls, a sagging cupboard, an old table with a Formica top, and straight-back chairs with vinyl cushions. The closest object of luxury was a potbelly stove in the center. More than a few times each winter, some or all of the group would use the cabin as a base for an ice-fishing weekend, and the potbelly stove proved its worth then. At other times, the cabin was a base for hunting and fishing or poker games. Or, as in the stag weekend last fall—for something more. The cabin was a symbol of defiance for the men who gathered there, an escape from the women in their lives, and accordingly, the unspoken rule was that no effort would be made to clean or fix it up in any way.

"I got one," Fowler said in greeting as both men rose, question marks on their faces. "Twelve midnight. Saint Andrews Church. Exactly like the tip said. He was half drunk, and he was at the corner of the church trying to start a fire. All I had to do was walk up behind him and snap the cuffs in place."

"Only caught one. The slowest and stupidest, right?" King said.

"The only one we saw." Fowler tried to keep his voice level. King's overstated racism always irritated him.

"Who knows he's here?" Anderson asked. Despite the heavy smell of whiskey on his breath, he looked fresh and clean shaven. The judge, on the other hand, with his sagging jowls on his overlarge head, looked old and tired.

"Two Car was with me during the arrest," Fowler confirmed. "But we haven't done any paperwork. And Two Car's not going to ask questions about where I took him. You know how much he hates them."

"So bring the savage in," the judge said, downing a large shot of Jack Daniels.

"Only after you understand how we're going to do this," Fowler said. "So listen close to how it's going to go once he's in here. And after I've explained, we're going to settle back and have a couple of drinks. The longer we leave him out there in the dark, the more scared he's going to be."

## 2:23 A.M.

"Let me ask you something," James McNeill said. "You had the best look of all of us. Did he have a rifle or shotgun?"

Clay shook his head. "Definitely no weapon."

"Good. We don't have to worry about an ambush."

"What if he gets into a vehicle?" Clay asked. They'd been in pursuit for less than five minutes, after a twenty-minute delay while McNeill dealt with his hired hands at the bunkhouse and while Latcher got his bloodhounds on the scent.

Now Latcher and the leashed bloodhounds ranged twenty steps ahead, breaking through underbrush with the help of Latcher's spotlight. This was the first time McNeill had spoken since leaving the ranch house, and Clay, staying close behind, had been waiting for the chance to ask his own questions.

McNeill pointed uphill. "Vehicle? No roads that way. None. The fool is maybe thinking he can lose the dogs, but he's wrong. Those hounds can track a sparrow through fog from here to New York."

"Did you send someone to look after Kelsie? Clay asked. In case he circles back?"

"Yup. And I hope you're finished wasting good air on useless talk. This ain't going to be an easy hike, and you'd be better off saving your breath."

The next half-hour proved the rancher's prediction to be accurate. They followed a trail that would have been difficult in daylight.

More than once, their quarry doubled back then jumped far to one side or another. At best, though, it only delayed the bloodhounds a few minutes.

The trail disappeared into a mountain stream. James and Clay guessed their prey had traveled uphill instead of downhill. Even though he almost never did it, Caleb finally decided to let the blood-hounds off the leash. He wouldn't have done it if they were tracking an animal, but he figured that the man they were tracking wouldn't hurt the hounds.

He sent one up each side of the water. Five minutes later, the dog on the far side of the stream brayed to show he'd picked up the trail again. Caleb leashed the hounds again, and they strained to pull him up a path in their eagerness to stay on a hot scent.

Soon after, the trail became a straight line, as if their quarry had decided he could not outsmart the bloodhounds and had chosen to outrun them.

Again, Clay found his focus heightened. The occasional braying of the bloodhounds, their obvious straining at the leashes, his own heavy panting, the flashlight beams darting into thick bushes and crevices behind large boulders, and the expectation of reaching their quarry at any moment—all of it brought him solidly into the present, where second by second all that mattered was the input of his five senses.

They half-jogged behind the bloodhounds, stopping every few minutes to catch their breath. After forty minutes of fast-paced pur-suit, McNeill called out to Caleb. "Up ahead's the mad trapper's cabin. You think he knows that?"

Caleb called out a command to his hounds, and they stopped. "Probably, Jim," Caleb said, his breathing ragged. "The way he's run-ning, he shows a good grasp of the area."

"Let's go slow then."

"Like if he's waiting inside? Got a rifle packed in there?"

"Yup."

"Jimmy, I like the way you think. We'll go real slow."

They went slow. The trail, however, skirted the cabin by at least fifty yards, and they relaxed. James pointed out the cabin as they passed, and Clay glanced at its dark, squat shadow in the moonlight but gave it little more attention. The bloodhounds were moving fast, and he wasn't going to be left behind.

# 3:03 A.M.

Fowler placed Harold Hairy Moccasin on a low stool inside the cabin, and the three stood in a circle around him, saying nothing as they looked down on a man with a burlap bag over his head and his wrists handcuffed together behind his back.

"What is this?" Harold Hairy Moccasin asked after a minute of silence. "You can't do this. I get one call, don't I?"

The gas lantern hissed steadily. The sheriff, the judge, and the banker didn't reply, didn't shift. Nothing gave away their presence to Harold Hairy Moccasin.

"I know you're there," he cried. "You gotta answer me. I have my rights, man. You hear me. I have my rights."

The judge, behind Harold, waited for a signal from the sheriff. Fowler noticed the judge was gently wetting his lips with his tongue. The new life in the judge's face and his obvious anticipation revolted Fowler, but he needed both of them here to see and pass on to the others that Fowler was doing what his job required, keeping the valley a feudal kingdom for their benefit.

"I have my rights!" Harold screamed. His feet tapped and his legs shook. "Where are you? Speak!"

Fowler had put the sack over Harold's head as soon as they cleared the streetlights of Kalispell. As they drove, he made it clear to Harold they were going into mountains, miles away from the nearest paved road. Without supplying the details, he'd made it equally clear that Harold should expect the worst. Fowler knew that the man would begin to imagine what would terrify him most and that the terror could feed on itself.

The judge silently mouthed a question. *Now?*

Fowler shook his head.

"Hey, man! I was walking to my truck to put gas in it! I needed to take a leak, so I stopped at the church, man, at the side where no one could see me. That's all. I wasn't going to light a fire. It just looked that way!"

Harold's voice grew pleading. "Someone, man. You gotta talk to me."

Fowler nodded.

The judge tapped Harold on his shoulder with an aluminum tent pole.

Harold spun so quickly that he nearly fell off the stool. "Who was that, man? What you doing?"

The banker poked Harold in the stomach with another tent pole. He spun again toward the new attack. "Get away, man. Get away!" Harold's voice rose in panic. He lifted his hands uselessly behind his back. "Get away!"

The banker and the judge alternated, prodding from one side, then the other. Harold twisted and turned in vain at each new touch, then finally gave up and let himself sag motionless.

To get a response, the judge whacked Harold across his head. Aluminum connected with bone.

"Oh, man! Oh, man!" Harold's wailing was muffled by the burlap sack.

Fowler shook his head angrily at the judge and motioned for both to stop.

"What's your name?" Fowler asked.

"Harold." He twisted his head in the direction of Fowler's voice. "Harold Hairy Moccasin."

"Why were you at the church?"

"I told you, man. My truck. It ran out of gas. That's why I had some with me. I needed to take a leak, that's all."

Fowler nodded at the banker, not the judge; the judge was too enthusiastic. Fowler intended to let Harold go and didn't want to hurt him bad, just scare him good.

The banker smacked Harold across the arm. Harold yelped at the unexpected blow.

"We don't like it when you lie, Harold," Fowler said. "Don't lie. Why were you at the church?"

"Come on," Harold said. "Just let me see. That's all I ask."

"You didn't answer the question, Harold," Fowler said, shaking his head at his two partners. "Get ready. We're going to hit you again."

Harold cringed and huddled into himself, waiting for a blow that did not come. After a minute of cringing, he began to whimper.

"Why were you at the church, Harold?"

"To burn it," he sobbed. "Now can I see?"

"Alone? Or with help? Answer me, Harold. Who are the Native Sons?"

"Come on, man. Where's my lawyer?"

Fowler pointed at both his partners. They began to rain light blows down upon the helpless man. Fowler cut his hand across the air, and they stopped.

Harold was sobbing. "Man, this ain't right. It ain't right."

"Harold," Fowler said, "what you don't understand is we're not interested in solving this for the public's benefit. We just want to stop the Native Sons. This is our valley. You mess with our valley, we mess with you."

The sobbing and whimpering continued.

Fowler softened his voice. "Maybe you understand now. Want to make a deal? We let you go, and you tell your friends to back off."

"Yeah," Harold said, his voice suddenly alive with hope. "We will! We will!"

"No chance," Fowler snarled. "We want names."

With names, Fowler could bring the others up one by one and terrify them, too, into leaving the valley. It would effectively end the trouble without giving the media a chance to descend and probe the valley's secrets.

"Names, Harold," Fowler repeated.

Fowler signaled again and more blows descended on Harold. The banker and the judge worked Harold over for a few more minutes. Fowler noticed the judge had begun to sweat.

"Ready, Harold?" Fowler said when they stopped. "We want your friends' names."

Fowler was surprised. He'd figured the little guy to be a coward. He'd figured him to break much sooner. It was impressive, his loyalty to his friends.

Time for more heat, Fowler decided. He wanted to get this over quickly so he could drop Harold off at some other point on the mountain and make him find his own way back so he wouldn't know where this cabin was. Fowler didn't enjoy this task; he just knew it needed to be done.

Harold had hunched over so much that he was almost off his stool. Fowler jerked the stool out from under him, and Harold crashed to the floor. The burlap around him showed circles of spreading bloodstains.

"Friends' names, Harold. Who are the Native Sons?" Fowler was forced to raise his voice to be heard over Harold's sobbing.

"Tell us, you miserable dog!" the judge snarled. Before Fowler could stop him, the judge brought his tent pole down across Harold's head in a sidearm swing with the force of a man striking a golf ball.

The crack was audible even above Harold's muffled sobs. Harold's body stiffened, then jerked spasmodically for ten seconds, then became still.

The judge looked at the banker and the sheriff and wordlessly shrugged an apology. He stepped over Harold and over to the bottle of Jack Daniels where he rewarded himself by pouring another.

## 3:12 A.M.

Ridiculously easy, the Watcher thought, squatting just inside the cabin entrance as the bloodhounds and flashlights passed by. All it had taken was a tight circle to come back down. Soon enough they'd discover the turn in his trail and realize he'd returned to the cabin.

He had needed to mark the FBI pig. He'd thought of leading them directly to the cabin and shooting as they appeared, but that was too uncertain. He didn't want to hit either of the other men. No, he had to be certain where the FBI pig was in their group.

Now he knew. Clay Garner was at the rear. Circling back like this had been a brilliant move. And he could shoot from closer by attacking from behind instead of waiting in the cabin.

The Watcher grabbed Nick Buffalo's rifle from where it was propped by the log wall beside the entrance. He stepped into the night air, away from the copper smell of Nick Buffalo's pooled blood.

He cocked the rifle and ran toward the disappearing flashlights uphill. He wasn't concerned about being heard. The dogs and crashing of the other men's footsteps would conceal any noise he made on his approach. And, as if he'd been fated to succeed, the breeze was blowing down the mountain, taking his scent away from the dogs, not toward them. Shooting the FBI pig would be child's play, especially since he followed a couple of steps behind McNeill and Latcher.

It took the Watcher only a minute to close in on the three. The light from their flashlights enabled him to clearly distinguish each man. Not that it would have been difficult in less light. Of the three, Clay Garner seemed a full head taller.

The Watcher ran to within twenty-five steps of his oblivious prey. He wanted to be closer to be more certain but needed to give himself distance to escape.

Close enough. He crouched on one knee and steadied the rifle against his shoulder. A head shot would be perfect but too risky. He couldn't afford to miss on the first shot.

He picked instead the outline of the man's broad back as a target.

This was a lot more fun than shooting deer, he thought. He squeezed the trigger.

The rifle's flat explosion rocked the night air. His target tumbled forward. The other two froze, only briefly, then dove to the side.

The Watcher fired three more shots, pointing upward at the sky. He only needed to establish confusion, enough to give him the chance to get back to the cabin. Then he turned and sprinted downhill, leaving behind howling dogs and curses. Ten seconds later, he reached the cabin and ducked inside. He stepped to the cabin wall where Nick Buffalo's body lay slumped in the dirt, then dragged the body back to the entrance.

And waited.

"He dead?" Caleb shouted. "He dead?"

No, Clay tried to reply, but couldn't. He was in shock. He'd had one foot in the air, ready to step downward, then without warning, like a bird flying into a picture window, he'd been dropped. It wasn't until his face was pressing into hard ground that he dimly pieced the explosion sound to a rifle shot and the rifle shot with the pain in his upper ribs and only then vaguely understood he'd been hit by a bullet.

He felt someone roll him over.

Light pounded his eyes. He wanted to shut them against the glare but worried it might be too easy to keep them closed, so he blinked frantically and soundlessly.

"Off his face," McNeill ordered. "Let's see where he took it."

The beam moved down his body and Clay realized that McNeill was using a knife to cut open his bulky sweater and shirt.

"Bad," Caleb said seconds later. "Real bad."

"Maybe not." McNeill's voice was calm. He was removing his

jacket, then his shirt. Clay heard ripping sounds. "We've got to wad this over the entrance and exit."

McNeill gently lifted him partway. "Get your hand under him and press this against his back. Hold it there."

Caleb did as he was told. Then McNeill lowered Clay's upper body.

"Wad this piece on the exit wound and hold it there, too." McNeill ordered. "It's not sucking. He's not bubbling. Let's hope it missed his lungs."

"Jimmy, what if he returns?" Caleb asked. "We're sitting ducks."

"Shut up. Keep your hands in place. We're not going to lose this man. Got that? Shut up and don't move."

Clay closed his eyes. He felt a jacket covering him up. Caleb's hands kept pressing against his back and chest.

"Clay? Clay?"

He realized McNeill was talking to him. Clay moaned.

"Look. Hang in there," McNeill said. "The worst is stopped. We're going to—"

Rifle shots thundered again.

McNeill swore. "Caleb, he's in the cabin."

"He'll keep shooting till he gets lucky!"

"Don't move. Just don't move." McNeill was up and gone.

Clay tried not to breathe. He felt stickiness on his back and on his belly. A detached part of his mind told him it was his blood draining away.

The nearby bloodhounds whined.

Clay felt the shock disappear and pain began to grip him. He decided to grimly count each breath. Anything to get him through. He moaned again. Then he began to drift through a hazy river of time marked by the rising and falling of his chest.

*I'm dead,* he thought. *Where's Sherry? Where's Samantha? I want them waiting for me in heaven.*

Clay felt wet warmth on his face. He realized he was crying.

He heard another barrage of rifle shots followed by loud shouting.

He began to lose count of the rise and fall of his chest. He couldn't keep his eyes open.

Brightness flared beyond his closed eyelids. *Heaven?* He fought to open his eyes again. Where were his wife and baby?

The brightness registered as flames. The cabin. The mad trapper's cabin. Burning bright.

Then there was a shadow above him. McNeill.

"Keep him going, Caleb. Press hard. Make sure the dressing doesn't shift. I'm going for a horse to take him back down."

Clay smiled at McNeill's foolishness. Clay didn't need a horse to get to heaven. Only a prayer.

*Dear Lord*, he began, *take me home to my wife and baby* . . .

The flames, the shadows, the pressure of Caleb's hands, and the pain of his own breathing faded away before he finished his plea.

# Day 18

"I'm out of here tomorrow, Miss Nightingale," Clay said a few minutes after Kelsie arrived in his hospital room. She was sitting near his bed, her hands folded neatly in her lap. She wore blue jeans and a light sweater; Clay wore hospital greens. "Thanks for your kind attention."

Clay smiled at the delicate furrows that appeared across Kelsie's brow. She was too polite to ask, so he explained. "Florence Nightingale. Famous nurse. A little before your time."

"Lady of the Lamps," she replied. "I do read, you know."

"I'm sorry. The look on your face said otherwise."

"The look on my face said I don't understand why you are leaving. Didn't the doctors say you needed at least another week?"

"I'm being transferred to a hospital in Virginia. There's a man out there who wants to bring me up to speed on my new assignment. He doesn't want me wasting time just lying around."

"Oh." The news seemed to put her into a quiet state.

During his convalescence, Clay had frequently wondered why Kelsie visited him in the hospital twice a day. He had a theory, and this seemed as good a time as any to try to help her.

"Kelsie," he said, "I want you to know that you don't owe me a thing. You can't blame yourself for what happened to me."

She studied him without any reaction.

Suddenly flustered by the girl's poise, Clay stammered a bit as he continued. "What—what I'm saying is that even though you don't owe me anything, if you think you do, you've more than repaid me with your time and concern. When I leave tomorrow, you can pretend all of this summer never happened."

"What about your investigation?" she asked.

The change of subject was so abrupt, Clay floundered again briefly. "Well, uh, they know Nick was the one. You're safe."

"Train investigation," she corrected him.

Clay frowned. "My SAC—"

"SAC?"

"Special agent in charge. He's intructed me to wrap it up. The engineer's reports are coming back inconclusive, and with no specific evidence to the contrary, all agencies are concluding the derailment was an accident." He grimaced. "Politics. Everyone already knew that would be the conclusion. Except for me. I came in thinking I'd bust something open and make a name for myself. Instead, all they wanted was an FBI seal of approval to cover everyone's respective rear ends." He shook his head. "I was that seal, all right. Just feed me some fish and pat my flippers."

Kelsie smiled at his feeble joke. "They gave you a new assigment, didn't they?"

"B.S."

"You just said—"

"B.S. doesn't mean that. It means Behavioral Science. Tracking down more animals like Nick Buffalo."

Kelsie closed her eyes briefly then let out a deep breath. "I think that will help a lot more people than being an FBI seal."

"Me, too," Clay said.

A nurse knocked on the door, and Kelsie stood. "My cue to leave."

"Hey," Clay said. "Thanks. You know. For—"

"For visiting?"

He nodded.

Kelsie moved directly beside him and took one of his hands in hers. "I want you to know," she said, "I never once came up here because I thought I owed it to you."

Her fingers were gentle on his. "Someday I hope to meet someone as kind and gentle as you. And I'll marry him."

Before he could reply, she leaned down quickly and kissed his cheek. Then she straightened and walked out of the room, leaving him to smile at a schoolgirl's crush.

# 2:07 P.M.

*A knock at the door brought all heads up from school desks. A week into school, and already the first-grade class understood the value of diversion.*

*When Mrs. Schmidke opened the door, the children saw a woman in blue jeans and an old sweatshirt. She was crying silently, her face contorted in pain.*

*Mrs. Schmidke put her arms around the woman and stepped outside into the hallway. None of the kids in the class spoke.*

*Why would a grown-up be crying?*

*Some of the kids looked at a boy sitting at one of the center desks. They knew it was his mother crying.*

*The boy didn't return any of their looks but stared straight ahead. He knew the best way to deal with anything that made him anxious was to pretend he was made of stone.*

*Mrs. Schmidke stepped back inside the classroom and called the boy's name.*

*Without expression, he stood and walked out to meet his mother. She squatted in front of him, gazed into his eyes, tried to speak, then sobbed and threw her arms around him. It wasn't until they were in the car that she finally managed to tell him anything.*

*"Your daddy's in the hospital," she said. She started the engine, sat back, and bit back tears. "He was in an accident. And he's hurt."*

*"Is he going to die?" Ever since making his very bad wish, the boy had worried that his father might die.*

*"No!"*

*His mother took a deep breath. "No," she said. "He's not going to die. All right? He's not going to die. Don't you worry. Everything will be all right."*

*She wiped her face. "I'm sorry you have to see Mommy cry. But don't you worry. Everything will be all right."*

*"Mommy?"*

*"Yes?" She brought the gear shift down, and they slowly drove out of the school parking lot.*

*"Are we going to see Daddy now?"*

She sobbed again. "No, son. It wouldn't be a good idea for you to see him just yet."

They passed the gasoline service station with the big signs he tried to read out loud every day she took him to school.

"You have to be brave for your mommy," she said. "She needs you to be a little man for her."

"Yes, Mommy."

"I have to spend a lot of time at the hospital."

"Yes, Mommy."

"And I won't be able to have you at home. Mommy doesn't want to leave you, but right now she doesn't have a choice."

"Yes, Mommy." He thought over what she had told him. "If I can't see Daddy right now, where are you taking me?"

"To see a friend." Her voice was high and cheerful, like the way she told him that the doctor was doing what was best and that needles only hurt for a bit.

A friend? All of his friends were in the kindergarten class. He didn't understand.

"Remember that nice lady who took care of you this summer when your daddy and I went on our short little trip? She is so happy that she is seeing you again."

She leaned over and patted his knee. "Don't worry, it will only be for a short time. And remember, she's very nice. She loves you like I do."

The boy grew rigid and stared silently at the dashboard until they stopped in front of that house and the old lady with rose-scented perfume reached in and pulled him out.

The Watcher sat on a bench outside the hospital. He kept his head down and his baseball cap in place. The bench was shaded by trees, but he didn't want to risk the slightest chance that Kelsie might see him from the hospital window.

He hated her. He loved her, and he hated her.

She was his. She shouldn't be visiting the FBI pig in his room. Not anywhere. But since getting her driver's license a few days earlier, she had made the trip into Kalispell every afternoon to sit beside his bed.

The Watcher wanted to go up there at night and kill him. He knew he could. He'd walked by on three different afternoons, pretending to visit someone down the hall, and had seen him hooked up to tubes, helpless. Aside from spending time with some old

Indian who came by every day, he was just waiting to take Kelsie's time and attention.

Not love, he told himself. He wasn't taking Kelsie's love. She was just visiting him because she felt guilty.

Still, the Watcher wished he could go in the hospital room and kill the pig slowly. What misfortune that Nick's rifle had been loaded with a hard-point bullet that passed straight through the man, not even nicking a lung. The Watcher badly wanted to finish what the bullet had begun, but if he did, then they would know that they had blamed the wrong person by thinking it was Nick Buffalo who had been shooting from the cabin and who had died in the fire.

After dental records had confirmed the blackened body was Nick Buffalo's, and after the twisted and burned rifle found beside the body had been identified as Nick Buffalo's, the sheriff had announced finding a confession and suicide note in Nick's mobile home, with confirmed analysis that the handwriting did indeed belong to Nick. The newspapers, radio, and television had been full of the story, speculating endlessly about the significance of an eagle-feather headdress left in plain sight on Nick Buffalo's bed. Everyone believed Nick had killed Doris Samson, shot Clay Garner, then committed suicide during a shootout with James McNeill. Only the Watcher knew different; only the Watcher knew what the feather headdress meant. He would have liked to keep it, for leaving a feather as a calling card somehow gave him comfort, but the Watcher also knew if he began with the feathers ever again with anyone but Kelsie, it might raise questions about how Nick Buffalo had died. He had, however, plucked a handful of feathers from the headdress, and he carried one with him now.

The Watcher's plan had worked to perfection. Not a single person in existence knew the Watcher still lived to watch and wait. He could hunt women to give him the power of life and death that he craved, and if he did it carefully, no one would ever know it was him.

Which was why he stared at the hospital with anger and wrestled with himself over a difficult decision. He had the note in his pocket—he had written it earlier that day. Should he deliver it or not?

First he had to decide if Kelsie would betray him again. If she did tell someone about the note, they would know the guilty man had not died in the fire; all of the Watcher's fine work to put the blame on Nick would be thrown away.

Finally, he decided Kelsie would not tell anyone about the note. It would scare her too badly, as if he had risen from the ashes to return to her.

Decision made, the Watcher stood and began to walk toward the hospital parking lot where she had left the truck. In the few minutes it took to reach the truck, he knew he had fooled himself. It wasn't only because he was angry that she was giving attention to the FBI pig. By the anticipation causing his belly to tingle on his approach to the truck, the Watcher knew he missed having power over Kelsie. Telling her to stay away from the hospital was simply an excuse to prove he still had power. If it hadn't been the FBI pig, he would have found another reason to let her, and only her, know he was still watching and waiting.

He reached the truck and opened the driver's door. She hadn't locked it. That was another sign his power had slipped. Soon she would know her Watcher still loved her. She would begin locking doors and looking over her shoulder, and he would know his power over her was complete.

The Watcher got into the pickup and made a charade of searching his shirt pockets for keys, as if the truck was his and he was getting ready to drive away. Then he slapped his head, as if he suddenly remembered where the keys were. He stepped out of the truck and slammed the door shut, the picture of someone angry at his own stupidity.

But the Watcher was far from angry. Tucked into her ashtray—sticking out so she could not miss it—was an eagle feather. And a folded note.

It was a good note. He looked forward to watching her at her window tonight. And although he would be on guard for another trap, he was certain it was such a good note that there would be no trap set for him this time. Or any other time after that. ▨

# PART TWO

# Kalispell
# June, 1996

# Day 1

In the sunlight on the second floor of the house, the Watcher surveyed the result of years of effort and called it good. He had worked the entire night through to make his self-imposed deadline, but he was not fatigued. He'd trained himself to need little sleep.

There was no one to hear him as his self-congratulatory words echoed off bare walls. That didn't bother the Watcher, of course. He enjoyed solitude. He'd spent weekends and occasional vacation time building his project, and every hour of work had been in solitude. Over the years, not a single person had been invited inside the house to witness the steady progression of construction. No one could have any knowledge of the project; he could not take that risk.

Because he'd been unable to hire skilled workmen, the Watcher had been forced to learn from handyman books and from his mistakes. He'd taught himself to measure correctly. He'd learned how to brace two-by-fours. He'd even mastered electrical wiring. He had drywalled, painted, and carpeted. Everything, including the installation of video cameras, he had done himself.

All told, the work itself had been extremely satisfying—almost therapeutic. Dozens of times over the previous years, he had felt the urge to kill come upon him. Practicality, not revulsion, had dictated he fight the urge, but there had been some exceptions. If too many were killed, however, it increased the chances that he would be discovered. Also, if he took time away from the project to seek his prey, the project's completion would be delayed. He would have to wait that much longer before he could make Kelsie completely his.

Time and again, this project had helped to slake his urge. By taking hammer in hand, pinching nails between his lips and becoming a carpenter, he occupied his mind and hands. He was not only building a structure of walls within walls, he was building a dream.

And the dream was finally ready.

## 10:12 A.M.

Clay sat in the middle row of church, frustrated.

First of all, there was the frustration he endured weekly at this church, his attendance a ritual because Kelsie had insisted upon it from the first day of their marriage. While Clay knew Kelsie was worth it, Clay felt too many of the people around—fidgeting and coughing and discreetly checking out hat and dress styles—were content to make sure God remained small enough to fit into this church building.

The lack of joy in this church also frustrated Clay. The man behind the pulpit was, by occupation, an avowed Christian. And Christians proclaimed a God of love had given them a lease on eternal life. Now, if a person really believed that, wasn't it the greatest news in the world? That dying didn't matter because you were just passing through a curtain to perfection on the other side? If a person really believed, wouldn't that person find some joy in the knowledge of faith, especially one who was self-appointed to preach that news? So why did this dried-out prune drone judgment from the pulpit the way he did every week?

Every week, Clay came to the same conclusion. Any nonbelieving person sitting in the pews using any degree of logic would have a reasonable right to doubt a message conveyed in such contrast to it contents. As near as Clay could tell, the best reason to join this congregation was because it was one of Kalispell's oldest and most respected social clubs.

On the other hand, if his old Indian friend George Samson ever spoke from the pulpit—a laughable idea because tolerance was another practice merely preached in this church—there'd be joy in

George's voice as he passed along his message. He wouldn't be a dried-out prune. And George was pushing, what, seventy by now?

Clay wished his frustration ended there, with amusing daydreams of George Samson shaking this congregation with some hard-edged truths and questions about the great mystery of God.

Instead, Clay's mind kept returning to the larger source of his morning's frustration, sitting to his left, still and attentive to the sermon, hands resting in her lap. She was perfumed, coiffed perfectly, filling perfectly a perfectly pressed tan dress. With one silk stocking knee crossed over a silk stocking thigh, there was just enough leg showing to distract him. She was utterly beautiful—utterly distant.

How he loved Kelsie! Being with someone you loved, in itself, was good, very good. But to be with someone and be able to share memories added to the good. And to be with someone with the security of looking forward to more memories made it even better. He had found all of this in Kelsie.

How he loved her. How he loved their memories. He grinned everytime he thought of the shock of mutual recognition on their first meeting upon his return to the valley after retirement from the FBI—she was the lawyer who had handled his real-estate deal, and she had looked up from her desk in disbelief at the sound of his familiar drawl after nearly seventeen years of separate lives. Then began six months of courtship, with her the delightful and subtle aggressor. The wedding had taken place here in this church. Then the honeymoon followed, where each morning he'd awaken expecting to find it a dream that a woman this smart and beautiful would love him in return.

A surge of affection hit him as he thought back over their six-year marriage. Sure, the last few months had been tough, but he hadn't helped, retreating into the silence of stubborn pride in answer to her growing silences. He reminded himself that she had it tough, running her career, doing her best with Taylor. No wonder she sometimes retreated into herself.

Today, after church, he'd pack a picnic basket. He'd arrange for someone to take care of Taylor for the afternoon and offer to take Kelsie on a romantic retreat. He'd take the first step back to her and hope that love would do the rest.

Clay reached over and took her hand. It was the first physical contact they'd had in a week.

She flinched. It pained him.

He squeezed her hand. It remained limp and unresponsive.

He maintained his grip, waited a full five count, hoping she'd understand how much it hurt to have such a small action rejected when he had memories of so much more. There was no return squeeze of affection. Slowly, he dropped her hand back in her lap.

Taylor tugged on the arm of Clay's suit jacket from the other side. Clay swallowed his sadness and anger and turned his attention to their five-year-old son. Taylor grinned and pointed down beneath his swinging feet at a small black beetle crossing the shiny tiles of the floor. Clay grinned and grabbed Taylor's hand. Anything to keep the little rascal from jumping down and hollering and laughing as he chased the beetle beneath the pews.

Taylor, at least, squeezed back.

Clay resolved not to give up. As they drove out of the church parking lot, he suggested the picnic. Kelsie didn't answer.

The only sound to break their ride came from the backseat. Taylor was humming on his beloved harmonica. For all the disadvantages that had been placed upon him by the presence of one extra chromosome, he had one natural gift: music. From birth, it had captivated him. As soon as he'd been able to crawl, he had moved to the stereo speakers and hummed with whatever music was playing. Taylor would never understand written musical notes, but he was a natural mimic. The harmonica had been an inspiration from Clay, who understood Taylor's stubby fingers and comprehension level would limit his dexterity with any other instrument. With the harmonica, however, Taylor could pour out his breath and emotions with amazing rhythm.

Kelsie waited until they were at the ranch to speak. "I think a picnic is a great idea," she finally replied as they pulled into the ranch yard. She looked away from Clay and out her window at the ranch buildings and corrals to her right. "Why don't you take Taylor and make an afternoon of it?"

Clay spun the wheel and parked beside her BMW.

"You don't understand," he said. His tone was light, but he was determined to make the day work. "I meant you and me. We'll drop Taylor off with Lawson. I've been thinking we could use some time to get reacquainted." He tried his best grin. "I know a great lake where we could skinny-dip."

"No," she said softly.

Louie Two, their golden Labrador retriever, was running circles around the parked Jeep, barking a welcome. Taylor carefully put his harmonica in his back pocket before pointing at Louie Two with laughter.

"No? We're married. I know the fact that we can legally skinny-dip takes a lot of the fun out of it, but . . ."

For the first time in weeks, she reached out to Clay. She put her hand on his shoulder and turned toward him. Neither had released their seat belts. As much as Clay wanted to slip loose and embrace her awkwardly across the armrests, he was afraid to move. What if he frightened her away?

"Clay, you're breaking my heart," she said, her hand motionless, her face still.

"Is it the thought of my untanned body whooping and hollering in cold mountain water?" Even as he tried to make light of her rejection, he knew something was seriously wrong.

"Please don't make it more difficult for me," she said. "I feel like I'm going to fall into a thousand pieces."

"Kelsie?" he asked.

Just then Taylor leaned forward and stuck his head between the seats. Clay was proud Taylor had learned to undo his seat belt and that he had learned to wait until the vehicle was stopped to do it. Usually Clay applauded or hugged him for his feat.

Clay lifted a hand to tousle Taylor's hair, but Kelsie interrupted.

"Not now," she said to her son. "Play with Louie Two."

Disappointment crossed Taylor's face. Kelsie took her hand off Clay's shoulder and turned back around the other way to unlock Taylor's rear door. Louie Two was outside, wagging his tail and panting. Taylor began to hum with happiness and pushed himself into the ranch yard.

Clay managed not to say what was on his mind. Couldn't Kelsie behave like a mother instead of a caretaker? This moment, of all moments, though, definitely did not feel like the moment to begin yet another fight that could turn into a cold war lasting for days.

Taylor heaved the rear door shut then clapped approval for himself and his accomplishment.

"Take Taylor on a picnic this afternoon," she said. "It'll be easier for both of us."

"I don't understand," Clay said, although the sick feeling in the pit of his stomach told him maybe he did.

"It will give me time to pack. I'm leaving you."

"Leaving?" Clay took some deep breaths. He'd known things were bad, but this was a baseball bat coming at his head with no warning. "Leaving? Just like that? One day here. The next day gone. No chance for discussion? Isn't this something two people in a marriage decide upon. Together?"

"Stay angry. That will help."

"Help me? Or you?" he asked. A mixture of rage, frustration, and searing pain filled him. He wanted to lash out. With words. With his fists. Instead, he gripped the steering wheel with both hands and stared unblinking through the windshield.

"I've got an apartment in Kalispell," she said.

"You've been planning this. Did you have a checklist? One through ten. Number nine was get the apartment. Number ten was finally let the husband know."

"I'm not responding to that. There's no sense throwing mud at each other. I'll get you my phone number as soon as it's installed. Until then, you have my cell-phone number." She paused, emphasizing her next words. "For any emergency."

Clay took some deep breaths to steady himself. "And what about Taylor?"

"I'm assuming you'll keep him. We both know why."

No words were needed, Clay thought. It was true. They both knew why. "He'll miss you," Clay said.

"I doubt it," she said.

"*I'll* miss you."

"Don't. I won't be back."

Taylor was banging on the door on Clay's side of the Jeep.

"Will you tell me why?" he asked. He wasn't going to beg, but he deserved more than what she was giving him. "I know it hasn't been good for a while, but—"

"It's nothing you did or could change. This is not about you."

"Another man?" There was the bruise on her right arm, one that she'd tried to hide. He'd wondered if it came from another man, someone who had gripped her in the heat of excitement.

"No." He noticed she hesitated slightly.

"Of course not," he said. The pause was like a sword piercing his heart. He couldn't hold back his bitterness. "Of course not. You're the perfect mother. The perfect wife. The perfect lawyer. The perfect churchgoer. Adultery wouldn't fit your image."

"I'm going," she said, "before this gets ugly. Please don't try to stop me."

"Go," he said, wanting to stop her.

As she got out of the Jeep on the passenger side, Clay opened his door and let Taylor climb onto his lap.

Clay watched Kelsie's near-perfect outline of shoulders, back, and hips as she marched to the porch. He ached to hold her again, to have her bury her head in his neck and drape her arms over his shoulders.

"Hey, cowboy," he said to his son.

"Cowboy, me," Taylor said, jabbing a proud thumb at his own chest.

"Cowboy, you." Despite his churning guts, Clay smiled at his son. "What do you say, cowboy? Picnic this afternoon? You and me and Louie Two?"

"Picnic, me," Taylor said, nodding fierce agreement.

The smile that was on Taylor's face most of his waking moments never appeared, however. Instead, there was a look of perplexed wonderment. With both stubby hands, he reached up and touched the shine of tears on his father's face.

# Day 2

As if Kelsie needed another reminder of her situation, when she dug into her shoulder bag for her car keys on Monday before leaving her office for lunch, she found the warning note that had been placed in her glove compartment with the snake the previous Thursday.

*Don't cry,* she told herself, *survive. Tears won't help. The important thing is to survive.*

She moved across her office. She took down the musical dancer jewelry box from a bookshelf, her hands trembling as she remembered the flashing triangular head and the unexpected suddenness of the snake's attack. She hid the note along with all the others in the false bottom of the box. The irony had long since been lost on her, that where once she had stored all the precious mementos of her childhood dreams, now she kept the notes that had destroyed those dreams.

Instead of going to a nearby restaurant for a salad that she knew she'd only pick through, Kelsie left McNeill, McNeill & Madigan and drove aimlessly for most of the lunch hour, trying not to think.

She wasn't remotely successful. The memory of Clay's stoic pain filled her with sadness. The growing legal quagmire on her desk remained to pull her into its depths. And always, underneath all her thoughts, fear festered.

Totally unrefreshed, she drove into the parking lot behind the two-story office building owned by McNeill, McNeill & Madigan. She turned off the ignition and leaned her forearms on her steering wheel then rested her forehead against her arms.

When she opened her eyes, she nearly gasped.

"Pretty," Lawson McNeill said. He'd arrived noiselessly and without casting a shadow upon her. He stood at the passenger side of the BMW, looking down into the roofless car. "Very pretty. Even in the harsh glare of midday sunlight."

"That's shallow and sexist and patronizing." She grinned and spoke with a light-hearted tone, hoping he hadn't noticed her startled reaction. "You've implied I'm aging to the point that daylight may be considered an enemy. And you've implied my physical appearance has importance in this situation. Judge me by my merits, Lawson."

"You are woman. Hear you roar?"

"Jerk."

"So talk to one of the partners if you've got a complaint about me." Lawson crinkled a grin. He was the second McNeill of McNeill, McNeill & Madigan. Since Earl Madigan's death from a heart attack two years earlier, they were the two full partners, overseeing three junior partners, two legal secretaries, and a good percentage of the legal revenue generated by the longtime residents of Kalispell as well as the tanned, famous, and rich Californians who were making the area their new, trendy mecca.

"I will talk to the partner. Next office meeting," Kelsie promised. She hoped banter would drag her from her dark mood. "Expect a memo."

"Sure. I'll sign myself up for sensitivity training." Lawson was still grinning, a handsome, blond, middle-aged man, sure of himself and his expertly knotted ties and thousand-dollar suits. Over the years, of course, Lawson hadn't lost his height nor a rangy grace in his manner of walking. He was slightly balding now, with a trace of a paunch, but in courting games he offset these minor afflictions with tortoise-shell glasses for the intellectual look and with a hefty monthly draw against the firm's ample profits. From his nearly awkward teenage years, Lawson had become extremely confident around women. Kelsie sometimes wondered if he made conquest after conquest to offset those shy teenage years. While the local women knew his habits, many didn't mind the gamble anyway, and there were always new California women to take interest in a chance at permanent domestic bliss with Lawson and his paychecks. Kelsie was often tempted to warn these hopeful candidates but had long ago decided it was as much *caveat emptor* as none of her business. If a woman couldn't see this one as Peter Pan in the first place, any warning would fall on deaf ears.

"Hey," Lawson said, "while I'm at it, I'll talk James into signing up for sensitivity training with me. We'll crash-course ourselves into becoming men of the nineties."

The thought of her sixty-seven-year-old father as a caring, nurturing "New-Age" man brought forth Kelsie's first real snort of laughter of the day. "Sure, Lawson. I'm visiting him tomorrow. I'll ask him for you."

She sobered at her own words. There were two reasons she needed to visit her dad. Neither was pleasant.

"Anything wrong?" Lawson asked.

Kelsie stepped out of her car before replying. "If you want to know, it's Emerald Canyon. Dad's name has come up."

Lawson held up his hands, palms outward, warding Kelsie off, although she was on the opposite side of the car from him. "I don't want to hear about Emerald Canyon. I have two rules about my legal work: no complications and profitable billing." He shrugged. "From what I can gather, Emerald Canyon breaks both rules. Right?"

Her turn to shrug. "This one's never been for the money—although money seems more possible now."

"My point exactly. That's why I don't want any details. Especially if you have a run-in with the old man. I'm on my way out to the ranch for an appointment with Clay. He's grouchy enough about agency-land regulations."

Kelsie hoped her outward smile hid an inward tightening. The ranch, she thought, where she did not live anymore. "Dad should hear about Emerald Canyon from me first. Not a stranger."

"You're a brave woman," Lawson said. He leaned against the top edge of the passenger window and stared across the car. "If it was politically correct, I'd pat your hand or your shoulder."

"Salute," she said. "That would be more appropriate. Remember my reputation as the ice queen."

Without warning, she felt tears fill her eyes. She was an ice queen in an old furnished condo that smelled of years of cats. Her last memory of the ranch was Taylor clinging to Clay at the porch, Clay with bewilderment and pain in his eyes. Ice queen indeed.

"Kelsie?" Lawson began to walk around the front of the car to reach her.

"Don't ask," she said. Lawson would eventually find out about her separation from Clay, but she didn't have the strength to tell him now. "Don't ask, all right? This is not a good time for me."

Kelsie marched to the office without looking backward.

Kelsie faced the computer on her desk with her office door closed, much as she had done for most of the morning. She told herself that self-pity would not help. She told herself that, in work, at least, she had control over events, and at this point any control would be a blessing. She told herself this might be the biggest case of her career, that she shouldn't let her emotional turmoil distract her.

After a half-hour with her eyes blank, she reached for the power switch on the computer. It felt like another person's body responding. She rubbed her face as she waited for the programs to load.

To her left, a clipboard was attached to a swivel arm. It would let her transcribe directly from the report on the clipboard to the computer. Normally she'd have one of the secretaries do the input typing, but the report, if true, was too important for office gossip. Typing also gave her an excuse to concentrate on anything but her lonely apartment and how she would manage to spend the first evening there.

She found the file she had been working on before the weekend, opened it, and scanned through the words on the screen to see if she wanted to make any changes to the draft following the preamble:

> . . . *this suit contends that the defendant's policy of approving zoning, building permits, and building inspections of the homes and businesses on shrink-swell soil and in violation of building code requirements, constitutes a "taking" of plaintiffs' property without just compensation in violation of the Fifth and Fourteenth Amendments of the United States Constitution.*

*This suit further contends that in April of 1974, the County Planning Department voted approval of development based on soil samples taken from the perimeter of the land in question, instead of requesting a complete survey of the land.*

*Moreover, this suit contends that members of the County Planning Department, County Administrator, Building Officials, and corporations involved with Emerald Canyon will be held liable for the negligence involved by voting said approval.*

Not only had this draft taken her triple the time she'd normally expect, she was capable of better and knew it. Given her emotional stress, Kelsie thought, she should be on a leave of absence. But the timing couldn't be worse for this particular lawsuit. Things were falling into place, and it was beginning to appear the suit had some merit. Besides, leaving work wouldn't help solve her problems. And she had problems to solve for others.

Emerald Canyon was a huge golf-course real-estate development. It had been a forerunner of a new development trend that in retrospect was obvious. Developers were no longer building golf courses for the sake of golf but for the astronomical prices buyers were willing to pay for a residential lot adjoining the golf course. Over the previous ten years, developers all across the country had used the tactic with overwhelming success.

Emerald Canyon, however, had begun twenty years earlier. Its success had been guaranteed by something few other developers could offer—a world-class resort as a neighbor, the Big Sky Casino, located on the edge of the Flathead reservation.

Like many other Native American tribes across the country, the Flathead tribe had turned to legalized gambling as a way to earn income. As spectacular as any Las Vegas resort—the project had been overseen by architectural and management consultants from the neon city—Big Sky Casino was in a perfect location, in a valley designed for winter and summer tourism.

The developers of the Emerald Canyon golf and retirement village had been shrewd enough to foresee Big Sky as a tourist mecca. On property adjoining the Flathead reservation boundaries, they had built two eighteen-hole golf courses to world-class specifications. Because of their foresight, they'd been able to obtain huge tracts of land at low prices. Not only had they been able to sell golf-course lots at a premium, but they'd also been able to sell hundreds of homes on the land that merely gave a view of Flathead Lake.

Many of these homes had been sold as retirement villas. Many of these owners were now relying on Kelsie and the report in front of her.

It was from an engineering firm in Great Falls, which she had received from the early-morning courier. Her lack of reaction to the report was further proof that her emotional stress was draining her professionally. At any other time, the gist of the report would have filled her with urgency and excitement. Any other time, she would have reacted immediately instead of letting the report sit on her desk all morning. Any other time . . .

She blinked herself back to the report, aware with chagrin that her lack of concentration was brutal. Kelsie began to transcribe directly from the engineer's report, inserting the significant part of the report into the middle section of her lawsuit.

> Based on recent core samples of soil taken throughout the entire development area, an outside engineering firm has confirmed that: "Substantial limitations to development stem from adverse soil conditions and pollutants . . . It is therefore imperative that design and construction criteria for development specifically deal with the site limitations dictated by the possibility of unstable foundations resulting from shrink-swell soil problems, and the final recommendation is that no development should be undertaken until pollutants are removed from the soil."

Kelsie scanned through the addition a few times, looking for typos. Content it was satisfactory, she glanced through the rest of the lawsuit until she came to the conclusion.

> In short, the shrink-swell soil problem came to light in 1993 as residents came to the County Board, one by one, with damage complaints. All complaints were ignored.
>
> By 1996, nearly 200 homes were found to have damage related to soils and shoddy construction. Over thirty residents have shown medical problems related to the major pollutant reported in the soil.

*The plaintiffs are each seeking $1 million in compensatory damages, as well as a $25 million pool for punitive damages, with liability for compensatory damages to be shared by members of the County Planning Department, County Administrator, Building Officials, and Corporations involved with Emerald Canyon.*

It was the last line that bothered Kelsie the most. *Corporations involved with Emerald Canyon.* Would there come a point, she wondered, where she might be forced into a position of conflict of interest? And if so, what choice would she make?

## 2:12 P.M.

Taylor McNeill-Garner sat cross-legged in a shaft of sunlight inside the large patio doors of the walkout basement. Beyond the doors were acres of pine trees, and through a gap in the pine trees was a glimpse of the lake, and beyond the lake a view of the abrupt blue walls of the Swan Mountains.

Taylor, however, gave the mountains no thought. He preferred the pretty way in which tiny pieces of dust seemed to dance in the shaft of sunlight. Once in a while, he tried to bite one of the tiny pieces. This would make him giggle.

From above, he heard the low hum of angry words. It broke his happy mood. Taylor McNeill-Garner lifted his head and frowned. He forgot about the pieces of light. He forgot about the teddy bear in his lap. He forgot about the music-maker in his back pocket. Anger distracted him, bothered him. And it bothered him most when anger came from his father or mother.

He couldn't understand the words coming down from the closed door at the top of the stairs. Taylor wasn't good with words, but he was good with feelings.

His feelings told him his daddy was angry. He spoke in a low, hard voice when he was angry.

Taylor smiled as a nice picture filled his head. He would go up the stairs and wrap his arms around his daddy's legs. That would make him feel better. Taylor unbent himself by pulling his ankles out from under his crossed legs. When he stood, he felt the teddy bear fall. Falling wasn't good. He knew that. It hurt. He picked up the teddy bear and kissed it on the forehead, just like sometimes his father kissed away hurts from his own falls.

Taylor made it to the bottom of the stairs. Far up, he could see the door. He would have to be careful. He didn't like to fall.

Then Taylor heard scratching on the patio door behind him. He teetered on the first step as he turned to the new distraction. It was Louie Two, the golden Lab, pawing to get in. Taylor grinned. Many times, Louie Two licked Taylor's face and made him laugh.

For a moment, he hesitated. His daddy was angry. Taylor wanted to hug him and give him warm feelings to take away the anger, but he also wanted to play with Louie Two.

Louie Two was closer.

Taylor reversed direction. Almost at the patio doors, he remembered. Louie Two was outside. Taylor slowed. He remembered these doors bumped his nose if he walked too fast. It had happened before. Other times, when he put his hand against them, they were cool to his touch. When he pushed against them, they didn't let him through. This was funny, because Taylor could see things on the outside, but not get to them.

Taylor stopped inches away from Louie Two and pressed his face against the glass. Louie Two pawed at Taylor's face, the dog's paws scratching the glass.

Taylor carefully sat down. He folded his ankles beneath his crossed legs. This was a problem. Louie Two was outside. He was inside. Who would open the door? He had tried them before, but he could never open them.

Movement outside caught his attention. One of the big people! Taylor grinned. Taylor remembered this one. Here was someone to open the door. Taylor pounded the heel of his palm against the glass.

The door opened, and a hand reached inside to help him to his feet.

Taylor took the hand and grinned again. The fresh outside air brought him smells and sounds. So many new things to smell. So many new things to hear.

Taylor stepped onto the patio. This would be fun. He walked with the man toward the depths of the pine trees.

# 3:37 P.M.

When he'd sold the ranch to Kelsie and Clay a few years earlier, James McNeill had moved from the original ranch house and built a smaller one for himself one mile down the road. The arrangement worked well. He was close enough to stave off loneliness, far away enough that each household felt private and separate.

As Kelsie drove along the winding road up into the hills to her father's home, she suddenly wished her father didn't live nearby the ranch, for she dreaded the possibility of seeing Clay's Jeep rounding a corner or topping a rise. She saw no other traffic, however, and with relief, she reached the house unnoticed. *Forty years old*, she thought, *and I feel like I need to sneak home.*

In the front of the house, she debated with herself. If she parked in sight of the road, Clay might notice and stop and cause a scene. But Clay and her father were good friends, and Clay visited once or twice a day. If she hid the car on the other side of the house, Clay might walk in unaware of her presence. She decided to park in plain view. Clay would be unlikely to cause a scene in front of her father, she thought. It would also be unfair to surprise Clay. Again.

When she called in through the kitchen door, James replied from the front room. She found him in his customary straight-back chair at the picture window, blanket folded over his legs, gazing across his beloved valley at the far mountain walls. She leaned forward and gave him a peck on his cheek then sat in sunshine on the opposite side of the room and placed her briefcase at her feet.

There was a long, low, walnut coffee table between them covered with back issues of *National Geographic* and *Life* magazines. The sofa at the back wall was black leather of simple design. Above the sofa was a large painting of a black wolf against gray poplar trees. No prints or paintings hung on the other walls, not because James had a spartan sense of decoration, but because he knew it gave added impact to the painting of the lone wolf staring out at the hills.

"Would you like me to make you some tea?" Kelsie offered.

"No, thanks," James said, with just a hint of a dry cough. "No sense pushing my bladder more than necessary these days."

The cough and comment were reminders of time's crusade against her father, like the deep wrinkles in his face, the waver in his voice, and the blanket across his legs in a room already so warm it caused little beads of sweat to apear on her forehead. He used a cane to walk now across the same land he'd once half-jogged with her as a girl riding upon his shoulders. Wasn't it bad enough she had these sad reminders to destroy the memories of the physical man he once was? Did she also have to risk destroying so much more of what she cherished about her father?

"A Tuesday morning visit," James said, without rancor. "This is unusual."

"Life hasn't been that usual lately." She waited. This was his opening, if he wanted to take it, to let her know Clay had told him about the separation.

"Oh?" He smiled. "Of course, I've always been interested in how you might define your life as usual."

Normally, she would have taken that as a compliment. Her father had always encouraged her to live by no man's rules—emphasis on "man." Unlike many of the others in the valley community, he never saw anything wrong in her pursuing her own career away from the ranch, if that was what suited her.

"First thing I've got to tell you—and I didn't tell you earlier because I didn't know if I would go through with it—is that I've moved out on Clay and Taylor. I found a place in town."

"That's interesting," he said, moving his gaze back toward the dark dots of spruce on the far hills.

"Interesting?" Despite her earlier reflections on the sadness of watching him grow old, she couldn't fight a surge of annoyance. "This is not a time for you to affect a nonjudgmental stance."

"You want me to tell you it's wrong?" he asked.

"No."

"You want me to tell you it's right?"

"No."

"You want me to blame Clay?"

"It's not his fault."

"You want me to pester you with questions?"

"I couldn't take it."

"I believe, then," he said, turning back to her so she could see him smile away any offense, "I'll allow my first statement to stand: That's interesting."

Kelsie sagged with frustration. When he put it in black-and-white terms like that, of course, he was right and she was a fool to snap at him. But why did it *feel* the way it did inside, against any logic? What *did* she want? She wanted to cry and someone to listen. It wouldn't make the problem go away, but it would help her. To have someone listen and not offer advice. Men were good for a lot of things—she loved James and Clay—but they never just listened; they offered advice, solutions.

Yet she lived and worked in a man's world. This was part of the price she paid. So she drew a breath, pushed back her frustration, and straightened on the couch to a controlled posture.

"Anyway, I thought you should know about the separation," she said. "In case Clay didn't get around to telling you."

"He hasn't."

Did she read judgment in his curt voice? Was he taking Clay's side? She couldn't bear it, but she knew she couldn't explain, either. Instead, she opened her briefcase and spread it on her lap, keeping her hands busy so her father wouldn't see she was trembling as she tried to put her emotions into neutral.

"Emerald Canyon, Daddy," she said, setting aside her cellular phone and taking out some papers. "Know much about it?" She'd been dreading the question for two weeks, rehearsing it for one. It felt wooden.

"Probably not much more than you do," he said.

A two-edged answer. Did he realize that? Or was his voice casual because he truly was casual?

"I've been researching its corporate background," she said. "I know more than you might think."

"Then this feels like you're on a fishing expedition. It's what your momma used to do to me. Ask me what I knew about something and hold back what she knew just to compare notes."

Kelsie kept her eyes on the papers. He was right, of course, but was he dodging the issue? "What do you know?" she asked. Anything not to have to accuse him.

He smiled sadly. "You've left Clay and Taylor. You haven't even slowed down to ask about your old man's health. All I see is this steel mind clamped shut on what appears to be lawyer business. Maybe I'll have some tea after all."

"No," she said. The injustice of his accusation—that she was cold and unfeeling—felt like a light bulb breaking in her stomach. "I want to talk about Emerald Canyon."

"Certainly," he said, his voice silkily polite. It was the way he handled anger. Just like Clay.

"Thank you," she said, equally polite, equally angry. "What do you know about Emerald Canyon?"

"World-class casino run by the reservation. World-class golf course. And retirement homes filling with more Californians than I could count in a month of Sundays."

"Anything else you know?"

He frowned at her. "The way that's come out, sounds close to calling me a liar. Were you a man, and were you anyone but my daughter, I'm not sure I'd tolerate further discussion."

"This is what I know," she said. "Emerald Canyon is in a unique location. It's within reservation boundaries, giving them the right to run the casino. It's on the edge of the reservation, though, making the nearby private non-reservation land valuable for expanded development, as has happened."

James shrugged. "I retired from cattle, not real estate."

He was going to make her say it, she thought; he was going to make her be the one to say it. Couldn't he at least spare her that?

"A Mr. George Samson owned the original piece of land within the reservation. He's a full-blooded Flathead, and by law he was entitled to sell the land to the county, which he did in the summer of 1973. Do you know what I find interesting?"

"George Samson," he said, although it wasn't in answer to her question. "Clay's friend. That was his land?"

"Yes." Her lips were tight. As if there weren't enough complications and pain, Clay would once again taste betrayal from the McNeill family. "The land title shows George Samson. Although the price—and I checked it against other land sold the same summer—was considerably higher than he would have received at fair-market price, a year later it was worth twenty times as much because of the Big Sky Casino, and worth fifty times as much within another five years."

"That's what you find interesting then."

"No." They were both getting closer and closer to the edge. Couldn't he ease off instead of pushing her there? "What I find—"

Her cell phone rang. It nearly startled her into spilling her briefcase off her lap onto the floor. With quick anger, she snapped off the power.

"What I find interesting," she said, "is six separate numbered corporations. These corporations purchased the land from the county at considerably less than what the county paid. Records of the minutes show that part of the conditions to purchase involved a promised cleanup of soil pollutants. I also find it interesting that the land was purchased six months before the announcment of the Big Sky Casino development."

James McNeill shrugged again. "Someone had a plan and gambled well. I tip my hat to them."

Kelsie pulled out a photocopy of a newspaper article. "I was sixteen that summer. You might remember a train derailment, the one that brought an FBI agent into the valley."

"I remember everything about that summer, the good and the bad. I'm just glad after all this time, the good's here and the bad's gone."

*A few months ago, I would have agreed with you*, she thought, *and how I wish I still could.*

"I've talked to Mr. George Samson. He said he would have preferred to keep his land," Kelsie said. "But because of the spilled bulk chemicals and how much time and effort it would take to clean it up, he was pragmatic enough to sell when the county offered what he felt was a high price."

"We both know Clay and George are good friends," James said. "It's my impression that George is happy with the next property he bought from the proceeds. It's higher up in the mountains, farther away from town."

"Are you listening to me? The land never got cleaned. Reports show work had gone into it. Bulldozers pushed dirt around, but it was never cleaned properly. The developers buried core samples that showed contamination and unstable soil."

"Why are you telling me this?" he asked abruptly.

They were at the edge. And he'd pushed.

"Because—"

The ringing of a cordless telephone interrupted her. He fished under his blanket for it. "McNeill," he answered. A pause. "Clay. How are you?"

He listened, glancing occasionally at Kelsie.

"Kelsie's here," James said after a while. "That's why." Another pause. "All right."

James McNeill listened a few more minutes while Kelsie fidgeted. She wouldn't have believed it if someone had ever tried to explain beforehand, the range of agony and stress that came with the end of a

relationship. Clay was a mile up the road, on the other end of a telephone line, and she was as distant from him as if she were dead.

James finally hung up. "Kelsie—" he began.

"No," she said. "I need to finish. Whatever you have, whatever
Clay has, it can wait."

"I guess it will, won't it?" he said, again with extreme, silky
politeness.

"It's taken me months, and it's taken connections only Clay could
get me through the Bureau, but I finally tracked down the names of
the people who owned those corporations."

She studied his face. He regarded her passively. He *was* going to
make her say it. "I want you to hear it from me first," she continued.
"I'm about to start proceedings on a $55 million lawsuit against those
six corporations. There's also a good chance the corporate directors
will face criminal charges. This scandal is going to rip apart the
power structure of the entire valley."

Still no reaction from her father.

"Daddy"—she took a deep breath—"are you going to help me on
this? Or will I have to see you in court?"

"You finished with what you have to say?"

She nodded, numb. This was not the reaction she'd expected.

"Good."

He rose from his chair and took slow, steady steps past the coffee
table toward the kitchen.

"Where are you going?"

"You've got me cranky, and I don't trust myself to say things I
won't regret. I'm getting my cane and my jacket, and I'm meeting
Clay. I suggest you follow in your car."

"Follow?"

"That call that came through on your cell phone. It was Clay. He's
been trying to get you to let you know."

"Know what?"

"Taylor," James said. "He's lost."

## 3:48 P.M.

"A fire?"

"A fire."

Across a table on the veranda of a large house on the shores of

Whitefish Lake, two men eyed each other with dislike neither tried to hide.

To Wayne Anderson, retired banker, Sonny Cutknife was hardly different from a phony television preacher. Maybe Sonny didn't promise cures in exchange for send-in donations, but he was grandly using a belief system that let him milk his followers. The shoulder-length ponytail, the beads, moccasins, and leather vest he couldn't even button because his belly was so fat. The man had to be nearly fifty. Wasn't it time to quit posturing that ridiculous counterculture stuff? It grated on Anderson that Cutknife held much of his position by spouting antiwhite and antiestablishment hogwash that was well received on the reservation while at the same time directing on a daily basis a personal mutual-fund portfolio worth well over a half-million and switching his leather-vest-and-beer routine for Armani and Courvosier once a month on trips to Manhattan.

To Sonny Cutknife, Wayne Anderson symbolized everything hateful about weak, effete, arrogant, white power. The man couldn't bench-press a bag of hamburgers, but because of an accident of Caucasian-male birth, he believed himself to be one of the masters of the universe. He had to be pushing his midseventies, Sonny thought, but still wore his hair glossy brown, as if he could fool people into believing that nature had decided to allow him, and only him, to bypass the aging process. Of course, his hair matched his wonderful taut skin that screamed of a dozen Brazilian facelifts. What was truly hilarious to Sonny was the man's total lack of common sense. All that bother and expense of trying to appear twenty years younger when he wore the clothes he'd kept in his closet over those twenty years, clothes which at the moment consisted of a brown polyester leisure suit and glossy snakeskin cowboy boots.

"A fire," Wayne Anderson repeated, giving Sonny a scornful smile that emphasized the waxiness of his unnatural skin. "That shouldn't be difficult for you, should it? If I recall, you tried to do the same to a local church at one time."

"I know what a fire is," Sonny growled. "And don't forget, we both have our secrets."

"Temper, temper. One would hate to have to put you on a leash." Out came the smile again.

Sonny swallowed the insult because he'd long ago vowed not to try to fool himself into believing he was anything other than what he was: a hired man looking for the easiest way to make the most money. There was even honor in that, admitting without shame your vices and living by them.

"Where do you want the fire?" Sonny asked, thinking when all the others lined up to throw dirt on Anderson's coffin, Sonny wanted to be there with a handful of rose-bed manure. He'd come back at night with his dogs, too, and all three of them would mark the gravesite with streams of disdain.

"Your office," Anderson said. "Burn your office."

"The administration office? On the reservation?" Sonny looked at him, disbelieving.

"None other."

"I don't understand."

"It's the computer age. We know you've delayed electronic recordkeeping as long as possible. We know you've been forced to finally install the system. Now would be a good time to get rid of all previous files before they're input. So make sure it's a good fire. We've decided it would be prudent to have all of the first twenty years completely destroyed."

# 4:01 P.M.

There were already two other pickups in the yard. One truck Kelsie recognized as belonging to Lawson, the other to Rooster Evans. She wondered how Lawson had gotten there so quickly, then she remembered. He'd had an appointment with Clay.

The three men were standing near the corral, two of them—Clay and Rooster—set apart by their cowboy hats. James drove his truck up to the group, trying to cut down on the walking he needed to do. Kelsie, in her BMW, stayed on his bumper and parked right behind him.

She opened her door and went to help James out of the truck. He shook off her help.

To Kelsie, his rejection added to the surrealness of the situation. How had it come to this—returning as a stranger to her own home? And returning because her son was gone? She forced her body through walking motions and rounded the front of her father's truck.

"Happened to stop by to ask about borrowing a tractor, and I heard the sad news," Rooster Evans said, pulling himself away from the knot of people. He remembered his cowboy hat and yanked it from his head. "Don't you worry, Babs, we'll have your boy within the hour."

Kelsie pasted a smile on her face. She remembered the cute poems he'd written for her when she was just a girl. Rooster was ever sweet, the only one to still call her Babs. He had taken her to the high-school prom, asked her a dozen times to marry him, and had not shown anger at her dozen firm refusals. He'd married a town girl a few years later; it hadn't stuck. The town girl had departed the Evans spread with healthy alimony, and he'd stayed, running the ranch under the watchful eye of his father, Frank, who continued to grow in orneriness with each passing year. Rooster's hair was still deserving of his nickname. It was paler red than the fiery color of his teens but still short and bristly. Light freckles still covered his forehead, arms, and hands. His hairline had receded, and there were tan lines across his brow from where he always wore a hat, but he still looked like the teenager she always remembered hanging out with Michael and Lawson.

"And if we don't find him then," Rooster said, "I'll take my plane up and Lawson will take his. We'll find him. I promise."

More than a few of the big ranchers had planes, for hobby, hunting, and convenience. Rooster, Michael, and Lawson, in fact, had once all shared in buying an airplane. That had happened much earlier, when Michael was still alive, when all three had been musketeers, raising gleeful cane throughout the valley, when Michael and Lawson were still friends, not bitter enemies over a matter that neither had discussed with anyone.

"Won't surprise me if we get five planes into the air," Rooster said. "You know how folks around here help out."

"Rooster, you always did know how to cheer me up," she said.

Rooster nodded shyly and stuck his cowboy hat back on his head.

Kelsie moved past him, conscious of her high heels on the packed dirt, conscious that the conversation stopped between Clay and Lawson. They were as uncertain of what to say as she was.

She waited for Clay to speak and noticed a purple sweater on the top of one of the corral rails. Didn't the sweater belong to Taylor?

Before she could ask, Clay took her elbow and pulled her away. They stopped at a corner of the corral. Her feeling of strangeness intensified at his coldness; she hadn't seen him since Sunday, but it seemed like years, and she caught herself studying him as if indeed—by the manner he stood apart from her—he was another woman's husband.

Age had softened the angles on his face, but character and strength were molded into place. His awkward frame had filled out over the decades, but he was far from fat, a result of the ranch work that demanded most of his daylight hours. His flannel shirt had faded; his new jeans had not.

He was staring back at her with intensity and some anger. Kelsie became aware of something that surprised her: She felt renewed desire for this man, the tall, rugged stranger. Why now when there was no way to go back to him? Why now in the face of crisis?

"I've already called Noah Latcher," he said. "I thought it might make more sense to try bloodhounds before calling the hired hands or neighbors for a search party. And I'm not real, real worried about Taylor. Not yet. Louie Two's gone, too, so I'm guessing they went together. Louie Two will take care of him."

"He's lost," she said. "Taylor is lost. You know that for a fact?"

"No, I don't know that. He might be under a pile of towels in the laundry room. I was just getting lonely up here and decided to find a way to get attention."

"I don't need this," she said angrily.

"Sorry. Let me remember to think of you first." His sarcasm was obvious. He grabbed her shoulders and stared her in the face. "I don't care what you need. Taylor is in the woods somewhere. We both know he doesn't have a chance of finding his own way back."

"In the woods . . . but how?"

"Lawson and I were upstairs. We had an appointment with some government yahoo going over those stupid environmental regulations for cattle on open range land. Taylor was downstairs. Safe, I thought. When Lawson and I went down, the patio door was open. No Taylor."

"You know he'll wander," Kelsie said. "Why wasn't it locked?"

"Look in my eyes, woman," Clay said. His voice was low. "Don't you dare put any blame on me. Some boys have a full-time mother. Some boys even have mothers who love them. Maybe if you had been at the ranch—"

"You and I made our arrangements long ago." Kelsie found it easy to respond with her own anger; it pushed fear and worry aside. "Taylor has Down's syndrome—I hardly need to point that out to you—which means he should not be left unattended. Which was another part of our arrangement. Obviously he was, and now he's gone. Instead of looking for someone to blame, why don't we concentrate on finding him?"

"Sure. Let's find him fast so you can get back on your way. Hate to inconvenience you and your little life too much."

"You rotten, miserable . . ." she began, her eyes stinging.

He'd turned his back to her and marched back to the small group.

Noah Latcher arrived ten minutes later, a single bloodhound in the cab of his pickup truck. He and the hound were reputed to be a couple sniffs better than old Caleb and his legendary brace in their day.

When he stepped out of the truck, Noah had a leather leash wrapped around his left hand. He wore jeans and a dirty white T-shirt with a photo of Marilyn Monroe on one side, Elvis on the other. He wasn't wearing boots but a pair of high-top running shoes, well worn and brown with mud and manure.

Noah didn't pause but nodded hello, opened the passenger door, and lifted the low-bellied dog onto the ground. He snapped the leash on its collar and unwound the leather strap from his hand. The dog sniffed disinterestedly at Noah's ankle.

"All right," he said. He had his old man's bulbous nose and shy way of speaking. "You got what I asked for over the phone?"

Clay stepped over, handing him the purple sweater from the wooden rail of the corral. "Taylor wore this all day yesterday."

"Good," Noah said. "Bring me and my dog to the last place you know the boy stood."

"You want all of us with you?" Lawson asked.

"Don't matter none to me," Noah said. "Nothing distracts this hound."

"Lawson," Clay said, "why don't you stay with Kelsie and James? You're not wearing the clothes for a trek through bush. Rooster, for that matter, you'll break your ankles climbing around in those cowboy boots. Fact is, if you have work, you might as well go on. I'll call you as soon as we find Taylor."

Rooster shrugged agreement.

"I'm going," Kelsie announced. "I'll be in sweats and hiking boots in less than a minute."

It wasn't that she pictured Taylor huddled somewhere frightened out of his wits and waiting to be rescued. No, she wasn't much worried about him. He couldn't have gone far, she thought, and the hound would track him, probably within a half-hour. She also knew he would be playing happily wherever they found him, and just as happy to be interrupted and taken home again. She wanted to go with the bloodhound because she didn't want to be sitting around the kitchen with Lawson and her father, enduring the awkward silences as they waited for Clay to return.

She changed into clothes she'd left behind and met them at the patio door of the walkout basement.

Noah gave the bloodhound the scent from Taylor's purple sweater, and the dog began to cast from side to side, its massive nose sweeping the top of the lawn. Within seconds it gave an excited "harumpph" and yanked at the leash, taking Noah in a straight line across the grass and toward the trees at the far edge of the yard.

Clay followed. Kelsie followed Clay. They had avoided eye contact and any more conversation since she'd arrived.

The trail was easy to follow. It cut among the trees in a slightly uphill direction, taking them out of sight of the house and ranch buildings.

"I don't like this," Clay said, stopping long enough for Kelsie to reach his side.

"Neither do I," she said. "I mean, he can't be far, but if he fell or anything . . ."

"That's not what I mean," Clay said. "Think of what Taylor would be doing on the loose in here."

The flitting shadows of a blue jay crossed Kelsie's face. It landed on a tree a few yards away and hurled insults at their intrusion. A small white butterfly dipped from flower to flower.

She understood Clay's concern. "He'd be chasing that butterfly," she said. "Crawling under bushes to look at beetles. Wandering over to try catching that blue jay."

"Exactly. Anything but hiking in a direction with a purpose. It's like someone has him by the hand."

Kelsie felt her first prickle of fear. To this point, she'd felt concern but not fear. Not until now. *It couldn't be . . .*

"Maybe he heard something ahead," Kelsie said, "something that drew him. Or maybe he was trying to keep up with Louie Two, and Louie Two was after a deer."

"No," Clay said. "You know Louie Two. It's the other way around. Louie Two keeps up with Taylor."

"He'll be fine," Kelsie said. "He'll be fine."

For a dangerous moment, it seemed Clay was about to put his arm around her shoulder. She moved forward and followed Noah and the bloodhound, letting Clay trail her.

The path took them in a large semicircle until it eventually reached the edge of the trees at the main road a half-mile beyond the ranch house. There was a ten-foot-wide shallow ditch filled with tall grass. The bloodhound took them through the ditch and up to the asphalt. It went left, then right, patiently sniffing. Then he began to whine.

"Problem, Noah?" Clay asked.

"Must be the oils in the pavement. He's not picking up the boy's trail. I'll take the hound to the other side of the road and let him cast about there."

Ten minutes later, the dog was still trying to pick up a trail.

"This isn't good," Noah said, calling them over. He unleashed the dog and gave him a command to circle wider. "I mean, the kid didn't just fly away."

"Unless he got into a vehicle," Clay said.

Kelsie's prickle of fear began to grow.

"Well . . ." Noah said, scratching his head. "If it was someone local, they would have brung him to the ranch by now. And if it was a tourist, they'd probably take him to the police station, right?"

Clay didn't answer. He crossed the road and returned to where the trail had first reached the asphalt. He squatted and looked in both directions. He grunted, rose, and walked up the road a couple of paces. "Here," he said, pointing downward. "See this oil patch." He reached down and smeared it with his forefinger. Dark liquid gleamed on his fingertip. "It hasn't all soaked through yet. It's pretty recent."

"Clay?" Kelsie asked.

"A vehicle was parked right here, long enough to drip oil. And it didn't leave all that long ago. I sure hope it was coincidence. If not . . ."

"Yes," she prompted.

"If not, it means whoever drove it away was waiting here for Taylor."

"What about Louie Two?" she asked. "He wouldn't let anyone take Taylor. You know how protective that dog is."

She lifted her hands and cupped her mouth. "Louie Two!" she called. "Louie Two!"

The only sounds to greet them were the buzzing of flies, the rumbling of a distant truck, and the bloodhound whining.

Then the tall grass began to shake. It took a few more seconds to realize what was causing the grass to move. At first, all they saw was Louie Two's head. Then they saw why he was dragging himself along. Someone had smashed both his back legs.

## 7:58 P.M.

*"You said Daddy wouldn't die," the boy said, holding his mother's hand tight as they sat in the church.*

*The boy didn't like the organ music. It wasn't happy music. Everybody was too quiet. And everybody seemed to be staring at him and his mommy.*

*"The angels need him in heaven, honey. That's where Daddy is right how. In heaven looking down on us."*

*The boy pointed at the long, dark box in front of them. "But didn't you say Daddy was in there?"*

*"Hush. His body is in there. That's what your daddy left behind when the angels took him to heaven. Just his body."*

*"Can we see him? I just want to say good-bye."*

*His mother's shoulders shook. He couldn't see her face because she had a black curtain in front of it. The black curtain hung from her hat. There was this sad music and grownups who were very quiet and he was scared and he couldn't see his daddy's face or his mommy's face. He felt alone.*

*"I want to see Daddy," he said, raising his voice. "Why can't I see Daddy?"*

*She took a handkerchief and pressed it against her face beneath the curtain. "Nobody can see him," she said. "The car accident burned part of him."*

*Burned? So his father was dead. And dead meant forever. He remembered that. He also remembered wishing that his father would die. That meant this was his fault. His wish had made it happen.*

*The boy became so still and so quiet that after several minutes his mother tugged on his hand. "Are you all right?" she asked him.*

*"I'm sorry," he said. "I didn't really mean it."*

*"You didn't ask anything wrong," she said. "It's just that I'm upset. Very upset."*

*Now it was his fault his mother was crying. He put his head in her lap.*

*"That's all right, honey," she said.*

*He pressed the softness of the black dress against his face and tried to block the sounds of the music from his ears. Then the music stopped. He looked up and saw a tall man with a white face and gray hair walking past the box that held his father.*

*"Ashes to ahses," the man began in a deep, slow voice . . .*

The Watcher let himself in the front door with a key. He didn't bother to bolt the door behind him.

He was surprised at the rundown condition of the condominium, but then he realized she had probably chosen it because of the garage below. The row of condominiums were all two-stories, built into a hill. The front side of the condos appeared to be one-story high and could be reached by a sidewalk. The backside of the condos all had garages on the lower story, with the living quarters above the garage. A stairway from the garage led directly upward into the living quarters, which meant condo owners could drive inside the garage, shut the electric garage door behind the car, and from the safety of the garage walk directly into the condo.

Hers was a two-bedroom layout. From the hallway, a corridor ran past the small kitchen and a small living room on one side and the two bedrooms on the other side. This was the hallway that led to the back door and the steps down to the garage.

The Watcher opened the back door and looked down into the garage with satisfaction. The same features that made the condo appear secure from an outside attacker made for an extreme disadvantage for the victim if the attacker was already waiting inside. Once Kelsie had her car parked in the garage, he could easily move her into the car, completely hidden from witnesses.

Smiling, the Watcher returned to the living room and resumed his inspection. Even though early-evening sun tilted through the patio doors, he flicked on some lights. The orange-brown shag carpet had been flattened from years of use. The paint was beige, the ceiling grimy.

From the living-room patio doors, he checked the sight lines into the condo. He was grateful. From the roof of the buildings on the opposite side, he should have a clear view inside. If he changed his mind and allowed her to remain here for any length of time, he could rent one of the opposite condos and watch her at his leisure.

The Watcher stalked from room to room going through her belongings and carefully putting them back in place.

The Watcher found himself returning to her bedroom. Even though she'd just moved in, already the scent of her perfume was starting to overcome some of the mustiness of the carpet and old furniture.

He looked for her bathrobe and found it hanging on a hook on the backside of the bedroom door. He put the bathrobe on, savoring her closeness to him. When he left, he would have to take something from her shower. A used razor blade, maybe, as a souvenir.

He turned slowly, hugging himself, and gazed at her bed. That was where she would be tonight: a perfect prize, there for the taking any time he wanted. And, after years of waiting until the situation was perfect, he was finally on the verge of possessing her. He had prepared his home for her. He had Taylor safely hidden close by—the day's activities had been hectic but worth it. All that remained for the Watcher was a few more details. Until then, he intended to savor the fruit of his careful planning and patience.

Still wearing her robe, he stepped to the bed. He sat on the edge, then leaned back until he fell, his arms spread-eagled. His feet on the floor, he smiled at the ceiling.

*Tonight,* he thought, *she will be here in the darkness. Here where my body now lies.*

The thought gave him satisfaction.

He knew she wouldn't be home for a while. With the trouble over the boy, she would be at the ranch for hours. That gave him time to enjoy her apartment.

He also needed to sleep. He had energy far beyond ordinary mortals, but even he needed to recharge. Ahead of him, in the darkness of the night, he would have need for strength. A few of the details did need attending to, and he could not afford to be careless this close to his final goal.

The Watcher kicked off his shoes and, still wearing her robe, crawled beneath Kelsie's sheets for a nap. Soon, he would share far more than her robe.

# 11:00 P.M.

Clay sat on the edge of the sofa, elbows braced on his thighs, hands clenched together. Kelsie paced their living room, stopping occasionally to look outside through the picture window into the night as if Taylor might reappear at any moment.

Over the years, Clay had been in dozens of homes filled with the same helpless horror and tension. He had seen mothers with red-rimmed eyes, fathers in stony silence. All of them had clung to him—sometimes literally—as the single expert who might be able to bring back their child. Most of them stared at the telephone as if it might ring any second with news of salvation.

Now the same scene was happening in his own home. Clay knew the odds after a child had been abducted: It was next to impossible that he would see Taylor alive again. Chances were good he'd never even view his son's remains. The more time that passed, the best he could hope for was an answer, that he wouldn't be left with years of alternating between unreasoning hope or the darkest imaginings of his son's fate.

And Clay's experience gave him plenty of fuel for nightmares. The screams of years of victims reverberated through his mind. Despair began to fill him. His little cowboy, gone.

"Kelsie," Clay said. "I need you to hold my hand."

She stopped pacing. He reached upward. She sat beside him on the sofa and wordlessly took his left hand in both of hers.

They sat in silence.

Images of Taylor flashed through Clay's mind. Breakfast, when Taylor insisted on buttering his own toast, a task that took fifteen minutes, and Taylor's laugh of triumph at finishing. Bath time, and the funny duck noises Taylor had learned to make. The day in a park when Taylor had put his arm around an old woman sitting hunched on a bench and hummed a happy song for her, and the tears of gratitude in her eyes when he left five minutes later. Taylor and his unfathomable fascination with watching professional hockey on television.

"I'm sorry about this afternoon," Kelsie said, rubbing his hand softly. "I'm sorry for the angry words."

"No," Clay said, "I deserved it. I was mad at myself for not watching him. I took it out on you. And, of course, we had no idea . . ."

He didn't want to say the ugly words out loud. *No idea that Taylor had been kidnapped.*

Unless Latcher's bloodhound had followed the wrong trail, it couldn't be anything else but. Someone had led Taylor from the ranch house into the woods and in a nearly direct line to the road. Someone had beaten Louie Two so badly the dog's back legs were broken, and he was now in the animal hospital. Someone had taken Taylor away in a vehicle that had been parked along the road.

After finding the dog, they'd called the sheriff's office, and Clay had explained it appeared to be an abduction. Search parties had gone out anyway, groups of neighbors scouring the ranch lands in all directions for as long as the daylight had lasted. Rooster, true to his word, had organized an air search. All with no results.

The sheriff's department had released information to the media outlets describing the possible abduction and included a photo of Taylor. The photo was recent, all the more heartbreaking to Clay because the image seemed to capture the soul of Taylor's happiness and vulnerability. In it Taylor was standing in waist-high grass, the blades blurry in the foreground. He was wearing a dark turtleneck sweater and had one fist up to his half-open mouth, tasting a knuckle smeared with strawberry jam. Taylor's brown hair was short at the front, long at the back, ponytailed in the manner of some of the singers he loved watching on the country-music videos. What tore at Clay the most were Taylor's eyes: soft, innocent, and with the almond-shaped beauty shared by most children with Down's syndrome.

What person would kidnap such a child?

Through the photograph, they could always hope that someone might spot Taylor in a restaurant or a gasoline station. Clay wasn't giving it much hope, though. Whoever had done this was smart enough to succeed in daylight, with no warning and leaving no traces. It was unlikely a dumb mistake would be made from this point on. Besides, it was too easy to keep a kid of Taylor's size and gentle disposition hidden in a van or a car's trunk.

The biggest question for Clay was as simple as it was inexplicable. *Why?* They hadn't received a ransom note or phone call. *Why take Taylor?*

One of Clay's first actions had been to call his former colleagues at Quantico, alerting them to the kidnapping and asking for a search of any recently released or escaped prisoners who might have had motive to revenge themselves on Clay. The preliminary results showed no candidates.

Clay sighed his grief. He'd seen the hopelessness and despair of parents who were missing children. He had always had sympathy for them but had never felt nor understood this level of agony.

Some monster had taken his son. And Clay knew all about monsters.

"Clay?"

He looked over. He realized he'd clenched his fist hard, crushing Kelsie's hand in it. He relaxed his fist.

She lifted his hand to her mouth and softly kissed the back of his hand, looking over it into his eyes.

He saw tears and tenderness. Without thinking, he reached with his other hand and pulled her close, his arm around her shoulders. Her head fit into the crook of his neck. Tears ran against his throat.

"I love you," he said, staring sightlessly at the far wall. "No matter what's happened and what we go through, I love you."

She kissed his neck. "I love you too. No matter what's happened. I do love you."

He kept his arm around her shoulders. She shifted her head and kissed his neck again, a long, lingering touch of warm lips against his skin.

Clay closed his eyes. It was bittersweet to feel such strong love against the curtain of his grief, uncertainty, and despair.

She kissed him again, then wrapped her arms around his back. He felt the hunger in her embrace and realized she was expressing what he, too, was feeling.

Neither moved, as if both were silently trying to deny their heightened awareness of the other. The hunger only grew.

Then she pushed away from him and flicked off the lamp on the table beside them. In the darkness, she began to unbutton his shirt.

"Kelsie, are you sure that—"

"Shhh," she said, her voice breaking. "Shhh."

Strange, he thought, the complexities of the soul. Taylor was gone. Both of them were frantic with worry. He was angry at her for leaving without an explanation. Yet an elemental, unreasoning need was driving them together.

She kissed him fiercely, and he tasted the salt of her tears.

He responded, amazed at the love and desire flooding through him. They clung to each other like survivors of a shipwreck. Too soon, the world and its pain would return, but for now, in this moment, they still had each other.

# 11:43 P.M.

The flashlight illuminated the rough earth walls, and shelves cut high into the walls. The Watcher focused the beam on Taylor.

Taylor squinted and smiled. "Cowboy, me," Taylor announced, happy for company. "Hungry, me."

The Watcher ignored Taylor. He set the flashlight on one of the shelves then stepped outside, leaving the door open. He had no fear the boy would escape by running into the night.

"Cowboy, me," Taylor called after him.

The Watcher returned, dragging a man. He pulled the man to the far wall and left him lying there. Then he went back and shut the door. When he turned around, he saw Taylor squatting over the motionless body.

"Cowboy, me," Taylor said.

"Simpleton," the Watcher said. "He's dead."

Taylor continued to look into the face of the body. He tugged on the dead man's sleeve.

The Watcher had better things to do than marvel at genetically wired stupidity. He pulled a box off the crude earth shelf and set it on the ground. He picked up the flashlight and searched inside. The contents absorbed him so completely, he didn't realize he was humming until he felt Taylor beside him, humming in the same way.

"Shut up."

"Hungry, me," Taylor replied.

The Watcher pushed Taylor away.

Taylor returned and hugged him. "Hungry, me."

"Idiot." The Watcher pushed him away again.

Taylor returned and hummed and hugged.

The Watcher pushed Taylor back. When Taylor stepped forward, he slapped Taylor's face.

Taylor looked puzzled, but he did not cry or move back. He merely smiled uncertainly.

The Watcher sighed. Obviously, he wasn't going to enjoy revisiting the memories called up by the contents of the box unless he took care of the boy. He reached into his jacket and pulled out two chocolate bars. "Shiny colors," he said, mimicking Taylor. "You like shiny colors?"

He put them in Taylor's hand. Taylor bit into the paper. It was so unexpected, but so logical, that the Watcher snorted laughter. "Hey, cowboy. Unwrap it."

Taylor bit again. He spat out the paper.

"Here. Let me do it." The Watcher peeled the wrapper off and gave the chocolate bar back to Taylor. Taylor crammed it in his mouth. The Watcher unwrapped the other chocolate bar and gave it to Taylor. Taylor offered the second chocolate bar to the dead man.

The Watcher shook his head. When Taylor got no response, he set the chocolate bar on the ground near the dead man's face.

"Idiot."

Taylor grinned.

Enough of this, the Watcher thought. He took a small plastic bottle out of his other pocket. "I'm leaving you water. In this bottle. Understand?"

Taylor grinned. He took the water and fumbled with the plastic top.

The Watcher reached for the bottle and opened it, then handed it back to Taylor.

Taylor tilted it. Some of the water ran down his neck. Taylor tilted and tilted. He wiped his face with the back of his hand when he was finished.

With a final disgusted shake of his head, the Watcher stepped outside, shutting the door behind him, leaving Taylor in the dark with the dead man.

Moments later, he opened the door again. He beamed his flashlight on Taylor, who was already beside the body.

"Cowboy, me," Taylor said quietly to the dead man.

The Watcher stepped inside, reached down, and took Taylor's hand. He wrapped Taylor's fingers around the handle of the flashlight. "Don't ask me why I'm doing this," the Watcher said. "You'll probably try to eat it."

As the man shut the door again, Taylor pointed the flashlight beam in erratic circles. He pointed it at the man who would not wake up. Taylor stared and stared. Then he grabbed the corner of one of the blankets the Watcher had left, pulled it over the body, and moved under the blanket too.

Holding the body, Taylor hummed himself to sleep, with the flashlight pointing at the rough wooden door of the prison. ▨

# Day 3

Rustling of clothes brought Clay to consciousness. His back hurt; he'd been curled on his side on the couch, with Kelsie sleeping spoon-style in front of him. His arms were empty now. He blinked and looked for his wife.

The yard light outside threw a glow into the living room. Everything in the shadows of this room was familiar to him: the wide mantelpiece across the stonework of the fireplace; the outlines of the lamps; the bookshelves across two walls; the paintings, their details now blurred grays and blacks.

During their marriage, Clay had faced plenty of nights when he'd known he would be too restless to sleep. To spare Kelsie, he'd take a blanket and move to this couch, staring at all those familiar objects, trying to keep his mind blank and, occasionally, managing to drop into restless sleep.

Tonight in her arms, for a few hours, he had slept as if dead. The strain of separation from Kelsie had driven him to exhaustion, and with her return, he'd finally relaxed enough to succumb to his tiredness.

Awake again, he took in the familiar night outlines of this room and another familiar outline. His wife. She was standing at the side of the coffee table, reaching behind her to zip up the skirt she'd worn when first arriving at the ranch.

"Honey?" he said softly.

The rustling of her clothes stopped. "I'm sorry I woke you," she said. "I waited as long as I could."

"You didn't sleep?"

"It doesn't matter," she said. "You did."

She leaned forward and put her arms into her sweater then straightened and reached up as she wriggled to pull it down over her head and shoulders. The image seared into his mind, a quick impression of the paleness of her flesh and litheness of her body. He smiled.This was one beautiful woman, one he loved. He might not understand her, but he loved her deeply. Something had driven her away from him, made her take an apartment in town. But she was back, and he could forgive.

This was the blessing in Taylor's disappearance. It had knocked down the walls between them. Together, they'd face the new problem. Once they got Taylor back, he and Kelsie could rebuild. Those were the thoughts he'd had falling asleep. These were the thoughts he had waking up and seeing his wife in front of him in the shadows of their living room.

Then it occurred to him. She was getting dressed.

"What time is it?" he asked, sitting up and pulling on his shirt.

"A little before five."

"Sun won't be up for another hour. Do we have to be in a hurry?"

"I do," she said.

"You do." It was an accusation. Not a question.

The silence became awkward.

"Clay," she finally said, "last night surprised me as much as it surprised you. It was like we needed each other. But maybe last night was a mistake."

"I'm your husband. I love you. We *do* need each other—especially now. How could it be a mistake?"

"Because . . ." she faltered, then found the courage to continue. "Because I don't want to give you the wrong impression. I can't come back."

He stood angrily. He grabbed his pants and hopped from foot to foot as he pulled them on.

"Tell me what is going on," he said, his voice low and intense. "Our son is missing. Do you understand? Missing. Abducted. Of all times, this is when we need to be together. You can't just walk out and leave me with questions about why. Not now. It was unfair when you first left. It's inhuman now."

"I have to go," she said.

"No!" For the first time in their marriage, he shouted.

She turned away from him. He jumped over the coffee table and spun her toward him. "No," he said again, almost pleading.

"I have no choice," she said. She began to cry. "Can't you trust me? I have no choice, and I can't even explain to you why I don't have a choice."

"You're going to explain," he said.

"Don't you think I want to? Look at me. I need you—infinitely more than you need me. I need you for me. I need you for Taylor. The last thing I want is to leave this house and leave your arms." She began to sob. "Clay, I don't want to be alone."

Her admission stunned him. He felt immediate guilt for being so hard on her. He put his arms around her, and she sagged against him.

"I don't understand," he said. "I just don't understand."

She didn't reply.

For five minutes, she hung on to him, sobbing with a reckless force that scared him. Eventually her wracking sobs began to subside. Her breathing grew less ragged, the rise and fall of her ribs less pronounced.

"Please," he said, whispering. "Tell me."

She pushed herself away. "If you love me," she said, "you'll let me go."

Drained, he watched with helplessness as she walked into the kitchen and out of the house. A few minutes later, the headlights of her BMW swept the ranch yard, and she was gone.

## 4:48 A.M.

Sonny Cutknife stood in front of the open filing cabinet in the corner of his office. He was almost ready to strike a match. It would be an irrevocable act and in some way, major or minor, would certainly change the course of his comfortable life.

He savored the moment, not because he enjoyed the thought of a fire destroying the administrative building, but because he enjoyed being aware of significant moments. Few were the men with the courage to forge their own destinies; most let life act upon them and, like corks on a wave, arrived at unknown shores. Not Sonny. He took pride in knowing it was his own hand on the rudder and that he charted his own course through the winds and tides of events around him.

It was the same with corruption. For some, Sonny knew, corruption was a gradual process. Small acts of laziness, minor unethical decisions, a series of shortcuts—all of it dust settling in layers, until one day the dirtiness was real and apparent, with no pointer to the transition from innocent to guilty.

Sonny, however, clearly remembered the moment and place he had sold out. It gave him a minor sense of virtue. Corruption had not taken him unaware; rather, he'd been in control of the process, and he'd known exactly what he was doing. It made him better than the hapless fools who woke up one morning and wondered with sudden regret where they had gone wrong and how they'd managed to fall so far. No, Sonny had understood the significance of his decision while making it. No matter what happened, he was not going to waste time on regret; something else he had decided as he deliberately allowed himself to become an apple—white beneath red skin.

The moment and place of his sellout had begun at the pool table in the bar of the Kalispell Hotel on a September evening a few months after Harold Hairy Mocassin had disappeared. Sonny had been leaning over a difficult bank shot, hoping to knock the eight ball into the side pocket, knowing if he missed slightly he'd probably scratch the cue ball and lose not only the game but also the last five dollars in his wallet.

Sudden silence had cut through the smoky air.

Sonny looked up briefly to see a sheriff in full uniform stepping slowly between tables, almost like a classic entrance in an old western, all eyes upon him, all breath held, all drinks poised in motionless hands.

Sonny, though, was too cool to react as the others. No white man—sheriff or not—was going to take him away from a pool game. Sonny dropped his head and resumed eyeballing the length of his cue stick. Out of the corner of his eye, he saw his opponent backing away from the table, taking his glass of draft beer with him. Sonny's peripheral vision told him why. The sheriff had reached the pool table and was staring at Sonny. Before, Sonny's shot had merely been one of many private dramas in the crowded bar. Now, it was the total focus.

He clicked the cue stick into the white ball. It was a perfect shot. He knew it as the white ball made contact with the eight ball, knew it as the eight ball hit the bank, reversed direction, and spun toward the corner pocket. Just as the eight ball reached the pocket, the sheriff plucked it from the table.

"What kind of nonsense is that?" Sonny asked, getting the right touch of belligerence into his voice for the benefit of his audience and especially for the girl in the corner with the halter top who had been pretending to talk with her friends while keeping a good eye on Sonny.

"You and me are going for a little ride," the sheriff said. "I'll try to explain then."

"I ain't going anywhere but to the bar for another beer."

"I got me a pair of handcuffs and a bad temper that says otherwise. Be a lot easier on the both of us if I don't need to use the handcuffs."

Sonny didn't think about it long. Maybe the man's hair was grizzled and he had some sag to his face, but he was still plenty big and drill-sergeant mean. If Sonny let himself get dragged out, it wouldn't show much dignity. On the other hand, with the sheriff looking like the bad guy, it was probably earning Sonny sympathy. With any luck he'd be back to cash in on it before the halter top at the table in the corner found someone else to pretend to ignore.

Sonny tossed his cue stick at his opponent. "Hold my spot," Sonny said. "And you remember. I won this game."

Sonny's cowboy hat was on a nearby table, along with a half-glass of beer. He grabbed the hat and put it on, tilting the brim just right. He paused to finish the beer. Going with the sheriff was one thing, but seeming like he was in a hurry was another. Finally, he ambled toward the door, following the sheriff to the police car parked outside.

"You'll sit in the back," the sheriff said. "Make yourself comfortable. We got a ways to go."

"A ways to go" turned out to be nearly an hour, an hour of no conversation at all. Sonny had tried once or twice to ask questions, but the sheriff hadn't even glanced in the rearview mirror at Sonny. They'd taken pavement into the hills until it became gravel, gravel until dirt, and had arrived at a small cabin just as the the sun began to set. Sonny didn't like the darkness, didn't like the mountain remoteness among the trees, didn't like the fact that he couldn't open the doors of the police car because the handles on the back doors had been removed. Sonny especially didn't like having all this quiet time to wonder exactly how much the sheriff knew about the Native Sons and if it had anything to do with why the sheriff was taking him here. By the time the sheriff parked the car, Sonny had forgotten his hopes for the girl with the halter top and had long since begun to worry about survival.

The sheriff opened the back door of the patrol car and invited Sonny to step outside. Sonny did, watching the sheriff's hands closely, dreading the sight of a billy club.

"Go on in," the sheriff said, pointing at the cabin. "You'll find someone waiting for you. My advice is to listen close."

The sheriff plunked himself back into the car and rested behind the steering wheel. Sonny thought it through, realized he had little choice, and let himself into the cabin with its lamplit interior of rough walls, sagging cupboards, and bunkbeds along the walls. There, for the first time, he met—and instantly hated—the tall, pale banker who introduced himself as Wayne Anderson.

"Look around," Anderson said. "Take a good look. This is the place where your friend Harold Hairy Moccasin died."

The casualness of the man's words scared Sonny, more than the words themselves.

"You'll die here, too," Anderson continued. "Tonight. Unless you make the right choice. So listen good."

"I'm listening," Sonny said, his mouth suddenly dry.

Sonny had been listening ever since. He'd been listening for twenty-three years, right to the moment of striking a match in front of the open filing cabinet.

Sonny had rigged it as simply as possible. Gasoline and kerosene, he knew, left traces that arson investigators could find. From what he'd read, they could piece a fire together from its origin.

Sonny didn't know enough about electricity to rig faulty wiring. So he had chosen candles, setting them upright in the files. He'd light them and shut the file cabinet drawers, leaving them slightly open to supply air. He also had some candles set up in the trash basket at the side of his desk. He'd draped the long curtains from a nearby window into the paper-filled trash basket.

What he hoped was that the candles would burn down and start all the papers on fire. Once the curtains caught, there was a good chance the wood paneling would begin to flame, especially since Sonny was leaving a few windows open to provide a draft.

What Sonny also hoped was the time it took for the candles to burn down was enough time for him to get to his girlfriend's. She'd be his alibi.

Sonny would blame a careless cigarette for the fire. Everyone knew he chain-smoked. The metal ashtray on his desk would not burn in the fire. He'd say he must have missed the ashtray and hit the trash basket with his final cigarette of the evening.

If the candles didn't work, Sonny would come back early the next morning and do it right with kerosene, taking his chances on an investigation. He wasn't really worried about it though, for he had his own plans.

He hadn't believed Anderson's excuse about deciding the new computer system made for the perfect opportunity to erase the years of paperwork. They could have chosen a time five years earlier or waited five years and simply burned down the computer systems. For all these years they had been content in hiding behind a legal labyrinth that had protected them so well.

No, Sonny, thought, something was in the wind. They were well-connected enough to hear of an upcoming investigation. Or maybe one of the surviving members of the group was defecting to go public. Or maybe inquisitive heirs were investigating the sources of an estate's revenue. Whatever the reason, they wanted to cover their tracks.

Sonny had been planning for this. He had not been stupid enough to think that this gravy train would stay on the tracks forever. He'd enjoyed the ride and had had every intention of staying on board while the train was running. But from day one, he had known that eventually something would derail it.

He had spent years putting together his own documents. Wayne Anderson might think a fire in the administration office would erase any links to Emerald Canyon. But Wayne Anderson was wrong. And Wayne Anderson and the surviving others—mistakenly secure in their assumptions of anonymity—would pay for the mistake. Sonny intended to sop up the last of the gravy before moving on.

Without any change in expression, he struck the match. He leaned forward and lit the first of the candles.

# 6:15 A.M.

Despite the extreme loneliness of sitting at the kitchen table with a cold cup of bitter coffee, Clay smiled as he watched a truck come up the drive of the ranch house. If the clouds broke, the sun was only minutes away from reaching the tip of the mountains—it didn't surprise him that these visitors would arrive with the light of a new day.

Clay smiled because even without the familiar light-green paint of the old Chevy truck, he would recognize his visitors by the stiff posture of the passenger. Old George Samson spent a great deal of effort and pride in carrying himself as a man thirty years younger. George also tended to concentrate on the scenery and never relaxed enough to enjoy conversation.

While Clay had spent his share of time driving George into town for supplies and occasional doctors' appointments, in this case, George's grandson Johnny was the recipient of the old man's focused silence. Clay could guess why they were at the ranch; he wished there was another reason.

As they parked the truck, Clay rose from the table and moved to the kitchen counter. He dumped wet coffee grounds into the trash, found another filter, measured fresh coffee, and began to brew a new pot, making it twice as strong—the way the old man liked it.

Johnny and George knocked before stepping into the back entrance. Johnny wore khaki pants and a button-down shirt. He was a schoolteacher on the reservation. Unlike some teachers who felt they needed to be friends with their students and were ineffective as a result, Johnny knew the kids wanted someone to respect, so he chose not to dress as they did.

George, hair dazzling white, was a denim ad in soft, faded jeans and soft, faded jean jacket. He'd finally allowed his doctor and Johnny to talk him into spectacles. Aside from the wire-frame glasses and slight shrunkenness he couldn't hide with any amount of excellent posture, he hardly looked older than when Clay had first spoken to him a quarter-century earlier.

"Morning," Clay called. "Sit yourselves down. I was just about to start some eggs and bacon."

It was a white lie. Clay didn't feel like eating. He didn't feel like doing much except for punching a fist through the kitchen window. What was there he could do to get Taylor back? Nothing. He, the great retired FBI hunter of serial killers, had so little information about Taylor's disappearance that all he could do was sit by a phone and hope for a call from the person who had taken his son. He planned to call the local sheriff to ask him to bring in the FBI, but even then, Clay knew that fieldwork rarely helped the victims; instead, it provided preventative measures by stopping the kidnappers from future crimes.

There were also his feelings of frustration about his wife—he knew where she was, but it seemed there was even less he could do to get her back. Clay was beat up good, and he knew it.

Johnny and George took chairs at the kitchen table, waiting with formal politeness as Clay cracked eggs and stripped lines of bacon into a frying pan. Only when Clay turned back to them did George speak.

"I didn't find out until last night. Johnny came up to the cabin," George said. He did not listen to the news and would not have heard otherwise. "We are here to help."

"Taylor?" Clay asked, knowing, of course, it was.

"Yes," George said. "Johnny was able to tell me only what he heard on television."

"I wish you could help," Clay said. "We've got Rooster Evans going up in his plane today, and the search parties will continue. But I'm pretty sure Taylor isn't out there."

"The reports were true?" Johnny asked. "He's been kidnapped?"

"Everything points to it." Clay found refuge in replying professionally, as if it wasn't his son who was missing.

"What can we do?" George asked.

Clay was glad they didn't offer trite consolations, such as Taylor would be fine, or he'd be back soon. Clay was glad they didn't ask questions in the manner of bystanders at a gruesome car accident. He'd been there, when people took pleasure in the curiosity of horror. *Who might have kidnapped him? Was it revenge? Any ransom calls? How was he taken? How are you sure it's a kidnapping? Do you think he's alive?*

"What can you do? Drink coffee," Clay answered. "Eat my bacon and eggs without complaining. I can't leave the house. I have calls to make; I need to coordinate the search efforts. Tell me a couple of bad jokes. I could use some company."

"Kelsie?" Johnny said.

"Not here." Clay grabbed the coffeepot and poured them each a cup. He didn't explain further.

George was a close friend. Johnny, almost as close. But Clay didn't buy into the female thing of easing pain by sharing it. The way men worked, Clay figured, if they didn't know each other well, baring the soul was plain embarrassing. And if they were good friends, they could read enough between the lines. Talk about anything—philosophy, baseball, women and how they drove you nuts. Argue about anything. But feelings? Hey, they were there, you knew that. And if you wanted to talk about them or listen, fine, but no probing. No advice offered unless asked. What it boiled down to was that silence was good enough sympathy. Sometimes sympathy was changing the subject and allowing a man his dignity.

"Maybe you should send us up in the air with Rooster," George said after he and Johnny absorbed the implications of Clay's brief answer about Kelsie. Gone at six in the morning? Gone during the crisis of Taylor's kidnapping? There could be no good reason for that.

"Let me in the airplane," George continued. A wide grin showed off new teeth. "With these spectacles, I see like an eagle again."

The offer touched Clay. One of the reasons George watched the scenery so closely while riding in a moving vehicle was to take his mind off the moving vehicle. George didn't go much for speeds over thirty miles an hour.

"Might be a good idea," Clay answered George. "I'll see if he has room in the airplane."

The bacon began to pop and sizzle. For the next few minutes, Clay tended the stove and listened with half-concentration to George and Johnny argue over the efficiency of George's eyesight, thinking how much good it did a man to have close friends, thinking back to his career days and how job and family tended to keep his peers at mere acquaintance level.

It wasn't until moving to Montana that Clay had first spent time with a friend who didn't always somehow turn the conversation back to work issues. That friend, of course, was George.

Mindful of George's kindness years earlier when Clay had been in the hospital, Clay had made a courtesy call to George at the new cabin he'd built higher in the mountains. The casual impulse visit had lasted an entire afternoon as they sat on the cabin veranda, sipping on lemon water, discussing subjects that ranged from stars to physics to baseball and history, with Clay impressed at the old man's reading habits and eclectic knowledge.

The visits had become weekly, the discussions more lively. It was inevitable that George challenged Clay's determination to see the world on strictly scientific terms.

"You made your living by sifting through evidence and drawing conclusions," George began one day about four years ago.

"Hard evidence," Clay corrected. "Forensic science. Fingerprints, powder burns, body fluids, autopsy reports. I did not speculate on the unmeasurable."

"That is fair," George said, a smiling playing at the edges of his mouth. "But tell me, does a good investigator or scientist disqualify any conclusion before weighing the evidence?"

"No. We try to keep an open mind."

"Tell me then," George said, "why do so many educated people decide God does not exist and shut their eyes to even considering His presence?" Before Clay could answer, George continued. "Spend the next week open to the search that He does exist behind the workings of this world. Look at everything as if you are a child. A child finds amazement in first holding the string of a balloon that floats. A child chases a pigeon in the park and laughs with delight when it flies away. Children see everything with a degree of awe. Pretend, then, everything you see is new to you. The complexity, the wonder of it all, will overwhelm you. When you return next week, tell me, if you are able, that this world is an accident of the universe."

The week between conversations became almost mystical for Clay. He watched Taylor wiggle fingers and toes, and marveled at the working of nerve impulses.

Instead of an annoyance to be swept away, a dew-laced spider web stretching across the steering wheel of his tractor became an incredible testimony to the unfathomable—that a tiny bit of soft-shelled protein was capable of intelligence, reproduction, and sophisticated food-gathering.

One afternoon, Clay spent a full half-hour examining a feather he'd found below the loft of the barn where the pigeons roosted. He pulled apart the strands of the feather, silk smooth and delicate, yet sturdy and practical in the design. Up close he could not see where one color of the pigment began or ended. At arm's length, he saw again the mottled brown and black of a feather. Strong and tough, yet so light it almost did not exist. Something so perfectly made was so common. And if something this ordinary held so much mystery and wonder . . .

Clay found joy in the taste of the morning's first coffee, in Kelsie's touch. He looked at his watch and tried to imagine the eternity of time. And the world, once so common, filled him with mystery. He began to understand how George could be serene and joyful into old age.

During their next conversation, Clay admitted to George that perhaps all of this mystery might be best explained by the invisible presence of a greater power.

"Clay," George said, "could you understand this greater power as eternal, a power beyond time and space?"

"If a person is looking for definition, sure."

"And could you give Him a name? God."

Clay nodded.

"How about Christ? Christ as God?" George said.

Clay shrugged. "No one denies the historical Jesus. A genius of philosphy, a teacher talented enough to impact history—"

George snorted. "Not a genius or teacher. Either lunatic or Son of God. No sane human teacher would claim something so preposterous. Unless he were sane and it was true."

"Well . . ."

"If you can imagine a God of great power, my friend, then you only have one stumbling block between you and Christ. Yes, it is a matter of faith. Ever read C. S. Lewis? All you have to do is accept that a God great enough to be behind the workings of the universe descended into the physical realms of His own universe and rose again. I believe once you understand and know that, the how and why of existence falls into place. You are not only seeing the sun in the sky, but by it, you are also able to see everything else. With that understanding, you will find peace. Not necessarily happiness, but peace."

Yes, Clay had found his peace: the valley, the friendship, a marriage and child, and faith. Happiness was too elusive; it depended on external factors, but peace could exist even in the depths of trouble. That was what Clay now wanted to cling to: peace, even in the chaos of this situation.

The telephone rang. Clay had the receiver to his ear before it rang again.

"Mr. Garner?" The voice was unfamiliar.

"Yes."

"We need you over at the Evans ranch. Frank, he's"—the voice faltered—"he's been killed. And there ain't yet been no sign of Rooster."

# 6:38 A.M.

*The boy approached the couch, holding two baseball gloves. Not that he expected much, but it was still worth a try. He raised his voice to be heard above the crowd's roar on the television. "Mommy said maybe we could play catch."*

*"Mommy, Mommy." It was a mimic of the boy's voice. "You're nearly eight, kid. Quit talking like a baby."*

*The man tilted a can of beer up to his mouth. "Get another thing straight. I didn't marry your old lady. She married me. In other words, I set the rules. Just 'cause she says something don't mean it's gonna happen."*

*He gestured at the television set with his can of beer. "No way I'm leaving. Extra innings."*

*"Maybe after?" the boy tried.*

*"Not a chance. I got to catch up on some sleep. I work hard all week supporting you and your old lady. I deserve a good rest."*

*He drained the beer in a final gulp. "Get me another can from the fridge, will ya?"*

*The boy brought back another beer, which the man accepted without taking his eyes off the game. The boy waited, not sure what he was waiting for.*

*"Hey," the man finally said, "make your own fun. Scram before I give you one upside the head."*

*The boy returned the baseball gloves to his bedroom. He pulled his collection of horror comics out from under the bed and flipped through, pausing at each new torture scene and taking satisfaction in imagining his stepdad the recipient of boiling oil, poison-tipped daggers, or the guillotine blade.*

*An hour later, the boy left his bedroom. He heard giggles from the couch. His mother had returned from shopping for groceries. He avoided the living room. He hated seeing his stepfather with his hands on his mother. The boy moved through the kitchen, quietly closed the back door behind him, and sat on the porch.*

*He closed his eyes, savoring one of his favorite scenes in the comic book.*

*A woman, bound on a table, in ripped clothing, was about to be skinned alive. The man with the knife above her had such pleasure on his face, the woman such terror. And she was as helpless as he was powerful.*

*The squawking of magpies caused the boy to open his eyes again. A skinny gray cat had entered the back yard, and the birds were crying angry alarm at its presence.*

*He watched the cat. He recognized it as belonging to Mr. Watson, the neighbor who yelled at any kids stepping onto his property. The cat slinked through the bushes at the fence then darted into the open door that led into the garage.*

*It gave the boy an idea. He stood, ran to the garage, and pulled the door shut. Now the cat was trapped.*

*After that, the boy took his time. He didn't have to worry about anybody in the house asking him questions. They never did. He stole back into the house and tiptoed into the basement workshop. He had a list in his mind of the items he would need: First of all, garden gloves because the cat would most certainly scratch and bite; then fishing line; hedge clippers; and solvent. Chemicals might be fun for experimenting. It would be interesting to see what solvent did to a cat's eyes. Yes, chemicals . . .*

The Watcher wore a longhaired wig and a baseball cap. He doubted anyone would notice him this early, but caution had kept him hunting for decades, and in going for the ultimate prey, he wasn't about to relax his vigilance.

As he walked up the sidewalk to the front of Kelsie's condo, the Watcher squeezed his left arm against his ribs, holding a Ziploc bag in place hidden beneath his jacket. Inside it was a cloth soaked in ether, the fumes contained by the plastic.

Over the years, the Watcher had searched for the perfect chemical. At his best, of course, he had no need for help, using conversation and seduction to get his victim to a place where they had no possible escape.

Occasionally, however, he did need his victims to be unconscious. He'd tried benzene, which had the advantage of being pleasant smelling and a gas at room temperature. Used in motor fuels and as a solvent, it was readily available and nearly instant in effect. Unfortunately, more often than not, it caused vomiting, and once, before he had understood dosage well enough, it had led to a fatal heart attack.

The Watcher liked Veronal. As a barbiturate, it was easy to slip into a drink. It produced unconsciousness instantly. It was difficult to obtain without prescription, though, and the Watcher did not like any paper trails that might lead back to him.

Once he'd even tried carbon tetrachloride because he knew it attacked the central nervous system, and, as he'd found, it did work. The drawbacks were its slowness and unpredictability.

In the end, he always came back to the good old standby, ether, also called chloroform. He'd first used it on Kelsie the summer she turned sixteen. All it had taken was an ether-soaked cloth over her mouth while she slept. She hadn't awakened or kicked—that's how quickly it worked. Yes, it had been a juvenile prank, using lipstick to write "I Love You" across her forehead, but then, he'd just been learning about the uses of the power of life and death.

The only drawback the Watcher had ever found with ether was uncontrolled hyperthermia, something he had not anticipated until later research showed him it was a genetic response that occurred in about 10 percent of the general population. It had happened to a college student, driving her temperature up over 110 degrees, and she had died long before she could be any use to him. Because of that incident, he'd begun his experimentation to find something perfect; in the end, he decided he'd take the one in ten risk that ether presented.

Fortunately, he knew Kelsie would not have that genetic response. She'd survived the lipstick night with no ill effects. He could use it on her again. And he was ready.

He'd rigged, as usual, a facecloth so that it was almost like a surgeon's mask, with strings attached to each end. The facecloth was damp with ether; the large Ziploc bag kept it ready. His much-practiced procedure was simple: Drop the cloth in front of the victim's face over her mouth and nose, pull tight on the straps, and knot them quickly, then step back and wait to catch her as she fell.

He mentally rehearsed his actions as he advanced on the condo, thinking through the layout of the place, knowing the only real danger would be if she managed to get to a telephone behind a locked door before he chased her down.

He checked his watch—it was 6:40 A.M. She might still be sleeping. Or in the bathroom getting ready for her punctual 7:45 arrival at the office. Or in the kitchen sipping on coffee. He had no way of guessing. Because of the daylight, she didn't need to turn on any lights in the condo.

She'd returned from the ranch two hours earlier. He knew that because he had been waiting and watching. Upon her arrival, the bedroom light had gone on then off. She'd gone to bed, probably hoping to rest for a few hours until daybreak.

It was an easy deduction that she'd spent the entire night with her husband.

She'd been warned against that. It drove the Watcher mad to think that she might share herself with another man. Now she would pay. He had not planned to take her this early, but it enraged him to think of her with her husband. It had always enraged him. Before he'd been helpless to do anything about it. Now . . .

Now she would pay the price. Her car was waiting in the garage of the condo. It would be a simple matter to load her unseen into her trunk and drive the car away.

The excitement of it, after years of planning for this moment, easily washed away any exhaustion he felt from the activities that had kept him up the entire night.

The Watcher opened the front door with his key. He pushed the door open slowly and listened.

Faintly, he heard running water inside. She was in the shower.

Perfect, he thought. Absolutely perfect.

## 6:48 a.m.

"Clay Garner," Clay said, introducing himself to the man in the green John Deere cap standing at the front of the Evans house. He was a thin man with a wizened face, smoking a cigarette, drawing deep drags then nervously flicking the cigarette to get rid of the ashes that never had a chance to accumulate.

"Jess Higgins. I'm the one who called you."

"How about the sheriff?"

Behind them, near a few pickup trucks, gathered in a group of about a dozen, were other ranch hands, speaking in low whispers. Johnny Samson and his grandfather had joined the group, and they stood watching with their hands in their pockets.

Clouds had moved in over the valley. Low rain clouds, gray like the grittiness Clay felt in his soul.

"I called him, all right," Higgins said. Wind gusts lifted the strands of hair that curled out from beneath his cap. "Right after I called you. He ought to be here sometime soon."

"Who's been inside the house?"

"Just me," the man said. "And I swear on a stack of Bibles I didn't do nothing. I walked in the kitchen door, looking for Rooster on account of he was supposed to be down at the shed to help me vaccinate some steers. And there he was. Dead. The old man, I mean."

"Take your work boots off," Clay said.

"My boots?"

"You'll be doing yourself a big favor." Clay didn't bother explaining that if this ranch hand had contaminated the crime scene, at least they'd be able to match any debris and trace evidence to his boots. "Take them off and tie the laces together. Leave them hanging over the top of the railing there."

The ranch hand was too scared to question Clay further. When the boots were in place, Clay continued.

"Just Old Man Evans dead?"

"That's all I seen. Sitting in the chair with his head tilted back unnatural. I'll be having nightmares, it was so unnatural. With a wide-open, big smile across his throat and a big puddle of blood on the floor. When I saw that, I backed out in a hurry."

"Where'd you call from?" The less time this ranch hand had spent in the house the better.

"A phone down at the barn."

"You didn't go anywhere else in the house?"

"Nope. Too scared. Just stepped into the kitchen, saw him on the chair, and high-tailed it back out again."

"Any sign of Rooster?" Clay asked.

"None. You think he's dead too?"

"Hard to say." Clay was torn about what to do. He was not an investigating officer. Although he knew enough not to disturb anything at the crime scene, he still didn't want to enter the house. First, it would rankle the sheriff. More important, it might compromise any evidence found at the scene. A good defense attorney could successfully argue the evidence inadmissible, based on an unauthorized civilian, who may or may not have distorted the findings.

Clay was patient too. Chances were the sheriff would invite him in and at the least share whatever he learned. Waiting another twenty minutes or so wouldn't make any difference to Clay. Twenty minutes would make a difference, though, if Rooster was somewhere else in the house, alive and in urgent need of medical help. Clay hated to think of his neighbor dying while friends and ranch hands waited outside. Yes, it was unlikely. If Rooster had been attacked, he was probably long dead, like his father. But if there was just the slightest chance . . .

Clay headed toward the back of the house. "I'd like you to come with me," Clay said to the ranch hand. "In fact, I'd like you to stand just inside the door and watch me." A witness, Clay hoped, would take care of any defense attorney who might try to say Clay introduced false evidence to the scene.

"You sure?" Higgins said. "My stomach ain't the strongest and—"

"Just watch to make sure I go straight through the kitchen. Then you can stare at your socks for all I care." The man nodded. Stocking-footed, he started to follow Clay.

"And if the sheriff gets here, let him know I went inside to look for Rooster. I won't be long."

"Leave the cigarette outside," Clay said as they reached the kitchen porch. He wanted this scene as pure as possible. Forensics had improved dramatically over the past ten years. Sometimes the crime was solved before the investigators took the last photographs.

Clay half-ran from room to room. There was no sign of Rooster. On his way back through the kitchen, Clay stopped for a full ten-count and studied the situation, trying to see it the way the murderer had seen it in leaving.

As the ranch hand had described, old Frank Evans was in a kitchen chair, throat severed so deep his head was tilted back.

Clay shivered. The tang of blood was like a kick in the stomach. It took effort not to look away. He'd been out of this for six years and was glad to be affected. One of the main reasons he had retired was because he'd become too detached from his victims, he'd become numb to almost all his emotions. Finally, he had decided life was too short to become a robot.

But now, even though he was feeling emotions, he knew they would only get in the way. He took a calming breath and pushed his feelings aside, stepping back into his past where dead bodies were merely pieces of meat.

Mentally he began to catalog what he observed. Nothing else

seemed to be disturbed or out of place. That told Clay something. Whoever killed Evans had not been searching for anything or had had enough time to search carefully; whoever killed Evans had been able to do it without a struggle.

No trails of blood led to the chair. It was safe to assume Evans had not been killed elsewhere and dragged to the chair. Instead, he'd been sitting there. The killer probably stood behind Evans, grabbed his hair, pulled the head back, and slashed with a knife. The autopsy would show whether the killer was left-handed or right-handed; it would also show the type of knife blade used. The killer was a strong man; a human throat and cartilage were tougher than most realized.

If the killer stood behind Evans's chair, either he had managed to sneak up or Evans knew him and had no reason to expect the assault. Clay would have to ask if the old man had been hard of hearing, which would have made it easier for someone to enter the kitchen without his knowing.

The blood at the base of the chair had stopped spreading, stopped dripping from Evans's soaked shirt. That told Clay the murder had happened earlier rather than later. Again, he could rely on forensics to help him there.

Clay saw one more thing of interest—real interest. He saw a boot-print in the edge of the pool of blood and more bootprints leading away, getting fainter with each succeeding step.

Clay squatted and with his hands above a bootprint, roughly measured the length.

He rose again and met Jess Higgins at the kitchen door. "Go and get your boots," Clay said. Higgins didn't ask why; he just rounded the house and returned a few moments later, carrying the boots. He handed them to Clay.

Clay didn't need to measure the ranch hand's boots against his earlier estimation. He merely lifted the boot and checked the soles for blood. There was none.

The footprints posed some interesting questions, Clay thought. If those were the killer's prints in the blood, why had he waited so long after slashing the rancher's throat? The blood needed time to reach the floor and form a puddle. The killer should have been long out of the kitchen by then. Had the killer waited beside the dead man, searching through the rancher's pockets or perhaps admiring his handiwork? Or had the killer returned after going through the rest of the house?

Or, if those weren't the killer's footprints in the blood, why hadn't that person called for help? Why had that person disappeared, and who was he or she?

Clay had a hunch. Most ranchers left their dirty shoes and boots on mats on the back porch, and the Evanses were no exception. He bent down and began examining the various types of footwear on the porch—from rubber boots to workboots to sneakers, and all soiled with mud and manure. There were only two sizes. Since only Frank and Rooster lived in the ranch house, Clay knew it was an easy conclusion that only their footwear was on the porch.

What disturbed him most was the fact that of the two distinctive sizes, one seemed to match the size of the bloody bootprint in the kitchen. The bootprint matched the size of Rooster's boots. And Rooster was missing.

Clay hoped it was a coincidence.

# 7:45 A.M.

Kelsie felt her head pressing against something hard and a sharp pain against her ribs. Her neck was bent, her feet tucked beneath her thighs, her hands stuck together and fingers numb. She heard a wind rush, a rumbling, a high-pitched hum of . . .

Kelsie tried to piece all of it together. Her eyes had watered badly, gumming the eyelids, and she blinked to try to focus. There was a crack of light above her in the darkness.

*High-pitched hum of . . . tires.*

She was in the trunk of a car, moving along a road at high speed.

Gradually it began to make sense. Her head was against the spare tire. She'd been folded, legs bent beneath her, neck twisted forward. Her ankles and wrists were bound—it felt like tape. The loss of circulation hurt her fingers. The sharp pain in her ribs was . . .

She shifted, trying to relieve the pressure. The pain ceased. She'd been thrown on top of a briefcase. Her briefcase? That meant she was probably in her BMW. She'd been exhausted upon arriving at the apartment and had stumbled in without removing it from the trunk.

Then, with an intake of breath, she remembered.

Her bathroom. She'd been in the bathroom. She'd just gotten out of the shower and was toweling herself dry. She heard a slight sound behind her and had begun to turn her head. She'd glimpsed a figure in the fogged mirror but had seen no more. A wet cloth had been put over her face. She'd gasped with horror, instinctively pulling in a lungful of air against the cloth that she thought was meant to smother her. Then blackness.

If she was in her own BMW, someone must have carried her down the stairs into the garage. That same person must have dressed her. Her fingertips were pressed against her waist; she could the fabric of a sweatshirt. Her legs were covered. Blue jeans?

Kelsie was surprised at herself, how calmly she was taking this. For twenty-three years this was the situation she had dreaded, anticipated, expected. For twenty-three years, it had been a sword hanging above her, twisting on a thread. Now that the thread had snapped, it was almost a relief.

Who had taken her? The question sprang into her mind as if she were observing another person.

That answer would almost be a relief. When the trunk opened, she would look into his face and finally discover the answer to a question she had taken to sleep every night since the summer of her sixteenth birthday. Who was the man who watched her? What would he do?

Kelsie began to imagine the worst. She told herself to stop. She told herself there was no sense in going through horror twice. The one time, when it actually happened, would be bad enough. She made up her mind to fight him with all her strength, to die fighting. When that trunk opened, she would . . .

*The briefcase!* It held her cell phone.

She twisted more, grunting with effort.

The car accelerated and rocked from one side, then to the other. The driver—her kidnapper—must have passed a car. Where were they going? More importantly, were they still in the valley's cellular zone?

It took a few minutes of effort in the cramped quarters of the trunk, but Kelsie finally got the briefcase free from beneath her body.

Fortunately, her abductor had bound her wrists in front of her, not behind her back. She flexed and bent her fingers, trying to get the circulation going. It took more minutes of fumbling to snap open the briefcase locks.

The car rocked over a few bumps. She froze, hoping the briefcase didn't turn over. If the cell phone fell out, it might land out of reach.

Gingerly, balancing herself by pushing against the interior of the trunk, she reached into the briefcase and felt around. She let out a deep sigh as her hands closed on the familiar shape of her cell phone.

She pulled it up in front of her face and hit the power button with her thumb. The key pad lit up. Her eyes, though, were on the display. What kind of reception strength remained?

Seconds later, she got her answer. The blinking display meant she was on the fringes of the cell zone. It was fifty-fifty whether her call would ring through. If it did, she might get nothing but crackle. The car might reach the top of a hill and give her a clear call, or it might hit a valley and disconnect. She might get thirty seconds, she might get five minutes.

One call, Lord, she prayed. Just one call.

With her forefinger, she punched in the number to the ranch house. Then she hit the send button.

For too many heartbeats, the phone remained dead. Then it crackled slightly before the blessed relief of the pulsating ring filled her ear.

*Oh Lord*, she prayed. *One other favor. Please let Clay be home.*

One ring. Two rings. Three . . .

The answering machine kicked in. Clay's rounded, drawling syllables greeted her. She wanted to smash the phone in anger and frustration. The reception began to crackle. Had they reached the end of cellular coverage? Or just a dip in the road?

*Hurry, hurry, hurry,* Kelsie pleaded as she listened to the familiar taped message. *At least let me leave a message.*

The crackling eased slightly and the answering machine finally beeped.

"Clay," she said, conscious that she might lose contact at any second. "He's taken me. The one from the beginning. He's finally taken me. In my car. Watch he doesn't kill you. Like the others before. Pray for me, Clay. Save me."

She took a breath. If you only had ten seconds to say something to the person you loved, what would it be? "The dancer has the notes. Look there. Then you'll know." The crackling intensified.

"I love you, Clay." She felt herself begin to sob. "I love you."

Dead air. She'd been speaking into dead air. How much had gotten through?

She pulled the phone away. When she was finally able to see through her tears, the display confirmed what she already knew: no signal strength. She was out of the cell zone and getting farther away every minute.

The tires continued to whine. The wind continued to rush.

Slowly, as if swimming through a dream, she managed to tuck the cell phone into the front of her jeans and pulled her sweatshirt down to cover it. Then she closed her eyes.

Eventually, the tires would stop whining, the wind rush would die, and the rocking of springs would cease. At that point, when the car stopped and the driver stepped out from behind the steering wheel, she could expect the trunk to open—and the worst to happen.

# 8:31 A.M.

James answered the front doorbell. It took him a few moments to remember the man standing outside, an Indian in blue jeans and vest. Fat, layered like slabs of Plasticine, had thickened the man's face. But the eyes were the same, as was the braided hair, except for strands of gray. Behind the man was a black Chevy four-by-four pickup.

"You worked at the ranch, right?" James said as greeting. "I'm sorry I can't recall your name."

When the man went to pull off his vest, James invited him in. The man ignored James and set the vest on the railing of the porch. The action puzzled James, especially when the man began to unbutton his shirt.

"I guess you want to play games," the man said. "Take a look, I'm not wired."

"Wired?" James wondered if wired was a term younger people used instead of drunk and if so, figured the man was indeed wired, especially as he took his shirt off and set it over the vest. The man's huge belly was a solid ball sprinkled with gray hairs.

"Wired. For sound. You don't need to pretend you don't know me." The man unbuckled his belt. "Bottom half's clean, too. Hope you don't have any shy women around."

"Hang on, mister," James said, grabbing the man's shirt and shoving it at him. "You and me have a serious miscommunication going here. You leave them pants in place and explain to me exactly what you're trying to say."

The man shrugged. "We'll waste a lot of time if you want to keep playing dumb."

James had had enough. "Don't stand on my porch and insult me. Speak clear or leave. What's your name?"

"Sonny Cutknife. I'm in administration on the Flathead reservation. You might recall when you guys put me there and why."

James felt like he'd stepped onto a stage without a script. "Put you there?"

"Put me there. Look, you can dance around all you want, McNeill, but I won't. I'll get straight to it. I've been feeding all of you through Emerald Canyon long enough. But I can see the writing on the wall. Anderson tells me to burn down the office to get rid of the files, I do it. All you got to do is listen to the news this morning, you'll know it's all been torched."

"Anderson?" James repeated. None of this made the slightest sense to him.

Sonny Cutknife shook his head in exaggerated disgust. "Wayne Anderson." He raised his voice. "Wayne Anderson. And twenty years of kickback fees from the casino to Emerald Canyon corporations for use of recreational facilities and certain permits from county council. Would I be talking this loud and this clear if there were recording devices? This is not a sting operation, McNeill. This is me coming to collect."

Sonny crossed his arms. "I don't want much. At least percentage-wise. I'm not greedy. Give me a million, and I'm on my way. Not only that, but I'm out of the country."

"You have me at a loss, Mr. Cutknife."

"A big loss, McNeill. I've got enough of a paper trail to nail you and your friends to the cross of my choice. Thought you were dealing with a stupid Indian, didn't you? Well, you were all wrong. Now's the time to pay for that mistake."

"You misunderstood me," James said.

"I don't think so. And don't try anything stupid like getting rid of me the way you did Hairy Mocassin. If that happens, you'll have attorneys swarming all over you."

James grabbed Sonny by the elbow and escorted him down the steps, off the front porch. "I have little idea of what you mean, and even less interest in pursuing it further," he said firmly. "You get in that truck of yours and off my property. Come back again making threats, and you'll find yourself facing a shotgun."

# 9:01 A.M.

*"You stupid, ungrateful brat." The voice thundered at the boy from across the kitchen table. "You eat the food I buy. You wear the clothes I give you. And how do you repay me? How?"*

*The boy ducked his head. He truly was sorry. Not for what he had done to the cat, but because he'd been stupid afterward. He should have buried the body in the woods where no one would find it.*

*Instead, he'd dropped it into the trash can and covered it with newspapers and rocks. The trash man had noticed the cat while emptying the can. He had noticed the missing limbs and the empty eye sockets. Now the boy was paying the price for his stupidity.*

*"Jed, hold your temper," his mother said. "Please? You know what happens when you fly off the handle."*

*"What!" he shouted. "What! Do you have any idea what he did to that cat? He's a sick kid. And he's going to get a taste of his own medicine."*

*The man stood and yanked his belt out from his pants. He folded the belt in half and held both ends in one hand. The looped belt gave him a solid strip of double leather. "Strip your pants, kid. Get your butt over here."*

*"Jed, he—"*

*"Your son's going to be lucky if I leave him any skin."*

*"Jed, you can't. He's just—"*

*"Shut your mouth, woman. Or you'll get the same. I'm the man in this house."*

*"No." It was a rare flash of defiance from her.*

*"No?" He grinned. "No? Then you make your choice, woman. Him or me."*

*"Jed . . ."*

*"Make your choice. Him or me. I do it my way, or I walk."*

*The boy's mother looked back and forth between the two of them. She licked her upper lip nervously. Then she got up from her chair and went to the kitchen sink. She kept her back turned on the two and busied herself doing dishes.*

*Smiling, the man crooked his finger at the boy.*

*The boy walked around the table over to his stepfather. He was deter-mined not to give the man the satisfaction of seeing any fear.*

*The first lash of the belt cracked across his skin. It stung so badly that the boy gasped despite his determination to be stoic.*

*The belt came down a second time, then a third. The boy bit his lip. Tears ran down his face, but he didn't make a sound.*

*The lack of reaction enraged the man. He brought the belt down again and again, trying to get the boy to cry out.*

*Soon, the boy lost track of how many times the belt whipped his bare buttocks. Soon, it didn't matter. The cold, sullen hate that grew and fed on the pain was more than worth the price.*

The Watcher drove slowly beneath the low branches of a spruce tree. The needles screeched against the rooftop. He put the car in park and cut the ignition. From beneath the tree, he could see parts of the small lake ahead. Large splats of rain brought rings to the lake's surface as if hundreds of trout were rising.

For several minutes, the Watcher remained in the car. He enjoyed the smell of the leather of the BMW's interior. It smelled of her per-fume. Good perfume, not like the rose perfume of his nightmares.

When he finally pushed the door open, he had to duck against the sweeping branches. Accumulated rainwater ran from the spruce needles down the collar of his jacket and onto the skin of his neck and shoulders.

He stepped out from the tree, shrugged, and smiled. The dis-comfort of the cold rain was nothing compared to all the pleasure ahead of him.

For a moment, he fought the temptation to return beneath the branches and open the trunk of the BMW. She was there waiting for him. After all these years.

He came so close to yielding that he actually checked his wrist-watch to see if he indeed had extra time. *No,* he told himself, *patience. Don't add risk to the equation.* His careful plans did not include immedi-ate satisfaction. The infinite rewards would come later with the clock-work smoothness of the events falling into place as long anticipated.

With a sigh of regret and joy, he began to work. Earlier, he had cut branches from other spruce trees and left them piled near the tree. Now, he placed them strategically until the branches hid from view what little of the BMW had been visible in the first place. Chances were extremely small that a hiker or fisherman would walk within a half-mile of the car, let alone five feet; now a passerby would actually have to crawl beneath the tree to see the BMW.

When he finished, the Watcher released another sigh. With so much done and so close to the end, he still had many details remaining.

After a final look back, he walked away. He had parked his own vehicle a mile away, reducing the chance anybody could link him to the BMW if, by freak coincidence, someone actually found it before his return.

His footsteps were muffled by the soft, wet ground. Within minutes, the lake and trees were out of sight.

Rain dripped across his face. He smiled as he walked.

# 9:14 A.M.

The house seemed empty, cold, and gray when Clay returned. Even with Johnny and George again in the kitchen, settling down with fresh coffee, the house seemed empty.

The rain had been building steadily until it was now at a full downpour. More reason for Clay to be depressed. Rain wiped away footprints, debris. There hadn't been much chance of finding Taylor anyway. The rain brought it down to zero.

If that wasn't enough, the Kalispell sheriff, Matt Brody, wanted to delay bringing in FBI help for a day or two. Clay had been part of the territorial squabbles before and had hated it then as much as now, except now he felt he was paying a personal price for it.

Back at the house, Clay's first move, after pointing Johnny to the coffeepot, was to head for the answering machine near the hallway phone. He had been gone at least two hours at the Evans ranch, enough for Clay to discover along with the sheriff that, aside from the bloody footprint, there was little to discover.

Maybe in the two hours someone had called with news about Taylor, he thought. Even a threatening phone call or a ransom phone call was better than nothing.

Clay hit rewind. The first message was an apology from Lawson; the weather made it difficult for an aerial search, but he would be checking every hour to see when he could take his plane up. Then came the endless messages from neighbors offering help or sympathy.

After a while, the voices became no more than a jumbled chorus. Clay was tired and gritty from lack of sleep and from worry and stress. All that kept him listening was the hope that there would be news about Taylor. Then, finally, came Kelsie.

Her voice—clearly hers despite the static hissing with it—brought Clay to full alert.

"Clay, he's taken me. The one from the beginning. He's finally taken me. In my car. Watch he doesn't kill you. Like the others before. Pray for me, Clay. Save me."

Ironically, the static fell away just as she drew her breath, and he heard the edge of panic in it. As she began to speak again, the crackling intensified. "The dancer has the notes. Look"—a white wave of crackling static blurred her words—"then you'll know."

Her voice faded as the hissing rose. "—you Clay." Sobbing. "I—"

Galvanized, he rewound and replayed her message. He replayed it three more times, copying it word for word into a notebook he'd had ready near the answering machine in case there had been a ransom call. He guessed at the amount of words lost to the static.

*Clay, he's taken me. The one from the beginning. He's finally taken me. In my car. Watch he doesn't kill you. Like the others before. Pray for me, Clay. Save me. The dancer has the notes. Look —then you'll know. — —you Clay. I— — —???*

Clay sat heavily on the chair beside the phone, hardly able to comprehend the message he'd put on paper.

*The one from the beginning.* What beginning? *Finally.* What did finally imply? He'd tried before?

*In her car.* If she was in her car with him, why was he allowing her to speak?

*Killed like the others before.* What others? Why would he kill Clay?

*Save me.* The terror in her plea ripped at his stomach like shards of swallowed glass.

*The dancer has the notes.* Dancer. Someone she knew? Trusted enough to keep notes? When she didn't trust Clay? A man? In the arts? Jealousy darkened Clay's thoughts.

*I— — —* ??? Clay underlined the question marks at the end of the final sentence. He had no idea how long she had spoken after beginning the sentence, no clue to its direction.

He stared fiercely at the notes, as if the intensity of his thoughts would bring sense to the words. It wasn't until Johnny lightly nudged Clay with a cup of coffee that Clay realized anyone had joined him.

"Bad news?" Johnny asked.

Clay didn't answer. He reached for the phone and dialed a number he knew by heart.

"McNeill, McNeill & Madigan. How may I help you?"

"Julie, it's Clay. May I speak to Kelsie?"

"Mr. Garner, I'm afraid she's not in."

"Did she leave a message explaining why?"

"Funny you should ask," Julie replied. "It's very unusual. She never keeps clients waiting, and two of them have already been here a half-hour."

Clay took the phone away from his ear and slammed it against his other palm. He was about to hang up when a thought struck him. *Lawson. Maybe he could help.*

"Julie," he said quickly, "can you put me through to Lawson?"

"He's on a conference call. Could I take a—"

"Julie, trust me. Put me through."

"But—"

"Now." Clay's voice hardened so drastically that Johnny raised an inquiring eyebrow.

Ten seconds later, Lawson came on the line. "What is it?" he asked. "Taylor? News on Taylor?"

Clay made a note of mental gratitude that Lawson had not wasted time by sputtering about the interruption. This, the Lawson who had a reputation for counting billing time down to the final second. Clay felt a surge of warmth for his brother-in-law.

"No news," Clay said, "and I appreciate your offer to take the plane up as soon as the weather breaks."

Clay stopped to get strength. "Lawson, I think Kelsie's been kidnapped too."

"Hang on."

Ten seconds.

"I'm out of the other call. You've got my full attention. What in Sam—"

Clay explained as well as he could. On Clay's end, Johnny listened impassively.

"Any of it make sense to you, Lawson?" Clay finished. "The one from before. Others killed."

"No," Lawson said slowly. "It doesn't make sense to me at all. Not unless it's a client. But even that doesn't make sense. You know as well as I do that she didn't do criminal law."

"This is important," Clay said. "And at this point, I don't care much about ethics, legalities, or the firm's reputation. Can you pull me a complete list of her clients? I'll be by within the hour." Before Lawson could answer, Clay said, "Better yet, could you pull the list and go through it first? Underline anybody you think might be off balance. And I mean anybody. We've got to start somewhere."

"Yes." Lawson's voice was crisp. "You'll get my list of clients too."

Again, Clay felt warmth for his brother-in-law. It was a generous offer.

"I'm calling the sheriff next," Clay said, then paused. The next question would hurt, especially if Lawson had the answer. "Lawson, Kelsie moved into town. But she didn't give me her address. I'm wondering if she passed it on to you."

There was a long pause.

"I need the sheriff to send someone over to her new place," Clay said. "With Taylor gone, I can't afford to believe this is anything but a kidnapping."

"Twelve-forty McDonald Drive," Lawson said.

Clay closed his eyes against the pain. She could tell Lawson but not him.

"Thanks," Clay said. He felt like a punching bag with the sand draining from a hole in the bottom. "I'll keep you up to date."

He hung up on Lawson, not wanting to hear any pity.

"Not good," Johnny said.

*That I don't even know where my own wife has moved? Or that she's gone?*

"Not good," Clay said.

He dialed the sheriff's office. It was small consolation that this might be enough to convince Brody it was time to bring in the FBI.

## 9:43 A.M.

The darkness continued for Taylor. Sometime after he woke, he became aware of the discomfort of his pants. His diaper was damp and cold. Usually his dad changed it.

"Me, cowboy!" Taylor shouted again and again into the darkness.

That always brought his father, usually with a smile on his face. If he was nearby, he would have turned on the lights and helped Taylor with his diapers.

There was no one.

Taylor moved away from the man beneath the blanket. He pulled his pants down, which took much concentration, especially in the dark. It took him another equally long stretch of time to finally remove the diaper. He dropped it on the floor, then slowly, awkwardly pulled his pants up.

He felt his music-maker, the harmonica, in one pocket and pulled it out. He brought the harmonica to his mouth. Then he stopped. Taylor felt a knot in his stomach. He had long since eaten the other chocolate bar. Since then, no one had come by to give him something to eat.

"Me, cowboy!" he shouted. "Me, hungry!"

No one answered.

"Me, cowboy! Me, hungry!"

Taylor waited. He was beginning to feel cold.

He found the blankets again, sat down, and pulled them over his legs.

He put the harmonica to his mouth and began to blow sounds. Taylor couldn't put his feelings into words, but he could use his heart to put it into sounds. He was sad.

# 9:58 A.M.

"They found Rooster's truck near the condo?" James echoed the information.

Clay nodded. They were sitting at the kitchen table. Clay had driven down the road to speak to James in person. Where he needed to take the conversation was not something he wanted to do over the telephone.

"Sheriff said it was found a couple blocks away. His registration, Murray Paul Evans, was in it." Clay hadn't pressed the sheriff for more information. He knew too well how rigidly many law-enforcement men protected their territory. A retired Bureau man with a personal stake in the situation would definitely be a threat. At the Evans ranch, they'd treated him as a bystander, not someone who could help.

"Rooster? Kidnapping Kelsie?" James was asking himself the

questions. "I've known him since grasshoppers could wrestle him to the ground. He doesn't seem the type. On the other hand, he's always been sweet on Kelsie. Long-suffering and sweet."

"Well," Clay said, "he *could* be the type: no mother; raised in relative isolation; time to brood and become obsessive."

"You don't sound a hundred percent convinced."

"James, if he kidnapped Kelsie, he's either stupid or doesn't care we know he did it. Leaving his truck nearby is about as plain as writing a letter saying he did it."

"Maybe he planned on coming back to get the truck."

"I've thought about that,"Clay said. "Maybe he took her in her car because he didn't want to risk any witnesses. Maybe he did expect to come back and get the truck before anyone knew she was gone. Maybe something happened, and he couldn't get back in time. Or maybe someone left his truck there and wanted it to look like Rooster's the one."

"Then who?" James asked.

Clay stared out the window. "That's why I'm here. There's not much I can do myself on this, at least in terms of a physical search. The sheriff and his entire department have those kind of resources. Difficult as it is to do, I've got to leave it in their hands. All I can do is ask questions."

He looked directly at James. "I'd like to know about the men in her past."

"There was plenty she wanted to leave behind and forget."

"I know this won't be easy," Clay said. "She's your daughter. My wife. I'll be asking you questions I never asked her. But we both want to find her, and time is precious."

*Or time doesn't matter,* Clay thought. *She could already be dead.*

James nodded. He looked older, grayer than he had the week before.

Clay read from his notepad. It gave them both the chance to focus on a third-party object.

"I returned to the valley in '89." Clay said. "Kelsie was thirty-three years old then. We married a year later."

"A fine wedding," James said. "You made a fine couple."

"She was thirty-four then," Clay wasn't going to let this become a conversation. "I wasn't her first boyfriend. Yet, in six years of marriage, she never once told me about any of the previous men in her life. It wasn't my business, so I never asked. And now I'm asking."

"I'll do my best," James said. It looked like it was taking the old man effort to breathe. "I know she had some difficult years."

"Was she ever serious with anyone?"

"In college she met a fellow. Down in Great Falls. She brought him home a few weekends. I believe they meant to get engaged. He seemed like a nice enough boy."

"And?"

"Turned out he wasn't as nice as it seemed. Had a drug habit."

"So she dropped him."

"No." James shook his head for emphasis. "No, she definitely didn't drop him. Fact is, when he died, it broke her heart. She quit school for a year. Doctors called it clinical depression, and they had to prescribe some fancy medication. She came back to live with me. Sometimes weeks would go by, and she wouldn't leave the house."

"Died," Clay said. *Watch he doesn't kill you. Like the others before.*

"From what I gathered, it was a drug overdose. The one time I tried to discuss it with her, Kelsie nearly went crazy. I had to call the doc, and he sedated her. You can see why it wasn't something any of us talked about."

"His name?"

"Couldn't remember if you gave me a hundred years."

"Would Lawson remember?" Clay asked.

James wrinkled his eyebrows in thought. "Let's see. Kelsie was probably twenty then, which means it was seventy-seven."

The old man did more arithmetic silently.

"No," James concluded. "I doubt Lawson would remember. Or even knew about it. He was back east at Harvard Law School. Determined to do it on his own. He wrote me plenty wouldn't accept help. He kept a job there, went about making a name for himself without relying on me. He was so determined to do it on his own, I can't recall him even coming back for a visit for six or seven years, not until Michael's funeral."

James shook his head. "Let me tell you, that was difficult on Lawson. You probably know that he and Michael had a falling-out."

"A little of it," Clay said. "Kelsie hasn't talked much about those years."

"No one knows why they fought," James said. "But it was an all-out fistfight outside a bar in Kalispell a few months before Lawson headed east. They simply stopped speaking to each other. I could almost see it going through Lawson's head at Michael's funeral, that

Michael had died and they'd never resolved whatever it was that tore up their friendship."

James grimaced. "Sorry. Old history. You're asking me about Kelsie, and I drifted . . ."

"Did Kelsie have any other serious boyfriends?" Clay asked.

"I guess it depends how you define serious," James answered. "Seems to me it was a couple years later—don't hold me to it exactly—she did spend some time visiting a fellow in Whitefish. It was winter, and Kelsie skied Big Mountain three or four times a week, when before she skied maybe once a month. Rumors reached me about a handsome instructor. I didn't mind, of course, because her old smile had returned. The only time I mentioned it, though, she made a big to-do about denying it."

"You never met him?"

"Never even knew his name."

"It ended that winter?" Clay didn't like this, digging into his wife's past.

"Before the end of the winter. She just stopped skiing altogether."

It was Clay's turn to do math. "She would have been twenty-three? Twenty-four?"

"Something like that. Whatever went wrong with the ski instructor, it put her off men. She didn't even date for the longest time."

James paused.

"Until . . ." Clay prompted.

"A rodeo cowboy. Fellow by the name of Tommy Bell. They took to each other like glue on paper. Reminded me of me and Maggie, how hot they were." James stopped himself. "My apologies, Clay."

"What's past is past, James. She married me, and I'm glad for it. Go on."

James rubbed his face. It took several moments before he said, "Tommy died too. He died with Michael in the whitewater rafting accident. They'd become good friends. They found Tommy's body. Michael's"—James looked away—"Well, Kelsie probably told you. They figured he got wedged in some of the underwater boulders."

Kelsie *hadn't* told him the details of Michael's death. Early in their courtship, Clay had once asked her about Michael. She visibly tensed and asked Clay not to mention the subject. They had ended the evening early, and a week had passed before she returned Clay's call.

*Watch he doesn't kill you. Like the others before.*

"She was in her late twenties," Clay said, wanting confirmation.

"Around that. Out of law school by then. She really threw herself into work."

"Any other boyfriends after Tommy?"

"Not until you returned."

"Did her choice surprise you?"

"She needed someone rock steady, Clay. I was glad for her. And for you. Things seemed pretty good."

Things had been good, Clay remembered, until Taylor was born with an extra chromosome. Then she gradually hardened. The office began to take more of her time and home less. Passion eroded to obligation. It became Clay and his little cowboy—his missing little cowboy—with her on the outside.

"You know she moved out," Clay said. "Last Sunday."

"She told me yesterday morning when you called about Taylor. She wanted to talk to me about Emerald Canyon. You know anything about that?"

"No," Clay said. "You think it has anything to do with her kidnapping?"

"I doubt it." James hesitated, as if he was going to say something else. He shut his mouth, opened it again. "When you find her, you going to stay with my daughter?"

Clay thought of the nights Kelsie had been gone, of the evasive answers she had given him. In her desperate message, she hadn't said anything about loving him.

"Yes," Clay finally said. "If she agrees, I'll go the distance. She's my wife."

"Love?" the old rancher asked. "Or Christian duty?"

"How do you separate one from the other?" Clay said. Not that, at this point, he could answer the question himself.

Their silence became uncomfortable.

"Well," Clay finally said, standing, "I've got to keep moving."

James nodded, not asking Clay about his plans.

Clay did not want to explain, for then he would have to explain his suspicions about Kelsie, suspicions that meant he was going to have to go through the contents of Kelsie's office. The sheriff might have already been there, but Clay doubted it. The sheriff had no reason to suspect Kelsie had been hiding something. The sheriff had no reason to suspect Kelsie had another man in her life, one who might be involved in the kidnapping and at the very least might have some answers.

Clay, however, wondered if Kelsie was having an affair. He wasn't sure he wanted to find proof of it in her office or anywhere else.

# 11:59 a.m.

"Julie, I hope you don't mind." Clay stood in the reception area of the law firm. He held a file folder in his hand, one she had handed him. "I need to spend time in Kelsie's office."

"No, no, no," Julie said quickly. "I don't mind at all."

Julie was short, brown-haired, and happily pregnant. She was also regarding Clay with the sort of expression saved for recent widowers. That, along with the nervous pity in her voice, meant Lawson must have told her some of why Clay had needed the file.

She busied herself by shuffling the papers on her desk as he walked past her. Clay's only relief was the fact that Lawson was engaged in another conference call. Grateful as Clay was for Lawson's help, he didn't want to talk to anyone at this point.

Down the hallway, he turned into Kelsie's office. He shut the door behind him, locked it, and surveyed the room.

Her desk—large, gleaming walnut—was bare, except for a stack of file folders of what Clay assumed contained ongoing legal work. Her telephone and computer monitor rested on an attached side desk. Clay knew Kelsie's work habits. She liked the sense of control given by having only one file open and spread out on her desk at any given time. At the end of the day, she would neatly return all the paperwork to an unfinished file, with careful notes attached to break down her billing time to that point. She had not returned to the office that morning; no files had been opened on the polished desktop.

The rest of the office was like any other law office in the country, with bookshelves, diplomas, and two chairs opposite Kelsie's desk for clients. Unlike any other law office, this one, though, held an eight-by-ten framed photo of Kelsie, Taylor, and Clay taken after church one afternoon in sunshine on the front yard of James McNeill's house. A much happier day than this one, Clay thought. Alongside that photo was one other, showing a much younger James McNeill, along with Lawson, Michael, and Rooster Evans, grinning proudly in front of an airplane they purchased together, their youth emphasized by bell-bottom blue jeans and long hair.

Despite the legitimacy of his visit, Clay felt vaguely guilty to be stepping uninvited into Kelsie's domain. He would need to go through her diary and her desk, looking for any clues that might explain recent events. Clay could not shake his nagging doubts about their relationship; given the opportunity, a jealous husband would be doing exactly this, checking on his wife for any signs of an affair.

To prove to himself he was not a suspicious husband, he stayed away from her Daytimer, although it would have been his first step as an investigating official. The Daytimer would give him a list of strangers and friends she had seen, a list of people to call with questions.

He should be going through her desk, too, looking for anything unusual. Was he afraid of what he might find? Or who he might find in her life?

Clay stared sightlessly at the bookshelf against the far wall. Suddenly an object came into focus: an antique music box on the top shelf, with a lid that opened to store jewelry in the velvet lining inside. Kelsie had inherited the music box from her mother. Once, during an afternoon when Clay had helped Kelsie rearrange the furniture in the office, she'd wound it. After opening and closing the lid, the tiny ballerina on top turned on a spindle to the tune of "Waltz of the Flowers" from *The Nutcracker.*

The music box seemed out of place. Aside from the family portrait—and Clay wondered if it was displayed for clients' benefit—the music box was the only sentimental object in the office. Clay believed he understood why. Kelsie had had a very special relationship with her mother. One afternoon, she had played her dancer again and again, telling Clay childhood stories he'd never heard from her before. Staring at the music box, it occurred to Clay that he could not recall that Kelsie possessed any other object from her life before they had met and married.

Then it hit him, so obvious he was furious at himself for not thinking of it sooner.

*Dancer. The dancer has the notes.*

He moved to it quickly and set it down on her desk. The end of the tune weakly tinkled as the ballerina came to the end of her dance.

Within seconds, he found the false bottom and pulled it up. A stack of notes filled the bottom. He removed the stack and went back to Kelsie's desk, reading the top note as he walked, so stunned by the words that he was hardly aware that he'd found his way to the chair.

> Darling, please show how truly you love me. Delay my request no longer. It is tedious and dangerous work to remove snake fangs. Next time I may not have the patience. Next time I may leave the gift for someone close to you. Remember the others.

The handwriting was in dark, heavy pencil. At the top, in Kelsie's neat handwriting, was a date, the previous Thursday. Clay was staggered by the implications of the note. Snake fangs? Had Kelsie been attacked by a snake? And not said anything to him?

He flipped the note over and read the next one. It was dated with Kelsie's handwriting two weeks earlier.

> Darling, here is my request. I have been very patient, enduring for years already the time you have spent with another man. Now, however, you must live separately from him. Find a place in town. If you don't, he will die. If he hears of me, he will die. Then, too, will your son. Keep the silence. You know this is not an empty threat.

Clay felt the strange mixture of rage, relief, and frustration. There was another man in Kelsie's life, but not in the way he had feared. Instead, it was much worse than he had feared. The monster had bludgeoned Kelsie with threats and terror . . .

Clay went through note after note, all with the same penciled block letters. They were arranged in reverse dates, as if Kelsie had put each note on top of the other as they arrived in her life. He felt sick as he read one from 1988:

> Your cowboy will ride no more rodeos. Michael is dead too. They would have lived, had you not defied me. Will you remember the lesson now? Save yourself for me. Someday, I promise, we will be together . . .

He flipped through more notes and saw one dated ten years earlier:

You wake up to this note, my love. Let me be the first to tell you. The ski instructor has moved on from this world. He went quickly, too quickly for me to enjoy. But the end result is the same. Again, it is only you and me. See how I love you? I tolerate no others and never will. Your love is my power, and my power is your love.

In March of 1976:

Nathan is dead, my love. The fool dared to attempt taking you away from me. The world will see it as a drug overdose, but you and I know differently, do we not? As always, I do this with the love that burns forever.

Another note sent waves of revulsion through Clay.

Undress near the window tonight, my love. You know how I love to watch. I need not mention the consequences if you disappoint me.

Clay bowed his head and rubbed his eyes. What an incredible burden she had had to carry for all these years! What had it been like for her? The information James had given him earlier in the day only hinted at her lonely torment: quitting school, broken heart, clinical depression. Clay thought it was a miracle the woman's spirit had not been broken.

He forced himself to return to the notes. The one at the bottom, dated the earliest, July, 1973, struck him with words like bullets.

My love, I am not dead. The world may believe I died in the cabin fire, but I promise you, I still carry my love for you. Do you now understand how far beyond the fools of this world I am? Even in the writing of this note, you should see how I am able to toy with those fools. There is no more need to pretend I am something I am not. The false scent given by broken grammar and almost crazed ramblings is gone. Why? I am assured you will not pass this note—or future ones—on to anyone. For if you do share the knowledge that I am alive, I will strike those nearest to you. They will pay the price for your betrayal. Do my bidding in all

things, my love, and all shall be good. Fail me, and more shall follow Doris and Nick into the dark beyond.

The burden had been upon her since the summer of her sixteenth
birthday, Clay thought. Everyone else in her life had moved on,
believing the horror over, and she'd been left to carry the agony for
the rest of them.

Clay placed the notes back together, in the order he had read
them. His hands moved with slow, precise actions, as if he were
brittle and the slightest movement might break him. And that was
exactly how he felt. Brittle, old, and sorrowfully afraid for Kelsie.

# 12:30 P.M.

James McNeill, sitting in his usual chair overlooking the valley, had
his cordless telephone in his lap. He knew he would use it, just didn't
want to. He was afraid of what he might find out.

Reluctant or not, he would make the call. Kelsie and Taylor were
gone. Clay had his own ways of trying to find them. James would do
what he could. If he found anything to help Clay, he would pass it
along. If the phone call gave James nothing, then he himself could
close the lid on this can of worms and leave an old friendship intact.

All of this because of Sonny Cutknife. James had given the unexpected visit much thought. Sonny Cutknife had come in, blustering
with his innuendos and an Emerald Canyon payoff. Earlier, Kelsie
had dropped her Emerald Canyon accusations. It was obvious, then,
that there was a dead and stinking skunk buried somewhere. Sonny
and Kelsie both figured James was it.

He wondered if Emerald Canyon had anything to do with
Kelsie's disappearance. What had she told him the morning Taylor
was kidnapped? *A $55 million lawsuit against six corporations.*
*Corporate directors facing criminal charges. A scandal ripping apart the*
*power structure of the entire valley.*

If she'd accused anyone else—say, an owner of one of those corporations—was the threat of a lawsuit and criminal charges reason
enough for that person to have kidnapped her? Especially if it might
seem like the kidnapping happened for an unrelated reason?

James wanted to find out. If if was information Clay needed, Clay
would get it, regardless of the consequences.

Sonny had given James one name, the name of a man James hoped was not part of those six corporations. If he was, James wondered, would years of friendship and favors be enough to get some of the truth?

There was only one way to find out. James began to dial.

The phone on the other end of the line rang five times. The phone was answered with a long pause before someone finally said, "Anderson residence."

James blinked. This was not Wayne. The voice was younger, stronger, and hesitant.

"I'd like to speak with Wayne," James said.

"May I tell him who is calling?"

"An old friend."

"I'd appreciate it if—"

"You tell Wayne if he's got to screen his calls, he's a sorry old twit trying to seem important."

James grinned. He knew that would get Wayne on the phone immediately, huffing and puffing with indignation.

James heard the sound of the phone being set down. There was muffled background discussion enough to puzzle James.

The phone was picked up. "Mr. McNeill," a voice said. "This is Sheriff Matt Brody. How are you today?"

Brody? What was happening.

"I'm fine," James said. "I'd also appreciate knowing what's going on. Why have some young snot ask me for my name if you already know?"

"Caller I.D. Anderson had it on his phone system. My deputy was merely trying to confirm it was you. When he passed on your message for Anderson, it seemed likely to be you."

*Had?* Anderson *had* it on his phone system? Why speak of Anderson in the past tense? For that matter, why was the sheriff at Anderson's? And answering Anderson's phone?

"This is a real coincidence," Brody said. "You were on my list of people to call. Partly because of Anderson and partly because of your son-in-law."

"Clay?"

"Yeah. He's not up at the ranch. Any idea where we can find him?"

"He called me maybe an hour ago to see if I'd heard anything,"

James answered. "Said he was looking for Russ Fowler. I told him about Russ being in the hospital. I assume he went there. You want to tell me what's happening?"

"With Clay? I'm not sure yet. I was on my way to his ranch when I got radioed here," Brody said. "As for this? First Evans. Now Anderson. Someone's on a hot streak right now. This is Kalispell, not Los Angeles. I'm supposed to deal with car break-ins and speeding tickets, not murder."

# 1:05 P.M.

"Let me tell you straight off so you don't sit there wondering," Russ Fowler told Clay. "It's a lymph node cancer. I intend to kick around awhile longer, no matter what the doctors tell me."

Clay wondered if he'd been able to hide his surprise when he walked into the hospital room and saw Fowler lost in the center of the bed. Clay remembered the former sheriff as a vigorous, barrel-chested man. If ever a person needed to understand the frailty of human life, Fowler would have provided the lesson, Clay thought. The skin on his skull and face had tightened to the point of shininess; on the rest of his body his skin sagged where muscle and flesh had disappeared.

"I've gotten used to most of it," Fowler continued. "Even the pain gets to be something you can't imagine you ever lived without. What I hate, though, is the food. Not that it's bad. I'd like it if I could tell it was bad. No, for some reason I can't taste. You can't believe how much you lose when you can't taste."

Clay was looking around. Fowler was in a private suite. How much would that cost? Where had Fowler gotten the money for it? No health insurance paid for private suites.

"You did good after you left the valley. What was it? Twenty-some years ago? I heard you moved up fast in the Bureau. Made a name for yourself. Glad to hear it."

Fowler was talking plenty, Clay thought. Probably trying to plug any silence before it got started. Curious as Clay was, angry as he was, however, he sat down and settled back in a chair. No sense warning Fowler.

"I heard about your wife," Fowler said. "Small town. People make a point of keeping me informed."

"It's exactly why I'm here," Clay said. "The night that Nick Buffalo died up on the mountain? I don't think he was the one who stalked Kelsie. And I've got the notes to prove it."

Fowler merely nodded, his eyes half-closed as if he wasn't too interested.

"Look," Clay said, "you did the wrap-up work while I was in the hospital. Everything came out nice and clean. If it was someone else, not Nick Buffalo, you would have seen some of those loose ends."

"That's right," Fowler said. "There were some loose ends. And it was convenient you were in the hospital while I put everything together."

"And?" Clay's anger grew. "What loose ends did you tie into a pretty little package?"

"I've been sitting on this for a quarter-century," Fowler said. He grimaced in pain and shifted positions. "I'll be honest. If I was healthy, I might be tempted to sit on it a while longer. Course, now I don't have much to lose anymore. And who knows, if there *is* a big judge up there, maybe Saint Peter will give me a break."

Fowler shifted again. "That night you got shot? You're right, when we pinned things on Nick Buffalo, we pinned the wrong man."

"You're going to tell me that in the course of an investigation, you and the coroner and whoever else mopped it up lied about the body in the cabin?"

"No, it was Nick, all right. I'm just saying he didn't shoot you. I believe he was dead beforehand. Whoever killed him left him there as the scapegoat. With what you tell me you know already, you could have guessed that."

"And you knew this for a fact?" Clay was growing angrier. All these years of believing Kelsie's stalker was dead. All these years of imagined safety. All these years of the monster lurking just out of sight."

"This never got out because we didn't let it get out. Behind the shell of the cabin, away from the burned-out area, we found sawdust in the grass where wind had blown it into the roots. A lab tech checked it against core samples of some of the half-burned logs of the cabin. Perfect match."

"Someone had sawn out part of the cabin?"

"After reading your report and listening to James McNeill give his version of the events, here's what I think happened," Fowler said. "You got shot. The shooter raced back to the cabin and kept shooting from in there. He started the fire and left through a hole cut in the back. No one was going to see him in the night, not with the flames as a distraction."

Fowler coughed up some phlegm and spat it into a cup. He took a few deep breaths. "There were other inconsistencies. The suicide confession note that the media loved? You might recall we were looking for Nick to ask him questions. First time we searched the place to pick him up for questioning, the note wasn't there. We didn't find Nick; we didn't find the note. When we returned after Nick was dead, the paint on the front door was scratched. Someone had jimmied the lock, probably with a screwdriver. One of the neighbors told us about seeing a light moving around the house late at night. It was an easy guess that someone had planted the note."

"The handwriting?"

"His. I couldn't hide a discrepancy that big."

"Someone forced him to write it."

"Sure. Plus there was the feather headdress on his bed. As you know, the feathers matched the ones left with Kelsie and the one we found in Doris Samson's mouth. Even though finding it seemed strange, it also tied everything together to end the case file. I've never understood why it was there. It wasn't there the first time we visited, but it was there the second."

Clay was leaning forward in his chair. "You buried all this information."

"Clay, there was a lot of pressure on me to have the case solved. I figured I'd pin it on Nick and quietly keep looking."

"You forgot to tell *me*."

Fowler looked away from Clay. "It wasn't forgetfulness. You were leaving the valley, and the last thing I wanted was you in my hair again."

Clay stood. "Whoever did this just walked. Did you stop to think that he might keep stalking Kelsie?"

"I did think about that."

"And?"

"And about every month or so I'd make a point of asking her if things were still fine. I figured if he showed up again, she'd tell me. It didn't seem right, though, to tell her why I was asking. If he hadn't shown up, I didn't want to get her scared for nothing by telling her he was still alive."

"Twenty-three years is a cold trail, sheriff."

"I've kept all my notes and records. I expect you'll want them."

"You expect right."

Fowler closed his eyes. His breathing stilled. For a few moments, Clay wondered if he had fallen asleep or if indeed the man had breathed his last breath.

"I'm not accustomed to asking another man his business," Fowler finally said without opening his eyes. "But I've been wondering this for some time, and of late, it has become a more compelling question."

"Go on," Clay said.

"How have you hung on?" Fowler asked.

"Hung on?" Clay didn't feel comfortable discussing matters of his heart. Not with a stranger. "Hung on? How can you ask? It's my wife and son."

"No," Fowler said, "I wasn't talking about Kelsie. How have you hung on to God? I've heard you're a churchgoing man. Me, I gave it up. You might remember I worked for the LAPD before taking the job here. Walking through the sewers of the worst that people can do—how could I believe in God with that kind of filth around me? You must have seen worse, plenty worse. How is it you still believe in a good God?".

Clay's mind flashed back to cases he had worked on: The woman whose entrails had been spilled from her body cavity, and a footstep in the entrails, showing how the killer had stood on them to let her crawl until she died, her intestines unraveling behind her like an obscene snake; the fifteen bodies of teenage boys that had been found decomposing in shallow graves dug into the cellar floor of a church deacon's house; pitchers of human blood stored in the refrigerator of a retired schoolteacher; and girls taken from street corners and found days later, torn like abandoned dolls. Clay had stepped into the caves of hell, peered into the minds of the demonic. It had driven him to the point of surrender, where he'd felt himself pulled into the swirling morass of dark, unreasoning evil. And beyond all of that, there was still in him the question that echoed through the decades, an angry cry of defiance to the God who had allowed a coal truck to take away the woman and child of a young man barely twenty. Did Fowler understand how often he had wrestled with the same question?

"Are you going to make a religious decision based on how I answer?" Clay asked.

"Don't feel responsible for my soul," Fowler said. "Whatever I'm wrestling with has nothing to do with you."

Clay stood, moved to the hospital window, and stared down at the parking lot. Fowler had asked the question with honesty. Despite his anger, Clay would reply in turn.

"If it means anything," Clay said after a minute of thought, "when I got around to believing, evil as much as anything else pointed me toward God."

Clay pulled a chair over to the hospital bed. He hated seeing the tubes pushed in the nostrils of the sagging old man, hated seeing spotted skin so close to the bone on his once powerful arms and hands. Fowler had never been a friend—in fact, had once been close to an enemy. Fowler had hidden key evidence that might well be the single biggest reason Clay now had to search for his own wife and son. Still, each shared the inescapable. Bodies disintegrate over time. What was happening to Fowler now would happen to Clay later. How could Clay not feel compassion for the man?

"Once I understood evil was real," Clay said, "once I understood it was something so tangible that I shuddered in its presence and in the destruction it left behind, I couldn't help but question the reason for its existence. What was it trying to destruct? I finally saw that evil took away love and anything good. As if it hated anything in the light of love and found a way to use humans to vent the hatred. It gave me a sense of something we'll never truly see or understand: a raging battle of two supernatural forces."

Clay paused, self-consciously looking at his blunt, work-worn fingernails. "Russ, I've been at the edge of that battle. I know evil is real. Later, when I began to wonder about the other side, part of why I was able to accept it was because I knew evil was real."

Clay paused as he struggled to find a way to explain. Finally he said, "Let me change the subject in a way. To try to understand evil, I asked around: psychologists, psychiatrists, priests. It was almost like I was making an unofficial scientific study. I was even able to convince the Bureau to fund some of my research on the basis that it could help our profiling."

Fowler regarded Clay without blinking.

"I was able to meet with a priest who had exorcised a demon

from a woman," Clay said. "You might try to tell me it was a priest who merely *believed* he had exorcised a demon and that she got better by the power of suggestion. I can't argue with that, except to say this was an intelligent, skeptical man who didn't want to believe it himself until, halfway through the exorcism, the demon began to speak. The priest said her face became reptilian, her eyes lidded like a snake, her voice hoarse with contempt. He said he's spent hours in front of a mirror since, trying to replicate the utter ugliness of her evil grin, and he doesn't believe it's humanly possible to move muscles in that manner."

"I'm not scoffing," Fowler said. "I won't challenge your priest without listening to him myself."

"Out of everything we discussed, one thing has stayed with me. The priest told me that Satan has no power except in a human body. I asked him to explain. He said there came a point, three days into the exorcism, when the demon repeatedly threatened to kill him and threatened to kill the possessed woman. The demon was snarling with homicidal fury, speaking through this woman, who was writhing in her restraints. The priest was terrified, yet at the same time he saw a way to pull the demon lose from the woman's body. He challenged the demon to make good his threat. Nothing resulted except more threats. An hour of the vilest threats followed, until the priest realized this demon, like all demons, was spirit. It could do nothing without human hands to help him. Hers were tied. The demon was helpless."

"Are you saying the serial killers you have hunted are all possessed by demons?"

"In a few cases, I would say yes," Clay replied. "That might surprise you, but you'd probably find a lot of police and investigators in those cases agreeing with me. As for the rest, I almost wish it were so. It would be much easier to accept if we could believe it was literally the devil at work, playing these killers as puppets . . ."

"But—" Fowler prompted.

"But after speaking to the priest, I began to see things in a new light. Satan—if you want to personify him—can't do anything unless we make the decision to do his deviltry. And that's what it comes down to: our decisions, good or bad. For most of us, the choices are forks at decision points—big or little—in the paths of our lives. For the killers, enough forks in the path have led them to a road where they've chosen far more obvious evils than our ordinary lies and greed."

Clay had never before articulated his thoughts to anyone. He found himself speaking quickly, as if he were afraid he might lose his words as they entered his mind. "I'm telling you all this because I'd seen so much evil I wasn't able to accept God until I'd found a way to understand it in a world He created."

Clay stopped, struck by another way to explain. "Russ, you know I love Kelsie. Could I point a gun at her head and force her to do my will?"

Fowler grunted out a no answer.

"Sorry," Clay said, aware he was talking more in one stretch than he had done in years, "but you've got me going, and I don't want to stop. If you accept that God created us in His image, I think you have to accept that He gives us free will. The way I see it, God won't put a gun to our heads, either, for the same reason I couldn't to Kelsie's. Love. I don't believe God lacks the power to destroy us or destroy evil. By His choice, it is with pain that He has allowed us choice. I believe He weeps to watch when we choose evil, and in so doing, choose to inflict punishment upon ourselves."

Fowler lifted a hand briefly, then let it drop. Clay accepted it as a sign of interruption.

Fowler drew a breath, and it seemed to Clay that the old man's lungs were brittle with effort. "So if we always have choice," the old man said. "Evil will always win."

"Russ," he said, softly, "if you don't understand the battle was fought and won on a cross two thousand years ago, then it will always appear that evil has won."

"How do you expect me to believe that?" Fowler croaked. "People don't come back to life."

"There's the great mystery, isn't it? Either Jesus was God and did. Or He was a nutcase and didn't. Which puts it back to a faith decision made of our own free will—while He watches and waits."

Fowler started wheezing. He tried a brave grin. "Think believing will help me as the end closes in?"

"Doesn't matter," Clay said, thinking of what his old Indian friend, George Samson, had said about the pursuit of truth.

It was not the answer Fowler expected, and his surprise showed in his face."Doesn't matter? Then what's the sense of believing?"

"If you want truth, truth's degree of helpfulness won't matter. If the resurrection story is untrue, neither you nor any other honest man would want to believe it, helpful or not. On the other hand, if it is true, you and every honest man won't care whether it gives help; you'll just want to believe."

The old man thought it through then finally grinned in appreciation. "You ought to become a preacher, son. Nothing like getting close to my deathbed for people to start coming in to save me by sugar spoon-feeding me or ramming it down my throat with guilt or threats of eternal hell. You put a practical edge on it. Truth as a reason to believe. I like that. A new twist."

Fowler began to cough. When he caught his breath, he said, "There are days it seems like I don't have long to decide, I can tell you that."

Clay could think of no reply that would not sound trite or patronizing.

Fowler continued. "You've given me plenty to chew on, son. Plenty. And the time was right for it. Thanks." With effort, he found more breath. "Come back tomorrow when I'm rested some. You should have plenty more to discuss with me by then."

"Such as?"

"Such as a boxful of files and evidence I've been hiding since that summer. Go down to Ron Duggan's. We called him Two Car. His address is listed in the phone book. He's a former deputy. Dumber than a bag of hammers, though. Bigger than a boxcar. He's been holding on to it for me."

"D-u-g-g-a-n?"

Fowler nodded absently. "I'm truly sorry about this," he told Clay. "For years now, I've believed the trouble was over. Now . . ."

He tightened his lips in a grimace of disgust. "Either it's a different man who took Kelsie, or it's one come back to life."

"What on earth—"

"Read through the files. Make your own conclusion first. It's the speeding ticket that tipped it for me. Then we'll talk. But I'm not sure it will do you much good. If I'm right, the guilty man—and I don't mean Nick—is long dead. Which is why I let the investigation die. If I'm right, you're looking for someone else, and I have no idea how to help you there."

## 1:38 P.M.

"Mr. Sonny Cutknife, please," James said into the telephone, irritated at the audible gum-chewing he heard from the secretary on the other end.

"Who's calling?"

"James McNeill."

"I'll see if he's taking calls."

"You tell him that—"

The secretary put James into a Muzak hold. He gritted his teeth as he waited. Any other time he'd have hung up.

"It's Sonny."

"Meet me here at the ranch," James said.

"I find this interesting. Any reason why?"

"You might recall our conversation this morning."

"I do."

"I've reconsidered," James said. "And I doubt you want the rest of my thoughts over the telephone."

"What time do you want me there?"

"Four-thirty."

"Clearing my schedule right now," Sonny said. "I'll see you then."

James hung up. Then he dialed another number—Johnny Samson's. James would need help for his discussion with Sonny Cutknife.

# 1:40 P.M.

As Clay drove through town from the hospital toward the address for Ronald Duggan, he was glad technology now gave him two tools that had been unavailable to him during his agent days—cellular phones and VICAP, the FBI's Violent Criminal Apprehension Program.

While Clay had not worked on establishing VICAP in the mideighties—he'd been in the field, not administration—he knew its history thoroughly, all the way back to the 1950s and a Los Angeles serial-killer rapist named Harvey Murray Glatman who became the real-life original for dozens of clichéd fictitious fiends with Glatman's MO of paying women to pose unclothed for modeling auditions as a way of luring them into seclusion.

Glatman's later confession had provided one of the earliest insights into the mind of a serial killer and a classic example taught by the Behavioral Sciences Unit in Quantico. From boyhood, Glatman had progressed from infantile sexual experimentation to making passes at girls to minor sexual assault, and finally, fifteen years later, to making his murder and rape fantasies a reality.

Because Glatman roamed from county to county in the already considerable urban sprawl of the Los Angeles area, jurisdictional barriers prevented investigators from connecting the murders. Had it not been for the persistence of an L.A. homicide detective named Pierce Brooks, who personally tackled the considerable task of combing the newspaper files and prying information from the police files of the separate counties, Glatman might have continued his slashing ecstasy for years.

It was the same Pierce Brooks, more than twenty years later, who fought for a grant from the Justice Department to begin a program that would overcome the police jurisdictional barriers. His dream was a computer system fed criminal data by police departments from all across the country, and accessed for data by departments all across the country.

VICAP became a reality in the mideighties, partially because the FBI pushed for it, partially because of the horrible reality of a society in transition. In the fifties and sixties, virtually all homicides were solved within a year of the murder—most fell into the category of murders committed by someone known to the victim.

As the seventies arrived, so did a new mobility, and a quarter of all murders were going unsolved. Serial killings and random murders both went from being rarities to being a terrible fact of life; seemingly unrelated murders didn't just occur across the span of counties, but were linked by interstate highways. A media frenzy pushed Congress into action, and VICAP, as a national central information computer, was born.

In retrospect, VICAP was so sensible it seemed inevitable. At the time, however, computers were more expensive, and most cops were suspicious of the new technology. Even with younger, more computer-literate officers entering into police work, VICAP faced a long adolescence. The VICAP form took an hour for a police detective to complete. Not all local police departments reported their current unsolved violent crimes to VICAP, let alone processed their backlist. Only near Clay's retirement did VICAP become an effective tool. Because of that, he'd never really had the chance to use it in his field operations.

He, of course, had never expected the need for it in retirement and wished, more passionately and with more pain than he would have believed possible, that he didn't have the need to access it now . . .

As Clay reached Highway 40 and turned east toward Columbia Falls, he reached for the other piece of technology that helped him occasionally as a rancher and that would have helped considerably more in his FBI days, his cellular phone. He dialed a number from memory and juggled the phone with one hand, coffee and steering wheel with the other.

"Flannigan," came the voice. Aside from less volume and more rasp in Flannigan's voice, Clay felt he could have been in a time warp, once again back in the days when he'd first called Dennis Flannigan because of a serial killer. Only now Flannigan had retired, and the serial killer had not.

"Dennis, it's Clay."

"Let me get back into my rocking chair, son. I fell out from surprise. Clay Garner? *The* Clay Garner?"

"Quit your griping," Clay said. "I sent you Tennessee whiskey for Christmas."

"And that Christmas card with your family photo. I can't believe someone that beautiful still keeps a mutt like you around."

Clay winced. Male banter, when insults meant affection, occasionally had its drawbacks.

"Dennis—"

For a moment, the reception faded.

"Sounds like you're in your truck," Flannigan said. "Knowing your West Virginia thriftiness, I don't think this is a social call."

"Not exactly. I need your help at Quantico."

"Sure." No hesitation, no questions, although surely he had some, Clay thought.

Clay decided not to force his friend to ask. "This one involves family, Dennis. If I go in asking questions and something leaks to the media, it will become a zoo. You know, something like serial killer stalks hunter of serial killers. It'll make things tougher than they already are, especially since the local here is dragging his feet on calling in help."

Long, respectful silence came from Flannigan's end. "Kelsie?" he finally asked.

"Probably Taylor too."

"Clay, that Christmas card remark. I—"

"Don't sweat it. How could you know?"

"Still . . ."

"Dennis, I need you to run a data search through VICAP."

"Let me get a pen and paper."

Clay jammed the brakes to keep from hitting a car that made a rolling stop before pulling onto the highway. California plates. It figured.

"I'm back," Flannigan said.

"Here's what I'm thinking," Clay told him. "Pull up a search on all kills within five hundred miles of Kalispell."

Whoever it was had been smart enough not to play in his own backyard. Otherwise, a concentrated pattern of murders would be too obvious. Clay was thinking the person needed a job to exist, which meant Kalispell had to be his base. At best, he'd be able to take two or three days off, unless he was able to limit his hunting to yearly vacations. That meant a leash of eight to ten hours drive to bracket the time he'd need to select, capture, and toy with his prey.

"Any particular type of kill? Style? Victim?"

"Make it a broad search for any unsolved murders on women between the age of twenty and fifty. Don't look for any particular MO. Pull them all. He's a smart one. If he's been doing this undetected for twenty-three years, he's disguised his pattern. It's a long shot—I think we'd have heard if he left the same signature on others—but pull up anything related to eagle feathers."

More static silence as that registered with Flannigan. "Did I hear you right? Twenty-three years? Eagle feathers!"

"You heard me right. I think it's the same one who brought me to your department."

"The one who stalked Kelsie when she was a teenager."

"Yeah." Clay watched for the turnoff to the county road that would take him to Ronald Duggan's place.

"Clay"—Dennis spoke with horror, not the hunter's excitement they'd shared during their careers together. This was personal—"after all these years, what would trigger him again?"

"If I could figure that out," Clay said, "I might have a chance of getting him."

Clay had seen his share of mobile homes, especially growing up. A lot of them did have the stereotypical discarded appliances out front, serving as bookends for rusting vehicles. This one, however, was among a patch of pine trees, and the yard was neat, the only vehicle in sight parked on tires, not wooden blocks.

Clay stepped out of the car, and a terrier bolted at him from a doghouse at the side of the home. It danced around his feet, feinting in and out, yipping alarm.

When Clay reached the door of the mobile home, he didn't need to ring the doorbell. Two Car Duggan was just inside the screen door, surveying his visitor.

From what Clay saw through the screen, this was a definite exception to the rule that owners began to resemble their dogs and vice versa. If Duggan was still in the force, they'd have bumped his nickname to Three Car. He wore broad suspenders over a graying T-shirt, probably because belts for someone of his girth were not commercially available.

Duggan didn't open the screen door. He didn't even greet Clay.

"Fowler sent me here," Clay said. The yappy terrier was at the bottom of the steps, still giving Clay full attention and volume.

"I know," Duggan said. "He called. I already got the box out. Open the door and it's yours."

Was it too much effort for the man to it do himself? Clay wondered. He opened the door. A file folder box was at Duggan's feet.

"Thank you," Clay said. As he stooped to pick up the box, he tried to ignore the smell of dirt and body sweat in the folds of Duggan's body.

"Could never figure out why Russ made me hang on to this," Duggan said. "The old lady always complained that it cluttered up the closet."

It was Duggan's wife, then, who kept things neat around here.

"Like I said," Clay told him, "thanks."

Clay carried the box back to his Jeep, hoping he'd step on the annoying terrier as it chased him in tight, noisy circles.

Clay was five miles back along Highway 40 when his cell phone rang.

"Garner," he said, curious. Few people had this number. Had Flannigan already found something of interest?

"Don't go home."

"Pardon?"

"This is Fowler. You got the box?"

"Yes. I haven't looked through it yet."

"Good. Don't go home. Make yourself scarce."

Unconsciously, Clay eased off the accelerator. Fowler was not the type of person to say things lightly.

"All right," Clay said. "How about telling me why?"

In the background, Clay heard a doctor being paged over the hospital intercom.

"Maybe ten minutes ago, the sheriff showed up. Here in my room. He was looking for you. He called Old Man McNeill, who told him you were headed here. But don't blame McNeill. He didn't know what they wanted."

"Which was?" Clay didn't like the implication he was hearing in Fowler's voice.

"They wanted you for questioning. Which is why the sheriff has already sent a car up to your ranch."

"But—"

"I know it wasn't you who took Kelsie," Fowler said. "I know that good and well. But I couldn't tell them, not without letting them know about the false reports and everything else. I had to keep my mouth shut and play dumb. I waited until they left. I'm in a wheelchair at a pay phone, and I'm glad I caught you in time."

"Me?" *What kind of nightmare is this?* "Me?"

"They found a watch underneath the bed at Kelsie's condo. With a broken strap. Like it had been kicked there or something during a struggle. The back of the watch is engraved to you. And they're wondering real hard how come it was you who told them you didn't even know where she lived when you called them up and sent them to the condo."

Clay thought of the engraved Seiko that Kelsie had given him one Christmas. It was a dress watch, thin, flat, and elegant. He rarely wore it, preferring the scratched Timex, which could take the abuse of work on the ranch. The Seiko could have been missing from his bedroom jewelry box for weeks before he would miss it.

"Clay," Fowler said, "they're real serious about this. They know she left you. And they know the same thing you do. Nine out of ten times in a situation like this, it's the boyfriend or husband. If you're onto something, best thing you can do is stay out of sight and not give them a chance to pick you up. Claim you didn't know there was a warrant out."

"What about Rooster Evans?" Clay said. "It looks like—"

"They want Evans too. No doubt about that. They're still looking. But they're also interested in you."

A quick glance in the rearview mirror showed no cops. Clay was already jumpy. He was also already making plans. He knew cops. If they decided to detain him, he'd be lucky if he got out of jail in less than two days—*if* he managed to clear himself. By then, Kelsie might be dead.

On the other hand, running would make him look more guilty.

He weighed his choices. Looking guilty or losing time in the race to save Kelsie. It was an easy decision.

"They won't find me," Clay told Fowler. "But how can I reach you? There's no phone in your room. I'm sure I'll have questions after I get through the files."

"Keep that battery on your phone charged. I'll wheel out here and call whenever I can."

"Thanks," Clay said. "And I mean that."

Clay waited for traffic to clear then spun his steering wheel hard, cutting a U-turn so sharply his tires squealed. He needed to get off the pavement and onto the back roads.

# 4:52 P.M.

James McNeill held a shotgun pointed at Sonny Cutknife. He and Johnny had marched Sonny to this isolated clearing at gunpoint, a half-hour walk of complete silence except for Sonny's questions, which went unanswered. James and Johnny wanted him nervous by the time they reached the post driver.

Johnny Samson had earlier thought he would find it satisfying, after all these years, to back Sonny Cutknife against a post driver and place his head beneath the poised hydraulic weight. After all, a quarter-century earlier, Sonny had done the same to him.

But he didn't find it satisfying. The man with the ponytail and massive gut and fringed leather vest was now a stranger, not the flat-bellied, rope-muscled bully of Johnny's memory.

They hadn't spoken to each other since that summer, their last encounter an angry shouting match over the disappearance of Harold Hairy Moccasin. Johnny had questions; Sonny gave no answers, just insolent shrugs.

The Native Sons were an equally distant memory. Johnny rarely thought about the bulldozer and the church-burning. He'd long since understood the confusion, grief, and youthfulness that had led him to his passive participation. While he regretted those few days in the summer of 1973, he now treated the memory with the same sad forgiveness a father might have for an errant son. Mostly, when he thought of the Native Sons, he remembered the truth of his grandfather's advice about choices. Had Johnny walked toward the church instead of away, he wouldn't be teaching school on the reservation; he wouldn't be married with two children and happy to return home every night after school.

"You heard Anderson's dead," Johnny said to Sonny, holding the man's ponytail so his head could not move on top of the fence post. It was an exact copy of how Sonny had once made him look up at the hydraulically driven weight. "Maybe now it's your turn to die."

"You been watching too many movies," Sonny said. "A shotgun at my back. Blindfolded silence on a long walk. Now this. I'm supposed to wet my pants?"

James glanced at Johnny, who raised his eyebrows in the equivalent of a shrug. With the tractor idling in the background to supply power to the hydraulics, this *was* supposed to scare Sonny.

Johnny figured the old man felt as foolish as he did. Earlier, they'd moved the tractor to an isolated clearing and set up the hydraulics.

"We want answers," James said. "I heard you once figured this was a good way to make a point."

"Another lifetime," Sonny said. "I'm surprised Goody-Two-Shoes here admits it ever happened."

"Might be one difference this time," Johnny said. He nodded at James, who reached over and put his hand on a lever. Sonny turned his head slightly, his total attention on the lever. "We're not bluffing."

James yanked. Sonny flinched. The weight above his head remained in place.

"What a shame," James said. "The hydraulics aren't connected properly. Guess we'll have to reconnect."

James took his time. He reached down among the hoses and

made adjustments. When he was finished, he wiped his greasy hands on his pants.

"I think it's ready now," James said. "I'll be happy to test it. Unless you've got some answers."

"How about the questions?" Sonny asked, not quite as confident as before.

James grabbed the shotgun from where he'd set it on the tractor fender then nodded at Johnny. Johnny released Sonny's ponytail, and Sonny eased himself away from the fence post.

"You'd really kill me?" he asked.

"My daughter's gone," James replied. "So's my grandson. I'm about ready to do whatever it takes."

Sonny straightened his vest. He adjusted his belly around his pants. "What do you want to know?"

"Emerald Canyon," James said. "You mentioned some of the others were dead and some of the others hard to reach. What's the setup? Who else is involved?"

"That's all you want to know?" Sonny was genuinely surprised. "You make this big production, and that's all you want to know?"

"And the summer when we were just boys," Johnny said quietly. "Harold Hairy Moccasin. I want to know about him."

Johnny was surprised at himself for blurting the question. He thought he'd buried most of the events from back then. But now, with Sonny right here . . .

"Let me have a smoke," Sonny said. He waved at James. "And put the shotgun away. I thought this was something serious."

Without waiting for permission, and ignoring the shotgun James kept at half-mast, Sonny fished inside his vest pocket, found a cigarette, lit it, and walked over to the tractor to turn off the ignition. He drew once on the cigarette and leaned against the rear tire of the tractor.

"Noise was getting to me," he said.

All the ways Johnny had imagined this going, thinking maybe they'd have to nick Sonny's ears or threaten to slit his nostrils; all the worry Johnny had put into wondering if he himself would be changed by becoming like Sonny, even for a good cause and only for a few minutes—and now the guy was relaxing with a cigarette and running this like it was his own conference?

"So what exactly do you want to know?" Sonny took another

heavy drag and turned his dark eyes toward Johnny. Although Sonny's face had fattened and sagged, those feral eyes still gleamed with danger. "And about that summer? Ancient history. If you need to know the truth, I called the cops ahead of time and told them about the church."

"What?"

"Yeah. Old Hairy was drinking beer, remember? When I left you to baby-sit him, I went into town and called the cops."

Johnny asked the obvious question.

"Why?" Sonny echoed. "Publicity. Didn't take me long to figure out the media people weren't going to help out by broadcasting our message. I mean, the entire valley's out of power, they've got tapes from the Native Sons, and all of them report it as a blown transformer? So I decided you and Hairy could make a little sacrifice. I sent them an anonymous tip, figuring once you got caught at the church, the rest of the stuff would come out and I'd get the publicity I needed to bring some more people to run the attacks. Only you—" Sonny blew smoke out in lazy curls and sneered disgust "—you decided to run back home. And when they caught Hairy, they didn't arrest him."

"He really joined a hippie commune?"

"Johnny, Johnny, Johnny. You didn't believe it back then, why start now?"

"Then . . ."

"They killed him, Johnny. Plain and simple. It could have been you they dragged to a mountain cabin and beat to death."

Sonny gave him a gold-toothed grin. Rumor had it he didn't need a cap, just liked the looks of it. "That was the first time this mess splattered all around you and missed completely. Second time, it was me taking it instead of you."

James had moved beside Johnny. They both stared at Sonny. It was quite a performance. Of course, Johnny knew, performing had been Sonny's strength, even before turning it to his advantage in tribal politics.

"See, Johnny." A timed pause. Another draw on the cigarette. "That fall, they came to me. It took them that long to put everything together. They came to me. Not you. You were second choice. They made me a deal. I took it. Which put me in, and they never had to make you the offer."

"They?" Johnny felt stupid. He was hanging onto every word coming out of Sonny's mouth. He knew it. Sonny knew it.

"The Emerald Canyon boys. Fits neat and tidy, doesn't it? As that seems to be the reason you were both in such heat to get me here."

Sonny shot his cigarette away with a flick of his fingers. He noticed Johnny's wince. "Five bucks, Johnny. I got five bucks that says you won't be able to just stand there. You'll have to track down the cigarette butt and make sure it don't start a forest fire."

James leveled the shotgun and fired, all in one motion.

Sonny stared at him in disbelief, then looked down at the hissing of air. Between his legs, the rubber of the tractor's tire was shredded in an apple-sized hole, with the force of the air actually blowing Sonny's pants like a flag in the wind.

"You get that cocky grin off your face," James said. "Find the butt yourself and stamp it out. Then get back to where you were and tell me about Emerald Canyon. I'm old, and in case you didn't notice, I don't have the patience I used to."

Sonny did as he was told. By the time he got back to the tractor, it was already tilted on a nearly flattened tire.

"Not only is my patience gone," James said, "so's my aim. Meant to put that buckshot a couple inches higher. Maybe next time."

"No next time," Sonny said. "All right? My heart's in bad enough shape as it is."

"Emerald Canyon," James said. "What was the deal they offered? And who were they?"

"They needed someone in administration to make sure the casino transferred some of the profits. They needed someone to make sure there would be no problems in developing the real estate. Me. In return, they promised me whatever money I needed for my campaigns and a percentage of the gross profits."

"They?" James asked.

"You don't know? That's the dumbest thing I—"

James used the pump-action to lever another shell into the barrel. "You're not talking fast enough for me."

"Wayne Anderson was one of them. He was the one who handled most of the transfers. Bermuda bank accounts, Swiss bank accounts. He put up a great smokescreen for the rest of them. There were five more all together. Fowler, the sheriff back then, he was in on it too. A couple others."

"Who?"

"Hey, I'm not stupid. I'm a lot of things, but I'm not stupid. Don't you think I did what it took to find out where all the money was going?"

"You're starting to sound cocky again," James said. "What's that fancy word doctors use today? Vasectomy. That's it."

He took aim just below Sonny's belt buckle and thoughtfully repeated himself. "Vasectomy. Fast and simple."

"Remember Thomas King, the judge who got shot by his wife?" Sonny's speech cadence picked up.

James nodded. Who in the valley could forget? She'd pleaded self-defense, proved it, inherited everything, and moved to Hawaii.

"King was one of them," Sonny said. "And two county council representatives. Both of them are dead now, but the money keeps going to their estates, funneled in from offshore. Anderson and Fowler have a few things on me that made it politically stupid to squeeze them. Frank Evans was in on it, and he's dead too. Now you see why I went to you for some spare change."

"No, I don't," James said. "Explain."

Sonny looked bewildered. "But you've got a Grand Cayman account too. I figure you've got close to six million in there. Which is why I came to you."

# 8:30 P.M.

"Welcome home, my love," the old lady said, closing the front door.

His mother's car was already pulling out of the driveway. She was on her way to an extended weekend in Las Vegas. She'd said she was going alone, but the boy knew better. His mother had found a new boyfriend. She wasn't even bothering to call them uncles anymore.

"It's nice to see you again. How long has it been since you stayed?" She answered her own question. "Since you and your mother moved out of town with that awful man. I think you were only six then."

He shrugged. Six years old was forever ago.

The old lady surprised him. She moved forward and engulfed him in her arms. Her rose perfume choked him. It filled him with panic, and he fought to push his face away from her chest.

"Let go!" It came out as a muffled shout.

She did not let go.

He half punched her stomach, and her arms dropped away. "That's weird," he said, sucking in air. "Leave me alone."

"Bobby?" There was a wildness to her eyes that disturbed the boy. He wondered if she was going to attack him. "Bobby . . ."

"Bobby?" His gut response was rage. It filled him with a frenzy of remembered hatred. He shouted, "That's not my name."

She took a stutter step backward, as if his voice was ice water thrown across her face. The glow behind her eyes faded. "I'm sorry," she said. "Forgive an older person's failing memory. You remind me so much of another boy I used to know."

The boy nearly put his hand over his nose and mouth. Her perfume really bothered him.

"Let's get you unpacked," she said. "I'm sure you're tired after the drive."

He shrugged. He didn't intend to waste much time in the house. It looked like a museum: doilies on everything, old velvety-looking furniture, blinds closed on every window. The sooner he started roaming the neighborhood, the better.

The boy brightened when he saw the location of his bedroom. It was a two-and-a-half story house. His room was at the end of a hallway on the second floor. With any luck, he would have a great view. In his suitcase was the low-power telescope he had received for his tenth birthday. Given privacy and much of the night, there was no telling what he might see through the windows of other houses.

"There you are, dear," she said, opening the door of the room and letting him step past her into the musty interior. There was an old-fashioned four-poster bed draped with a lacy bedcover. Beside the bed was a standing wardrobe closet. "Unpack and come down when you're ready. I'll have tea and cookies waiting for you."

"Sure," he said.

She closed the door. He set his suitcase on the bed and opened the bedroom window. He crawled out, found a drainspout, and climbed down to the yard.

"Tea and cookies," he said under his breath. "Tea and cookies. Stupid old witch."

He left the yard and didn't return for three hours. There was an urge upon him. Happily, he was able to satisfy it, for in the new neighborhood cats were much more trusting than in his regular neighborhood.

In the three hours away from the old lady's house, he found and killed two neighborhood cats, using only a pocketknife and his imagination, sitting *in the center of a large drainage culvert to ensure the privacy he needed for his experimentation.*

*It seemed as each cat died, the smell of the old lady's rose-scented perfume returned to his nostrils. He washed the blood off his hands in the trickle of water running through the culvert and left the bodies of the cats behind as he returned to the old lady's house for tea and cookies.*

In his hospital bed, head tilted forward by the pillow below his neck, Russell Fowler grunted at the arrival of an orderly in one of the light-green uniforms he was learning to hate. This one backed into Fowler's room, pulling a trolley. Then he closed the door.

"I'm sleeping," Fowler said. Couldn't they at least send female nurses? He hated being touched by a man.

The orderly's shoulders lifted and dropped in a shrug as he pulled the trolley over to the bed. Without saying a word—still facing away from Fowler—he lifted the bed sheets at Fowler's feet.

"Give me a break," Fowler said. "Can't you guys do this stuff during the day?"

The orderly ignored him.

Fowler could not see below his knees without sitting upright completely. He didn't have the strength to move, so he stared at the ceiling and tried to maintain dignity.

Poke and prod. That's all these people did. Fowler felt like he didn't even own his body any more.

"Hey," Fowler said. He realized the orderly had put a blood-pressure cuff around Fowler's calf just below the knee. "Doesn't that usually go on my arm?"

No reply. The orderly bent over Fowler's leg. He began to pump air into the cuff with the hand-held rubber bulb.

Although he had yet to see the orderly's face, Fowler noticed he wore white translucent rubber gloves. That was never good news. "Not another prostate thing," Fowler said. "Tell me you're not going higher than my knee."

Mute as ever, the orderly returned to his trolley and reached for something else. When he lifted his hand, he had a large needle in his hand.

Fowler groaned. Poke and prod. With more poke than prod. He shook his head. At least this time they weren't turning him over to jab the needle in his rump.

The orderly stood motionless, waiting.

Fowler's toes were going numb. What kind of blood pressure test was this? he wondered. And with a needle?

The orderly lifted Fowler's leg in one hand. He leaned over and with the other hand, jabbed the needle into the back of Fowler's calf. Then he dropped Fowler's leg.

"Happy now?" Fowler said.

"Very."

Fowler struggled to his elbows. He knew the orderly's voice.

The orderly turned to him, finally showing his face. Only it wasn't an orderly. And Fowler had been right about knowing the orderly's voice.

"You!"

"The human heart is amazing," the man said. "It circulates blood through the entire body in about four minutes."

"I don't understand," Fowler said. "We're in this together. You've made plenty of money. There's no need to do this."

"I'll explain then. I'm pulling the plug on my life here. Time to start a new one somewhere else, so I'm wrapping things up, tying up all the loose ends. Choose whatever cliché you prefer. The end result is that I also need to pull the plug on everyone in our little group. First Old Man Evans, then Anderson, now you."

The man held up the needle. "Simple, actually. Find a vein. Inject a bubble of air. I doubt anyone will look for the needle mark."

He yanked the Velcro loose on the cuff around Fowler's leg. "That should help the blood flow, don't you think? Start that little bubble on its way up?"

He glanced at his wristwatch. "I give you two minutes. Then, pop. There goes the heart."

Fowler looked frantically for the call button to alert the nurses' station. He saw it, reached out but not quickly enough. The other man pulled it out of Fowler's reach.

Fowler played his ace. "I've got files to be released in case of my death," he said, his voice tinged with panic. He'd known he was dying for some time, but he wasn't ready for it this soon.

"That infantile blackmail is only effective while I live here. When I say I'm pulling the plug, I mean it. Whoever I was will no longer be. If you're lucky, at the most the files will make for good newspaper copy."

Another glance at his watch. "Do you mind if I stay with you as you die? I've seen it countless times. The final moments, I mean. But you know, it never loses its fascination."

Fowler was no longer listening. He had dropped back down from his elbows and was staring at the ceiling. The reality of death was finally hitting him, cold and hard. He was not ready. What had happened to the invincible body he'd been so sure of all his life? Please, he thought, couldn't he go back and change the paths that had taken him here? He was dying with an untouched $5 million Swiss bank account, and he'd trade it all for the peace he'd seen in Clay Garner's face earlier in the day.

"Russ, I'm guessing about a minute. The bubble's probably well past your hips now. Remember, every beat takes it closer."

Fowler missed Thelma. Divorcing her had been a big mistake. He wished she was sitting beside him, holding his hand. If a man had to die, there would be some comfort in that.

"Thirty seconds, Russ. Get ready for the big bang."

Russ Fowler did something he had never done in his entire adult life. He began to cry.

# 10:30 P.M.

Clay had covered eight miles of forested ridges in the daylight available after parking and hiding his Cherokee off a rutted dirt road in a neighboring valley. The final two miles he had to cover in darkness, and he was grateful when he finally reached the gravel road that led to George Samson's cabin.

Clay stepped onto the veranda of the cabin. He eased out of the straps of the knapsack on his back and knocked on Samson's door. "It's Clay," he called.

The door opened seconds later. George Samson was fully clothed with no trace of sleep in his face. "I was afraid I'd have to go out there and track you down myself," George said. "He shook his head in mock disgust. "White people. How we lost to you is beyond my imagination."

Clay stepped inside and pointed at the lantern hanging from a ceiling beam. "We have telephones and electricity. Some of you still haven't figured that out yet."

George smiled. "Sit down, my friend. I'm glad you're here."

"Me too."

Clay set the knapsack at his feet and eased into a large stuffed armchair, vintage 1950s. Clay had always felt good in this cabin. George preferred a simple life: water from a well, cooking on a butane stove, no television, radio, or clock. The unhurried simplicity was calming.

George had sold the original land near the Flathead reservation and purchased a quarter section higher up in the foothills, leaving an ample savings account to take care of his minimal yearly expenses. With this cabin, however, he'd shunned even a telephone line. The cost of running utility poles this high into the hills was not the reason. With Johnny grown, there was no need to worry about emergencies. George had decided he didn't need a telephone for himself.

His furniture consisted of the armchair, a matching sofa, the kitchen table and chairs that George had crafted himself, and floor-to-ceiling bookshelves that took up three walls. More than once Clay had stopped by early in the day and done nothing but read, with George doing the same, the only break in their companionable silence being when George brewed tea.

"Johnny drove up and told you?" Clay asked.

"Johnny drove up and told me. He didn't say much except to expect you."

"That's because I didn't tell him much. Cell phones are not secure."

"You are welcome to stay as long as you wish."

"It's not that easy, George. I imagine tomorrow you'll have visitors from the sheriff's department. Once they figure out I'm not going home, they'll start checking my friends. This is a logical place."

George, sitting on the sofa opposite, smiled again, deep shadows in the wrinkles of his face. "The root cellar is not a logical place. I've already set up a mattress and sleeping bag and lantern. Even if they were looking for it, I doubt they'd find it. I dug it into the hill, and it's protected by brush."

"Works for me," Clay said. He doubted any of the sheriff's men would think of a root cellar. They'd grown up with wells, electricity, and telephones. Clay had grown up with an outhouse in the back and a pump-well out front, much the way George lived now. Clay knew about vegetables and berries preserved in rubber-ring glass jars. He knew about root cellars, where the poorer folks stored everything they needed kept cool during sweltering summers.

"Do you want to talk?" George asked.

"Not much more to say than the obvious," Clay replied. "I'm worried sick about Kelsie and Taylor. From what I've learned today, chances are she—they—have been taken by someone who's stalked her for years."

"Years?" George said softly. He understood.

"Years." Clay looked at his hands. "Not once did she turn to me for help. And of all the people in the world . . ."

". . . you would be the one who could help."

"Something like that." Clay didn't voice the rest: how her distance had increased over the years, how she had left him without warning, and how badly it hurt.

"What will you do?" George asked.

"I've got a friend back east. He's got the fax number to Johnny's school. We're hoping a computer search gives me a place to start, and he'll fax what he finds to Johnny. Until then . . ."

Clay gestured at the knapsack. He'd stopped at a camping store and paid for it with a credit card, making sure to complain obnoxiously to the sales clerk over the price. It wouldn't hurt—if the sheriff got serious about a search—to give the impression he'd gone for an extended trip into the woods.

"It's loaded with some files and evidence that Russ Fowler saved into his retirement. Remember the night I got shot at Mad Dog's cabin? Fowler knew all along that something wasn't right. The person who shot me from the cabin? It wasn't Nick Buffalo."

George's normally impassive face took on a look of surprise.

Clay told George about Kelsie's message, the notes in the music dancer, and about the conversation in the hospital with Russ Fowler.

"That means it probably wasn't Nick Buffalo who took my granddaughter either."

"No, George. Probably not."

Clay could not read the older man's face. The murderer of his granddaughter had been walking as a free man for a quarter-century, and George merely nodded.

"You get some sleep," George said. "Tomorrow, you and me, we got some work to do."

Clay did not sleep. He kept the lantern lit and sat in his sleeping bag.

Clay wasn't bothered by the confines of the root cellar. He could stand inside if he remained severely stooped. The root cellar extended ten paces into the hill. Spade marks were still clear in the dirt walls, with four-by-four lumber supports every few feet.

Earlier in the evening, George had moved all the food toward the back to make room for Clay. Beneath deer haunches, hanging from the ceiling, there were jugs of milk, yogurt, cheese, fresh fruits, and vegetables. A root cellar was remarkably efficient; with the cool earth to shield its interior from the sun, temperatures rarely rose above forty degrees, even in summer. Before modern refrigeration, Clay knew, people often placed blocks of ice in root cellars to lower the temperature even further.

With the heavy sleeping bag and mattress, in fact, the root cellar actually provided a comfortable place of rest. Clay's habit at the ranch house—summer and winter—was to sleep with the window open, so he preferred cool air on his face.

Instead of attempting to sleep, though, exhausted and stressed as he was, Clay opened the sheriff's files for the first time.

He first found photocopies of police reports. The same typewriter had been used on all of them. The bottom half of the *s* was missing, and the *o* was blotted. He smiled wryly. If law-enforcement agencies all had one thing in common, it was the dislike of filling out reports and—in the pre-computer days—the usual infighting for too few typewriters, most old and barely functional.

His smile disappeared as he concentrated on the police reports. He skipped the attached autopsy results and instead scanned the summaries.

There were three full-length reports, all murder investigations. The first one detailed the 1976 drug overdose death of a twenty-one-year-old Caucasian male named Nathan Yancey. He'd been found on the couch of his walkup apartment, the needle still in his arm, blood samples showing he'd taken a hot dose of heroin tar. Yancey had plenty of needle tracks, including dozens on his inner thighs, a place experienced addicts shot up in order to hide the puncture scars. Final conclusion: accidental death.

The second report, dated March, 1978, had an attached photo of Richard Lee Patterson, a blond-haired ski instructor with a confident grin. Richard Lee Patterson, according to the report, drank too much beer and stepped into a hot tub with improper grounding. Death by electrocution had made a mockery of the confident grin. Final conclusion: accidental death.

The third report contained much more speculation than hard fact. It covered a 1988 whitewater-rafting accident that killed two young men, Thomas Joseph Bell and Michael James McNeill. An intensive one-week search had failed to find the body of Michael James McNeill. Tommy Bell's body had been found washed ashore, three miles downstream of the inflatable raft, which had been trapped by the branches of a low, overhanging tree. The coroner reported that water in the lungs was consistent with death by drowning. A large bruise on the head made for an easy conclusion. The water had swept him into a boulder and knocked him out. Blood samples showed alcohol content to be .15, high enough to explain carelessness on a dangerous river. Final conclusion: accidental death.

As Clay read through the reports, he fought a sense of revulsion that almost became physical nausea. It confirmed the horror of the series of notes he'd found in Kelsie's dancer. Although the reports had been filed by the sheriff's office in three separate counties, they had one thing in common, one thing not listed in the reports. Nathan Yancey, Richard Patterson, and Thomas Bell had all made the same mistake: They'd all fallen in love with a woman named Kelsie McNeill.

Again, Clay realized the torture Kelsie must have faced in the aftermath of each death. The dancer notes clearly explained that the murderer blamed Kelsie for the deaths. She had borne the guilt for years, unable to share her fears, unable to ask for help.

Clay had assumptions only Kelsie could confirm. After the first death, Nathan Yancey's, perhaps the stalker had disappeared long enough to let her believe she might be able to risk another relationship. And again, after the ski instructor, murder number two, perhaps there had been another lengthy illusion of safety to allow her to come out of her solitary cave.

Clay pushed his mind from the subject and sifted through the remainder of the folder. On the back of the first file folder, he found an ambiguous note. In the lantern light, Clay squinted to decipher the scrawled writing.

*7:12 A.M. on July 12, '73—southbound, 87 m.p.h.—325/I-15—*
*Conrad—cross ref: K1200598.*

The speeding ticket Fowler had mentioned? Clay tried to translate.

I-15 was simple—the interstate highway. Conrad? Clay was pretty sure it was a town somewhere north of Great Falls. Maybe "325" referred to the mile marker on the interstate.

On the file folder, below Fowler's terse note, Clay wrote out the long version of what he believed it meant. At 7:12 A.M. on July 12, 1973, a southbound vehicle had been clocked at 87 miles per hour at mile marker 325 on I-15 near Conrad, Montana.

Clay didn't need a map to visualize the location. In a direct line from Kalispell, Interstate 15 was well east, on the other side of the Rocky Mountains. The highway ran north-south from the Canadian border, down through Great Falls, Helena, and Butte, continuing south to the Idaho state line. As a rookie FBI agent assigned to the train crash from the office in Great Falls, he'd traveled the highway more than a couple of times on his way to and from Kalispell.

Clay stared at the information. Who had been ticketed? What was that person doing on the interstate at that hour? Why had the person been traveling so fast? Where had the person been headed? And most important, why had Fowler decided the ticket was significant?

Then it clicked. July 12 was the night that Clay had been shot at Mad Dog's cabin.

His skin prickled at a conclusion that leapt into his mind. South on I-15. Did Fowler believe this person had been driving away from Kalispell?

Clay frowned, doing his best to recall the route from Kalispell to I-15. Highway 2 was the only road, a two-lane blacktop cutting through the mountains over to Shelby, 160 miles east. Clay had always driven during the daytime when traffic was heavy. It usually took a little over three hours. There were sixty miles of mountain road before the land leveled and the road straightened across the beginning of the Great Plains.

Clay tried to see if the math would work. He remembered he'd been shot just after three o'clock in the morning. He estimated it would take a person an hour to hike from the cabin down the mountain to the nearest road. Another half-hour from the ranch to Kalispell. Then, at night, speeding with no traffic, it would take two hours to Shelby instead of the usual daytime three. The town of Conrad was what, less than a half-hour south of Shelby on I-15? Especially at speeds averaging eighty-five to ninety miles per hour?

It added up to four hours. At high speeds, then, with no traffic, yes, the person who had received the ticket could have been at Mad Dog's cabin at three o'clock in the morning and reached—just barely—mile marker 325 on I-15 by 7:12 A.M., the time Fowler had written down.

Still puzzled, Clay set the file aside and leafed through the next file folder. As he set the first folder aside, the report on Nathan Yancey's death slipped out. Clay picked it up and noticed a single handwritten line written across the back of the final page: *M. has no alibi for the night in question.*

He went to the other reports. The back of the report on the ski instructor's death showed the same terse words: *M. has no alibi for the night in question.*

For several minutes, Clay stared at the shadows on the dirt wall of the root cellar. The obvious question went through his mind again and again. Who was M?

He finally turned to the last file folder. He found only a series of fingerprint cards. He glanced through them a couple of times, but nothing made sense. There was writing on the back of the cards, in light pencil that was difficult to see by the yellow lantern light: *M's prints match corkscrew.*

M? Murray Paul Evans, better known as Rooster? Corkscrew? The murder weapon found in Doris Samson's body?

When they spoke next, Fowler would have a lot to answer for. Why hadn't Fowler acted on the obvious conclusions? What had triggered him to gather the three separate reports?

Clay shut down the hissing of the gas lantern. He lay back, not expecting to sleep. His mind would keep sorting through what he'd learned, trying to find impossible answers. It was the way he was built, and the way he had handled cases through the years.

There was one crucial difference with this situation, however. It was not merely a case. Even if he could shut down his mind, sleep would be impossible because of his worries and fears and the sense that time was slipping away.

Was Kelsie still alive? Was the monster with her, delighting in some of the horrors that Clay had witnessed over the years?

It would have been easier on Clay if he had never tracked serial killers. Where other men could place their hopes and prayers in God and accept their own helplessness, Clay was driven by the sense that he should be able to do something. It made the helplessness and urgency that much worse. Where other men had no idea of the evils one human could do to another, Clay knew them too well. More than once, mercy had dictated that he lie to a grieving husband, holding back the details of the terror of his wife's final moments.

What details awaited Clay?

# 10:47 p.m.

*The boy woke from a nightmare, staring wild-eyed at the dim grayness of the ceiling. It took him a moment to remember. His mother was in Las Vegas and wouldn't be back for five days. He was at the old lady's house in the second-floor bedroom.*

*The boy heard heavy breathing. Then a cold hand touched his throat.*

*The old lady was sitting beside his bed!*

*"Bobby . . ."*

*He hated that sound; he hated her touch.*

*He flailed his arm to strike at the old lady. His hand, which was above his head, wouldn't move forward. He tried to hit her with his other hand. It took him several seconds to realize he'd been bound to the bedposts.*

*"It's okay, Bobby," she said. "Your mommy is here."*

*"You stupid old witch!" he screamed. "Let me go!"*

*She turned on the lamp beside his bed.*

*For a moment, he forgot to scream. She was wearing a blond wig. Her face was ghost white with powder, her lips a slash of red.*

*"I'm calling the cops!" his voice rose. "Let me go!"*

*"Bobby, you ran away today," she said. "That wasn't nice. I worried about you the entire time."*

*He tried to kick at the bedsheets and discovered his ankles were tied to the other bedposts.*

*"Bad boys aren't allowed to go outside." She kissed his forehead. "Mommy is going to keep you in bed until you learn your lesson."*

*"Untie me! You can't do this!"*

*She smiled. Her lipstick, smeared from the heavy kiss, looked to him as if she had just drank blood.*

*"Bobby needs to learn not to raise his voice."*

*She kept smiling as she pinched his nostrils. She waited until he gasped open-mouthed for breath, then shoved a sock inside his mouth.*

*"Can Bobby stay quiet now?"*

*He fought a gag reflex. He nodded frantically.*

*"Good. Mommy likes it when her little boy listens."*

*She pulled the sock out and let go of his nostrils. The boy drew shallow, scared breaths.*

*"Mommy's going to read you a bedtime story," she said. "Listen closely. We're going to have so much fun for the next few days, you and I in our little room here together."*

It was late evening. The Watcher had worked hard the entire day, juggling his schedule to take care of Anderson and Fowler and managing the difficult task of moving Taylor without getting caught. For lesser humans, it would have been impossible.

And now was the payoff . . .

For one delicious moment, the Watcher placed his hand on the trunk lock of the BMW. He had not yet covered his face. All he had to do was lift the trunk lid, and she would finally understand.

No, he told himself sternly. There was power in remaining hidden. He'd exalted in that power over the years as he waited to have enough wealth to make everything right for their new life together. He'd gloried in the secret that she could not know who it was who watched her. When she was ready to give herself to him, then, and only then, would he reveal himself to her. Oh, what a moment that would be . . .

The moment of temptation passed, and he lifted his hand. He was far too disciplined to succumb this late in his game. Secrecy was power. Power was secrecy.

He pulled a black hood over his head to match his black raincoat and the black gloves he was wearing.

He popped open the trunk. For a moment, she was still. Then she exploded into a frenzy of kicking.

He'd been ready, of course. His eyes had adjusted to the remaining evening light. Hers would be blinking at the sudden contrast after the darkness of the trunk.

He easily dodged her kicks—she was hampered by her bound ankles—and clamped his gloved hand over her mouth, pinching her nostrils with his other hand.

She bucked and twisted.

He smiled beneath his hood. Ether took away all the fun of a struggle, and he preferred causing her to lose consciousness this way when he had the luxury of time. Such wonderful spirit she showed. That meant it would be all the more sweet when she surrendered later to his complete control.

He continued to press with his hands. The kicking and twisting gradually grew weaker. When it finally subsided, he kept one hand across her mouth and the other holding her nostrils closed for another ten seconds. He doubted she was faking her unconsciousness, but why take chances?

When he let go, he waited and watched.

He placed a hand on her upper ribs, enjoying the sensation of the steady rise and fall of her lungs. His love.

After a few moments of admiration, he peeled the hood from his face and placed it over her head, backward, so she wouldn't be able to see through the eyeholes.

He pulled her out of the trunk, then he checked her wrists and ankles to make sure the bonds were still in place. Satisfied, he picked her up. He moved out of the trees and toward the floatplane on the nearby lake.

It took some effort to carry her onto the pontoons and then into the floatplane. He had had practice moving bodies in such a manner over the years. The only difference was that now he held a living body, not a dead one. The Watcher set Kelsie down in the cargo area. Beside her son. The float plane would take them to another faster plane. Then, all three would fly to their new home. A family.

## 10:54 p.m.

Consciousness was a surprise to Kelsie. Her last memories were of waiting in the trunk so long she'd screamed against the pain of her cramped muscles, so long she'd been forced to release the contents of her bladder. Her memories were of the horrible hooded face, of the hands on her mouth and nose. In her last memories, she had believed she was dying.

But she was alive.

Her wrists and ankles were still bound, however, and she was lying on her side. This time, however, the darkness around her face was complete. It took her several moments to realize a hood had been placed over her head.

It took her only a few more moments to understand she was on a small airplane. The engines droned. Occasionally the floor shook from the unmistakable sensation of passing through turbulence.

She heard another sound, one that took her longer to figure out because the wind and engine noise seemed to pluck the notes away at random.

"Taylor?" she cried.

The harmonica stopped playing. She felt a small hand on her shoulders.

"Taylor!"

His hands wandered to her face, feeling for the source of her cry.

"It's Mom," she said. "Taylor, it's your mom."

Taylor hugged her.

She held her hands in front of her. "Pull the rope, Taylor." It was a long shot. She doubted Taylor would understand the need to have the knots untied, let alone have the dexterity to actually do it.

She was right. He pulled at her hands first, then her wrists, then at the ends of the rope.

"My face," she said. "Take this off my face."

His hands felt for the source of noise. From the sensations on her face, she guessed he had leaned over and was resting his head against hers.

"Let me see," she explained. "Lift this off my face."

Taylor remained pressed against her. Her usual frustrations returned. Words were the way she earned her living, yet words were not effective with her own son.

She felt the warmth of his breath through the cloth hood. "Mom's here," she said. "Everything will be all right."

The airplanes engines continued to drone vibrations into her body. *Everything will be all right?*

She was on an airplane, hooded and bound by a man who had been stalking her since she was sixteen. It sounded like a small jet. Even a small airplane covered one hundred miles every hour. She knew that from hours of conversations she'd shared with Rooster, Lawson, and Michael. Twin engines pushed the speed up another seventy-five miles per hour or more. A jet travels four hundred miles per hour. Every passing minute moved her miles away from Kalispell. How could any searchers ever find her?

Taylor lay down beside her. He cuddled spoon-style in front of her, the way he usually did Saturday afternoons with Clay, when Clay fell asleep on the couch watching golf.

Kelsie felt remorse at the endless opportunities she'd missed with Taylor. If she had it to do over again . . .

*Stop,* she told herself, *you aren't dead yet.*

She told herself she was a survivor, and she'd fight as long as she could.

The engines droned, Taylor fell asleep, and Kelsie counted the seconds. She didn't know how much good it did, trying to figure out the amount of time they were going to be in the air, especially since she had no idea how long she'd been unconscious from the beginning of the flight. But counting was all she could do. The alternative was to wonder what lay ahead of her when the airplane landed. ◪ ◪

# Day 4

Clay waited, awake, until his watch chimed an alarm. He called Johnny Samson, spoke briefly, dressed, and stopped by the cabin. George was already up.

"Take this coffee," George said, meeting him at the door with a cup. "The less time you spend here in the cabin, the better. Go on up to the bench. I'll be there soon."

Clay accepted the coffee and the instructions.

Dew soaked the bottom edges of his blue jeans as he walked through long grass up the hill beyond the cabin. Clay wore a sweater and jacket so the early-morning chill did not affect him. Sunshine felt good on his face. He was grateful for a clear morning; after a sleepless, worried night, clouds and rain would have been an extra burden.

The bench was not far from the cabin. George had built it from logs and set it into a clearing, which took advantage of a western exposure. Clay had been there on occasional evenings. In still air, with long shadows through the pine trees at the edge of the clearing and with the sun's rays softened by dusk, the bench was—as George had expected it to become—a peaceful place for contemplative thoughts.

Clay pulled his cell phone from his back pocket and sat on the bench. A distant chittering squirrel was the only noise to break the silence. He left the cell phone on the bench, cupped his hands around the coffee mug, and closed his eyes.

He was exhausted. There seemed little hope the day would bring him rest. Or progress. He'd spent the night going through Fowler's files again and again, but without speaking to Fowler first, little made sense. Nor had word from Johnny been encouraging.

At the sound of footsteps, Clay opened his eyes. George was carrying a basin with two hands. He had a towel draped over his shoulders and a gentle smile on his face. As George walked closer, Clay saw the basin was filled with hot water, for vapors were rising into the chill air.

George set the basin on the bench near the cellular phone. He folded the towel and draped it over the back of the bench, then reached into his back pocket and one by one handed Clay a shaving brush, razor, and tube of shaving cream.

"First thing you do," George said, "is put on a good face. You feel lousy inside, I understand. Shave, take care of yourself, like today is a day worth getting ready for. It will give you strength."

George was right.

When Clay's hair was slicked back and his face fresh from the hot-water shave, he did feel brighter and more alert.

"I called Johnny," Clay said.

The old man looked puzzled.

Clay pointed to the cell phone. "You think you're out of reach of civilization, but you're not. He says, as of last night, no fax arrived. He'll call me as soon as it does."

"Anything else?"

"Johnny tells me I made the news. You are now officially committing a felony by harboring a fugitive from the law."

George sighed. "This makes it worse for you."

"It doesn't matter," Clay said. "If I don't find Kelsie before the sheriff finds me, it will be too late."

"You're sure?"

"Everything in my experience points to it."

"What will you do?"

"Wait for a call. From Johnny. From Russ Fowler. He told me he'd check in. I've got questions about the box he left me. Aside from that, there's not much. I mean, if I go back into town . . ."

"Teach me," George said. "Tell me what you're looking for. It can't hurt to have another pair of eyes, old as they are."

"Sure." Clay smiled. He knew exactly what George was trying to do—get Clay away from waiting helplessly with nothing to do. "Maybe after this you can apply to the Bureau."

They chose a spot just off the road, well screened by bushes, just below the cabin. If any cars passed, specifically cars from the sheriff's department, Clay would have plenty of time to slip into the woods and escape.

For chairs, they used firewood, tilted on end. The air was already warm. In the thinner mountain air, it heated in daytime as quickly as it cooled at night.

Clay put the contents of the knapsack on a blanket between them. There were file folders filled with the reports and photographs, notebooks, and fingerprint cards. What George didn't know was that Clay had already removed anything to do with Doris. He felt it would be extremely unfair for the old man to have to view the autopsy reports and crime-scene photographs of his own granddaughter, even if it had happened nearly a quarter of a century earlier.

"From what little you've said over the years," George said, surveying what was on the blanket, "I have gathered your job was to look into the minds of killers."

"When wolves roamed this valley," Clay answered, "ranchers hunted wolves by thinking like wolves, trying to look through the eyes of wolves, trying to understand what wolves would do in a given situation. My job was similar. I caught killers by learning how to think like them, by coming up with profiles based on their crimes."

Human hunters preying on human victims . . . What was happening to Kelsie right now as he and George spoke?

"I can tell by watching your face this is difficult," George said, breaking Clay's thoughts. "Perhap . . ."

"No. It's not like I could get my mind anywhere else anyway."

They sat quietly for a few minutes. A flock of chickadees, small black-and-white bundles of flitting energy, darted among the branches of the trees searching for food. When the collective chirping faded, Clay spoke again.

"There are some assumptions I can make. It won't hurt to share them with you. After all, whoever did this has been close to Kelsie in some way for a long time."

"I'm listening," George said.

"There are two types of killers," Clay said. He'd lectured on this plenty of times, but he had never expected to be lecturing because his own wife had disappeared. "Organized and disorganized. Someone who has kept himself hidden for twenty-three years is not disorganized. So we're looking for someone who has the characteristics of an organized killer. Simple conclusion, right?"

Clay outlined for George everything he had been refreshing himself on during the night as he went through the evidence files. Whoever it was, chances were he came from a dysfunctional home. More than likely during early childhood his mother had been distant or neglectful, and later, when a male role model was important, he had been abused or punished by a father, stepfather, or mother's boyfriends. He'd never learned what a normal, loving relationship was. All serial killers, without exception, had been subjected to serious emotional abuse during their childhoods, and many to physical or sexual abuse, leading them to lonely childhoods and disturbing fantasies that would eventually be acted out in adulthood.

Clay explained an organized killer was this boy turned man, and unlike the antisocial unorganized killer he had good verbal skills and a high degree of intelligence, someone capable of gaining control over victims with a con, someone smart enough to stage crime scenes to throw off investigators. This would be someone who might take trophies from his victims—not necessarily things of value, but reminders, like articles of clothing—someone who might take photographs for the same reason. Clay remembered one killer who had dozens of victims' necklaces hanging in his closet and often gave them to girlfriends for added secret pleasure.

Clay also knew, from dozens of interviews with serial offenders, that an organized killer felt superior to everybody. Monsters like John Wayne Gacy, who confessed to killing twenty-seven young men over six years, and Ted Bundy, executed for murdering an estimated thirty-five to sixty young women across a dozen states, laughed at the police too stupid to catch them and thought they could outwit psychiatrists.

These were men who, like good con artists—self-confident and with good verbal skills—had no difficulty attracting women but were unable to sustain normal, long-term relationships. Some, in fact, maintained girlfriends while hunting for others to kill. Nothing in relationships satisfied them. Something in their childhoods gave them tremendous anger toward women, and they often related later that their partners were not women enough to turn them on.

Clay finished his minilecture with a wry grin. "Disorganized killers are unpredictable and devoid of normal logic. The only reason we catch them is because of the mistakes they make at the scene of the crime. An organized killer is much different. The only good news about searching for an organized killer is that he leaves a pattern.

"Trouble is, I can only hope a fax comes in at Johnny's school and that it has enough information to help. Until then, there is too little to work on to let me start profiling. Nothing to give me a pattern yet— if there is one. He could be so smart there's nothing to find."

George pointed to the folders. "And these?"

"Some of it is the same mystery as before, twenty-three years earlier when I couldn't solve it then. Autopsy reports. Coin marks and eagle feathers."

"Explain," George said. "Eagle feathers?"

"It's called a signature. It's not necessary to know how the crime is committed but what the murderer does to fulfill himself. I think, though, this one was smart enough to change his signature. He went to a lot of work to convince us Nick was the killer. Why alert us otherwise with something as unusual as the feathers?"

Clay continued and told him about the eagle feathers and where they'd been found, without mentioning the one in Doris's mouth.

"Coins," George said. "You also said coins."

Clay chose his words carefully. Despite George's insistence otherwise, he was reluctant to speak about Doris's murder as if it were just another case.

"In one situation," Clay said, jabbing the ground in three spots to show the triangular configuration of the placement of the marks, "we found perfect round circles, as if dimes had been set down, then removed."

George frowned in puzzlement.

Neither said anything for a minute. They were accustomed to silences together.

"Do you know why Fowler did this?" George finally asked. "What would motivate the sheriff into letting a guilty man escape while Nick Buffalo, an innocent man, was not only murdered but burdened with false accusations?"

The old man *was* sharp. "I don't know," Clay said.

"Should you not also wonder why he went to the effort of saving these files? After all, it's direct proof of a coverup that could have cost him his career and sent him to jail. Why risk letting anyone find out later?"

"Another good question," Clay said. "One I hadn't considered. My mind has been on the person behind this, not on Fowler."

George nodded agreement. An ant had crawled up his pants and onto his hands, which were resting on his knees. George lifted one hand and examined the ant closely.

"Intricate," George said. "With everything man has been able to accomplish, there is no way he could build a computer that can do everything this fragile insect can, let alone scale down the computer to this size."

Clay was glad for the diversion. Talking about profiling serial killers had made him feel the filth again. He stood and stretched, willing the phone to ring: Johnny with news of a fax or Russ Fowler, calling back. Clay had a question about the information on the speeding ticket. Mainly, why was it included?

George lowered his hand and with a puff of air sent the ant into nearby grass.

"I have been thinking, my friend," George said. "Do you think Rooster Evans fits this profile? Abused in childhood, a trophy keeper, someone who hates women."

"It's not that easy, George. How can we know he's a trophy keeper? What do we know about his childhood? I'd have to be able to search his house completely, interview people who knew him or the family, and I can't do that while the sheriff's got men looking for me. Even if I could, it's a job for federal agents, an entire team. They're not here, and how could I direct them when I'm considered a suspect?"

"We should draw up a list then," George said. "People in Kelsie's life now who were in her life then. Isn't that the one thing you know for sure about this man? That he was there then and now? With the list, Johnny and I can ask around about them, see who fits your profile."

Clay grinned. George showed keen insight, and working with him did ease some of his tension and worries.

George was also right. Twenty-three years earlier, the stalker had had knowledge of the private details of Kelsie's life and schedule—

right down to knowing where she hid her diary. Now, he'd known enough to engineer her kidnapping and, most likely, Taylor's.

"A list," Clay repeated, with another grin. "Now you're a mind reader."

He reached into his jacket for his shirt pocket and pulled out a folded sheet of paper. He handed it across the blanket to George. During the night, Clay had spent a half-hour's thought, trying to remember which of the ranch workers had been on the McNeill spread the longest.

The paper he gave to George had three penciled names:

> Rooster Evans—neighbor, now missing after
>              death of father
> Berry Burrell—current ranch worker
> Frankie Lopez—current ranch worker

As George examined the paper, the cell phone rang. Clay snatched it up from the blanket.

"Garner."

"It's Johnny."

George was gesturing for something to write with.

"Did you get a fax?" Clay asked. He handed George a pencil from his front pocket, and the old man began to scratch at the paper.

"No, but I heard a couple of things I thought you should know."

"All right," Clay said. Tenuous as this connection was, it still linked him to the outside world. He found himself gripping the phone tightly enough to hurt his hand.

"Russ Fowler," Johnny said. "He's dead."

"What!"

"Natural causes. But it's still strange. You call James; let him explain."

"Sure," Clay said. "I've been trying to reach him anyway. I'll keep trying."

Clay said good-bye. This was unbelievable. *Fowler. Dead. Was it a coincidence? Or—*

George handed him the paper. He'd added to the list.

> Rooster Evans—neighbor, now missing after
>              death of father
> Berry Burrell—current ranch worker

Frankie Lopez—current ranch worker
James McNeill
Lawson McNeill
Sonny Cutknife
Johnny Samson
Clay Garner

Clay scanned it. "No, not James. We both know that. And Lawson was with me when Taylor was kidnapped."

"Of course it wasn't any of the McNeills," George said. "Just like we know it wasn't you or Johnny. But you didn't ask for a list of possibly guilty people. You wanted a list of *all* people in her life then and now."

"Fair enough," Clay said. "Sonny Cutknife. Why is the name familiar?"

"He worked at the ranch with Johnny back then. Now he's the administrator out at the reservation. A real weasel. I put his name on the list because he also knew Nick Buffalo. He might not be in Kelsie's life, but he does live nearby."

A dim memory came back to Clay of a confrontation at the ranch with Johnny and two others. He could picture Sonny. Clay dismissed him immediately. All of his experience showed him that the vast majority of serial offenders were white men.

He was about to voice his opinion when the phone rang again.

"Clay." It was James. With a bad-news-tone that filled Clay with instant dread.

"Is it Kelsie? Taylor? Have they been found?"

"No," James said.

"I've been trying to reach you all morning," Clay began. "I—"

"I've been at the airport. Lawson's dead. His airplane exploded on the runway last night. They've just recovered his body."

# 6:30 a.m.

Kelsie felt hung over. It didn't surprise her. Even with the hood over her head, she'd known what happened when the airplane finally landed. A damp cloth had been pressed against the hood over her face. She twisted her head away from it, but the unseen hand had pressed harder until she was forced to inhale a dizzying sweetness that sent her again crashing into the darkness.

Now Taylor was beside her, staring into her face. Kelsie sat upright with slow, groggy awkwardness. Her hands were free. Her feet were free.

Taylor grinned and patted her thigh.

Kelsie gave him a distracted hug. She was trying to understand the situation. She was no longer wearing her soiled sweatshirt and blue jeans. Instead, she was now in a sweatsuit and conscious of the fact she did not have on any panties or brassiere beneath it. Taylor was in a smaller version of the sweatsuit in the same bright colors.

Someone had dressed her. Again. The same someone had taken away the cell phone she had tucked into her blue jeans.

Who was he? What did he want from her?

She turned her attention to the one question she might be able to answer: Where was she?

Taylor, sitting beside her, hummed and rocked with happiness. She looked over his head and around the room.

It seemed to be a living room. A sofa and easy chair were arranged around a large coffee table. The carpet was thick and luxurious. A large-screen television filled one corner. She saw a magazine rack, plants, assorted knickknacks, and various framed prints on the walls. Beyond the living room, she saw a kitchen area complete with dining table and four chairs on a hardwood floor.

Something bothered her. Looking around, she realized it was the lack of windows. The closest thing to a window was a small, square dark piece of glass in one wall.

Kelsie stood. Taylor stood with her and took her hand. The roughness of the skin of his hands had always repulsed her and reminded her that Taylor was indiscriminate with what he touched. At the ranch, Taylor explored anything of interest—his hands could have been anywhere, from pulling apart a dead bird to examining deer droppings. But they only had each other; Kelsie managed not to pull her hand away from her son.

They walked to the kitchen area. She saw cupboards, a sink, and a microwave. No dishwasher, no stove, no refrigerator. Again, there were no windows.

It occurred to her that there was no door leading out of the kitchen. Instead, the far wall of the kitchen—which she hadn't been able to see from the living room—opened to another large room, making the entire layout of the living quarters L-shaped, living room to kitchen to sleeping area.

She moved out of the kitchen with Taylor still humming and still clinging to her hand. In the sleeping area were two beds, one king-sized in the center of the room and one twin-sized, which was against one wall. Was the small one meant to be for Taylor?

In the far right corner was an open bathroom area containing a vanity, pedestal sink, toilet, and shower stall, all behind a waist-high wall to give a sense of separation from the rest of the area.

The walls, with fresh ivory-white paint, were decorated with tasteful prints. There were no windows in the bedroom area either, only the occasional small dark plates of glass where windows might have been.

Kelsie guessed the entire living space to be close to twelve hundred square feet. It was new, luxurious, but without windows, it seemed like a prison.

The thought went through her mind, and then she froze. *A prison.*

Kelsie looked around wildly for a door. It wasn't until she returned to the living-room area that she found it, painted the same color as the walls and without a doorframe.

She tried the handle without much hope. It was securely locked.

"Cowboy, me," Taylor announced. "Hungry, me."

She wondered if there was food in the cupboards. She and Taylor returned to the kitchen area. She found food, plenty of it. Nonperishable items such as rice and noodles, all stored in large plastic containers. There were pouches of powdered milk and powdered juices. She found sugar, spices, and coffee. Nothing, however, was in a metal can.

She found plates and cups, all made of the kid-proof rubber that parents bought when they had small children. She found forks, knifes, and spoons also made of bendable hard rubber.

What was going on?

"Cowboy, me," Taylor said again.

"Yes," Kelsie said, distracted. "Cowboy, you."

Something else was strange about this. She finally realized there were no lamps and that the light fixtures were recessed into the ceilings, covered by large circles of thick plastic.

She left Taylor in the kitchen and walked through all the rooms again. It took her a while longer to realize another oddity. There wasn't a single breakable object. She couldn't reach the glass light bulbs beneath the plastic covers. The dishes in the kitchen, of course, were indestructible. The big-screen television did not have a glass screen. The furniture was heavy wood. Even the bathroom mirror was of polished steel.

*Prison.* She couldn't help the conclusion. *Prison.*

She guessed that over five hours had passed before the airplane landed. How could she expect anyone to find her? This prison could be anywhere from San Francisco to Minnesota.

There was another conclusion, more chilling. Her kidnapper had put incredible resources and planning into this room—it spoke of great purpose.

"Hungry, me," Taylor announced again as he followed her into the bedroom area. He hugged Kelsie's legs and put his head against her thighs.

Kelsie heard a light crackle. She patted her sweatpants and found the source of the crackle. It was a piece of paper. She took it out and unfolded it, dreading what she might read.

The words were very simple. And they filled her with terror.

*Welcome home, my love.*

## 9:51 A.M.

*Hours later, the boy begged to go to the bathroom. He promised he would be good if only she untied him. He promised he would allow her to tie him back to the bed if only she let him go to the bathroom.*

*She refused. She said she had to show him that he must learn to behave.*

*He begged more. He called her Mommy.*

*"I love you, Mommy," he said, swallowing his revulsion. "I love you. I'm sorry I hurt you. I love you."*

*She began to cry.*

*He sensed her resolve weakening. "I love you. Bobby thinks you're the best Mommy in the world."*

*She threw herself across him and sobbed.*

*His instinct was to attempt to buck her off. However, he endured her perfume, and he endured the smeared tears across his face and hair, in the hope that she would untie him.*

*"Mommy loves you too," she said. "Mommy's sorry for Halloween. Mommy didn't mean to hit you. Can you forgive Mommy for letting you fall down the stairs?"*

*"Yes, Mommy," he said. He was smart enough not to ask her to untie him. The request might make her suspicious.*

*Finally, she pulled herself away from him and slowly untied the bonds that held his wrists and ankles to the bedposts.*

*He waited until he was standing. Then he reacted quickly and furiously. "Stupid old witch!" he shouted and kicked her in the stomach. She dropped to her knees, and he punched her in the head. Then he pushed her onto her back.*

*"Stupid old witch," he shouted at her prone body. He was tough. After the beatings he'd taken in his life, he was tough. No old lady was going to scare him.*

*He ran from the bedroom, down the hall, down the stairs, and to the front door. It didn't matter how far he had to run, he'd find someone to help him get to the police. Then she would really pay.*

*He yanked at the handle of the door. It turned and twisted, but it did not open. It was bolted shut.*

*He snapped on the front hallway light. The bolt was a key lock. He needed the key to open the door. He dashed to the back door. Same thing.*

*Windows! he thought. He ran into the living room. Iron security bars had been placed on the outside. No burglars could get in. No one could get out.*

*The second-floor windows did not have security bars, he thought. He'd already escaped through his own bedroom. But the old lady was in there.*

*He'd try another room on the second floor. He'd jump if he had to. Anything to get away from the crazy old lady in the blond wig.*

*He ran back up the stairs and tugged at the doors down the hallway. Each one was locked.*

*"Bobby . . . Bobby . . ." Her moaning voice taunted him from his bedroom.*

*Where could he go? Ahead of him at the end of the hallway, he spotted a small door. He ran to it and pulled. He nearly gasped with relief when it opened. He saw a set of stairs leading up to the attic. He hesitated. Would he be trapped up there?*

*"Bobby . . . Bobby . . ."*

*What choice did he have? Maybe she would first look for him downstairs. Maybe there was a window onto the roof. Maybe there was a good hiding spot.*

*He hesitated too long.*

*"Bobby!" she shrieked as she stepped out from his bedroom.*

*Blood was running down her face.*

*He took one step and closed the door behind him then fled up the stairs into the darkness of the attic.*

*Were the spider webs his imagination, the result of reading all those horror comic books?*

*He couldn't see. It was nearly dark, with the only light coming from the moon through a small window too high in the ceiling for him to reach without a chair.*

*The door at the bottom of the attic stairs opened. "Bobby!"*

*He bumped into chests and boxes as he tried to find a place to hide. The front of his thighs hit something with soft edges. He reached with his hand. The mattress of a bed? Yes!*

*His first thought was to crawl under it. But then he had another idea. He stripped the top blanket off the bed. Maybe he could throw it over her and get past her. Maybe then he could somehow lock her in the attic and call the police.*

*"Bobby!"*

*There was a small snap as she flicked on the light at the bottom of the attic stairs.*

*For one, long, unbelievable moment, the boy froze in the sudden brightness.*

*Then he screamed.*

*On the bed beside him, now exposed because of the blanket in the boy's hands, was something he dimly recognized as another boy.*

*This one, on the bed, was dried, shrunken leather over bones. Skull hollow, eye sockets empty, jaw fallen away.*

*The boy finally understood the shrunken leather was a vest over a skeletal body and that the feathers in disarray around the skull came from an Indian feather headdress.*

*"Bobby . . ." the old lady called again.*

*The boy leaned against the wall and slid down until he was sitting. He curled his knees up against his body and hugged himself, waiting in silent terror as her footsteps creaked up the attic stairs.*

The Watcher drove in satisfied silence. He was exhausted but juiced on caffeine and adrenaline. Since ten o'clock the night before, he'd flown over four hours on the way out and four hours back, with an hour in between to transfer Kelsie from the airplane into the house. He hadn't been able to leave the valley until just before sunrise. Still, he was making good time. Kalispell and his old life were already two hundred and fifty miles behind. He could have been farther ahead, but Highway 93, the two-lane from Kalispell to the interstate at

Missoula, had slowed him because he refused to risk a speeding ticket or hitting a deer, not with so much accomplished already, not with this journey the final and only barrier between him and the woman he loved.

Others, he thought, would have stayed on 93 through Missoula, taking it south nearly to Idaho Falls before turning off to remain on a two-lane road as far as possible. Others, however, did not have the experience and nerves he did. Two-lane roads did have less traffic, but that was a disadvantage, not an advantage. The best way to hide was among hundreds of vehicles, not dozens.

No, the Watcher knew the best routes were the interstates. By remaining eight miles an hour above the speed limit, the car was essentially invisible to state troopers. He planned to average a steady seventy-three miles per hour, putting him through Idaho Falls, through Pocatello, and into the wide, broad valleys north of the Utah state line.

Flying, of course, would have been much better. But he'd made his plans, and he would stick to them. Driving took the risk of getting caught from minimal to zero.

Yes, he admitted to himself, even if driving was tedious, he did have reason to be satisfied. Each minute put more than a mile between him and the life he had left behind in Kalispell. Each minute brought him more than a mile closer to home sweet home.

## 10:15 A.M.

Waiting, waiting, waiting. The tension—minute after minute after minute—made Kelsie want to scream.

The door would open eventually. She hadn't been placed in such an elaborate setup just to be ignored. And when it opened, then what? Who would it be? What would be done to her?

Again and again, she told herself not to speculate. Instead, she went through the living quarters repeatedly looking for anything she could convert to a weapon. She found nothing of use, nothing she could hide in her clothing and use to attack her attacker. She found nothing that could even be destructive to herself or the apartment.

There was no glass anywhere. The shower stall door was plastic. The microwave door was solid metal.

She believed she understood why there was no stove. With the burners, she would be able to light a fire.

Where before she had puzzled over the lack of canned foods, she now understood. Sharp lids could be fashioned into crude knives.

The rubber eating utensils had no sharp edges. She couldn't cut the blankets or towels into strips, which—she shuddered in speculating that it was anticipated she might get desperate enough to take her own life—would make it possible to hang herself. All of the electrical cords—to the television or lamps—were barely more than a foot long.

For that matter, there was nothing metal to insert into the wall plugs. The edges of the wood furniture were rounded. She couldn't hurt anyone, including herself.

In short, whoever had placed her in the living quarters had planned carefully. That made her predicament more chilling—the obvious meticulous attention to detail.

She had enough food to last her for weeks. The microwave would let her heat and boil the noodles and rice. Bottles of vitamins had been provided—to make up for the lack of fresh foods? There were even boxes of disposable diapers; whoever had done this knew her situation intimately. That, of course, was not a surprise to Kelsie.

Hour after hour after hour, she waited. She slept, she paced, she watched television. Some of the channels had been blacked out; she finally realized the local channels were unavailable. She could watch HBO, MTV, TNT, and all the other national cable networks, but there was nothing to give her an indication of where these living quarters were.

Everywhere she went, Taylor bumped along behind her, humming or playing his harmonica. She would bend down to look in a cupboard; he would bend down beside her. She would sigh in frustration; he would sigh. She would sit down; he would try to crawl in her lap. She went to her bed; he curled up beside her.

Her original relief at finding him alive had become the constant vague irritation she'd always felt at his bumbling presence. It wasn't right—she felt guilty because she knew a good mother wouldn't be frustrated—but the more time that passed in the prison, the more she grew angry at Taylor for his ceaseless devotion. All she wanted was some peace. From the tension. From Taylor.

The minutes kept stretching. Each of those minutes with Taylor reminded her that she had failed both as a mother and as a wife. And each of those minutes reminded her that Taylor's handicap was a punishment she deserved from God for letting three men die as a price for loving her.

# 12:03 p.m.

Clay was at the bench on the uphill side of the cabin, biting into a sandwich he didn't feel like eating, when the cellular phone rang.

"It's Johnny. I don't have good news about your fax."

"What?" Clay asked. If Johnny wasn't going to waste any time with preamble, neither was Clay.

"Floyd, the principal here, was standing at the fax machine when your friend sent his report."

"You can't get the fax?" Fowler was dead. Feeble as the hope was, this fax had been Clay's best chance. What else could he do when all that linked him to the world was a cell phone?

"Worse, Floyd called the sheriff. Your name was on the report, and your name's been in the news. Floyd's trying to be a hero."

"It was sent to your attention, wasn't it?"

"Yes. I was in class and just got out for lunch and—"

"That's not what I meant," Clay said. "Your name's on the fax. They're going to be asking you some tough questions. I'm sorry."

"I can deal with it," Johnny said. "I'm more worried about you. If they hadn't figured yet where you might be, they'll sure have good reason to guess now."

"I'll watch for them." Clay tilted the phone against his ear with his shoulder. With free hands, he wrapped the remainder of the sandwich.

"There's more." Clay picked up the hint of excitement in Johnny's voice.

"Tell me," Clay said as he began walking down to George's cabin.

"It's a man named Sonny Cutknife. He's disappeared. You know about him yet?"

"I do. I talked to James about an hour ago."

*Sonny Cutknife!*

Clay had finally reached James McNeill later in the morning. James had passed on everything he'd learned about Emerald Canyon, including the fact that his name was on one of the corporations. While Clay hadn't been able to make any more sense of it than James, something was definitely linking Emerald Canyon to Kelsie. It also formed a link to Frank Evans and by extension, his son Rooster.

Clay was also very conscious of the list of names in his pocket. Rooster was on the list, but so was Sonny Cutknife.

"I mean, Sonny's really disappeared," Johnny said, "and not trying to hide it. He left a letter of resignation for the administration secretary. He's gone. I heard it at lunch already, and the rumor is all around the reservation. Especially how bad the secretary took it. She was his girlfriend and didn't see it coming."

"Do me a favor," Clay said. "Find out what you can about Sonny's childhood."

"He was adopted," Johnny said, almost immediately. "I remember him telling me that. White parents who took him out of a foster home. He really hated them. You want me to try to get their names?"

"Definitely," Clay's heart began to surge. White parents. Adopted. Bad childhood. It might seem too simple of a thumbnail sketch, but how many others on that list were likely to have the same profile? And Sonny had disappeared. If the stalker was Sonny, there would be something in his past to point toward where he'd gone. And where Sonny was, Kelsie and probably Taylor would be too.

Could Clay outguess Sonny? Only if he knew more.

"George said you worked on the McNeill ranch with Sonny," Clay said. He'd reached the cabin and was staring down the road, looking for the first signs of approaching vehicles. "How long had he been there?"

"At least a couple of years."

"What do you think. Is he mentally stable?"

Johnny waited, as if he were measuring his answer. "That summer he once threatened to kill me. He stuck my head in a post pounder and asked if I wanted my skull to pop like a watermelon."

"Find out as much as you can about him." This was the first sign of progress, and Clay felt stronger because of it. "Nothing is too trivial to report. Nothing. Can you talk to me tonight?"

"Sure. Where?"

Clay wondered how long before men from the sheriff's department appeared on the gravel road.

"That's a good question, Johnny." To Clay, it looked like he'd better start putting distance between himself and the cabin. With the ridges and dips of the mountainous hills, he wasn't sure how long he'd be in cell-phone range. "How about calling me on the hour and half-hour?"

"Done deal," Johnny said. "This is a small place. I'll have plenty on him by the time we talk again." Johnny hung up.

Clay dialed another number. He hoped the battery on his phone would last.

"Dennis, it's Clay." With his left hand, Clay pressed the phone against his ear. He held a pen in his right hand and was poised to scribble notes on the back of a file folder across his lap.

"You got my report?" Flannigan asked.

"It came in but someone else got hold of it. I don't have time to explain. Can we talk now and talk fast? I don't know how much battery time I have left on my phone."

"Fire away."

"Can you sum up what you found? I'm ready to take notes."

"Hang on," Flannigan said. "The report's on my desk. I'll pick up the extension there."

Clay closed his eyes. The sun warmed his face. Under any other circumstances, he'd welcome a peaceful moment like this, high up in the quiet hills. Now, however, he felt jangled, his nerve ends gritty, his stomach sour. There was so little he could do, so much that had to be done.

"Clay, I've got it in front of me."

"I'm listening."

"Here's the short version. You asked for any unsolved murders within five hundred miles over the last twenty-three years. In statistical terms, the answer is none. None, at least, that would be related to this. The ones that did come up I went through myself. None of those deaths fit what you're looking for."

Clay had no hesitation in trusting Flannigan's judgment. It was the results that bothered him. None? It didn't make sense. Once the monster had a taste for blood, it was almost impossible to stop.

"We're at a dead end with VICAP?"

"No," Flannigan said, "and that's part of the longer version. "You told me to pull up a search on women between the ages of twenty and fifty. On a hunch, I went back in to VICAP with something more specific. I took away the boundary you gave me and opened it to the entire country. I asked for hits on women with a similar appearance to Kelsie. Tall, blonde, and young. Guess what?"

"You wouldn't be telling me unless you found something."

"Thirty-two." Flannigan's voice rose. "Thirty-two! Scattered far and wide and with no kill pattern I could see, no time pattern that made sense. A bunch up and down the Atlantic states. The Midwest, Southwest, all over the place. Maybe that's why no one else connected them. Maybe there isn't a connection. But thirty-two? If it's true, this is a major killer, and no one has any idea he's been hunting."

Clay knew it was possible. It had taken a lucky break for anyone to discover that John Wayne Gacy had killed over thirty young men in less than seven years, in the far tighter geographical circle of his home near Chicago. A body count of thirty-two over twenty-three years in the entire country would be practically invisible, even with VICAP.

"He's probably taken more," Clay said. "Those are only the ones registered in VICAP. You can figure that others weren't reported. And figure also that some were killed and their bodies never found. You know how many thousands of missing-persons cases don't get solved."

"That's the other thing," Flannigan told him. "Bodies. I called up another request. I got to thinking if your man does live in Kalispell, maybe he picks up his victims from *outside* the five-hundred-mile circle you gave me. Maybe he takes them home from there. The computer gave me ten hits. Bodies found over the last fifteen years within that five-hundred-mile circle. These bodies—well, some were identified, some weren't. What's got my attention is that five of the seven bodies with positive I.D. were lookalikes. Tall, blonde, young. Of the ones that couldn't be identified, autopsy reports show bone structure of young Caucasian females."

"Couldn't be identified?"

"Clay, that's what's got me convinced you're onto something. All five bodies dumped within the five-hundred-mile circle had one thing in common: They were found in remote mountain-hiking areas. Some had been there so long that the animals had scattered the bones."

"He takes them on camping trips," Clay guessed aloud. "Gets their trust, puts them in a situation where he can play with them as long as he wants without any danger. We're looking for someone who's familiar with backcountry."

*Rooster Evans fit. So did Sonny Cutknife.*

"Whoever it is, he's a sicko," Flannigan said. "You haven't heard the worst of it."

Clay did not want to hear. Already, Taylor had been gone for two days, Kelsie for one. If the monster had taken them on a forced march into any of the nearby mountains, they could be anywhere among tens of thousands of square miles of mountain and trees.

"Give it to me," Clay said slowly.

"He likes breaking bones."

"Repeat that."

"I've never heard of anything like it. Each one without exception showed broken bones. Everywhere. As if he had taken a sledge-hammer to them."

Clay took several deep breaths to compose himself. If there was ever a time to detach himself from his emotions, this was it. "Any of the others found elsewhere fit that MO?"

"A couple of others," Flannigan said, "but also in remote areas. So it still fits."

"Right," Clay said. "Anything else you can tell me?" he asked.

"Plenty of details. I haven't been able to put a profile together. Maybe you can. But there're thirty pages of details. It'd be a lot easier if I could get it to you somehow."

Movement in the trees below caught Clay's eye. It was George carrying two backpacks. He pointed back at the cabin.

"I'll get you a fax number as soon as I can," Clay said.

"Sheriff's men," George said as he approached. "I left as they were driving up."

"Wait for the fax number," Clay told Dennis. "But right now it looks like I have to go."

An hour's hike higher into the hills from the cabin, George and Clay took their first break. The old man's effortless stamina impressed Clay greatly. Of the two, Clay was the one who called the stop.

"Not used to packing," Clay said, pride forcing him to pretend he was breathing normally. "How do you do it?"

"Old Indian trick," George said. He found a log to sit on. "It is a matter of intelligence, not strength."

"*Intelligence* brought you up the hill?" Clay knew he was being set up.

"No, intelligence led me to insist on packing both knapsacks. I loaded yours down with everything heavy I did not wish to carry."

Clay snorted. He set his pack down. "Have any idea where we're going?"

"Away," George said. "That seemed safest."

"Any other ideas?" Clay was glad for the banter but could not escape the desperate sensation of time—measured in Kelsie's heartbeats—sliding away while he could do nothing but run.

"We rest," George said. "We talk. For I have been thinking about something peculiar. Tell me again about the night you were shot by the person you thought was Nick Buffalo."

Clay did.

"It looks different now," George said. "You know Nick didn't pull the trigger. You know it was someone else. Tell me again, how did that someone else arrange it to look like Nick?"

Clay repeated Fowler's speculations. "The reports showed sawdust in the grassroots. Fowler guessed—and I agree with him—whoever did it cut a hole in the back of the cabin. Say he's got Nick's body in there. He runs back to the cabin, starts shooting like it's Nick shooting. Then he lights a fire and leaves out the back."

"Do you think he carried Nick up to the cabin that night while you were chasing him with a bloodhound?"

"No. He'd definitely have placed the body there ahead of time."

"What would have happened if hikers came along? Or ranch hands? If they found Nick's body in the cabin beforehand . . ."

"Slim chance," Clay argued, "since most people thought the cabin was haunted. Or," he continued, "maybe he covered the body with a blanket."

"To me, my friend, this does not sound like a person who leaves things to chance."

Clay was forced to agree, half-amused at the surgical precision of George's thinking.

"Let me ask you something else. Do you think this person carried Nick's body all the way up to the cabin?"

"No," Clay said. "Too much work. Impossible at night. Also, there's the chance of someone seeing him during the day. If he was smart, he'd try to get Nick to meet him there."

"So . . ."

"So Nick knew him."

*Sonny Cutknife? Rooster Evans? Or someone else?*

"Looks like it," George agreed. "Now after the person killed Nick, if he didn't leave the body in the cabin, where would he have stored it?"

"Not on the hillside," Clay said. "What are you thinking?"

"Is my cabin modern?"

"No. I've got to rattle the outhouse before I go in there, just in case a skunk's inside." Clay smiled. "You thinking he kept the body in the outhouse?"

"Where did you stay last night, and why did we decide it was a safe place?"

It hit Clay. *Root cellar. Few were the people of this generation who might know an old trapper would have a root cellar.*

George smiled at the look of comprehension on Clay's face. "The root cellar."

"The cabin site might be a nine-hour hike from here. Are you willing to risk the time it takes on the off-chance our guess is right?"

Clay nodded.

"You told me earlier that we are after a predator," George said.

Clay nodded again.

"Do predators not have lairs?" George asked. "And if we find his lair, will we also find Kelsie and Taylor?"

# 4:15 P.M.

Something brushed Kelsie's hand. She woke from her nap with a violent lurch, expecting from the depths of a dream the man with the hooded face to be looming above her.

"Cowboy, me," Taylor said. He looked up from where he was licking her hand and gave her his usual grin. "Love me. You."

She pulled her hand away and wiped it on the blanket. "Play. Go. Leave me alone," she said, shivering with the afterrush of adrenaline. She pointed at the kitchen. "Go."

Taylor shrugged and hopped down from her bed.

He hummed as he walked. It was a lurching gait that had often embarrassed Kelsie in public places. It had taken Taylor over a year to learn to crawl, nearly four years before he walked. Whenever she took him somewhere, which was seldom, she felt pitying glances from other parents.

Some parents, she knew, institutionalized their Down's syndrome children. That would have been her choice. She'd mentioned it in passing to Clay once. Clay's response had been unnerving silence, followed by his leaving for a long walk. The subject had never come up again. While Clay loved his son, to Kelsie, Taylor was a stigma. Somewhere deep inside, Kelsie believed if she had not allowed men to die because of their love for her, Taylor would have been born a normal child.

She also knew the high marriage-failure statistics on couples with handicapped children. If Clay hadn't been so enduring—something she loved him for but was often helpless to show—their marriage, too, would have ended in divorce. As it was, it hadn't been good for a long time.

Lying in bed, Kelsie thought about Clay and wondered if they could find passion again. If she learned to stop using work as an excuse not to face what she didn't like about herself . . .

Kelsie laughed bitterly, loud enough that Taylor stopped and looked back at her. How could she think about a future? This was her life, an apartment prison. Her cellmate, Taylor, was the one person she'd spent years trying to avoid. Kelsie had no illusions. This was probably the best it would be. Sometime soon, she and Taylor would not be alone.

The clattering of cupboards interrupted her brooding.

"Taylor," she shouted.

The clattering stopped, only to be replaced by the discordant strains of a harmonica.

She sighed and got out of bed.

She was helpless in many ways in this prison, but there were a few things within her control. She walked to the kitchen area and found Taylor sitting cross-legged on the floor there. He pulled the harmonica from his mouth at her approach. He gave her another grin.

"Is that the only expression you have?" she snapped. "An idiot's grin?"

The grin faltered at the tone of her voice. "Cowboy, me?"

She reached down and snatched the harmonica from his hand. "I'm equally sick of this," she said. She threw it on the countertop and jerked Taylor to his feet. "I'm putting you in bed, and that's where you're staying."

He stumbled along behind her. At his bed, the narrow one near the bathroom, she pulled the covers back, lifted him onto the mattress, and covered him.

"Sleep, you," she ordered.

"Sleep, cowboy," he agreed.

As soon as she turned her back on him, he jumped out of bed and followed her.

"Taylor . . ." she warned in a low voice. She took his hand and repeated the entire process.

"Sleep, me," he agreed once again.

This time she made it to the couch in the living room before he reappeared.

"Taylor!" Once again, she put him in the bed.

Once again, he agreed, "Sleep, me."

She was on the couch, leaning forward with her head in her hands when he tugged on her sleeve.

She exploded. "You stupid, stupid child," she screamed. "Surely you can't be that retarded that you don't know how to sleep!"

He regarded her with serious eyes. "Cowboy, me?"

"Retard. Retard, you," she said. "Hear me? Retard, you."

He flinched at the volume of her screams, but he didn't back away.

She drew a breath, and in that brief, quiet moment, Taylor spoke. "Retard, me?" He stepped up to her and hugged her leg.

She stared down at his head. *Retard*. The word pierced her. She'd called her son a retard.

He reached up for her hand. Numbly, she let him take it. He kissed her hand. "Make better," he said. "Love me. You."

A tear ran down Kelsie's face, then another.

There'd been a morning, so long ago it seemed like it had happened in a book. It was shortly after her mother had died, when Kelsie still daydreamed and thought romance was forever. Kelsie had been back of the barn. The air had become completely still, the way it got before a storm. She had heard distinctly one plop of rain on the hard earth. Then the second plop. A third. She saw at her feet the dark splotches of those first few large raindrops. For some reason, the moment had seemed magical, as if she'd been given a great lesson she couldn't understand. She'd been given the privilege of hearing—out of all the rain that would burst forth in a thundering deluge—the very first three drops.

One tear. Two. Both fell on Taylor's upturned face. He smiled and licked at them with the extended tongue peculiar to children with Down's syndrome.

Before, seeing yet another sign of his handicap would have revolted her.

Now? Drained of her defenses, she saw him differently for the first time. This was her son, her only son. His walk, his humming, his joy, and yes, even his large, ugly tongue, all of it belonged to her son, the son who was holding her leg.

The third tear fell. And the pent-up rain finally burst. Without shame she pulled Taylor to her and held him in return.

## 9:00 P.M.

As darkness fell, Clay and George looked for a campsite. They estimated there was less than a mile left to reach Mad Dog's cabin, but with night upon them, they knew a search for the root cellar would have to wait until morning anyway.

George chose the meal as his responsibility; Clay chose shelter. As George assembled a fire, Clay found a knocked-down sapling. With a hatchet, he lopped off the branches then set the long pole chest-high in the crotches of two trees some ten feet apart. Clay unfolded a sheet of plastic from the knapsack and tied it over the support pole. Next he set a line of rocks across the back of the sheet so that the plastic formed a primitive roof, angling downward from the pole. It would not shield them from a sustained storm, but for what they needed, it was sufficient.

For his part, George was efficient. Clay enjoyed watching the old man work. George had hiked at a steady pace all day and showed no strain of fatigue. Food, a pasta mix from a freeze-dried package, was ready by the time Clay had unrolled the sleeping bags onto the earth floor beneath the shelter.

They ate in silence sitting cross-legged on the ground. They let the hush of the wilderness drop upon them with the darkness.

George had left a pot over the fire to boil water. When both had finished eating, George suggested coffee.

"Decaf?" George asked. "You need sleep. I could see it in your face all day."

Clay managed a smile. He knew George was right, but did not expect sleep to come any easier than the night before, decaffeinated coffee or not.

"Decaf," Clay said.

Again, extended silence. Clay was on his third cup of coffee before George spoke again.

"You and I," he said. "We've had many such nights like this, yes? We trade thoughts and speculations on many matters. We puzzle at the ways of God, seeking to increase our understanding of Him."

Clay sipped his coffee. He knew George well enough. The old man drank in silence, too, waiting until he had properly framed his thoughts to begin. Clay wouldn't interrupt until George asked him a direct question.

"I think, my friend, you and I are like babies playing with pebbles on the beach, unaware of the existence of the ocean, let alone the infinite wonders hidden in the depths. Life and this universe is an unfathomable mystery. Even scientists will tell you that the more answers they find, the more questions are raised. And where is God in all of this? We try to decide. You and I push our pebbles around and arrange them and take comfort in holding them, but our intellect simply does not have the capacity to understand God and this mystery."

Clay stared at the glowing embers of the dying coals. His wife and son were gone, in the hands of a monster. He was virtually helpless against that threat. Another ten hours would pass before he could take what little action was within his power. Ten hours that could be an eternity of unimaginable terror for the two people he loved most. And after that? Clay had no guarantees that any of his efforts or the authorities' efforts would ever lead to finding Kelsie and Taylor alive. Chances were just as good that their bodies would never even be discovered. Clay had never been in the grips of such black, unrelenting despair.

"Listen to me," George said.

Clay lifted his head.

"Clay, sometimes I tremble when I contemplate my own death. It is not something far away and vague to me. It is not an intellectual exercise. Someday soon my heart will stop beating. When I die, will I go into a void of nothingness? Or will I find the face of God and answers to the mystery? After a lifetime of choosing to believe I have an eternal soul, I still face doubts daily. Has everything I've done been nothing but the flailing of flesh dissolving into ashes? Or will I be released from the prison of this body to roam the heavens?"

"And?" Clay's voice was soft.

"This mystery of life and death and the beyond is so overwhelming that after a lifetime of searching for truth, I have had to return to the faith of a child."

George's voice dropped. "I have to accept that I'm so little I can't understand my Father's ways. I have to trust with the blind faith of a child. He and Love wait beyond in a way I can only dimly glimpse now. That blind trust, after a lifetime of straining to understand, is the only strength and peace I can take into the face of death."

"You have a reason for telling me this," Clay said. "You have a reason for telling it to me now."

"Think of a rope, my friend. You can believe the rope is strong, but how will you know unless you test it? Not until you are hanging from that rope over an abyss will you know whether it was worth trusting."

"Now I'm hanging from that rope?"

George nodded slowly. "It is in the set of your shoulders and the fear in your face. You are hanging from that rope. As am I. It is my own death I contemplate. It is the death of your wife and child that you contemplate. The reality of what we believe is tested by these realities."

George rose abruptly. "I am going to my sleeping bag now. I hope as you watch the fire, you will find peace in this. If what we believe is true, then death, no matter how horrible, is not the end. If death is not the end, then all of our lives' sorrows will pass into joy. I pray we find Kelsie and Taylor. Yet if we don't, you will not be gone from them long, nor them from you, because there is the other side of the curtain of our life on earth, a place where these sorrows will be forgotten. If you do not believe this and trust this as a child holds his father's hand along a path in a dark forest, your faith is meaningless. If you do trust this, there is nothing more valuable on earth than your faith."

George patted Clay on the back, then shuffled toward the shelter.

Clay stared at the fire. His despair turned to tears, and with his tears, finally, came the lifting of a burden.

Much later, when he crawled into his sleeping bag, he slept without the nightmares that had haunted him since Taylor's disappearance.

# 10:21 p.m.

Kelsie remembered a gangster movie, one that had almost introduced a phobia into her life. In the movie, the assassin had slipped into the office of his victim. He was armed with a simple garrote—two short handles of wood, connected by a four-foot length of piano wire.

Execution had been simple and horrifying. His victim was sitting at his desk, concentrating on paperwork. The assassin soft-shoed himself behind the victim, looped the wire into a circle, dropped it over the victim's head, and yanked the wooden handles in opposite directions. Brutally quick and strong, the assassin exerted so much force that the victim's head had been partially severed from his body.

Ever since seeing the movie, Kelsie had been uncomfortable with strangers sitting behind her in theaters, on airplanes, or anywhere else. The image of the garroted man would flash into her mind, and she would shudder at how easily the method worked and how little chance the victim stood.

Now, she realized, if she could, she would garrote the man to protect Taylor and herself. She began to devise a plan. Instead of piano wire, she would use a length of string. Instead of wooden handles, she would use one of the sturdy, hard rubber knives on each end.

She did not expect that the string would actually cut through the flesh of her captor's neck. She did expect to be able to pull tightly enough to strangle him, however. If somehow she could get behind him and if somehow she was able to loop the garrote over his neck, she would fight with all her fury. Nothing would shake her from his back until he finally fell.

That was her plan. All she needed was a length of string strong enough to handle the pressure. She did not find string, of course. But that would not stop her.

She took a dish towel, moved to the couch, and began pulling at the fringed edges.

Taylor sat at her feet and hummed with contentment. Occasionally, Kelsie would stop her work and drop her hand to rub his shoulders. Taylor needed touch far more than he needed words.

Thread by thread, Kelsie intended to weave herself a line that would not snap. It did not bother her that the task would take patience and consume time. She was glad for something to do. She was certain that if she did not find a way out, there would be years of time, in here, ahead of her.

# 11:46 P.M.

"Bobby . . ."

The old woman's voice broke the boy's spell of terror. He stood, averting his eyes from the skeleton on the bed.

"Bobby . . ."

The top of her head, blond wig grossly twisted, appeared at the level of the attic floor. The boy looked around for something he could use to strike her.

He saw nothing.

"Bobby . . ." Her slow ascent reminded him of the zombies in his horror books.

He looked around wildly again. He saw the skeleton. He reached for the weapon, grabbing it before his revulsion could defeat the instructions from his brain. When he lifted his right hand, he was holding a thigh bone.

"Bobby . . ."

He drove forward, screaming and swinging hard. The bone caught her across the shoulders and neck. It took her by surprise, and she fell backward, tumbling down the stairs. When the boy dared to peek, he saw the wig resting on a step, just above her impossibly twisted body.

He threw the thigh bone at the far wall and slowly made his way downward, half expecting the old woman to rise and clutch at him.

She lay motionless. He jumped over her and into the second-floor hallway, then slammed the door behind him.

He was breathing in short gasps, but most of the panic had ended.

How could he get out?

Her purse, he thought, he'd find keys in her purse.

Then he remembered the first cat and how a trashman had found it. He had made a promise to himself then never to get caught again.

The old lady was dead. What would they do to him for that?

He knew he had to find a way to hide her. He found matches. But, first, on impulse, he went back up the stairs and took the feather headdress from the dried-out corpse. It was a trophy. Little Bobby had died, but the boy had survived. *He hid the headdress in some bushes at the back of the yard, then returned to the house and held the flame of a match to the base of the living-room curtains until they were on fire.*

*Later, when he had to cry to fool the policemen and the firemen, it was very easy. All he had to do was think of her clutching hands and her perfume and how she called him Bobby.*

The lights of Las Vegas, glowing some fifty miles ahead, brought new energy. He had driven all day with only three stops for food and gas. By rights, he should have been exhausted. He wasn't, of course. If he continued past Vegas, there were only three hours left until he reached Kelsie in the castle he had built for her.

As he drove closer to Vegas, he began to reconsider. Why arrive so tired he couldn't fully enjoy the first meeting with Kelsie—the first real meeting, the one that counted for the rest of their lives together. Why not stop in Vegas and sleep?

For the next forty miles of driving, he had good intentions. He would rent a cheap room and just sleep. He would forget other sweet, sweet memories and not let Las Vegas distract him. But the excitement in him grew as the distant glow turned into neon reds, blues, greens. It wasn't just excitement over Kelsie. It was the long familiar predator's excitement. He surrendered to it before reaching the city limits.

Despite the excitement, he did not rush. Instead, he checked into a motel. He spent a half-hour making sure his mustache was secure, another five minutes selecting a wig. He dressed casually elegant—cashmere jacket, Polo shirt, and fresh jeans.

He did not rush his cruising either. He wandered from casino to casino, alert for a potential victim. Nearly a half-dozen times he moved in closer to a woman, then backed away. For aside from her looks, the woman had to have the certain edginess, which experience had taught him meant the best chance of success. She had to be constantly surveying the room, as if looking for a man, which naturally she was.

After two hours of soda water and lime juice, he saw one. She was moving from slot machine to slot machine, dropping coins and pulling without any real interest in the results. She wore a black dress with spaghetti straps and black stockings. Her blonde hair brushed the skin of her bare shoulders. She'd been drinking, which was obvious by the careful way she moved to keep her balance. Perfect.

The Watcher moved closer.

This one was older than he preferred. The excitement, though, could not be denied.

He waited until her back was turned. He walked up behind her and spoke with enthusiasm. "Kelsie?" he said. "Kelsie McNeill?"

She turned her head, and he backed away, stammering. "I'm sorry," he said. "You look just like someone I know."

This was the crucial moment. If she smiled, it meant either sympathy or interest. Either did just fine.

She smiled, the wrinkles on her face emphasized by her heavy makeup.

"I guess it was too much to hope for," he said. "Ten years and a thousand miles since breaking up. Again, I'm sorry."

He backed away, then stopped. "Look," he said, "this is stupid, but I'm in sales, and I've got a lot of money and, honestly, money doesn't help at all when you're lonely. I was wondering if . . ."

The woman's smile grew broader.

"Honey, you got the money, I got the time." She stepped closer, into a ray of light from the ceiling. Food edged the corners of her mouth. She squeezed her arms together, accenting her cleavage. "And, honey, if it makes you feel better, go ahead and call me Kelsie."

She took his arm and led him away from the slots and toward the bar.

# Day 5

"George, did you pack a candle?" Clay was on his knees, peering at a small wooden door set into a frame that sagged back into the hard dirt walls of an embankment. It had taken them two hours to find the root cellar beneath the sweeping branches of a spruce growing out of the side of the hill, twenty paces from the last rotting timbers of Mad Dog's cabin.

"Candles are very light." George grinned to dispel his own tension. "They go in my knapsack, not yours."

Clay was too distracted to notice George's attempt at a joke. He was totally focused on the door. Weathered wood, stained with the acid runoff from spruce needles. It hung straight, however. The hinges on the door were bright, the padlock new.

*Predators have lairs. Predators always return to their lairs.*

For a moment, Clay wondered if the predator was inside waiting.

Then he shook his head—he wasn't thinking straight. The lock was securely bolted on the outside. It would have been impossible, then, for someone to crawl inside, shut the door, and lock it on the outside. If anyone was in there at all . . .

"Kelsie!" he shouted, banging on the door. "Taylor!"

He listened for muffled moans, which would tell him they'd been gagged. Instead, he heard a faint buzzing sound. He couldn't be sure if he was imagining it or not.

George knelt down and handed Clay a candle and a couple of wood matches. "Lock looks strong," George said.

"Did you load any sledgehammers into my knapsack? Felt like it."

George took a Swiss Army knife out of his pocket. "Use a screwdriver on the hinges."

Five minutes later, candle and matches tucked in his back pocket, Clay was working on the final screw. The buzzing had not gone away—in fact, it seemed louder to him now. Once before he'd heard such buzzing. He prayed now that he was wrong.

"George, maybe you should stand guard by the tree." George did not need to see inside the root cellar, not if Clay's terrible premonition had justification.

George backed out.

Clay hesitated. It was agony. Wild elation and hope filled him. The lock and new hinges were proof enough their guess was probably accurate. Could Kelsie and Taylor be waiting for him on the other side bound and gagged?

*Predators have lairs. Predators always return to their lairs.*

Dread terror consumed him. The buzzing. Would he be opening the door to the cruelest crime scene any killer could invent?

Clay pried the door away from the frame. The padlock splintered as he yanked it away completely. A sharp copper smell hit his face. Few people would know that smell. Few people had stood over a disemboweled body. Few people had seen frenzied flies blanket day-old blood. "Oh, God," he prayed.

The nightmare was coming true. He scrambled backward on the verge of vomiting. The stench, unbearable in a normal situation, was that much worse because he didn't know if the body was Kelsie's.

"What is it?" George asked.

"Give me a minute," Clay lied. "I'll be fine."

The peacefulness of the sky, the gentle breeze, the gurgle of the nearby stream, and the green of the mountainside mocked him and his utter dread. Clay wanted to run. He wanted to deny the root cellar and the body inside had ever existed.

But he had to know. As he crawled back under the tree, he could hardly support his weight on his trembling arms, in his fear at what he might see. At the open door, he lit the candle and pushed it inside ahead of him.

What he saw first were cowboy boots, pointing upward, and the dim outlines of legs covered by a blanket.

The sight shot him with electric relief.

*Rooster Evans.*

Clay had seen what he needed to see. It was not Kelsie or Taylor. No other bodies lay in the confines of the root cellar. Let the sheriff deal with this one. He began to back out.

Something in the corner caught his eye. In the candlelight he saw it was a diaper.

*Taylor! Had Taylor been here?*

Clay ran the candle around the edges of the root cellar, looking for anything to give him an indication of what had happened to Taylor.

He caught the darker shadows of a crude shelf cut into the dirt wall, about chest high. Clay moved closer to the shelf. In the flickering, smoking candle light he saw curled edges of paper.

He reached for the paper with his other hand. A quick glance showed it was a photograph. He decided to look at it outside, in the light of day.

He took a quick look around the cave but found nothing else.

As he left the root cellar, he realized tears were falling down his face, tears of relief. Not until seeing the cowboy boots turned upward had he known the extent of his agonized uncertainty.

"Oh God, oh God, oh God," he kept whispering. "Thank You. Thank You. Thank You."

Once outside, he crawled out from under the spruce tree, stood, and faced George again.

"Rooster Evans," Clay said to the unspoken question. "Ripped up bad. I hope it happened after he died."

What Clay didn't say was that Rooster had been ripped up so badly it was like a message left behind for Clay—taunting done by the killer.

Clay held up the piece of paper. "I found this, too."

They studied it together in the sunlight. George glanced at Clay, a look of horror on his face. "Like Kelsie," George said in a whisper, "but not her."

The black-and-white close-up of the woman's shoulders, neck, and face did resemble Kelsie. A little younger, a little coarser, but the same shoulder-length blonde hair, the same type of cheekbones.

Clay understood George's expression. This woman's eyes were wide with fear—with good reason. A gloved hand at the edge of the photograph held a fillet knife, and the tip of the blade was an inch under her skin with a two-inch red track showing where he had begun to cut.

"A trophy," Clay said. He was forcing himself to step out of his emotions and assess the photograph with his years of experience. He knew he was seeing something important, but he couldn't quite figure it out.

The quality of the photograph was good, very good, as if taken by a professional and developed by a professional. A photograph like this would require a setup ahead of time. It would require a . . .

"Tripod," he told George. "Tripod."

"I don't understand."

"Coin marks, remember? Set apart in the corners of a triangle. Back then, he'd taken photographs using a tripod. How else could he and the victim be in the same shot?"

George nodded slowly. In nearly three-quarters of a century of living, nothing had prepared him for the evil implicit in such a photograph.

Clay, however, had moved well beyond the emotional impact of the image of the dying woman. "We've got to get moving," he said. "Back toward town."

"Town? But—"

"Black and white. Easy to develop and print. Do you think he ever dropped his film off at a one-hour developer?"

"Oh. You mean—"

"I mean as soon as we get back into cell-phone range, we're calling every photography shop in a radius of a hundred miles. Let's pray that someone on the list in my back pocket has been buying supplies."

## 9:14 A.M.

*The boy had learned to understand the glazed look on his mother's face. He had also learned to hate it.*

*"Mrs. O'Connor called this afternoon," she said. She sat in an old robe at the kitchen table. The ashtray beside her overflowed with half-smoked cigarettes. The sherry bottle beside the ashtray was almost empty. "She says if you don't stop following her daughter Teresa, they're going to call the police."*

*His mother poured the remainder of the sherry in a glass. She wasn't even trying to hide it from him anymore.*

"I'm worried about you," she said. She was practiced enough that, even this late in the day, her slurring was hardly noticeable. "Is this something all fifth-grade boys do?"

"What do you care?" the boy said. He leaned against the kitchen counter, sneering. So he liked to follow Teresa. Was there a law against that? Besides, she deserved it, kissing all the other boys in the class except for him.

"What do I care? I'm your mother."

"You're a drunk." It was the first time he'd said it, as if he was testing her.

She rose unsteadily from the table and stumbled toward him. He smelled the sherry, thick and sweet, on her breath.

She drew her hand back, and he waited, almost relieved by her reaction. Maybe she did care. Punishment was love, too, wasn't it?

Then she turned away. "Get out of my sight," she said. "I don't need this kind of hassle."

He didn't know he was going to do it until he was actually doing it. He pushed her, catching her in midstride, and she fell hard.

She screamed.

"Mommy!" he said. He kneeled and tried to put his arms around her shoulders. She pushed him away.

"Mommy!"

She managed to get to her knees. Blood welled from a cut on her bottom lip.

"I'm sorry, Mommy," he said.

"You're a freak," she said. "Don't think I don't know about the things you do. The telescope in your room. Your little experiments in the basement. Those moldy feathers on that stupid headdress? Your magazines? I don't want to look at you."

"Mommy!"

She managed to stand and without a word left the kitchen. Seconds later, she returned and snatched her half-glass of sherry from the table.

"Make your own dinner," she said.

He knew she was going to her bedroom. She slept most of the day, except when she was drinking.

The boy waited until he knew she was asleep. He tiptoed into her room and took a twenty-dollar bill from her purse. That would get him dinner.

He stayed away until well after dark, and when he returned, he saw a big, old, rusted car in the driveway. Another boyfriend. Why did she always choose another man instead of him?

*Usually it didn't make him feel sad or lonely. He had learned not to feel. But this time—unforgiven and with the picture of his mother helpless on the floor and the blood on her lip because he had pushed her—the thought of another boyfriend made him miserable.*

*He sat on the curb for a half-hour, trying to work up the courage to move into his small bedroom past the lights and noise that would be coming from behind her closed door in the trailer.*

*He wanted to teach his mother a lesson; he wanted her to pay attention to him. And he remembered how easy it had been to solve his problem the night the old lady died in the attic.*

*The boy left the shadows of the street and quietly walked into the kitchen. Matches. He needed matches.*

The Watcher eased himself into his own house. There was a security pad, hidden behind a fake light switch. He flipped the lid and disarmed the system.

"Welcome home, my love," he whispered.

He stepped through the kitchen. Gleaming copper pots hung above an open stove range. The kitchen was six hundred square feet, as well-equipped as the best restaurants. He'd hardly had a chance to use it. All of this was about to change, of course. This was where he would cook wonderful meals for his love.

The Watcher was almost giddy as he moved through the house. In all of his years of preparation, in all of his time in the house, during all of his carpentry labors in complete and necessary solitude, it had never once felt like home to him. Now, of course, it did. His love awaited him. Upstairs.

He was in no rush, however. Although he had showered and slept in the hotel in Vegas—before and after satsifying his hunger with the grimy, drunken blonde—he still felt the exhaustion of the hectic pace of his last few days.

He would sleep again. He wanted everything to be perfect when he joined Kelsie. Rest first, he told himself. It was easier to abide by his decision because of one other thing that made him dizzy with anticipation—the survellience cameras in Kelsie's apartment. He had installed the wide-angle lenses beneath the plastic caps that covered the light fixtures. Kelsie could not know of their presence, which, of course, made it all that much more delicious.

The Watcher had no need to walk through the rest of the house to check for intruders. Not only had he taken the precaution of a security system, he had also installed discreet survellience cameras on the exterior to allow him to watch the grounds. Yes, he would admit to himself, he was a control freak. But was there anything wrong with that? From his bedroom he could monitor not only Kelsie's apartment but also much of the neighborhood. He could do the same from another bank of monitors just outside Kelsie's room. Unlikely as the possibilty was, the Watcher had prepared for the day visitors might try to enter his fortress. He wanted the chance to be as well warned as possible. And should that day ever happen, he'd prepared for escape too. With money, everything was possible.

Satisfied and exultant, he hurried to his bedroom. It was huge—the entire house was over forty-five hundred square feet—and he had installed a large-screen television at the base of the bed. Hidden beneath the bed were the video machines, cables, and wiring that led to the video cameras.

The Watcher undressed slowly, savoring his anticipation. He hung his clothes on hangers. Finally, in a thick robe, he propped pillows against the headboard, lounged on his bed, pressed his remote control, and began flicking buttons.

On the large-screen television, the kitchen camera in her apartment showed no sign of Kelsie or Taylor. Neither did the bedroom and shower cameras.

He clicked to the living room camera and smiled. *What a beautiful woman!*

She was sitting on the couch, reading a magazine. Taylor was curled beside her asleep. Her blonde hair was neat and brushed. He liked that: It meant she was taking care of herself.

Life was complete now. He could be with her when he wanted. Or he could content himself in this manner. The Watcher finally had his mate.

## 10:11 A.M.

Clay set his knapsack on the counter and stood for a full count to twenty wondering when the deputy on the other side would look up from his desk.

"Help ya?" the deputy finally said, the opposite suggested in his immediate return of attention to paperwork on his desk.

Clay read from a sheet on the nearby bulletin board. "'White male, six feet two inches, slightly graying hair, no distinguishing features or tattoos, considered armed and possibly dangerous.' Interested?"

"Huh?" The deputy glanced up again, did a double take in sudden recognition of Clay, and clutched at his holstered revolver.

"Settle down," Clay said. "Would I walk in like this if I meant trouble?"

"Brody!" the deputy hollered, reluctant to take his hand off his holster. "Brody!"

Sheriff Matt Brody shuffled out of his office down the hall. He walked with a slight limp. Clay would have guessed him to be in his midforties. He wore round wire glasses on a round face just short of chubby. He was of medium height, medium build, his shirt a little tight, showing bulges of belly fat that oozed around his side like mayonnaise spilling from a sandwich.

"It's Garner," the deputy said. "Clay Garner, you know the guy we're—"

"Sit, Mac," Brody said.

The deputy sat.

"Good boy," Brody said. He turned his attention to Clay. "I'd like to know where you've been. We've been trying to bring you in for questioning, and the fact you stayed away so long doesn't put you in a good light."

"It's not me," Clay told Brody. He didn't want to waste any time. "It's not Rooster Evans. He's dead, probably killed the night Frank Evans died."

Clay pushed on before Brody could interrupt. "I do know who it is. That's why I'm here."

Clay spread the files from his knapsack on Brody's desk. "These came from Russell Fowler. He had them in storage for years. You can read through the reports, but I'd rather you did it later and take my word on it for now. Fowler kept notes that he did not include in the official investigations on these murders. From the notes, I believe Fowler suspected the same person killed them all but didn't have enough proof to act. All of them had one thing in common: The dead men were close to Kelsie in the years before we married. The same person who murdered those men now has Kelsie. He is the same person who killed Rooster Evans. I wouldn't be surprised if he was responsible for Fowler's death."

Clay pointed to some handwritten notes on the sides of the files. "Fowler's handwriting. You can have it analyzed later, but time is short. Fowler put enough together to show that his suspect had the means, opportunity, and lack of alibi for all the murders. Nowhere, though, has he written a name. It was as if he wanted to gather this material together in case he ever needed to assemble enough proof to prosecute but was guarding against the wrong person finding it first."

"That doesn't necessarily mean guilt," Brody said. "Maybe Fowler kept this aside because he knew he had nothing but speculation."

Clay unfolded the well-worn piece of paper with his list of names.

> Rooster Evans—neighbor, now missing after
>              death of father
> Berry Burrell—current ranch worker
> Frankie Lopez—current ranch worker
> James McNeill
> Lawson McNeill
> Sonny Cutknife
> Johnny Samson
> Clay Garner

Clay borrowed a pencil from the top of Brody's desk.

"Dead," he told Brody, and scratched out Rooster's name. Clay continued. "Rule James and me out." He penciled out himself and James.

"Lawson . . ." Clay paused. It was difficult to think of Lawson dead, and even more difficult to think of Lawson dying in a plane crash. "Lawson was with me when Taylor was kidnapped." He marked off Lawson's name.

"I can't see it being Burrell or Lopez," Clay continued, crossing off their names. "They're still on the ranch. If you've got the report Flannigan was trying to fax to me—which I assume you do—you'll also have his summary. The victims were missing from a wide-ranging area. I don't think ranch hands have the money or opportunity to leave work long enough to go that far afield that often.

And if you check the dates that some of the victims were reported missing—which I did with my former colleague Dennis Flannigan on my way here—you'll see they were taken during calving season. There's no way either of those men would be off the ranch then." Clay crossed off their names.

"Sonny Cutknife and Johnny Samson. Both worked on the ranch over twenty years ago, and both are no strangers to the hill country. And if you remember the FBI report from Flannigan, whoever did this probably took the women on extended camping trips."

"Sonny Cutknife skipped town," Brody said. "That should tell us plenty, is what you're probably saying."

"Sheriff," Clay said softly. It got Brody's attention.

"Yeah?"

"I don't think it's either man."

What had Fowler said in the hospital? *I'm not sure it will do you much good. If I'm right, the guilty man is long dead. Which is why I let the investigation die.*

Clay flipped over one of the file folders. He read out loud his own translation of Fowler's brief note. "At 7:12 A.M. on July 12, 1973, a southbound vehicle had been clocked at eighty-seven miles per hour at mile marker 325 on I-15 near Conrad, Montana."

"A speeding ticket?" Brody asked.

"You'll notice the reference. K1200598. I asked Flannigan to get a search started. He's having a difficult time. We're talking about a twenty-three-year-old speeding ticket buried in some old file cabinet in any one of three or four courthouses on the other side of Montana. He doesn't have the pull to find out what you might be able to do by calling in some favors."

"If the ticket is still there."

"If the ticket is still there," Clay agreed. "Conrad is small-town Montana, not New York. I'm guessing chances are good it's filed somewhere. At the least, it's worth the effort."

"You want to know who got the ticket."

"I believe I already know." Clay took the list back. He wrote a name beneath the others on the list and folded the paper. "Do what it takes to find out who was issued the ticket. If that name matches the one I wrote, will that be enough to convince you to start a massive manhunt?"

"Tell me first how you got the name you just wrote."

"From a photography supply store," Clay said.

"I don't understand."

Clay explained the trophy photo and its implications. "I didn't bother checking against current purchasers," Clay went on. "I figured the killer would be smart enough now to buy out of town or out of state. But I don't know if he was that smart back when he started. It didn't take many calls to find out who was in business twenty-three years ago. Kalispell was even smaller back then. It only had one store where a person could get supplies to develop his own photos. I managed to reach the owner who is now retired and in Florida."

"Yeah?" Brody's voice was filled with skepticism.

Clay held up the piece of paper. "The name I just wrote? He bought enough developing paper and chemicals and was enthusiastic enough about it as a hobby that the owner still remembers him."

Sheriff Brody returned to his office twenty minutes later.

Clay hadn't enjoyed the wait. While he was sure enough of his own findings, if for some reason the name didn't match, he'd have an uphill battle trying to convince Brody to start a manhunt.

"It was a ticket paid late," Brody said. "Which is probably why it crossed Fowler's desk back then."

Clay unfolded the paper and handed it to Brody, who read the name Clay had written earlier.

"Yeah," Brody said without enthusiasm as he read the name Clay had circled. "That's who I got, too. A dead man. Michael McNeill."

"Dead," Clay replied. "Or missing and presumed dead?"

## 11:07 A.M.

Brody had given Clay the fax confiscated from Johnny Samson's school and let him use a small office down the hallway. It smelled of greasy food. The imitation woodgrain desktop in front of Clay was scarred with cigarette burns.

Intent on the pages on the desk, however, Clay was blind to his surroundings. He spent an hour going through the fax from Dennis, looking for any pattern that might point him to Michael McNeill's whereabouts. It was one thing to know who had taken Kelsie. It was another to guess where. McNeill had remained alive and hidden for years since his faked death. Where was his next lair?

The type became a blur in front of his tired eyes. None of the faxed information in front of him showed that Michael had ever taken a woman and her child. He wouldn't break the pattern unless he had a good reason.

On the other hand—and Clay could not avoid thinking it—if McNeill stayed with the pattern and forced Kelsie to go on a hiking trip into the mountains, just as he'd done with her lookalikes, then Taylor would be in the way. And that meant Taylor was probably—

No, he told himself angrily. Taylor was alive. There *was* a break in the pattern. Years had gone by while Michael was safely invisible under a different identity, stalking and murdering women who resembled his sister. Now, he'd actually taken Kelsie. Something had changed the pattern, triggered him to go beyond the serial killing, something that made it necessary to take Taylor and keep him alive. That's what Clay was going to believe.

Clay went through the faxed papers yet again. Eighteen pages in total. Dennis had pulled up everything possible from VICAP. There was a complete background on each of the women, including whose bodies had been found and where, and who was still missing.

None of it told Clay one crucial thing. *Why?*

It was inhuman to think of a brother stalking his own sister for decades. What would posess him to haunt his own sister? Clay wasn't looking forward to breaking the news to James McNeill.

*Michael McNeill?*

Within a few days, Clay knew, he might understand more. Something in Michael's past would have led him to choose this type of evil. Clay knew Michael's mother—Kelsie's mother, too—had died when they were young. Did that have anything to do with it? Or was it something that might have happened away from the ranch? Had Michael been abused by a schoolteacher, scoutmaster, or even—and Clay hated it whenever he heard—by a preacher or priest, anyone in a position of authority?

Evil grew from evil. Somewhere in the days to come, they'd find the evil that had brought Michael to the point of desiring his own sister then muting the desire with women who looked like her.

A psychologist would say Michael killed the women because he hated them for the same reasons he was attracted to them. He'd loathe himself for wanting his sister then loathe the women who represented his sister.

Clay sagged back into his chair, thinking about Michael and the horrors of his actions. Brody walked into the office.

"Any progress?" the sheriff asked.

Clay pointed at the papers. "Nothing beyond what I told you earlier. We need a manhunt. Everything here indicates he'll have taken her"—Clay winced at the implication Taylor was dead and corrected himself—"taken *them* into the hills. When I review the missing women and the dates they disappeared, it confirms that this has been his MO for years. Who knows how many other bodies haven't been found?"

Brody nodded agreement. "A real animal," Brody said with disgust.

"What I'm thinking is we still have time," Clay said, not responding to Brody's remark. He didn't want to think about an animal holding his wife and son. "From where all the other bodies were found, he took them deep into the woods, maybe by horseback. Maybe by foot. Some of the sites might have taken him days to reach."

"Are you suggesting an air search?"

Clay nodded. "Yes. But we need to keep it from the media. If Michael isn't in the hills, we can't afford to let him know that we know he's still alive. If he is in the hills, we can't be sure he doesn't have a radio. The last thing we need is to tip him off as we begin looking for him."

"I know it's your wife—" Brody began.

"Wife and son." Clay was not going to let anyone talk him into believing his little cowboy was dead.

"Wife and son. I understand you want to do everything you can. But even if we find them by an air search, what next? Drop men from the airplane? I mean, by the time anyone gets there on foot, he'll be long gone."

"Air search," Clay insisted. He knew Brody was right but couldn't get himself to agree to it. "Parachute the men. If dropping them from the air is what it's going to take, we have got to do it."

As he was speaking, something clicked in Clay's mind. He dug through the papers in front of him and reread the summaries of two autopsies. "Time of death impossible to determine. Bones weathered and broken, probably due to large scavenger animals local to area—"

"Dropping them from the air," Clay repeated. The photo in Kelsie's office of James, Michael, Lawson, and Rooster flashed into his mind. The four of them were standing in front of the airplane that the three men proudly purchased together. "Michael was—*is* a pilot. He could have dropped those bodies from the air."

Clay smiled grimly at the sheriff. "I need an atlas," Clay said. "An atlas, a pencil, and a ruler."

Brody watched over Clay's shoulder.

"Here's what I'm thinking," Clay said. "Most serial killers cruise the interstates. It gives them great range. But what if Michael extended his range by flying? Not only would it give him a far larger territory and disguise his killing pattern, but it would also allow him to accomplish something that is normally very difficult, dumping the bodies. He does it very simply. On his way home, he drops them from his airplane into rugged mountain country where the bodies might not be found for years, if ever. It's frightening to think of how many bodies are scattered that will never be found."

"I'm with your thinking on this so far," Brody said.

"Look." Clay swiveled the ruler to line up two *A*'s he had penciled onto a map of the continental United States. "*A* marks where this woman lived in Salt Lake City. The other *A* marks where her body was found, directly west of Butte, in the Deerlodge National Forest."

Clay drew a line, connecting the two points, then continued the line northward. "If he picked her up in Salt Lake City and dumped her while he was flying, do you think he took a detour home? I don't. I think it would be such a foolproof method, he wouldn't waste a couple of hours flying an indirect path home. I think it's safe to assume this straight line was his flight path."

"Clay moved his ruler to a couple of *B* points on the map. "This victim lived in Seattle. Her body was dumped west and north of Missoula, in the Bitterroot Mountains."

Clay slashed another line, from Seattle to where the body had been found, and continued the line farther until it intersected the first line he'd drawn.

"Let's move onto someone else." He slid the ruler over two C points he'd earlier marked on the map and drew a third line until it intersected the first two. "Picked her up in Denver. Dumped her in the middle of Yellowstone Park."

"Missoula," Brody said unnecessarily, pointing at the spot where the three lines met. "He's flying into Missoula. Do we look for him there?"

"I don't think so," Clay said. He consulted his notes. "These three women were all murdered before Michael supposedly died in the whitewater-rafting accident. He probably used Missoula as a base to remain relatively free of questions he might get from people who knew him here in Kalispell. I'm guessing, though, once he was thought to be dead, he'd find a base much farther away. In Missoula, there would be too much chance someone from Kalispell might fly in and see him at that airport."

"He could be anywhere in the country then."

"Yup. But look where I've marked the D's and E's."

Clay drew a fourth line, connecting San Francisco and a mark in the Sierra Nevadas, northeast of Bakersfield. "This woman was murdered *after* Michael was presumed dead."

He penciled a fifth line. "Same with this woman. Missing from Albuquerque, found in the desert mountains southeast of Kingman."

Clay circled the point where both lines met.

"Here," he said. "It's a long shot, but we don't have much to lose. All it's going to take is a phone call to the airport there."

## 3:30 P.M.

"Kelsie, my love."

Kelsie almost dropped the plate she was washing at the sink. After close to two days of dread, the unexpected voice hit her like raw voltage.

Even as her heart began to race, however, she knew the voice did not come from anyone in her living quarters. The voice was slightly distorted, with some echo, and came from a speaker above her. Hidden behind the ceiling vent?

She fought the impulse to look upward and managed to keep her hands in the soapy water.

"Kelsie, my love, I want to give you notice that I will be appearing soon. This will give you time to prepare yourself for me. A long, hot bubble bath would be appropriate. And you have probably noticed the selection of perfumes among your toiletries. I prefer the Escape from Calvin Klein, but you, of course, may have different tastes."

Unhurriedly, although adrenaline was making her shaky, she pulled her hands from the sink and wiped them on a towel.

She turned, looking for Taylor. He had moved into the kitchen behind her and was peering upward, trying to find the source of the unfamiliar sound.

"Oh, yes," the voice said. "Your son. I will make suitable arrangements for him during our time together. After all, you and I will need our privacy."

Kelsie thought of not replying to the voice. She realized, however, that whoever had put her in this room had almost complete control. She would have to reply sooner or later. Then another realization struck her. Whoever was speaking knew that Taylor had just moved into the kitchen.

*A video camera?*

She took Taylor by the hand and led him into the living room. The voice followed her there with an audible click as it transferred from the kitchen speaker.

"Go ahead, my love, sit on the couch. Make yourself comfortable."

Again, she refused to look upward. Her guess was that the observation lenses were hidden behind the plastic covers that protected the light bulbs.

Inwardly, she shuddered at the new knowledge. Everything she did—and perhaps had done since arriving—was in plain sight of her stalker.

She remained standing.

"Speak to me, my love," the voice said. "Don't you find relief after all these years that we can communicate?"

"Why?" she said. The anguish came from all those years of terror, anguish she couldn't hide, no matter how calm she wanted to appear to be. "Why me?"

"If I could have asked you to marry me," the voice said, "I would have. Long ago. I would have courted you and won you. I am much better for you than the others."

"The others you killed."

"I knew how good it would be, you and I together. I couldn't let them stop it. You will understand when you love me in return."

"You are holding me prisoner," Kelsie said. Was there some way she could get into his mind? "I don't think that shows love."

"Oh, but it does. I have loved you a long, long time. And now, you will be able to return my love for a long, long time. Don't consider this a prison but a home."

"No!" The strength in Kelsie's voice surprised her. Defiance, however, was one of her few choices. "You are a monster."

"You will see differently. And even if you don't, you will be wise to pretend. For I hold your life."

"But not my soul or my will. You are a monster. Every waking moment in this prison I will show you how much I hate you."

"Actually, my love, in less than an hour, you will do just the opposite."

"There is nothing you can do to me to make me submit. I will die before I let you touch me." She meant it. Twenty-three years under his control had been enough.

"I don't think so," the voice said. "Taylor is not here because I love him too."

Unconsciously, she hugged her son tighter.

"You see, my love, you will have a choice. Give yourself to me or lose your son. And I promise, you will watch him die slowly and terribly over many weeks, perhaps months. I have had practice at the art of torture."

The voice stopped, giving her a chance to understand.

"On the other hand," the voice began again, "for as long as you continue to please me as my wife, he will remain safe and healthy."

Another pause. "You have an hour to think this over."

# 3:45 p.m.

"So this is Lake Havasu City," Brody said, stepping onto the runway. Jet turbines wound down to silence behind him. "I hear they moved the entire London Bridge here. Remember, where I was pointing out that island as we came down? The bridge connects it to the town.

Some guy—McCullough, you know, McCullough as in McCullough chain saws—dredged the channel to make it an island then bought the London Bridge. He started the town from scratch, right here in the middle of the desert."

"Yeah," Clay said. He was deep in his own thoughts, hardly knowing what he'd just agreed to, hardly aware Brody had pointed out anything from the air.

As they approached, they had seen brown folded ridges of desert mountains and endless sand and brush of the valley flats. Sparkling deep, deep impossible blue among the arid pastels was the Colorado River, which widened to a lake because of a dam some thirty miles downstream.

From the air, the layout of Lake Havasu City was easier to read than a map. The airport was located a few miles north of the town on a two-lane highway that ran from the hills north and continued south and out of sight into the shimmering distance. The town with its thirty thousand residents sprawled over the western slopes of a small mountain range, overlooking the water and mountains that rose desolate on the other side of the lake.

Garner and Brody headed toward the airport terminal building. Neither carried luggage. Either Clay had guessed right, or he hadn't. They'd find out within the hour. There was no need to stay overnight.

"This is nuts," Brody said. "Absolutely nuts."

"It can't be all that nuts," Clay said. "You made the call here yourself. You know McNeill has made this his base. All we can do is try to track him from here."

"I'm not second-guessing that. I mean it's your money on the jet charter. What I'm talking about is nuts is this heat. I'll bet it's over a hundred degrees."

Clay's mind was on how he wanted to break into a run across the sticky, soft asphalt. If he needed a reminder of the urgency, all he had to do was recall the photograph of a blonde woman and the gloved hand and the fillet knife. He and Brody were measuring time in minutes. Kelsie might be measuring heartbeats as stretches of tortured eternity.

On the surface, flying to Lake Havasu City might have seemed like a gamble. It wasn't. They had nothing else to bet on. With no hesitation, Clay had agreed to pay the thousands of dollars to hire, on little notice, a corporate jet out of Kalispell, slashing an eighteen-hour drive to well under three hours of airtime. Clay had tried to use the airtime to nap. He'd had little sleep the previous two nights, and events were beginning to blur.

"Maybe it's a great place to spend the winter," Brody was saying, "but you got to wonder about the summers. Could you imagine some old couple moving down here from Michigan, retiring in a mobile home, and having to live through this kind of heat? I mean—"

"Brody." Clay said it with a weary tinge that the sheriff understood immediately.

"Sorry," he said. "Some cops get quiet when they're closing in. Others are talkers. Me, I'm a talker."

"Take a look again," Clay said to the fuel attendent. Clay held a photo of Michael McNeill, enlarged from the newspaper article on his whitewater-rafting death. "He might have been wearing a wig or a mustache. Look at his eyes. Nobody can disguise their eyes."

The fuel attendent leaned over the photograph. He hadn't stopped wiping his hands on a greasy rag from his back pocket since stepping into the airport manager's office. He probably didn't feel comfortable on the clean carpet, Clay thought, not in dirty coveralls.

"Ain't never seen him before." He frowned, a movement that wrinkled his freckled, bald skull. "How many times does a feller have to tell you? And in an airport this small, I see most everybody."

"It confirms what I pointed out, Mr. Garner," Charles Teebolt said in sanctimonious terms. Since they'd paged the fuel attendant to join them, the airport manager, tall and slight with a puffy blond toupee, had not stopped glancing down at the fuel attendant's dirty work boots on the carpet. "That is not the Michael McNeill who signs in and out for that particular aircraft. Are you quite satisfied? May this worker get back to his duties?"

Brody was outside. He'd spotted a coffee machine and a tray of doughnuts at a quarter apiece. Not that his absence mattered to the lack of progress in the office, Clay thought.

Clay left the photograph on the manager's desk. Picking it up would have been like giving up territory, and Clay wasn't ready to quit. He had nothing else to hang on to.

"We called from Kalispell," Clay persisted. "Before we left, you confirmed numerous flights into this airport by a Michael McNeill."

"Yes, yes," the manager said. With hand gestures, he was shooing the fuel attendant out of his office. "We keep impeccable records. I assured you of that over the telephone."

The fuel attendant seemed relieved to step away.

"You told us he flew a Cessna Citation," Clay confirmed, hoping for anything to clear this up. Impossible that both men had never seen Michael before. Was he that good at disguise? "Registration N00925J."

"Yes, yes. A Cessna Citation registration N00925J," the manager said. He smirked. "I simply don't make errors. Perhaps if you would have faxed me this photograph I could have saved both of us some time and trouble."

Clay slammed his fist on the desk in frustration, taking little satisfaction that the smaller man jumped.

"What is it, Hughie?" Charles made up for his fright by snarling at the fuel attendant, who was shuffling back inside the office. "I thought we were finished with you."

"But—"

"Move along," Charles told Hughie. "You know what they say about time and money."

Hughie shifted his weight from foot to foot. "It's about that Cessna."

Hughie turned to Clay. "See, I don't forget a plane. That feller you showed me, he don't fly that plane. I know that for sure."

Clay drew a breath and tried to speak slowly. "Another man flies it?"

"Yeah."

"That's what I've been telling you all along," Hughie said, actually stamping a foot with impatience.

"Would either of you recognize his face if you saw it?" Clay wanted to shake the man to get an answer more quickly.

Hughie shrugged. Charlie rolled his eyes as if Clay were a moron.

"What kind of car does he drive?" Clay asked the fuel attendant.

Hughie shrugged again.

Clay thought of Sonny Cutknife. "Is the pilot Native American?"

"You mean an Indian?"

Clay nodded, accepting the implied reprimand for political correctness.

"Nope," Hughie said.

Hours earlier, Clay had believed he knew *who,* and only needed to find *where.* Now he was certain he was in the right area but was back to the beginning on *who.* The most frustrating thing was that Michael McNeill was the perfect fit. Everything pointed to him, from the fingerprints on the corkscrew that had killed Doris, to his accessibility to the family. A faked death was the perfect way to disappear.

"Are you finished yet?" Charles asked. "I do wish to send this man back to work."

Clay was thinking maybe they could get Hughie and Charles to work with an artist and come up with a composite sketch. If they came up with a sketch and if they showed it around enough, they might come up with a name. They didn't have time, though, let alone the manpower. Something like this could take a day, two days of concentrated help from the local cops. And the whole reason he and Brody had flown in was to keep the local cops from getting involved.

"I said, are you finished?" Charles snapped. "I would—"

"Quiet," Clay commanded.

Hughie grinned, caught Charlie noticing, swallowed the grin, and quickly left the office.

Clay wanted to bang the desk again. Better yet, he wanted to hit the smug man and stop his whining superiority. Something was bugging Clay, something that had just crossed his mind.

*Michael McNeill was the perfect fit.* But if he wasn't the Watcher, that meant that from the beginning, someone had taken great pains to set him up.

If Clay could come up with the photograph of that someone, it would save all the trouble and uncertainty of a composite sketch. They could start here at the airport by showing the photograph around.

"If you don't mind, I do have my paperwork." The little man was actually ready to push Clay out of the office.

*Michael McNeill was the perfect fit. Too perfect?*

Clay ignored the man. Instead, he reached over the desk and grabbed the telephone. "What's your fax number here?" he asked as he was dialing a number in Kalispell.

"I beg your pardon."

Clay pressed the phone to his ear and listened to it ring, but continued to speak to Charlie. "Fax number. You said I should have faxed you a photograph ahead of time. Well, I'm about to have it sent."

In the airport restaurant, Clay got lucky on his second hit. Brody was out in the heat, moving around the airport runways with his copy of the faxed photo, talking to employees and asking the same question Clay was.

"See him before?" Clay asked.

"A few times," the tiny waitress said, squinting at the photograph. She was wizened, an elf in an apron.

Clay felt the hunter's surge of adrenaline, the excitement of a hunch well-played. "Anything you can tell me about him?"

"About Mr. Wilkens?"

"You know his name?" Clay's intensity nearly drove the waitress behind the counter.

"Mr. Wilkens," she repeated. "One day, he left his wallet behind. I was looking in it—to see who it belonged to, not 'cause I wanted to to take anything. But for all the yelling Mr. Wilkens did, you'd think he didn't believe me."

"First name?" Clay asked, not daring to hope. Wilkens was enough. It was much, much more than a composite sketch.

"Thomas," she said. "Thomas Wilkens. That was the name on his credit cards and driver's license. Does that help?"

Clay was already running toward a pay phone to call the Bureau. A false I.D. to the point of credit cards and driver's license meant there was a good chance he used the same name in that area.

With the right kind of help, it would not be difficult to find if someone by the name of Thomas Wilkens lived nearby.

## 4:30 P.M.

"Have you decided?" the computerlike voice asked over the speaker.

It had never been a decision for Kelsie. Even before, when she wanted to be a caretaker, not a mother, she would have seen herself dead before letting anything happen to Taylor. Before, however, her motivation would have been guilt, not the love she'd found.

"Let him live," Kelsie said.

"Good. We will be a wonderful family."

She might surrender for now, Kelsie knew, but she was going to kill this man. Somehow, sometime, she was going to kill him. She had the garrote hidden under her pillow. Even if it took days, weeks, or months of pretended love to have him relax his guard, she would find a way to strangle him. Those thoughts gave her the strength and hope to endure the unendurable. Whatever he did to her, she would survive. And Taylor would survive.

"There is the door near your bed," the voice said. "Stand well back. When it opens, send Taylor outside."

It seemed her heart stumbled. "Outside? But you said he'd be safe."

"Yes, my love, he will be safe. I have never broken a promise to you. You know that. From the beginning, every letter I've sent to you, I've fulfilled."

"Then why take him away from me?"

"You, my love. I want your wholehearted devotion. Taylor will remain outside. I have a special vest for your son. One with explosives set on a timer. When we have spent our time together, he will be allowed to return. If anything should happen to me, he will die. It is that simple. All that work on that garrote of yours was admirable but wasted. Remember, I have been watching you. I know everything."

Kelsie trembled. Her thoughts of defiance seemed like brittle grass in a wind. "How do I know you won't just kill him?" she asked.

"Kelsie, my love. Don't you understand? Just as you must keep me happy, so I must keep you happy. Taylor will live. For that way, I may return again and again and again."

## 4:32 P.M.

Within twenty minutes of Clay's call, he had the address of Thomas Wilkens. For all the Bureau's faults, when necessary it could pour on manpower, which it's agents had done with phone calls and their considerable authorization, discreetly checking with local utility records, phone records, state motor-vehicle records. All of it had pointed very conclusively to a man named Thomas Wilkens living at 289 Desert Quail.

Clay immediately rented a car. He drove, and Brody read the map. The house at 289 Desert Quail was on a cul-de-sac backing onto a golf course. Clay guessed it was a quiet, exclusive neighborhood.

The drive into town from the airport took them through a light industrial area, with scattered pods of mobile homes visible from the highway. Closer to the town center, the scenery became commercial—restaurants, hotels, gas stations.

Clay turned left, up into the hills on a main street named for the town's founder. They passed shopping malls with clean parking lots and hesitant old drivers. Higher up, the area became seriously residential—houses with graveled front yards instead of lawns, cactus instead of rose bushes.

"You understand," Clay said, breaking five minutes of silence, "I'll be taking the legal heat. If you go in without a warrant, you lose your career even if he *is* our man, even if Kelsie's in there."

Brody nodded.

That was the reason Clay didn't want local law involved; there was too much procedure. All Clay wanted was Kelsie and Taylor safe—if they were still alive—and the best way to keep them alive was by acting as quickly as possible. If they were alive, Clay didn't care what kind of legal mess he created. If they weren't alive, he'd care even less.

Clay turned twice more. As they climbed higher up the hills, the houses grew bigger.

"Ever noticed that in rich neighborhoods, it's like a ghost town?" Brody asked. "Nobody walking the streets. Cars inside garages. In poor neighborhoods, people are out, sitting on front porches gossiping. Rich neighborhoods, no one knows nobody."

"Exactly," Clay said. "This man is not stupid. If you were keeping prisoners, wouldn't you prefer a ghost town?"

Moments later, Clay braked at a corner in front of a street sign marked Desert Quail. He wasn't going to drive into the cul-de-sac.

"I'll need a gun," Clay said. "Yours."

"You're still under official custody. You know that."

"And I've done all this so I can lure you to a secluded spot, shoot you, and make a desperate getaway. Give me a break, Brody. We're talking about my wife and my son. I'm going in to get them out."

Brody unsnapped his holster and handed Clay his pistol.

"It's four forty-nine," Clay said. "If I'm not back in twenty minutes, that's your cue."

"You sure you know what you're doing?"

All Clay needed was a way to get up to the house without being noticed. He had an idea—an all-or-nothing idea. After that—

"Maybe this isn't such a good idea," Brody was saying. "They could fly a SWAT team in from Vegas in under an hour. How about local backup? And what if—

"Brody," Clay interrupted, "you're talking too much again."

# 4:50 P.M.

*The boy stared straight ahead as the truck stopped.*

*"We're here," the driver said unnecessarily. The boy had not spoken in three hours. He had rebuffed any attempts at conversation. The man felt he was speaking more for his own benefit rather than the boy's.*

*"I know you haven't had an easy few days," the man said, not unkindly. "But all of us will be doing our best to make it home. Because it is your home. I'll treat you like my son, and the others will treat you like a brother."*

*The boy did not reply to this either. He still smelled smoke and burning rubber. He still heard the wailing sirens of the firetrucks. He still saw the great geysers of water arched against floodlights.*

*Why hadn't his mother come out of the trailer? Why had she stayed inside? The firemen told him she had died without knowing what happened.*

*But the boy knew what had happened.*

*He had lit the kerosene-soaked foundation of the mobile home. He had started the fire that killed his mother. It was just supposed to scare her, not kill her. Nothing else but the nightmare of that night filled his thoughts.*

*"Step outside . . . son." The man's voice was awkward.*

*The boy got out of the truck slowly, reluctantly.*

*Two children close to his age came out of the house. The older one, a boy, did not run, but walked with grave dignity. The younger one, a girl, ran with a smile on her face.*

*"Hello," she said when she got closer.*

*"Hello," the boy said. A curious warmth filled him. In his back pocket was the only possession the fire had not taken. It was a photo of his mother when she was a girl. He'd always loved the photo, had spent hours looking at it, wondering about his mother at that age.*

*This girl, this shyly smiling girl in front of him, could have stepped out of that photo.*

*"Everything is going to be okay," she told him. "You'll see." She stepped forward and hugged him. She stepped back and took his hand.*

*"Come with me," she said. "There's a lot to show you."*

*The girl's brother followed them, and all three spent the rest of the day wandering around. The boy showed proper amazement at everything they pointed out for his benefit.*

*That evening, the girl took him for another walk. "Don't tell anyone," the boy told her, "but I love you."*

*"Of course you do," she said. "I love you too."*

*The curious warmth filled him even fuller than it had in the afternoon when he had first seen her smiling and running. "Maybe we can get married."*

*She laughed. "You say the sweetest things. But nobody would let us."*

*She laughed again when he pouted, and she hugged him. "Let's keep walking," she said. "It's going to be fun having you live with us."*

The Watcher pulled open the door, half-expecting Kelsie to try to force her way out in a frenzy of kicking similar to the one she'd launched from the trunk of her car. Instead, as Kelsie had agreed, Taylor stepped outside.

The Watcher locked the door again.

"Yabba-dabba-do," Taylor said. He grinned.

The Watcher could not help but grin back. He was softening, and he blamed it on his excitement at finally being with Kelsie.

He held out his hand, and Taylor took it without question, allowing the Watcher to lead him to a closet down the hall.

"Sorry, my little friend," the Watcher said. "You'll need to sit in here for a while. But at least there's a light, and it's better than a bomb set to a timer."

The rigged bomb-jacket, of course, had been a bluff. Why complicate things, as long as Kelsie agreed to his demands?

The Watcher shut the closet door on Taylor and locked it from the outside. Now everything was ready. Kelsie was waiting.

He allowed himself to hope she would be pleased when she saw his face. After all, they had shared much of their lives together. He told himself, however, it did not matter if she was not pleased. After a while, she would be happy that he loved her so much he would throw away his old life for her and go to all this effort to show his love.

The Watcher closed his eyes. He inhaled deeply, held his breath, then released it. He felt a strange, heady mixture of tension, pleasure, and nervous anticipation. At no other time and with no other woman had he felt this kind of peace and tingling warmth.

With a final sigh, he turned the key and pulled the door open to greet his lifelong love.

Her voice echoed disbelief. "You?"

## 4:54 P.M.

Clay kept his hat low over his face and consulted his clipboard as he walked on the sidewalk into the cul-de-sac. He had his guess as to the real identity of Thomas Wilkens and knew, even if he was wrong, that the killer would recognize Clay immediately—no person could stalk a man's wife without knowing the man and his habits almost as intimately as the wife's.

Clay assumed that Wilkens would not be watching the street with suspicion, let alone be watching the street during the next two minutes. The hat, workshirt, and clipboard—purchased hastily at a discount department store—were merely needed to fool neighbors who might otherwise call the police and to buy time on the minor chance Wilkens might glance out the window during Clay's approach from down the street. These were huge houses, set well back from the street, giving Clay protective distance from any casual inspection. All Clay needed was thirty seconds to get unseen from the sidewalk to the front door of 289 Desert Quail. It was a good gamble; Clay figured chances were small that Wilkens sat at his front windows. If the gamble failed and Clay did not get those thirty seconds, even the most elaborate disguise wouldn't help with what he had planned.

His quick survey from beneath the bill of the cap showed the five houses on the cul-de-sac to share classic desert architecture—tiled roofs, light pastel exterior walls, and three-car garages. Clay didn't know real estate well, but he figured each to be worth a million easily, each to run over four thousand square feet. What better place to keep someone prisoner than in the depths of the intimidating privacy of these mansions on the hill?

Clay walked slowly, pretending to check off various boxes on an imaginary paper on his clipboard, keeping his face turned away from 289 Desert Quail.

Clay had gone through the possibilities as he drove from the airport. Thomas Wilkens was the stalker, or he was not. That simple. The three-story mansion looming ahead belonged to a killer who had kidnapped his wife and child, or it did not.

If it didn't, Clay would accept the price. He'd face jail terms for breaking and entering, with added time for carrying a weapon. Not much of a price, he thought, compared to the alternative, risking the loss of Kelsie and Taylor.

If the mansion did belong to the stalker, chances were no one else lived there. Serial killers were loners—too many secrets to share. And if the house did belong to the killer, another set of two possibilities existed. Wilkens was either inside, or he wasn't.

If he wasn't, any mistakes Clay made wouldn't matter. If he was, Clay had to do this correctly and quickly, because of the final set of two possibilities: Kelsie and Taylor were inside the mansion, or they were not.

If not . . .

Clay pushed the thought out of his mind. Clay had made his best conclusion based on the patterns in the information back in Kalispell. This was not the time to second-guess himself.

He reached the sidewalk. With long strides just short of a lope, he moved toward the front door. These were the crucial seconds. If Wilkens happened to be watching at this moment, all surprise was lost.

Once into the shadows of the enclave at the front door, Clay did not relax. Although he was completely screened from any inside observer, and largely hidden from the street, he still had to assume the worst, that Wilkens had seen him and was already reacting.

Clay took the roll of packing tape out of his back pocket and peeled off a strip. Earlier, he'd picked a pebble from the street. He placed it squarely in the center of the tape and pressed the pebble into the doorbell. Clay squeezed the tape on both sides of the pebble onto the doorframe, holding it tightly in place, pressing against the doorbell.

Chimes inside bonged repeatedly.

This was his second gamble. If Wilkens was inside, he'd have to come to the door. Clay didn't expect Wilkens to open the door, but the constantly ringing bell would at least bring him to the door to look through the security peephole. All Clay wanted was the distraction to get Wilkens to the front of the house.

He ducked and sprinted around the garage, angling toward the backyard. There was a gate, locked. Clay hit it without slowing and tore it off his hinges.

He was going into this blind, and he knew it too well. He had no idea where the back door was. He was hoping he'd find a walkout patio and sliding glass doors, and he had no idea whether or not he'd set off a security alarm. Once inside, he faced another problem: He would be totally unfamiliar with the layout of the house. Which was why he wanted Wilkens at the front door—away from Kelsie and Taylor if they were inside.

As he'd hoped, there were sliding glass doors. Easier to break.

He kicked hard. On the third kick the glass shattered. To his relief, no alarm went off.

Every second now was crucial. He had to assume Wilkens had heard the breaking of glass and was now turning back from the front door.

Clay cleared out the glass and ducked inside, the pistol in his hand and cocked to fire. A blast of cold air hit him. He'd forgotten how hot it was outside.

He sprinted across carpet, the room and its contents a blur to him. He guessed the direction of the front door and dashed up a set of stairs, ready to fight or fire, dive or tackle at the first sign of movement.

Within seconds, he reached the wide hallway leading to the front door, almost skidding as he stopped on the glazed tile flooring.

The echoing bongs of the doorbell taunted him. The man had not come to the door at all. Did that mean he wasn't there?

"Clay Garner," a voice reached him from a hallway above. "You're looking in the wrong place. Come upstairs and join us. But do us all a favor, and get the doorbell silenced."

Clay whirled his head.

"Keep the gun if it makes you feel better," the voice instructed. "But it won't do you any good. I've got Kelsie and Taylor as shields. After all this effort on your part, wouldn't it be a shame to watch them die?"

Before moving, Clay memorized what he could see of the interior from where he stood. He'd dashed through the kitchen and a dining room to reach the front-door hallway. In the other direction, a wide, curving stairway led upstairs. At the top of the stairs, he could see that one hallway led left and another to the right. The walls were lined with large modern prints. Vases of dried-flower arrangements had been placed on various tables in the front hallway and dining room.

Clay unbolted the front door and removed the tape and pebble from the doorbell. The silence was eerie in the gigantic, empty house.

Clay closed the front door but left it unlocked. He took the stairs slowly, his footsteps absorbed by the rich carpet. At the top, he hesitated. The hallway to his right was longer, and there were open doors on both sides. The hallway to his left was much shorter and led to a single closed door at the end.

His instinct told him to go toward the closed door, but before he could act upon it, the speaker voice confirmed it.

"Come join us. We're behind the door at the end of the hallway."

Clay advanced. He wasn't sure if there was any other way to play this. The voice might be bluffing. Kelsie and Taylor could be elsewhere or—he gritted his teeth at the thought—already dead. Either way, Clay could not control the situation. He had to respond as though Kelsie and Taylor were on the other side. He had to hope he could delay events until Brody called in for local backup.

Clay pushed the door open with his foot and turned sideways, pressing himself against the wall. Not much protection, but if someone was going to shoot at him, it was better than giving his entire body as a target.

"Spare the drama." The voice did not come from a speaker but from directly inside. Clay knew that voice.

He stepped through the doorway, pistol chest-high and at arm's length.

The sight was so unexpected, it disoriented him briefly. This entire half of the second floor was wide open, like a warehouse loft. The walls were unfinished, the floor was rough wood. Filling the back portion of the huge open room was a smaller room, like a box within a box. Large television cameras, mounted above the smaller room on metal frameworks from the ceiling faced downward, toward the room. Video cables trailed everywhere.

The sight did not distract him for long. Against the outside wall of the inner room stood three people. Kelsie was alive and unmarked. Taylor held her hand. Behind and between them, with the barrel of a pistol pressed into Kelsie's ear, was Lawson McNeill.

## 4:59 P.M.

Sheriff Brody looked at his watch for the tenth time in a minute, wondering for the fifth time in that minute if he had shot his career by agreeing to this, wondering if he should just go ahead and call for backup immediately.

A four-door Lexus, gleaming waxed green, cruised past the parked car and turned into a driveway just up the street. Seeing the car reminded Brody of fat-cat lawyers, and lawyers turned his mind to lawsuits, and for the sixth time in the same minute, he wondered if he had shot his career. Then he thought about his own wife and their two kids and what he might do if they'd been taken by a monster who preyed on women and dumped them from airplanes. He'd be doing the same as Clay.

And if he was the one out there and Clay was in the parked car, he'd want Clay giving him a decent shot to rescue his family.

Brody began to strum his fingers on the steering wheel. All right, then, he wouldn't make the call until twenty minutes had passed. But did time have to move so slowly?

## 4:59 P.M.

"Set your gun down," Lawson said. "Kick it away from you."

"No." Clay kept the gun trained in Lawson's direction.

"Who do you want killed first? Taylor? Or Kelsie?"

Clay's gun did not waver.

"Think about it," Lawson said. "This is not your normal hostage situation. I can kill one and still have the other for protection. And it's not like I'll be particularly upset to pull the trigger. As you might guess, one more dead person on my list won't keep me awake at night."

Without the gun, Clay would be standing uprotected. With it, he knew without a doubt, he would watch Taylor or Kelsie die.

Clay set the gun at his feet and kicked it away. This was the moment of truth.

Lawson did not shoot Clay. Instead, he forced Kelsie onto her knees and kept a grip on Taylor's shoulder. He smiled his satisfaction from behind tortoise-rim glasses.

"I must admit," Lawson said, holding his pistol at his side, "this is a surprise."

He gestured at a bank of small television monitors at his side. "If it weren't for my outdoor surveillence cameras, it would have been far more of a surprise, since I didn't have the alarm system on. Very kind of you to alert me with the doorbell."

Lawson's cold smile stayed in place. "Let me satisfy your curiosity. Behind me is my guest room. Thanks to the wonders of modern electronics, I can observe my guest from my own room, down the other hallway. I can also watch for intruders from there. On occasion, of course, I must indulge myself in person here in the guest room. I always thought it would be prudent to put in monitors of the grounds here as well. Your presence is ample demonstration of how wise I was to protect myself."

"Are you all right?" Clay asked Kelsie. "Has he hurt you? Taylor?"

"We're fine," she said, taking a gulp of air.

"It's nice to see concern between the estranged," Lawson said. "Misplaced concern, Clay. These two will not be hurt. You, on the other hand . . ."

"I presume you built all of this yourself," Clay said, forcing admiration into his voice. Anything to waste time. "This must have taken years to set up."

"I was still at law school when I began to dream of this solution to my frustration. Unfortunately, I didn't have all the money I needed. This house, as you might guess, cost a fortune. So did my renovations. Of course, I also needed a large retirement fund. But I was patient. And, as you can see, it was worth the wait."

"I know you're a great lawyer, but how did you manage to get this much money?" *Stall*, Clay told himself, *pander to his ego and stall*.

"*Was* a great lawyer," Lawson replied. "Remember, the rest of the world thinks I'm dead. As for the money, I had my sources. Ask Kelsie about it. She's the one who started knocking down the walls."

"Emerald Canyon," she said. "You were one of the corporations?"

"In James's name, of course. Not that it was difficult to set that up. I've done plenty of trust work for him. I made plenty off the development, and we were skimming part of the casino operations. The money was so good, in fact, I might have delayed all of this another couple of years. But when you started investigating the corporations . . ."

He shrugged. "Clay, I'm sure you'd call it the trigger factor. Me, I call it common sense. If Emerald Canyon fell, I needed to bail out anyway. So why not retire, get rid of everyone involved, and take Kelsie with me into my new life?"

Lawson was enjoying his time on stage. Clay did nothing to discourage it. *Had it been twenty minutes since leaving Brody in the parked car?*

"Yes," Lawson said to Clay. "Trigger factor. I've studied everything in your field, Clay. I'm as expert as you are. I had to be, if I wanted to remain undetected. All the other fools who have been caught wanted to show off to the world. Not me. I just wanted your wife. I had to wait until everything was right. You should be impressed by my patience and foresight. For twenty-three years, I've left enough evidence in different places that if anyone ever looked closely, they'd blame Michael."

"Starting with a speeding ticket?" Clay asked. "Remember, the night with Nick Buffalo?"

"You mean the night I shot you in the back." Lawson laughed again. "The speeding ticket was child's play. We were in Great Falls—the alibi I needed—and I got Michael drunk and borrowed his truck and wallet. You know, on the way back, I was begining to worry I'd never run into a cop. You know the old saying about never seeing one when you need one."

Taylor plunked himself onto the floor beside his mother and began to stroke her hand.

"Actually," Lawson said, "it started even earlier. When I chose to take Doris Samson, I took a corkscrew Michael had used and left it in her body. It put his prints on the murder weapon."

Lawson smiled. "She was wonderful, you know. My first. And so easy. I knocked on her door in the middle of the night, pointed a gun in her face, took her to the motel and discovered what I already knew, the excitement."

"Didn't you step into a bear trap meant for Michael?" Clay was revolted at the silky pleasure in Lawson's recollection but kept his revulsion hidden. "Explain that."

"Meant for me, so no one would ever suspect me. I didn't step in it. I let the jaws close slowly, then began to yell. Believe me, even then, I wasn't acting."

"Michael," Kelsie said. "Did you . . . did you . . ."

"Kill him?" Lawson chuckled. "With much pleasure. He had become my one big worry. He caught me watching you outside your bedroom window one night."

Clay was glad Lawson was into the rythym of showing off and explaining. "The fight," Clay said. "You two had a fistfight and a falling out."

"Michael told me to leave town," Lawson said. "To never come back. Otherwise he said he'd tell everyone who I was. Michael, of course, thought I was a harmless peeper. He had no idea I was also taking care of the fools who dared try taking Kelsie from me."

"One by one," Clay said, "you got rid of them."

"Kelsie was disobedient for many years," Lawson said. "She would forget her lesson and allow another man to get between us. When it was convenient, that man would die. I'd leave just enough clues behind that anyone who thought each death was more than an accident would find evidence to point to Michael. And, of course, the notes gave me power over Kelsie."

"Let me tell you something I find amusing," Lawson continued with a smirk. It was if he and Clay were the only ones in the room. "I've had no one else to share this with. Fowler was the only one smart enough to see anything. He put it all together and came to me. He thought it was blackmail, and he was simple about it. He let me understand that what he knew about Michael would always give him leverage against me and the family. He called it his ace card. I think he wanted something against everyone."

"Everyone?"

"Emerald Canyon. Fowler didn't trust anyone in the group of us who put Emerald Canyon together. He wanted to be sure if the house of cards ever began to collapse, he wouldn't be the fall guy. It's a long, tedious story, involving political corruption and a small train derailment you failed to investigate properly."

Clay nodded, pretending thoughtfulness. "Taylor. How did you arrange that? I mean, I was with you at the time."

"Brilliance on my part. You might recall I arranged the meeting with you that afternoon. All I had to do was convince Rooster to take Taylor while I kept you busy. Which he did, believing it would be enough to stop Kelsie from investigating Emerald Canyon any further. Rooster, of course, had a vested financial stake in it, one he shared with his father."

"Then you killed him."

*Brody should be calling in the locals any minute.*

"Then I killed Rooster. Unfortunately, I didn't have the luxury of enjoying his death—I didn't have time. It was a two-for-one night. His father was next."

"Staging," Clay said. "You staged that crime so it might look like he'd done it."

"I'm glad you noticed. Yes, Rooster's bootprint in the blood was clumsy, but I was improvising. Same with your watch under Kelsie's bed. I just wanted confusion. Before I flew Kelsie and Taylor down here, I had a few others to take care of. Then I could leave Kalispell for good." Lawson spoke in casual, chilling tones. "You probably know which ones. Anderson. Fowler. I needed all ties to Lawson McNeill ended so that I could begin over here. The more confusion happening, the better."

"Who was in your airplane when it crashed? I mean, which body?"

"Sonny Cutknife. The final person who knew all of the Emerald Canyon details. I didn't want anyone ever beginning a search for the money trail that could lead to me. Teeth, of course, are never completely destroyed in a fire. So I pulled his in case they tried a dental-records match. Naturally, I pulled his teeth before I killed him. Tiring and nasty work, but fun."

Kelsie whimpered. "Don't worry, my dear," Lawson soothed. "I won't hurt you."

The hatred Clay was trying to contain overwhelmed him. He wanted to throw himself in a headlong dive at Lawson. But he held himself in check. The locals would come in silently, flashing lights only. They'd find the front door open. Any minute they could be coming up the stairs. Then this stalemate would take a different turn. Lawson would have to negotiate for his life . . .

"Why?" Clay said. "Why all of this? Why this obsession?"

"Funny you should ask. Kelsie had the same question. My answer to you is the same as to her. Because it's what makes me feel good."

"But—"

"Very simple," Lawson interrupted. "Psychobabble analysis about an old lady who accidentally killed her own son and put me in his place. Or that's just a handy excuse—you choose. Anyway, I'm curious about something. Actually, very curious. How did you find me?"

Here was another chance to stall, Clay thought.

"You dumped your kills from your airplane," he said. "Right?"

Lawson nodded amused agreement.

"Once I realized that, I got a map and began to draw lines from each victim's hometown to Kalispell. The locations of the bodies fell right along those lines. Two, however, didn't fit the pattern. When I drew lines from where you took them to where the bodies were found, the lines intersected here in northern Havasu. After that, it was a matter of calling airports in this area to see if your plane had ever landed here. Turns out that Lake Havasu City was a regular stop. After that—"

Lawson glanced at his watch. "Have you stalled long enough?"

Clay didn't answer.

Lawson grinned. "You are as obvious and stupid as any other cop."

He lifted his pistol, sighted briefly in Clay's direction. "I've had my fun with show-and-tell. But now it's over."

He pulled the trigger.

It was a flat snap, lost in Kelsie's scream. Only a .22-caliber pistol, the bullet wasn't enough to knock Clay down. It was enough, though, to shatter bone at close range. The bullet took Clay flush in the kneecap of his right leg.

# 5:09 P.M.

A tapping on the passenger window surprised Brody. He'd left the car running to keep it air-conditioned, so all he had to do was hit the window button to slide it down.

"Yeah?" Brody said to a middle-aged face above white-pressed shirt and a silk tie.

"I've been watching your car for fifteen minutes," the man said. "This isn't a neighborhood where we encourage strangers to loiter."

"Really?" Brody said.

"Really. I must ask you your business here."

"I must ask you to shut your mouth. There's broccoli in your teeth."

To the man's credit, he didn't check for broccoli. Maybe he was accustomed to dealing with the lower class and their crude jokes, Brody thought.

"I'm afraid I'll be calling the police," he said. "Perhaps you can explain your activity—or lack of it—to them."

Brody glanced at his watch. He grabbed the phone on the seat. "Don't sweat it, my friend. I'll save you the effort."

He began to dial. As the phone rang on the other end, Brody slid the window up, almost bumping the man's nose.

## 5:09 P.M.

Clay wobbled, frozen in disbelief, unable to draw a breath in the wash of overwhelming agony.

"Truly," Lawson said, "you didn't expect to live, did you?"

"Cops," Clay gasped. "On the way right now."

"I anticipated as much. Aren't you worried that I show so little fear?"

Kelsie tried to rise. Lawson pushed her down.

"What's going to happen is this." Lawson kept his pistol trained on Clay's forehead. "Step one, I push a little button, like this."

He reached toward the stand that held the television monitors and jabbed.

A dozen small explosions rocked the walls behind him.

"Fire," Lawson explained. "If you knew anything about me, you'd know my fondness for fire. It gets rid of a lot of trouble. I've had this backup ready from the beginning."

He moved back to Kelsie. "Step three. Kelsie, Taylor, and I go to a special vault hidden beneath this house. A fireproof vault, well stocked, well vented. From there, I activate a few other firestarters and poof, all of this is gone. I've spent my millions with great care, wouldn't you say?"

Clay wasn't saying anything. It was all he could do to remain standing. "Tonight, tomorrow night, whenever it seems safe," Lawson continued. "Kelsie, Taylor, and I will leave the ruins of this house and merely cross the golf course to a smaller property I've purchased on the other side of the fairway. It's a bit more primitive, but it is suitable. Especially if the world thinks we're dead."

There were already circles of flame on the scorched walls of the smaller room where the explosions had burst.

"Did I forget to mention step two?"

Lawson walked closer. "Yes, step two. That's where I leave you crippled up here to die in the fire. I've always believed that would be the worst way to die."

Lawson smiled and took careful aim at Clay's other leg. The pistol snapped again. Clay had started to sag. Instead of punching through his kneecap, the bullet tore through the meat of Clay's thigh.

Clay toppled, still sucking for air that would not fill his lungs.

Lawson's laughter was surreal against the crackle of flames.

From the floor, Clay twisted and looked up. He wasn't sure if he saw it right. A black snake looped through the air and settled around Lawson's neck.

Clay's vision cleared, and he understood. With Lawson intent on Clay, Kelsie had ripped a video cable loose from one of the monitors. With a hand on each end, she was now pulling, almost climbing up his back.

Lawson clutched his pistol in one hand and reached for his throat with the other, trying to pull the cable free. Kelsie bulldogged and hung on.

Lawson staggered and spun around, trying to throw her off. She screamed, frenzied in her attack, still on his back.

He spun again and again.

On his side, watching for Lawson, Clay began crawling toward the pistol he'd thrown onto the floor earlier at Lawson's command.

The flames began to roar. Oily smoke began to cloud the room. Clay screamed as his shattered knee bounced on the floor.

Lawson threw himself backward into a wall. Kelsie still clutched the cable around his neck.

Lawson stepped forward and rammed backward again. This time Kelsie flew onto the floor. Lawson reached down, grabbed her wrist, and jammed his pistol in her face.

Clay strained to reach the other pistol as Lawson began to drag Kelsie toward Clay.

Finally, Clay managed to close his fingers around the butt of his own pistol. A foot came down and pinned his wrist to the floor.

"Watch closely," Lawson gasped to Kelsie. "This is how a bullet shatters a skull."

Clay moaned. He tried to pull his hand free, but Lawson continued to press his foot down on Clay's wrist.

Then a weight dropped on Clay's back and shoulders and head. "Daddy, mine," Taylor shouted. "Daddy, mine."

Lawson hesitated. A millisecond, but hesitation enough.

Kelsie swung around with her free hand, punching Lawson in the groin. He stutter-stepped backward, releasing Clay's hand and wrist from underneath his foot.

Clay turned his hand upward and squeezed the trigger.

Lawson staggered again, bringing his hands down toward the blood on the front of his pelvis. His dropped pistol clattered past Clay's face.

Clay didn't have the chance to shoot again. Kelsie had taken Clay's arm and was trying to pull him up to his feet as flames climbed the walls around them.

"We've got to go!" she shouted.

He screamed as he put pressure on the leg with the shattered knee.

Kelsie got him onto the other leg, and he half collapsed against her. She pushed him up again and threw his arm over her shoulder.

"Taylor!" she screamed as she dragged Clay toward the hallway. She didn't look back until she reached the door. "Taylor!"

Through the smoke and flames, she saw why he hadn't responded.

Lawson, on his belly, had Taylor by the ankles. Taylor couldn't run. He was screaming, crying, reaching out for Kelsie. Lawson's face showed calm control.

A wall fell behind Lawson, sending a crash of sparks that temporarily blocked Kelsie's vision of her son. "Taylor!" she screamed again.

Clay had fallen against her, passed out. His weight nearly toppled her, but she knew if she set him down, she'd never get him up again. The fire was still contained to this half of the upper floor. All she needed to do was move Clay down the hallway, and he would be safe. But the fire in this room had risen so rapidly she knew she would not have time to take Clay and then go back for Taylor. Yet if she went for Taylor, the flames might engulf Clay where he was.

A curtain of smoke parted. Lawson still had Taylor by the ankles, still showed calm control.

"Oh, please," she cried. Clay's weight made her lurch. "Please give me my son!"

Lawson yanked hard, pulling Taylor down beside him.

"No!" Kelsie screamed. "My boy!"

Lawson pulled Taylor to his side.

"Please!" she screamed. "Let him go!"

Lawson looked up at her, smiled, kissed Taylor on the forehead, and released him.

Slowly, Taylor got to his feet. Another portion of the wall collapsed, landing on the back of Lawson's leg. Unhurried, Taylor patted Lawson on the head, then turned and ran toward his mother.

She dragged Clay ahead, away from the heat and the smoke. Taylor reached her side. Down the hall, when she looked back, she saw nothing but the dancing bright orange and red of fire. ▨

# Day 6

Kelsie snapped open the blinds. Light flooded the hospital room. Clay regarded her silently.

"You were right about Lawson," Kelsie said.

She stepped to the bed and placed a file folder on his lap. "Here are the newspaper articles and the police reports. The fire that killed his mother was not an accident. They never did know who did it."

"Lawson. If he killed his own mother  .  .  .

"It's spooky," Kelsie said. "Dad showed me childhood photos of Mother and my aunt, Lawson's mother. At that age, I looked almost identical to both."

"Spooky," Clay echoed. He wasn't much interested in the past.

Kelsie nodded. "Dad tells me that Lawson's mother was an alcoholic and had a lot of different men in her life. Of course, these weren't things I'd know when I was a girl and Lawson first came to stay with us."

"Of course," Clay said. He was sure if they looked into it enough, they'd find neighbors who complained about missing pets. It was all part of the pattern.

Kelsie lifted Clay's hand and kissed it gently. "You're not saying much," Kelsie told him. "Maybe flying you back here from the Lake

Havasu hospital wasn't such a good idea. The doctors there didn't think so, but you were so insistent . . ."

The concern in her voice touched him deeply. He wanted to tell her he ached with love for her. Instead, he shrugged and kept his silence.

"What's the matter?" she said. "You've been like this for the last two days. Are your legs hurting that badly?"

"Emerald Canyon," he said instead of answering her question. "What's happening there?"

"Most of the legal work is coming together. Dad has been able to tell me a lot about it. He says he and Sonny had a little discussion before Lawson killed Sonny. I wonder why Sonny told Dad so much. When I asked Dad, he just smiled and told me not to worry about details."

"That's nice," Clay said.

She lifted his hand and shook it. "What is it?"

Now or later, he thought. Might as well be now. "I know of course, why you left me," he said. "The notes. You were afraid that if you didn't leave, I'd end up like the others."

"You said you understood," she said. "That was the most difficult thing I have ever faced, leaving you and not being able to tell you why. If Lawson had known I told you anything, he would have killed you. Like the others. You already said you realized I didn't have a choice."

"You had a choice when you married me." He let that hang briefly.

"What do you mean?" There was enough strangeness in her voice to know he'd guessed right.

He gently pulled his hand away. He loved this woman. He wanted to bury his suspicion, but if he did, then it would always be there. Finally he spoke. "Before meeting me, it had been five years or so since your previous boyfriend. Enough time had passed that you thought maybe you'd try again. But this time, you were going to pick someone your stalker would be afraid of. Someone like me, with my kind of background."

She studied him gravely.

"In the back of my mind, I'd always wondered why you courted me," he said. "I've never been particularly attractive to women. I was older than you. But I loved you, and it didn't matter to me."

He shook his head sadly. "Some women trade themselves in marriage for the money of a rich man. You traded for protection."

"Clay . . ."

"I love you," he said. "That won't change. But you don't need protection anymore."

"Clay . . ."

"What I'm saying is that you still have your apartment in town. Now would be a better time to leave than later . . ."

His words hung in the air for a long, long time.

Kelsie stood abruptly and headed toward the open door.

The sight stabbed Clay, but he wasn't going to beg her to stay. Not now. He'd begged before and it had nearly killed him when she left.

She closed the door and turned back to him. "You're a fool," she said softly. "I won't lie. I did feel safe with you. But that reason alone wouldn't be enough for me to love you."

She smiled as she moved back to the side of his bed. "This is the second time you've been in the hospital for me. Remember? The first time I was sixteen. I had the biggest crush on you. I don't think all of that crush ever went away."

She leaned forward and kissed his forehead. "We're not where we were in the beginning. I made some mistakes. I built some walls. I've never been able to deal with Taylor. But I think we can make it better than before—if you let me."

She surprised him with lips soft on his neck. "When your legs are better," she said, "you owe me a picnic. And a swim in the lake."

"Sure," he finally said.

She lifted the covers, moved onto the bed beside him, and put her arms around his shoulders. She kissed him again. Less softly this time, more deeply.

"Just hold me," she whispered. On her side, she worked her leg gently around his shattered knee and fit herself into the warmth of his body. "Don't ever let me go."

Slater Ellis is in a race...

against time,

a hit man,

and a professor who plays God in his spare time.

If he loses, so does the human race.

# DOUBLE HELIX

A NOVEL BY

# Sigmund Brouwer

| | DATE DUE | |
|---|---|---|
| NOV 1 9 1997 | | |
| DEC 1 0 1997 R | | |
| APR 1 0 1998 | | |
| OCT 2 9 2003 | | |
| | | |
| | | |
| | | |
| | | |